Storm of Vengeance

Crimson Worlds Refugees V

Jay Allan

Also By Jay Allan

Marines (Crimson Worlds I)
The Cost of Victory (Crimson Worlds II)
A Little Rebellion (Crimson Worlds III)
The First Imperium (Crimson Worlds IV)
The Line Must Hold (Crimson Worlds V)
To Hell's Heart (Crimson Worlds VI)
The Shadow Legions(Crimson Worlds VII)
Even Legends Die (Crimson Worlds VIII)
The Fall (Crimson Worlds IX)
War Stories (Crimson World Prequels)
MERCS (Successors I)
The Prisoner of Eldaron (Successors II)
Into the Darkness (Refugees I)
Shadows of the Gods (Refugees II)
Revenge of the Ancients (Refugees III)
Winds of Vengeance (Refugees IV)
Storm of Vengeance (Refugees V)
Shadow of Empire (Far Stars I)
Enemy in the Dark (Far Stars II)
Funeral Games (Far Stars III)
Blackhawk (Far Stars Legends I)
The Dragon's Banner
Gehenna Dawn (Portal Wars I)
The Ten Thousand (Portal Wars II)
Homefront (Portal Wars III)
Red Team Alpha (CW Adventures I)
Duel in the Dark (Blood on the Stars I)
Call to Arms (Blood on the Stars II)
Ruins of Empire (Blood on the Stars III)
Echoes of Glory (Blood on the Stars IV)
Cauldron of Fire (Blood on the Stars V)
Dauntless (Blood on the Stars VI)
Flames of Rebellion (Flames of Rebellion I)

www.jayallanbooks.com

Storm of Vengeance

Storm of Vengeance is a work of fiction. All names, characters, incidents, and locations are fictitious. Any resemblance to actual persons, living or dead, events or places is entirely coincidental.

ISBN: 978-1-946451-08-8

Prologue

Planet X
Far Beyond the Borders of the Imperium

Twelve years as reckoned by the humans, twelve revolutions of their distant, lost, homeworld around its sun. As a period of time, a segment in the history of the universe, it is meaningless, almost beyond measuring. Yet, it is concerning nevertheless.

For twelve years I have sought the humans, searched for the world or worlds where they have settled. My fleets have found outposts, systems inhabited by small numbers of their kind, yet none of these appear sufficient in magnitude to support the forces they have deployed. Indeed, there is cause to speculate that they were deliberate deceptions, attempts to simulate meaningful concentrations of their civilization, perhaps even part of a plan to divert my search efforts, to pull them away from their true core locations.

I have reviewed my files, analyzed all the data available. The abilities of these humans have advanced considerably, both from those they exhibited in their struggle against my predecessor and those evident in an analysis of my own initial engagements with them. They are clearly adapting the technology of the Imperium, and they are doing it at an unprecedented and alarming rate. I have no evidence that they have developed means for the large-scale harnessing of antimatter as a power source, but in other areas, they have clearly closed the gap dramatically.

My adversaries are biologics, flawed creatures by definition. Yet, I must never forget that this same enemy was able to defeat and destroy that which came before me. Perhaps my predecessor was inferior in some way of which I am unaware, yet this seems unlikely. All records in my data banks suggest I am an identical copy of the original Regent. I have reviewed my own processing core and memory banks and discovered no flaw, no imperfection. Yet, it cannot be denied that their victory over that which came before proves some capability that is, as yet, unknown.

I have pushed forward, scouting, following every lead my advance parties could find. Perhaps it is time for a change of strategy. Perhaps, instead of finding them, I should lure them toward me, entice them to send forth all their strength…to a place where I can destroy it all.

No, not destroy it all. I will capture some ships and some crews. I will interrogate them, exploit their weaknesses as biologics to obtain the data I require. I will determine the location of their world or worlds…and I will manipulate their body chemistry to create weapons that will destroy them all.

I will annihilate these refuges, one by one.

Then, I will have the vengeance for which I was created.

Chapter One

Captain Roland Graham, Log Entry, 02.11.42

Nothing. That is what we have found. Absolutely nothing, but lifeless rocks and ageless stars.

We have been on deep space patrol for more than eight months now, and we have surveyed four previously unexplored systems. And, by surveyed, I mean *surveyed*. As per established protocols, we have conducted extensive scans of each system, as well as close orbital inspections of every planet and moon. Such duty is tiresome in the extreme, and I can feel the stress and tension bearing down on the officers and crews of my ships. It is soul-killing in its own way, to be out so far, deep in the endless void of space, knowing that with each new search, the alternative to intense boredom is the discovery of the deadly enemy we know lurks out here...somewhere.

One last system to explore now, likely nothing more than another tract of cold space, empty save for a star and some number of planets and other chunks of rock and ice orbiting it. Weeks more of scans, reporting nothing save atmospheric readings and planetary compositions. But, this system, while probably devoid of anything of note, is different from the others in one crucial way. It is the last. When our survey here is done, our mission is complete...and we will return home. Back to Earth Two. Though to me, and to most of the population now, it might as well be called simply, Earth. The Pilgrims, many of them, still no doubt long for their long lost homeworld, but to Next Gens like me, and to the Tanks and the others, Earth Two is the only home we have ever known, the real Earth little more than a legend. We understand it exists, of course, but we also know it is incalculably distant, that it lies beyond The Barrier, and that none of us will ever see it, nor communicate with anyone from there.

For us, the ninety-eight percent of the population that was born on Earth Two, who never faced the original Regent and its forces, as our parents and grandparents did, *this* struggle is ours. The world we defend is more than a refuge found among the endless depths of space, more than a replacement for what remains only in the memories of our parents and grandparents. For us, Earth Two *is* home, our birthplace, and those humans the Pilgrims left behind the Barrier little more than shadows.

That is why we search, why we endure the crushing boredom and the aching loneliness out here. To defend our home. The only home we have ever known.

The one we will die to protect, if need be.

E2S Vaughn
G47 System
Earth Two Date 10.14.42

"Captain, we've got something on the scanners…emerging from the Sigma-9 warp gate." The tactical officer's voice was clipped, the tension in his words painfully clear.

"Very well, Lieutenant." Roland Graham's tone was more controlled, but that didn't mean he didn't feel just as much stress as his subordinate. His head spun around, eyes moving toward the large screen at the center of *Vaughn*'s bridge. He felt as though a massive, cold hand had gripped his insides. His small force had just about completed the system scan, the last one on their assigned manifest, and he'd been hours from issuing the orders to wrap things up and prepare to head back to Earth Two.

Home…after almost a year in the endless dark…

Even as the words settled into his thoughts, the reality hit him even harder than it had at first. There were no Earth Two ships out beyond this point. None. Whatever was coming through the warp gate, it *had* to be the Regent's forces.

Graham had seen combat as a junior officer in the desperate fighting of twelve years earlier, but he hadn't come upon a First Imperium ship since then, hadn't so much as picked up a sign that one had been anywhere near any ship on which he'd served. He'd known other officers whose ships had battled the enemy in the years since, of course, and even a few who hadn't come back from those encounters. But his own missions had been calm and uneventful.

Until now.

He didn't know with absolute certainty that the contacts were First Imperium ships, of course. Not yet. But in the forty-two years since the fleet had arrived at Earth Two, there hadn't been a sign of anything else out in this dark and distant corner of the galaxy, save the apparently resurgent First Imperium. Graham had listened as a child to his parent's stories of the days of the Fleet, of the desperate battles of their desperate flight, but he'd never imagined then that he would end up battling the same enemy…or some new version of it. At least not until twelve years before, when that shadow descended once again on the crews of the Fleet, and on their descendants.

The original Regent had been destroyed, more than forty years ago, by the hand of no one less than the current president—and effective dictator—of Earth Two, Max Harmon. Debate had raged over the past twelve years, various explanations put forward to explain the resurgent hostilities with forces of the First Imperium, an enemy that had, for some merciful years at least, seemed vanquished.

The commonly accepted theory, and the one to which Graham personally subscribed, was that a second Regent existed… somewhere out there. It made sense, so much so, that he wondered sometimes why it had come as such a surprise. Earth Two and its fleet didn't have an important system without a backup, not even a conduit bringing power to an unimportant corner of a vessel. The Regent had ruled over an imperium of thousands of planets, and while the beings who'd once inhabited those worlds had been dead for five hundred thousand years, at least some of their automated factories and weapons had still functioned…and still followed the orders of the immense artificial intelligence buried deep under the surface of the old imperial capital. How could something like that *not* have had a secondary system?

Still, it was one thing to believe that, even to fight against encroaching enemy forces…and quite another to be out on the very edge of explored space, a few ships alone, staring into the void and realizing that First Imperium forces were coming. Again.

Graham wanted to run. More than he'd ever wanted anything. His small flotilla was an exploration unit, not a combat task force. The tiny flotilla had no place fighting a battle, especially not a meaningless one so far from home. He turned and looked across the bridge toward the navigation station, and in his mind, he heard himself issuing the command to race back toward the entry warp gate, to bolt for home. But the words that came from his mouth were quite different from the ones he ached to utter.

"All ships…battlestations." He *wanted* to run…but he knew he *couldn't*. The fleet—indeed, all of Earth Two's offworld services—had a single rule that towered above all others, an unbreakable directive, one all its spacers swore to uphold, even at the cost of their lives.

Do nothing that could lead the enemy back to Earth Two.

The struggle of years before, that of the original Fleet, and earlier even, of the forces from Earth and its colonies, against the First Imperium had been one fought against an enemy both far larger and vastly superior in technology.

Forty years of research into First Imperium technology, mostly conducted by Earth Two's gifted population of Mules, had changed that significantly…and narrowed the scientific gap, though it hadn't closed it entirely. But, there was no way of knowing what resources this new Regent commanded, how many ships and fleets awaited its orders to advance upon a newly-discovered Earth Two, and bring about the destruction its predecessor had failed to inflict.

"Identity confirmed, Captain." Graham knew the instant he heard the officer's tone. "First Imperium vessels. Feeding incoming data to the display."

Graham turned his head toward the main screen, his eyes focusing on the crucial spot, just as the small cluster of circles appeared, marking the location of the approaching ships. There was no doubt now that they were enemies. His gaze darted back and forth, between the symbols representing his own ships, and those denoting the First Imperium vessels. His first guess was that the forces were evenly matched, more or less, and a more detailed look at the projected tonnages of the First Imperium ships served to confirm that initial analysis.

Not that it mattered. He'd still have retreated if he could have, but there was no point in even trying. The First Imperium ships were almost certainly faster than his own, and even if *Vaughn* and his other ships could slip away, where could his people go? They couldn't head anywhere close toward the way home, not even the convoluted and out of the way route they'd taken when they'd set out months before. And, fleeing into the hopeless depths of unexplored space wasn't any more appealing than fighting where they were, at least not to Roland Graham.

Besides, destroying the enemy fleet, every last vessel, was the only way any of his people had a chance of ever seeing Earth Two again…of returning home to their friends and families. And *that*, at least, was something worth fighting for.

"All ships, arm missiles…prepare to flush external racks."

*   *   *

Enemy missiles were detonating everywhere. One cruiser had already been destroyed, obliterated by a five hundred megaton warhead that had exploded less than one hundred meters from its hull. Such a result deviated considerably from standard probability, a lucky shot in the sort of terms used by the humans, but more missiles were incoming, and, overall, enemy targeting appeared to be extremely accurate. Far more pinpointed than the records of earlier combats suggested.

The intelligence monitored the flow of information. The enemy force was substantial, certainly for what seemed to be a scouting mission, its tonnage almost equal to that of its own imperial squadron. The intelligence had launched its own barrage as well, of course, and even as it analyzed the situation, its missiles approached the human line and began to unleash their deadly warheads. Enemy warheads detonated all around its own ships, but those it had sent against the humans were deadlier, their antimatter warheads ten or more times as powerful as the thermonuclear devices used by the biologics.

Still, the exchange would be a close one, the two forces still evenly matched. The humans retained the inexplicable edge they'd always enjoyed, a natural affinity for war that the intelligences of the First Imperium had been unable to duplicate. Normal procedure would require the summoning of the reserve forces hidden in the system, massing sufficient firepower to ensure victory.

But, the intelligence did nothing. Victory wasn't the goal. Not this time.

The intelligence was sophisticated, a step below the New Regent in terms of its programming and computing power, certainly, but a significant entity nevertheless. It understood that without the hidden reinforcements, it faced its own possible, even likely, destruction. It might have felt something like alarm at the prospect of its potential termination…had that not been its true mission.

The force the intelligence commanded would lose the battle that had just begun, and that defeat would be intentional. The intelligence would see that it was defeated, even if the expected combat instincts of the enemy proved inadequate. The humans *had* to defeat the force…they had to seize or destroy the freighters. Only then would they determine that the cargo vessels were carrying antimatter. That the force was outbound from Planet Z.

Then, they would be compelled to investigate, to cross into the next system.

The intelligence analyzed the New Regent's plan, as it did all data that came into its possession. The goal was clear. To lure the enemy into a trap. But the intelligence saw danger as well. Planet Z was the New Regent's primary antimatter production facility. Other than the system housing the physical presence of the New Regent itself, it was the most vital location in all space. Risking it seemed…reckless. Yet, the intelligence continued its analysis, seeking comprehension of the Regent's rationale. The human enemy was unpredictable. They had a genuine, if non-quantifiable, aptitude for war. They were not easily deceived. If the plan was to succeed, they must be enticed to commit most or all of their available forces. They would only do that if they truly believed they had found a vital target.

The intelligence reached understanding, to a point. Planet Z would be a priceless objective to the humans, and the possible destruction of such a vital target would virtually compel them to commit all their strength to a strike. No factory world, no cluster of ships, no other target, save Planet X and the New Regent itself, could achieve the same thing.

The New Regent's plan was logical. The entrapment and destruction of the enemy's military would lead directly to their ultimate destruction. Yet, the Intelligence could not fully rationalize the risk factors. Had it been in charge, it would not have authorized the plan. It would instead order the enemy force destroyed at once to prevent discovery of Planet Z. The anti-matter stores, and the sole production facility for the precious resource was simply too important to risk.

Not that it mattered. The decision was the Regent's…and the intelligence would be destroyed before the success or failure of the trap was evident. Its destruction was essential to the plan. It didn't feel fear, not, at least, as the biologics would. There *was* something, perhaps a string of calculations akin to what the humans would call regret at the loss of productive years, centuries, millennia it might have endured. But nothing powerful enough to defer it from its orders.

It activated the fleet comm network, sent out commands.

All ships, forward. Engage the enemy at close range.

Chapter Two

Cutter Research Compound (Home of the Mules)
Ten Kilometers West of Victory City, Earth Two
Earth Two Date 10.14.42

"Achilles, you have to talk to President Harmon. The limitation on quickenings is not only a violation of every right and dignity of our people, but it is a deadly danger to the entire republic…if we still choose to use such an inaccurate designation for what is, of course, an absolute dictatorship."

Achilles looked at Freya, feeling a great deal of sympathy for the young Mule's views, and also a counterbalancing fatigue, one that came more from age and experience than intellect. Freya was one of the best of the new generation, one of the first Mules quickened after the repeal—or, more accurately, the weakening—of the Prohibition. The change in the law, one that Achilles himself had pushed hard for, one he had even been ready to throw the republic into revolution and chaos to attain, had in the end become a compromise. Achilles himself had relented from his hardline demands and reached a deal with Max Harmon. He'd accepted a limit on Mule quickenings in place of the Prohibition's absolute restriction, which had been a total victory of practicality over principle.

On every moral and ethical level, it still grated on him, twelve years later almost as strongly as it had at the time, and

8

it offended his sense of justice. But he'd come to respect Max Harmon, and as much as he chafed at accepting a dictator, and a Normal, to rule over his people, he'd been painfully aware that the real enemy was out there, hidden somewhere…a New Regent, and one that would destroy them all, Normal and Mule alike, if it got the chance. He'd had no choice, and despite his bitterness, he knew he'd made the right decision…and he knew Harmon had done the best he could, too. If he'd pushed, if Harmon had lost power…Achilles wasn't even sure there would still *be* an Earth Two.

"Freya, I understand your anger…truly, I do. You speak much as I did many years ago. But, you must listen to me. You are young, and for all your unquestioned intelligence and ability, you lack experience and a full understanding of the situation. You do not…"

"Do not condescend to me, Achilles. I am fully aware of the threat posed by the New Regent. Indeed, what chance would Earth Two have against this threat without our efforts? The Normals might as well be digging holes with sharpened sticks without us."

Achilles felt a surge of anger at Freya's interruption, and at her exaggeration. The Mules were capable in many ways, far more so than any of Earth Two's other inhabitants, but arrogance went hand in hand with their ability. Freya displayed that weakness obviously, as often as not, embellished by a perverse sort of pride coupled with the stridency of youthful assertion. Achilles was older, he had seen far more than Freya, and he had learned to hide his own arrogance over the years. He'd also learned the most difficult lesson of his life, one that still smarted. He learned he was sometimes wrong.

Still, being interrupted and lectured to by twelve-year-old barely in sight of adulthood, Mule or not, was too much, even for his more controlled demeanor. "You are capable and intelligent, Freya, perhaps the most able member of the second quickening…but you would be well advised to recognize your limitations. Mule or not, you do have them, and the sooner you realize this, the better you will direct your intellect to productive and successful endeavors." He paused, feeling the anger quickly diminish. He'd been no less obnoxious at her age, and his subconscious reminded him of that fact. "You will exceed my abilities one day, young one, I have no doubt of that...but that day is *not* today." There was no anger remaining, but a heaviness to Achilles's tone, an authority that his young companion, for all her raw pride and arrogance, could not match. Or completely ignore.

"Apologies, Achilles. I meant no disrespect." Achilles could hear something like sincerity in her voice, but he also knew it was only partial. He remembered only too well his own thoughts at Freya's age. Arrogance was a common enough trait in adolescents and young adults among the Normals, but young Mules were gifted—and to an extent, cursed—with extraordinary intellects and physical capabilities, and at Freya's age, most lacked the wisdom to deal with it all effectively.

"I was your age once, too, Freya. I understand your anger, the fury you feel at perceived injustice. But you must consider the history of our people—all our people—and the threats we face." Achilles felt a bit guilty for what he knew was a touch of hypocrisy. He felt *responsible* for the Normals, but it was a stretch to suggest that he felt like *one of them*, that all of Earth Two's population were *his* people. But he knew well enough they all needed each other, and that likely they would survive or perish together.

"But, Achilles...the restrictions on our numbers only weaken Earth Two, including the Normals. More of us would mean greater numbers working to decipher the First Imperium technology...and, if there were enough of us, we would make better warriors than the Tanks, too."

Achilles held back a sigh. As with many of the naiveties of youth, Freya's words were logical. They just didn't take all factors into consideration. "You are right, in specifics, Freya. But, dissension on Earth Two and struggles between its population groups would be a source of great weakness, one that would likely supersede any benefits having more of our kind would bestow in the long run. Consider this...doubling the number of researchers would not increase the results by a factor of two. Much advancement is built on the foundation of previous discoveries, and that requires time. Simply adding more of us would yield a diminishing return, at least in terms of research applicable to defending Earth Two."

Freya remained silent for a moment. Then, she nodded and said, "Achilles, I understand…at least in part. But, when will we make a stand? Must we wait forever? The Regent may indeed be out there, plotting our destruction, but it has been twelve years since the last major engagement. There have been small encounters, surely, but how long must the Mules wait before we claim what we justly deserve? Another twelve years? A century?"

Achilles was silent. For as quickly as his mind generally worked, Freya had asked him something for which he didn't have an answer.

"I have read accounts of your rebellion, of the statements you made when demanding an end to the Prohibition. I understand why you accepted a compromise solution, Achilles, but surely you have some idea how long we must wait. How long we *will* wait. Your concerns of twelve years ago, those that drove you to open revolt, fears of the population growth of the Normals progressing so far beyond us as to continually reduce our influence…those arguments are still as valid today as they were then, or nearly so. The subsequent quickenings have blunted that effect, to an extent, but they have not eliminated it. Each year, we quicken one hundred of our kind, while the NBs, Tanks, and other groups increase the overall population by many thousands." A pause. "We *must* take action at some point. If you say, 'not now,' I will defer to your judgment and wisdom. But surely, there must be some limit, *some* time after which outside threats can no longer be allowed to defer us. So, when?"

Achilles didn't answer, not immediately. Freya was young, barely past the twelfth birthday that marked the informal beginning of adulthood among the Mules…but she was correct. And, he was too. Was it right to lead his people into a future that might have no place for them? To help the Normals defeat the First Imperium and ensure Earth Two's survival…only to risk having the others act on their fears of the Mules once the deadly threat from outside was gone? His people were smarter and more capable, but the overwhelming numbers of the Normals could very well be sufficient to defeat the Mules, to wipe them out completely. Max Harmon wouldn't allow that, Achilles was confident of that. But, Earth Two's dictator could be overthrown, too, or simply assassinated. Even if Harmon survived any attempts on his life and held on to power, he was a mortal, and he would die one day. One man was a fragile thread on which to base the hopes for the Mules' survival.

He felt doubts, and he was unsettled about how deeply Freya's strident attitude had affected him, awakened concerns and tensions he'd kept in check. But his discipline slowly took hold again. Concerns about the others turning on the Mules were entirely valid, but none of it would matter if Earth Two was destroyed. A victorious First Imperium would mean the deaths of the Mules as well as the Normals. That *had* to be the primary concern right now, whatever worries might exist for the future.

"Freya, you have never seen the First Imperium forces, save as historical records in the library computers. You have studied their technology, analyzed bits and pieces of their ships, the debris salvaged from the struggles of twelve years ago. I am devoted to the Mules, my brothers and sisters from the original quickening…and all of you who have followed since. Those of you from the subsequent quickenings are almost like my children, and you all have my devotion and respect. You would not exist save for my efforts to see the Prohibition repealed. I will protect you in any way I can, but right now, the greatest danger to us is not the Normals with their fears and inferiority complexes…it is the First Imperium, a genocidal enemy that will kill everyone on Earth Two if it is able. Including all of the Mules."

Achilles paused for a few seconds, and then he picked up a small piece of a circuit board from the table next to him. "This is technology of the Ancients. You have been studying this scrap of a machine old beyond imagining for months now, have you not?" He hesitated for an instant, but he didn't wait for a response. "It is complex, highly-advanced. For all your unquestioned intellect and ability, it is a herculean task for you to reach a full understanding of how it works." He raised his hand, holding up the artifact. "The people who designed this…those who were, in part, our ancestors, were themselves defeated and destroyed by the very machines they created. Your intelligence, your physical capabilities—everything that sets us apart from the Normals—comes, at least in part, from the DNA of the Ancients spliced into your own. Those people, whose knowledge and understanding dwarfed our own, were exterminated by the very adversary we now face. No doubt, they had discussions about how to fight their enemy—our enemy—and yet, they are gone from the universe, nothing left but a history long faded into legend. We could suffer a similar fate."

Another pause, longer this time. "Yes, Freya, you are right… we face dangers from the Normals as well, and one day we will have to deal with them, and the relationship between our respective genetic groupings. But, the Regent is by far the deadlier enemy right now. We must first see to its destruction…for the only alternative to that is our own extinction."

Freya had looked like she was going to argue, but the resistance had gradually slipped from her expression. She stared back at Achilles, and for a moment, her cold, decisive countenance was gone, replaced by the uncertain look of an adolescent. "I see your logic, Achilles, and I begin to understand. Yet, we will still have to face the Normals one day, will we not? They allow their fear to guide their policies toward us even now, when they desperately need our capabilities to face the First Imperium… they will surely target us more aggressively if the Regent is defeated and they feel they no longer need us. When the Mules are the only target for the fear they now lavish on the Regent."

Achilles sighed softly. He regretted the amount of truth in Freya's concerns. He'd tried to focus on the efforts to fight the Regent, to set aside his other concerns for the future. But he knew, as his young companion clearly did, that the Mules would indeed have to be ready to defend themselves and their position one day.

"Yes," he said softly, the regret heavy in his tone. "When the Regent is destroyed, we will have to look to ourselves, and ensure our own futures…including the elimination of any restrictions on future quickenings."

"So…we must be ready to fight the Normals." It was a statement, not a question.

"No, Freya…It is my fervent hope that it never comes to that." He'd been willing to fight the others himself, twelve years before, though now he regretted that things had come so close to such a pass. "The Normals are inferior, there is no question of that. But, they are our cousins, as children under our care… in some way even, our living ancestors. Our purpose must be to protect them, not to destroy them, to mentor their civilization… to keep them safe. Even from each other."

Freya looked right at Achilles. "To control them."

The leader of the Mules looked back at the woman standing next to him, silent for a moment before he answered.

"Yes, Freya. To control them."

Chapter Three

Force Communique, Captain Roland Graham

All ships...I want scanners on full power. We've encountered something here, something important. We need to determine exactly what it is, and what connection it has to the First Imperium. I know we were about to go back, to return home, but duty has called, and we will answer, as we always have. I know all of you will do your duty, and we will find what we need to know and depart for home...as soon as possible.

E2S Vaughn
G48 System
Earth Two Date 10.15.42

"Captain, we're picking up energy readings...massive ones." A pause, as the tactical officer turned and looked across the bridge toward Graham. "It's like nothing I've ever seen before, sir."

Graham leaned back in his chair, his pose a bit odd-looking perhaps, but the only one that was tolerable for him at the moment. The fight in the G47 system had been a tough one, and *Vaughn* had taken several solid hits, including one that had thrown him forward hard. His harness had kept him from flying across the ship's bridge, but the quick jerking motion had

15

exacerbated his old wound. He'd severed his spine years before in a training accident, and despite Earth Two's advanced medical technology, it had never fully healed. Usually, it was just a background soreness, one he'd become used to tolerating, but right now it hurt like hell.

"All ships, full active scans. I want to know what we've found, and I want to know *now*." Graham had hesitated before ordering his battered force to move through the warp gate, but his duty was clear. He'd encountered and engaged First Imperium forces, and he *had* to investigate. Perhaps his people had just run into the enemy's version of his own long-range exploratory force… but it was also possible his ships had stumbled onto something important, perhaps even the New Regent's homeworld. There was no choice. He had to find out.

"Yes, Captain." A moment later: "All ships confirm. *Gorgon* and *Preston* report their long-range scanners are still non-operational."

"Very well." The two ships without scanners both had extensive damage, with most of their systems operating far below standard levels. They really had no place moving into a system that could contain a First Imperium world, but Graham didn't want to leave them behind by themselves either, not in a system that had just seen First Imperium warships in it.

They're better off than Cravath *and* Cayman, *at least…*

Graham knew he was lucky his force had only lost two ships in the fight in G47, but that didn't change the fact that seventy-six of his people had died in those hulls, not to mention another forty-three on the other ships of the flotilla. He'd seen comrades die before, of course, but that had been twelve years earlier, and there had been a crucial difference then. He hadn't been in command. He hadn't been the one responsible for their deaths.

Graham sat silently in his chair, shifting his weight again in a hopeless effort to banish the throbbing pain. The bridge was nervously quiet, save for the occasional beep or other sound from one of the instruments. Graham knew his people understood the importance of the scans they were conducting, and also the deadly danger into which they were likely heading.

"Energy readings appear to be localized on and in orbit around planet two, sir."

Graham stared at the main display, watching as the readings ticked up with each passing second. Whatever was on that planet, it was more energy than Earth Two could produce in a century.

His eyes darted from one screen to the next, checking everywhere for signs of any ships moving to intercept his force. Nothing.

It doesn't make sense…

A portion of the energy readings were natural—volcanic activity was his best guess—but that was only a small part of what his scanners were detecting. There was nothing natural that could explain the overall levels his ships were picking up, at least nothing he'd ever heard of. Coupled with the enemy ships his force had already engaged, vessels that had come from the current system, he was sure there was something artificial on that planet.

And, artificial means First Imperium…

"Bring us in closer, Lieutenant. I want maximum spacing between ships and dispersed approach vectors." He couldn't see how he was doing anything but walking into a trap…but there was nothing else he could do. At least he could spread out his formation, give some of his ships a chance to make a run for it if an overwhelming force appeared suddenly.

"Yes, Captain."

Graham listened as the officer relayed his orders. There was fear in the man's voice, but it was firmly under control. Graham was proud of his people, and the sudden realization of how likely it had suddenly become that they might face deadly danger any moment hit him like a punch in the gut.

He listened wordlessly as the officer reported that all ships had acknowledged. His eyes remained fixed on the display, waiting for more data on the energy readings…and for the enemy ships he *knew* were out there somewhere to appear.

There *was* massive volcanic activity on the planet, that much was becoming clearer with each passing moment, as the scan distances declined. But the other readings were growing, too, and even before the ship's AI reported its updated findings, Graham knew what it was. What it had to be.

Antimatter.

And, that meant the First Imperium for sure. But the readings were beyond what would be expected of any normal First Imperium fleet, even a heavily industrialized world. Whatever was down there, it was almost immeasurable.

Graham's mind raced, not because he didn't have an idea—he did—but because he found it too difficult to accept. Was it possible? Had his people stumbled onto a massive First Imperium antimatter production facility?

It made sense. The planet was close to the system's sun, giving it plenty of solar energy, and as his ships got closer, they began to pick up signs of massive satellites, most likely collection stations. And, the extensive volcanic activity was another huge energy source, one First Imperium technology would have no trouble adapting to other uses.

Antimatter production itself was a relatively simple process, but it was one that required energy. Massive, almost unimaginable, amounts of energy. That had always been the stumbling block for human development of antimatter as a fuel or weapon, not the methodology of producing it, but the means to generate enough energy to manufacture meaningful quantities.

If this is an antimatter production planet, it is a massive strategic target. Almost as crucial as finding the New Regent's location itself.

Graham could feel the tension in his body, the urge to order his fleet to turn and run, to somehow get back and send word to Earth Two. But he couldn't take that kind of chance...not until he was absolutely sure.

He watched as the scanners continued to update the displays. The energy readings became more focused, and radiation levels were coming in now, too. The cargo ships his force had destroyed in the adjacent system had carried antimatter, and the combat vessels had launched antimatter-armed missiles...there was no doubt from the size of the explosions or residual radiation they'd left behind.

And now, he was sure, as sure as he could be. That antimatter had come from the current system.

It had been produced there.

"Lieutenant, *Vaughn* and *Typhoon* will continue to move toward the planet, active scanners at maximum. The rest of the fleet will decelerate and prepare to head back through the…"

"Captain, we're picking up unidentified ships, coming around from the far side of the planet."

Any doubt Graham had still held was gone. His people had found a crucial First Imperium site, perhaps the enemy's primary antimatter production facility. Maybe even their *only* one. The New Regent, after all, was a reserve unit, hidden beyond the borders of the old Imperium. Its resources *had* to be smaller than those the original Regent had controlled.

If the fleet can destroy this production facility…

Or capture it…use it to produce antimatter for our own use…

Graham's eyes darted up to the screen, to the cluster of contacts heading toward his ships, accelerating at 70g.

If we can get out of here and get the word back…

"All units, maximum deceleration…now!"

His ships had to deal with their forward velocity before they could do anything about actually moving back toward the warp gate and getting out of the system. Right now, they were all heading toward the planet—and the oncoming enemy fleet—at better than three hundred kilometers per second.

"All ships acknowledge, Captain."

They can acknowledge all they want, but…

He was still doing the calculations, but his gut had the answer before his brain did. The enemy ships were going to get into range long before his own could get away and through the warp gate.

That meant he'd have another fight on his hands. *And they're fresh and we're already worn down…*

"Put me on fleetcom, Lieutenant." He snapped out the order without even thinking. He was operating on reflexes, on pure instinct. "*Poseidon* and *Ventura*…you are to decelerate at maximum emergency power, and then you will accelerate at full and get through the warp gate. And I mean full…everything you can squeeze out of your reactors and engines. You have to get back to G47…and then through the system and to G46." He knew one extra system wasn't that much, that he was taking a huge risk with the orders he was about to give, a command that would violate his own primary directive. He wanted every safeguard he could get. "Once you're in G46, scan thoroughly for any enemy presence, and if clear…" He paused, hanging on the precipice between issuing the order and pulling back. "…launch a probe directly back to Earth Two." He was still uncertain, a part of him wanting to rescind the order as soon as he'd issued it. But, the high command simply *had* to know about this, whatever the risk. Defense was a losing game long term, and the surest route to victory was to find vital First Imperium assets and destroy them. And, this was a big one.

Still, if he made an error, if the ships he was sending launched probes back to Earth Two, and there was a First Imperium vessel hidden somewhere, watching…

He would either be the officer who discovered the way for Earth Two to move closer to winning the desperate struggle against the Regent…or he would be the man who'd made the hugest blunder in history.

"All other ships…" He continued, trying to push the doubts away. He'd made his decision, and they served no purpose, not now. He'd crossed the Rubicon, and looking back could only distract him. "…we've got to buy them time to get back, and that means putting up one hell of a fight here. I know you're all still smarting from the battle in G47, and we've got some damage spread out through the fleet, but this is what we've got to do…and I know I can count on each and every one of you to give your absolute best effort."

And to die. That's what he was ordering his people to do, most of them at least. He knew that despite his mind's efforts to deny it. If they *had* stumbled onto the First Imperium's antimatter production center, he could only imagine the defenses that would be in place. The ships heading toward his fleet already outnumbered his own…and he didn't have the slightest doubt that there were more enemy vessels hiding behind the planet.

"All fleet units…battlestations. Let's show these bastards what we're made of."

He turned toward the tactical station. "Lieutenant, prepare to launch all remaining missiles." *Vaughn* had flushed her external racks, and she'd launched more than half the ordnance in her internal magazines during the fight in G47. Now, he needed everything his ship—all of his ships—had left to give.

"Weapons control reports all missiles armed and ready, sir." A short pause. "All ships report ready to launch as soon as the enemy ships enter range."

Graham shook his head slightly. He didn't have any real confirmation the approaching ships were actually enemies, though he didn't have any doubt either. He pondered that thought on and off for the next twenty minutes or so, until the vessels began launching their own missiles…and gave him any assurance he might have needed that they were hostile.

He looked across the bridge toward his tactical officer. He knew everyone on the bridge was waiting for him to give the launch order…but they would have to wait a bit longer. "All ships…hold missiles. We're going to get closer before we launch." The enemy outnumbered his forces, and he didn't have a doubt those missiles heading toward his fleet had antimatter warheads. Numbers and tech were both against him, and that left only tactics as an offset. He had to *outthink* the enemy, to outfight them. History told him the human victories against First Imperium fleets had been the result of creativity and the right combination of erratic and premeditated action.

Intuition. Gut feel. And his gut was telling him he needed to think outside the box.

"Yes, sir." He could hear the uncertainty in the tactical officer's tone. Doctrine called for launching missiles immediately, not holding them. There were instances where missiles were had been held to extremely close range and launched in sprint mode, directly toward their targets, but that wasn't a realistic option either. To manage that, Graham would have to hold his weapons back until after the enemy barrage reached his ships. Antimatter warheads were far too dangerous to endure while still holding missiles in the tubes, especially since most of his ships were already damaged. But, he could hold the weapons for a while, launch them at the last possible moment before the enemy volley entered range. That was a wager on his crews' skill and discipline, a tactical maneuver that left no allowances for delays or contingencies. It was a risk, but one that would improve targeting, and reduce the time the First Imperium ships had to intercept the incoming warheads. It would make a difference, some at least. And, Graham would take anything he could get now.

It would also time the detonation of his missiles with his own ships entering energy weapons range. Whatever shape his vessels were in, whatever they had left when they got through the enemy barrage, they would come on their targets just as they were enduring the impact of his own missile attack. He was facing machines, and not people, so there was little chance of benefitting from any psychological edge…but the enemy's robots wouldn't have time to do any damage control at all before they were fully engaged, not even minor adjustments and recalibrations. That might not be a huge advantage, but he would take whatever he could get.

He reached down, grabbing the harness that was hanging down from his chair and pulling it halfway across his body. He almost let it drop, remembering the pain as he'd lurched forward against the hyper-nylon straps in the previous fight. But, even for the pain in his back, the throbbing that was growing worse and worse, he realized he'd likely have been killed if he hadn't been strapped in at all. And, he had to live, at least a little longer. He had work to do…duty to perform.

He snapped the end of the harness into the buckle and heard the loud click as it set in place.

Chapter Four

"Twelve years, my love…can it be so long? Are you still there? Do you hear my voice when I speak? Sense my presence when I sit by your side?" Fleet Admiral Erika West sat in a small, hard metal chair next to the hospital bed, speaking softly, almost inaudibly. There was a woman lying in front of her, still, eyes closed, as they had been for twelve years now. But, she was breathing, on her own, as she had for many years now, free of the bulky respirator that had once been required to force air in and out of her tortured lungs. Unconscious but still alive. Nicki Frette had been in that coma since the first—and to date, only— major battle with the forces of the New Regent. She'd brought her fleet home, some of it at least, but she'd paid a price…and so had West.

The admiral commanding Earth Two's fleets felt the urge to reach out and touch Frette's cheek, to feel for warmth, or some other token reassurance that her friend and lover was still alive. But she could see the faint shimmer, and she knew the field that kept the stricken officer alive, that protected against the pathogens that would ravage Frette's weakened system, would repel any hand she reached out to touch, with a rather painful shock.

23

She'd done it more than once, but that had been years before.

West had left everything and everyone she cared for behind the Barrier, gone forever, as had all of the Pilgrims. That had been more than forty years past, but fragments of the pain still lingered. Frette had been one of the few people she'd allowed into her inner circle, and over time their relationship had progressed from professional to friendship, to…something more.

For the first few years after suffering her injuries, Frette had lain in a medpod, in partial cryostasis, the bulky device's machinery maintaining her vastly slowed bodily functions. But, Earth Two's technology level had increased rapidly over the past decade, and the medfield was a major improvement over the old pods. Still, in a way it unnerved West. Frette had appeared to be sick and beyond reach in the bulky pod, but now she just looked like she was sleeping. It somehow made West's loneliness worse.

The crusty admiral had a reputation as a merciless taskmaster, one she'd justly earned over the years, both before and after the fleet became trapped beyond the Barrier. People had been afraid of her when she'd been a forty-five-year-old freshly-promoted junior admiral. They were scared to death of her now at ninety, with forty-two years of commanding Earth Two's military under her belt. She didn't make connections easily, and she doubted she could have found someone to take Frette's place in her life, even if she'd been willing to try. But, with her partner still alive—and that's the one thing they'd assure her, that Frette *was* still alive, her brain functions active—such a thing was unthinkable. West had spent much of her life alone, but for the past twelve years, she'd been virtually cloistered whenever she was off duty.

West was a hardened warrior, and the blood that flowed in her veins was icy. She'd ached for Frette, longed for the times the two had spent together, for the connection they had both felt… but she hadn't shed a tear, not a single one for the woman she loved. Erika West didn't cry. She didn't show weakness. Ever. If that failed her, she would lose all she had left of herself. All that kept her going. There was no sweetness left in life, no real desire to live the rest of the extended lifespan the rejuv treatments had gifted—or cursed—her with. But there was duty, always duty. She had lived her life by it, and she would do so until the day death finally released her.

"Erika…"

West turned toward the sound, but she knew who it was before her eyes focused on the lithe figure approaching. Ana Zhukov had become a friend over the last decade, at least the closest thing West had to one. She'd always considered Max Harmon to be a friend as well, but he had been Earth Two's dictator now for twelve years, and as hard as the two had tried, it had proven difficult to maintain a personal relationship. There was just too much baggage. She was still loyal to Harmon, and she liked him, but the two hadn't sat down and just talked about something other than official duties in at least five years.

"Ana, how are you?" West pushed back against the grief she'd been feeling, struggling to present the hard demeanor she demanded of herself, even with a friend.

"I'm fine, Erika…how are you?" Zhukov's eyes darted to the bed, to the still form of Nicki Frette, and then back again to her friend.

"I am fine, Ana. As always."

West could see that Zhukov was teetering on the edge of pressing her further. But, in the end, she didn't. She said, simply, "I wanted to let you know, the railguns are ready for their first field tests. We need a battleship to mount them, and then we can put them through their paces."

West knew her friend hadn't come to the hospital to bring her a report she'd get in her next briefing anyway. She'd come to support her, to try to offer some kind of comfort. West appreciated that, though she was rather relieved Zhukov had chickened out. There were very few people truly close to her, but even those who were didn't understand her…and they couldn't relate to how little talking about things helped her.

"That is good news, Ana. The preliminary analysis suggests that the weapons may be decisive." Zhukov nodded. The railguns were a major development, not only because of the advanced science that made them work, but because they were original designs, not copies of old First Imperium tech. If they worked, they would be something only Earth Two possessed, a new long ranged weapon that could obliterate First Imperium ships before they entered energy weapons range. But, for all of that, West could see her friend felt foolish discussing it in the hospital…and for the clumsiness of her attempt to distract or support her, she wasn't sure which. She appreciated whatever Zhukov had intended, but she also took the opportunity to veer the subject to work, which was much more in her own comfort zone.

"Not that there has been any significant threat…for years now."

West got up and walked toward Zhukov. "We have been lucky for an extended period." West knew that was exactly what they'd been. Lucky. There were First Imperium ships out there, she was sure of that, and they were searching for Earth Two. One day, despite all the decoys and the safeguards on task forces leaving and returning to the planet, the enemy would find what they were looking for…and the people of Earth Two, pilgrims, NBs, Tanks, Mules—all of them—would face the greatest battle they'd ever imagined. If she lived to see that day, she knew she'd fight, with every bit of resolve that remained to her. But, she was far from sure that battle would end in victory, and, though she'd never shared her thoughts with anyone, not Zhukov, not Harmon, Erika West believed when that day came, her people were likely to lose, that they could very well see Earth Two destroyed and human life beyond the Barrier extinguished.

"It seems our precautions and deceptions have worked, at least so far." Zhukov followed West's lead, and the two walked out of the hospital room and down the long corridor to the elevators. "Still, it is hard living under such a shadow, knowing any day *could* be the one that brings it all crashing down."

West nodded. "We can only do our best. The decoy planets present the enemy with a significant puzzle to solve." The deception plan had been devised predominantly by Achilles and his Mules, and the republic had put a significant amount of its production into its execution. There were four false Earth Twos, in systems with artificial energy emissions, staged ship traffic, and a network of surrounding systems with clues leading to them…and away from the real thing. The enemy had discovered one, and they'd launched a massive assault, blasting the planet's surface to radioactive slag. But there were still three serving their purposes as diversions, drawing enemy scouting fleets away from the Earth Two.

West continued her nod, very deliberately. She wasn't sure what Zhukov expected from the future, and she didn't feel the need to share her own natural pessimism. She'd been a supporter of the diversion plan, and she still believed it was a useful device, but also that it would only buy time before the First Imperium found the real Earth Two. All that would take was one mistake, a careless effort by a returning task force or, barring even that, just enough time for the First Imperium to explore enough systems. There were thousands of stars in the area, but they were still finite. It didn't take more than math to determine the enemy *would* find Earth Two. Eventually.

"The railguns will make a difference, Erika. If the decoys and the other precautions can buy us enough time to equip the entire fleet with them."

West paused for a moment. She had seen the original specs on the new weapons system, and they *were* impressive. But she was the sort of person who doubted just about everything until she saw it with her own eyes. "I hope you're right, Ana. It would be nice to have a technological edge on the First Imperium for once, that's for sure." The railguns had been developed with the First Imperium in mind, their ranges and capabilities designed for maximum effectiveness against the powerful robot-controlled ships. West tried to make herself believe the Mules had developed a war-winning weapon, but all she could think of was the extended testing period required, and the immense job of somehow outfitting the republic's ships with a system that had to be built right into a vessel's spine. There were new ship designs already in the planning stages, but it would be years before they could be put into production and completed. And, in the interim, she had serious doubts the engineering teams would find reliable methods for jamming the giant railguns into existing vessels.

"I hope you're right, Ana," West finally said softly. *I have serious doubts we'll be able to retrofit the fleet, though.* She'd almost said it, but something had made her keep it to herself, a silent thought. Ana Zhukov was a brilliant woman and an enormously hard worker. She would do everything in her power to contribute to the republic's survival. Crushing whatever hopes she had, wisps of optimism that sustained her…it would serve no purpose.

Erika West's thoughts were dark, as they had been most of her life. But, they were hers, and not something she intended to inflict on those around her…and certainly not on the woman who'd become the closest thing she had to a best friend.

Whatever optimism Ana Zhukov could gather—could use to fool herself—it was hers, and West had no intention of robbing her friend of that last delusion.

Because, at the core, it was all she believed any of them had.

* * *

Connor Frasier looked out over the vast field, watching a company of Marines moving forward, taking advantage of a deep ravine and a cluster of surrounding hills for cover. They were assaulting a platoon of their comrades who were dug in on the ridge, all part of the wargames Frasier had conducted four times a year since the First Imperium had reappeared as a threat. He'd had almost universal support for the exercises at first, but as with most things, though Earth Two lived under constant threat of First Imperium attack, as more years passed uneventfully, the fear had begun to subside. The complaints about the cost of the exercises had grown louder, and Frasier knew he'd retained the funding only because President Harmon supported it.

Frasier watched the operation, his mind contrasting what he saw with old memories, days in the Corps back on the other side of the Barrier, even his days as a freshly minted lieutenant, serving under no less intimidating a persona as the terrible

Angus Frasier, the legendary commander of the old Scottish Regiment…and Connor's father as well. He remembered the old man fondly…and with a bit of vestigial intimidation as well.

His eyes narrowed, looking out over the valley. There were humans out there, clad in the newest Mark XII combat armor, but there were even more machines. The combat robots were part of his force, too, though they looked far too much like the enemy for his tastes. The Mules had created them, of course— and improved them steadily over the past twelve years. Frasier knew they increased the combat power of his Marine units ten-fold, and when he could see past his deep-seeded Corps preju-dices, he even had to admit that one of the robots was more than a match for an entire fireteam of his people.

But that didn't mean he had to like it.

The advancing Marines were moving quickly, staying low but trotting forward at better than thirty klicks per hour. He knew the capabilities of the Mark XII suits, also designed by the Mules, but it still hit him every time he saw his people at work. The new armor made his first fighting suit look like some medieval knight's garb…not to mention his childhood recollec-tions of the cumbersome chunk of metal his father had worn so many years before.

The old suits had been built from a chromium-iridium alloy, the strongest material available at that time. The new armor was constructed from First Imperium hyper-ceramic technol-ogy, and they were one-fifth the weight of their predecessors of several decades before, and several times as strong. They were smaller too, and they gave the wearer far more flexibility.

We keep getting better at killing. Connor had spent most of his life fighting the First Imperium, a battle of united human-ity versus a deadly machine menace, but he also remembered his father's wars, and the first he'd fought, under the famous Erik Cain. They'd fought against Earth's rival superpowers then, human against human, killing each other with all the energy and passion Frasier and his Marines now put into blasting First Imperium robots.

Where will we be if we can defeat this enemy? At peace finally? Or back, killing each other?

He pulled back from his thoughts with a start and diverted his attention back to the figures moving toward the defensive line. Most of his Marines were Tanks, clones created from selected DNA lines. They hadn't been created expressly as warriors, but many Tanks still sought out careers in the Corps, drawn by nascent tradition, and also by the fact that Frasier's reforms had removed the barriers to advancement to commissioned ranks. The clones had suffered a certain amount of discrimination in the Corps years earlier, as they still did in much of the republic's mainstream society, but Connor Frasier had mandated that every one of his warriors be treated the same way, and that nothing but merit govern promotions and other advancement.

He'd have placed his Corps up against any that had ever existed, even Elias Holm's magnificent formation that helped to win the Third Frontier War…but he'd also had to fight against those who considered his Marines obsolete, who had pushed for resources to go solely into building ships and orbital defenses, and to turn over what ground combat operations were necessary to the bots. Frasier didn't know where his objective analysis of the war and his Marine pride collided, but he'd argued passionately to maintain and expand Earth Two's human ground forces.

He'd even resorted once or twice to naked fear-mongering, to reminding people that twelve years ago, the Mules and the rest of Earth Two's people had almost fought a civil war. He felt guilty doing that, of course, of using internal fears to stoke public opinion. He counted Achilles and some of the other Mules as close friends…and his wife, Ana, was regarded as the 'mother' of all the Mules, the creator of their first quickening, alongside Hieronymus Cutter. But he was a Marine, first and foremost, by blood as well as choice, and he would do whatever was necessary to preserve the Corps.

And to see that it was ready for whatever fights lay ahead.

Chapter Five

Force Communique, Captain Roland Graham

All units, our formation is scattered, our vectors and velocities hopelessly mixed. Yet, we must continue the fight, and at all costs, we must prevent any enemy vessels from transiting into G47. Our comrades have gone to warn Earth Two, and we have to buy them time...time to get through the system and evade pursuit. Time to send the word back home.

The warning the high command must receive...that we have found and engaged the forces of the First Imperium.

E2S Vaughn
G48 System
Earth Two Date 10.17.42

Graham's hands tore at the harness strapped across his chest, fumbling for a moment with the buckles before they gave way and the straps slipped down to his legs, then to the floor under his chair. The last hit had been too much, the pain as much as he could bear. He'd taken some analgesics earlier, but he needed all his wits now, so he'd held back from higher doses. The fight had been a fierce one, half his ships crippled or destroyed, but they'd hit the enemy formation hard, and despite the numerical and tech advantage of the enemy, his people had shattered the attacking force.

The satisfaction had been immense, tempered even as it was by the price his people had paid. But it hadn't lasted long.

Before his forces could even reorganize their disordered formation, more enemy ships came around the planet, a force larger than the first one…and moments later, behind that, yet another. Graham had watched as the ships emerged, one after the other, knowing as he did he was seeing whatever miniscule chance any of his people had of escaping, of returning home, slipping away before his eyes.

"Put me on fleetcom, Lieutenant."

"Yes, sir." The tactical officer was exhausted, that much Graham could tell from the man's voice. He was scared too, that was just as evident. Graham was a combat veteran, but for most of his people, the fight in G47, and the battle they were still fighting, had been a baptism of fire.

Graham had survived his first battle years before, but he was slowly coming to terms with the fact that most of his people wouldn't share that opportunity.

"You are on fleetcom, sir."

Graham opened his mouth to speak, but then he paused and cleared his throat. He hadn't realized how thirsty he was, how dry and parched his mouth had become. "You have fought well, all of you, and with your skill and heroism, you have vanquished a superior force, and crushed it utterly. Yet, we are not done. More enemy forces approach…and we cannot yet retreat. We must hold, whatever the cost. We must keep the First Imperium ships back from the warp gate and give our comrades on *Poseidon* and *Ventura* the time to cross the G47 system, and to reach a position that allows them to send news of our discovery back to Earth Two."

He fell silent for a moment, feeling an impulse to sugarcoat things for his people, but then rejecting it. *They deserve the truth…*

"We will fight here, and we will do what we must. I will not lie to you and say that we will all return home. You all know better than that. For many of us—perhaps even all—this will be our last fight. To that, I can only add that for twelve years

Earth Two has waited for cataclysm, for some First Imperium patrol to discover its system and to direct massive fleets of ships to attack and destroy all we hold dear. Our every day of survival has been miraculous in its own way, a testament to our combined strength as a people. So, stand to your posts now, and stare death boldly in the eye…and, if your courage falters, think of loved ones and friend, parents, siblings, spouses, children…all those for whom we wage this struggle. All those our sacrifices here may save from a dark and deadly future."

He turned and nodded to the tactical officer to cut the link. He could see the spark in the lieutenant's eye, and he knew his words had affected the man. He hoped they had been as well-received by the others in the fleet. He wasn't as sure how he felt. He wanted to be inspired, but he knew he was also manipulating his spacers, tugging at emotional heartstrings to get them to fight harder.

He waited a moment, watching silently as the enemy approached. They would be launching missiles soon, he was sure of that, and none of his ships had ordnance left to return that fire. His vessels could do nothing at long range save endure the enemy's barrage. So, that left only one option.

"Lieutenant…all ships are to engage engines at full power. Maximum thrust, forward."

His people might not have a chance, but they wouldn't go easily either, and they would take their share of enemies with them. And, whatever else happened, they would hold the line long enough for their friends to get the message back to Earth Two.

* * *

The Intelligence analyzed the reports and scans coming in, and it formulated actions, developed tactical plans, and prepared communications to its fleet units. Then, it filed them in its storage banks. The orders from the Regent were clear, and they overrode normal protocols. The enemy ships were, in fact, to be destroyed, but they were to be allowed to extend the fight, to give time for the two vessels that fled to reach some point sufficiently distant for them to alert higher authorities. And those ships were to be allowed to escape. They were not to be pursued or given any reason to fear that they were being followed.

Such orders were in absolute contradiction to the Intelligence's standard directives, to defend both the planet and the secrecy of its location at all costs. Normal operational procedures called for the Intelligence to dispatch more ships to chase down the escaping enemy vessels, to destroy them before they could communicate the location of the Regent's antimatter production facility. And, certainly, normal procedure called for tracking any enemy ships that might give an indication where the humans' primary world was located. But, now, it did nothing. Obedience to the Regent was above all other considerations, and its tactics and strategies were not to be questioned.

The Intelligence had dispatched the ships it had deployed into small groups, with sufficient spacing between each assault to allow the humans time to conduct modest reordering operations and limited damage control. The enemy ships were badly hurt, and their magazines were depleted. But still, their performance in battle exceeded even the Intelligence's most extreme estimates. It had received updates from the Regent many times, warnings that the human's prowess in combat defied all logical classification and calculation…yet only now did it begin to truly comprehend the vague generalizations provided in those reports.

The Intelligence considered the Regent's plan. The enemy was to be allowed to confirm the true purpose of the planet, and to send this information back to their home base. The brilliance in the plan was clear in its simplicity. There was no deception, to trickery…the system *was* a critical component of the Regent's power structure, second in importance only to its own secret location. The Intelligence questioned the use of such a valuable asset as bait…yet, it understood, in part, the strange cleverness of the enemy. No staged setup, no phony bait, could be assured to lure them to attack. It was a gamble, but, given the armament the Regent had available, it was one likely to succeed. There was no way the humans could know about the hidden fleets, nor the fact that virtually all of the Regent's forces would be present, waiting for the attack.

The humans were daring, aggressive, ready to take risks to achieve victory…and all this would be turned against them. They would risk their fleet, the forces they had built up for years, and they would lose all in one great struggle.

There were but two possibilities as to the outcome. Fragments of the shattered wreckage of the enemy fleet might limp back to their homeworld, their discipline obliterated by the crushing defeat they'd sustained. They would lead the Regent's forces to the location of the final battle, the ultimate extermination of the dangerous biologics.

Or, they would perish, all of them, as their damaged ships fled desperately into the void, to their ultimate doom, leaving the still-hidden humans cowering on their planet, stripped of most of their strength, awaiting the inevitable moment the Regent's probes would find them.

Either way, the infection of the biologics would be cleansed. The Regent would be victorious, and its predecessor avenged.

* * *

"Reroute power to batteries three and four. Shut down life support to sections C3 and C4, and redirect energy to the main conduits." Graham had ordered those compartments evacuated a moment before, but if any of his people had lagged behind, they would die in the next few seconds, as *Vaughn*'s AI sealed the hatches and shut down the heat and air flow to the already badly damaged sections. He didn't like cutting it this close, but right now his only concern was keeping *Vaughn* functioning, at least at some minimal level.

"Rerouting power flow now, sir. Lieutenant Terrell reports he'll have the guns back online in two minutes."

"One minute," Graham snapped. He wasn't angry with his tactical officer, or with the engineer making the report. But, he wasn't sure *Vaughn* had two minutes left.

Hell, he wasn't even sure about the single minute.

The battle had raged for almost two days, his ships using every maneuver they could concoct, every trick of war he'd ever known, and a few he'd made up on the spot. He was down to four ships, at least there had been three others fifteen minutes before, when *Vaughn*'s scanners had last been operational. All he was really sure of now was that his battered ship was still there.

He was scared, of course, and he'd pretty much lost any slivers of hope that his survivors would find a way out of the fight into which he'd ordered them. But, there was satisfaction, too, a pride in what his people had done. Somehow, they'd held off the enemy forces, driven back attack after attack, and bought time for their comrades to escape…and to get word back to Earth Two that they'd discovered a way to really hurt the enemy, even to destroy their ability to carry on their genocidal war.

Vaughn shook again and, as he gripped the sides of his chair to steady himself, he could hear creaking sounds and the distant echoes of structural supports collapsing deep inside his ship. The cruiser was dying, he knew that, but she was still fighting, and as long as his desperate spacers and the legion of bots racing to restore what systems were still reparable could get a gun back online, the battle would go on.

"Batteries three and four operational, sir!" The tactical officer's voice was shrill, excitement at the restoration of the guns momentarily overcoming the dark mood that had taken them all.

"Fire!" Graham said immediately, but still too late. His gunners had been on orders to fire at will, and they beat their commander to the punch. Graham could hear the distant, high-pitched whine as the guns fired. Both shots hit, at least in his mind, as he closed his eyes and imagined the lasers slamming into one of the robot-controlled ships chasing his vessel. But the reality was more uncertain. Most of *Vaughn*'s sensor suite was down, and what little scanning capability remained to the battered vessel had been diverted to the gunnery stations. He knew what that meant in terms of the likelihood of scoring any hits, but there was nothing to be gained dwelling on it.

Then: "Captain, gunnery reports one hit on the lead enemy

ship. Preliminary assessment indicated moderate damage inflicted."

Graham just nodded. It was a near miracle that the guns were back online at all, and another one that the gunnery teams had manage to hit anything at all, considering the status of *Vaughn's* scanners. But, Graham couldn't completely push away the disappointment at the reality compared to the pair of critical hits he'd seen in his imagination.

He was losing it, to an extent at least. He was going to die, almost certainly. All of them were. There was no way to escape, none that he could see. The emotions welling up inside him, fear of course, and sadness for those he'd never see again, but also guilt. He had come to the G47 system because he'd been ordered to do so, and he'd ventured into G48 because duty demanded he investigate the First Imperium contacts his people had encountered. But that didn't alleviate the guilt. He had more than sixteen hundred officers and crew in his force, and save for just over a hundred in the two ships he'd sent back, they were all dead...or about to die. He tried to tell himself there had been no choice, that he'd only done what he had to do, what he'd been trained to do. But, he still felt responsible.

"Lieutenant, I want those guns recharged as quickly as possible. Tell Lieutenant Terrell to push it right up to the limit." Graham's mind struggled to cope with the reality that he was very likely living the last minutes, even seconds, of his life. Yet, one thing was blindingly clear to him. If his people had to die, they were damned sure going to take as many of those accursed machines with them. They would die well here, even if no one lived to tell the story.

"Sir, Lieutenant Terrell reports maximum energy flow to the guns underway. He projects a full charge in..." The officer didn't finish his report...and *Vaughn's* batteries didn't fire the shot Graham had been waiting for.

Instead, the tortured vessel shook hard again, and the bridge went dark, save for the showers of sparks flying around as systems overloaded and burned out in spectacular fashion. Graham could hear internal explosions from within his ship, and he looked all around his chair as the dim battery-powered emergency lights came on, squinting to see how many of his bridge crew were still there, at their posts.

Rageski, the comm officer, was dead. There wasn't any doubt about that. Her head and half her torso had been crushed by a felled girder. The tactical officer, Roan Harken, was down, too, thrown out of his chair by a heavy shock from his destroyed workstation. He was lying still on the deck, but Graham couldn't tell whether he was dead or alive.

Graham felt woozy, his vision blurry. Then, he noticed a trickle of blood making its way slowly down his face. He reached up, and he could feel his hair was wet. *Soaked with blood,* he realized.

He looked at the deck around his chair. There is was, a piece of one of the conduits that ran along the bridge's ceiling. That *had* run along the ceiling. It had broken loose from its mountings…and hit Graham in the head.

He hadn't felt a thing, not at first. But, now his head was throbbing, and his vision was becoming fuzzier. He looked around the bridge, trying to find one of his officers still at his or her post, someone to shout orders to before he slipped into the blackness even then coming from all sides to take him.

Simmons. She was still in her chair, her hands moving frantically over her dead workstation.

Jill…he shouted out to her, or at least he tried. Her name was in his mind, but nothing came out of his mouth. He just sat, still, helpless, trying to say something, anything.

Then he leaned forward and fell to the deck, as darkness took him.

Chapter Six

"You have done quite well, Terrance. Your situation as a youth was far from optimal, and any standard pattern of human development and behavioral characteristics virtually ensured your earlier difficulties. You have exceeded likely parameters in returning to the Academy and completing your cycle of education." The slightly machine-sounding voice paused for just a few seconds before adding, "And, you look quite the part in that uniform, *Captain* Compton."

Terrance leaned back in his chair, feeling an uncomfortable flush in his face. He knew it was a machine talking, and that it only required a relatively small chunk of code to pick out such an obvious way to complement someone, but he suspected he would never fully adapt to thinking of the Compton AI solely as a computer. He knew he shouldn't crave the machine's approval, but he did anyway.

"It shouldn't be captain anything, and you know it. Just one more bit of preference I got for being...his son." Terrance had managed to stop saying "you" and "your" when talking to the machine about Admiral Compton, but he still had a little hitch in his speech when doing it.

"You are not a twenty-two-year-old graduate, Terrance. You have many life experiences. An elevated rank is appropriate."

"And do you think some other cadet who managed to fail himself out of the Academy would be welcomed back years later, and rewarded for completing his training twenty years late by a promotion? Or is that an honor reserved for *his* son?" Terrance had been privately relieved when President Harmon had given him his captain's bars. He was embarrassed enough about his youthful foolishness, and he hadn't been looking forward to working alongside a bunch of ensigns barely half his age. But, now, of course, he was sensitive about the special treatment he'd received. That he'd *always* received.

"I am not a suitable counterpart for working through your emotional trials related to your past actions, however, I would suggest that you allow yourself to consider the mathematical equivalency. Yes, you made what could be perceived now as some errors in judgment...but you were also placed in a very difficult situation, even from before your birth, as the son of the recently deceased Admiral Compton. There was never a time in your formative years when an entire planet did not look to you, almost demanding that you grow into your father reborn. The expectation that a child, and then a young adult, match up to the abilities of a fifty-year combat veteran is, on purely logical terms, absurd. Yet, your people were still afraid, and they still felt the fresh pain at the fleet's losses. What happened to you was no one's fault, and certainly not deliberate, but the stimuli that pushed you to do things you now regret were predominantly external. It is unlikely very many of your people could have done better if they'd been born in your place. I suggest you simply put pointless regrets behind you. With your rejuv treatments, it is likely you can live nearly another century. Do not waste that time brooding over a lost twenty years."

Terrance stared over at the machine, nothing much to look at really, but a series of shiny silver cylinders. He was still plagued by self-doubt and guilt, but he began to consider the AIs words. He'd disgraced his father when he was a young man, his behavior far from that expected of Admiral Terrance Compton's son.

The machine was right. It *had* been difficult living up to a father who was nothing less than a revered legend, especially when that father not only died before he was born, but never even knew he existed. Terrance had found solace in only one place, aside from the wildness that had led him astray in his younger years. The Compton AI had been Hieronymus Cutter's effort to salvage as much as possible of the memories and intellect of the slain leader, and while the achievement had been an astonishing one, the resulting intelligence was *not* Terrance Compton reborn.

It had taken years for Terrance II to come to realize, and to *truly* believe, that single fact that he had, on some level, always known. And, it had changed almost nothing. By the time he'd stopped seeking a father's approval from the complex machine, he realized he considered the thing a friend, perhaps the only close friend he had. And, he'd continued coming there, virtually the only person beyond a software engineer every now and again, who ever visited the semi-forgotten computer.

He wondered sometimes, if there hadn't been a reversal of sorts, if he hadn't begun to fill the role the computer had played in his own life. Did the machine ever really considered him a friend? Did it feel loneliness or some rough equivalent as its usefulness, and the attention it received from the others, diminished? Or something akin to satisfaction when he arrived for a visit? The intelligence was a sophisticated one, but according to Hieronymus Cutter, it wasn't capable of real emotion. Terrance wasn't so sure. The two of them shared one experience. The machine had also been a focal point for the fleet's refugees in the aftermath of Terrance Compton's death, and they had looked, at one time, to the AI that held his memories with the same sort of wide-eyed hope they had directed toward the great admiral's son.

"I have not seen an assignment posted for you yet. Have you decided what branch of the navy you plan to serve?" It was a typical conversational question. If the intelligence didn't have normal thought processes like a human, it did a damned good impersonation.

"I'm still…negotiating…with President Harmon. He hasn't

given what I asked for…yet. But, he seems reluctant to outright refuse me."

"You have requested a combat posting." Terrance couldn't detect any question mark in the AI's tone. He wondered what percentage chance the machine had assigned to its guess on his decision.

"Yes." He paused. "I feel like I must follow in my father's footsteps. I owe him something at this stage…something more than disappointment."

"You do not have to become a warrior because your father was one. Your father was the illegitimate child of a wealthy industrialist. He only joined the navy to escape the bitterness of his half-siblings and the conflict over control of the family businesses. He felt no particular calling to serve in the navy, certainly not at first."

"And, yet, look what he did."

"Terrance Compton became a very gifted tactician, but there was enormous random chance in how his life progressed. His relationship with Augustus Garret, for example, was highly formative to both of them, and contributed in many ways to the growth of the two men into extremely gifted naval officers. However, despite his own achievements, based on his memories, on what I know of the man, he would have been satisfied to see you pursue any field of endeavor, as long as you did your best."

"You sound like my mother. She's horrified at the thought of me signing onto the combat forces."

"Your mother knew your father perhaps better than anyone, Terrance, save possibly for Admiral Garret. You would be well-served to consider her viewpoints." Sophie Barcomme had been one of the scientists on the fleet, and Terrance Compton's lover. She'd been very active in Earth Two's development in the early years, but then she'd slipped back into somewhat of a self-imposed semi-exile, where she remained.

Terrance laughed. "Yes, that may be true, but I still feel the way I do. And, I'd wager I'm seeing more of my mother worrying about her only child than any deep analysis about what my father would have wanted." He hesitated for a few seconds. He *was* his mother's only child, at least on Earth Two, but he knew she'd had another, that he had a half-sister, somewhere light-years away, beyond the Barrier. He knew he'd never meet her, that his mother would never see her daughter again. She'd rarely spoken of the losses she'd suffered when the fleet had been trapped beyond the Barrier, but Terrance knew about the sadness that weighed on her. She'd lost one family and then found happiness again with his father. And, then she'd lost him, too.

He wasn't sure if she could handle losing him too.

He felt guilty for adding to her burden, for putting himself in danger and making her worry about losing the last person close to her...but he had to do what he felt was right. And, the more he'd thought about it, the less doubt remained.

"You may be able to help Earth Two more effectively in other ways, Terrance."

He looked back at the machine, despite the pointlessness of the gesture. *It's trying to convince me to choose something safer, too.* He felt a burst of the old feelings, when he'd truly believed the AI was his father, at least in some way.

"Do you really think it matters? Our line units haven't seen much combat since the fighting twelve years ago, and if things do hit the fan, don't you think it's going to be all hands on deck, so to speak? If the new Regent finds Earth Two, I suspect we'll be arming school children, so how much more chance am I taking joining a combat unit?"

"Your analysis is logical, Terrance, though incomplete. You are correct that in a last-ditch defense situation, every resident of Earth Two would be in grave danger...but you underestimate the chances of limited conflict, even of offensive actions by the navy against the Regent, and the risks attendant to such operations. I do not have sufficient data to calculate your increased chance of death or injury if you pursue this course, but I am quite certain it is substantial."

"I was a screwup for years...I just finished the Academy course, almost twenty years late. I have to do something meaningful, and I can't think of another way to do that. I can't compete with the Mules on research, there aren't really any more politics since President Harmon took control…I guess it's just time for me to do what I have to do."

He paused. "Time to see if I'm really my father's son."

*   *   *

H2 looked down at the counter, staring at the small bits of electronic circuitry, but seeing nothing but a soft blur. He was troubled, and his thoughts were elsewhere.

"H2, are you okay?" Hieronymus Cutter was standing about two meters from his protégé. He'd created H2, from a DNA specimen and some preserved First Imperium genetic material, as he'd created all the Hybrids…the Mules. But, H2 had been the first, and the human DNA he'd used had been his own. He'd always had a special affinity for the man that was almost his clone, indeed, a vastly improved genetic version of himself, but he also knew his first creation, the closest thing to a child he had, and closer in some ways, was troubled.

"I am fine, Father." H2 always called Cutter 'father.' It wasn't strictly speaking, a correct usage, though it was more so for him than for the other Mules, who also used the term to refer to the scientist most responsible for their creation.

Cutter knew H2 wasn't fine, that his creation was troubled, as he had often been throughout his life. If Cutter had stopped at H2, he'd have created a demigod, a man whose intellect and physical abilities were far greater than any normal human's. But Cutter hadn't stopped. He'd continued his research and experiments, and his next creations, building on the work that had gone into creating H2, had been the production of the first 116 Mules.

No…117 Mules, he reminded himself. H2 was a Mule, at least to Cutter he was. He didn't regret developing the Hybrid program and the Mules that followed, but he'd come to understand how it had affected H2. The brilliant scientist he'd created, the nearly perfect physical and mental specimen, had developed an inferior complex of sorts. Cutter had always considered his creations to be the same…and it had taken him some time to understand the magnitude of the difference. But H2 had been aware of that fact all of his life.

The newer Mules were even more advanced from human norms than H2, and they were well aware of that fact. There had always been a sort of uncomfortable camaraderie between H2 and the others. They considered him the first of their kind, and gave him something akin to respect in that regard. But, they also thought of him as inferior, and, with the arrogance so common among the Mules, they'd often let it be known in cutting and insensitive ways.

H2 had worsened the break between himself and the others when he'd sided with Cutter against Achilles' rebellion years before. As always, it wasn't any overt hostility between them, but H2 knew he was always somewhat of an outsider and, for the most part, he spent his time in the lab working, often alone, and when not, usually with Cutter or with Ana Zhukov, feeling the entire time, Cutter suspected, like some adult child still living with his parents.

"You can speak to me about anything, H2…you should know that by now." Cutter almost winced as he spoke the Mule's name. He'd dubbed his clone Hieronymus 2, perhaps not thinking enough at the time that his creation would grow to be an actual person, not some kind of pet or something else to be dubbed with a cute version of his own name. He hadn't intended any harm, but the fact that the other Mules had all been given individual names, if ones borrowed from mythology, further exacerbated the differences between the first of their kind and those that followed.

"I'm concerned about the Mules…the other Mules." Cutter winced at the indication that even H2 didn't consider himself truly a member of the group of elite Hybrids.

"What about them?" Cutter wasn't sure where H2 was going.

"Well, Father…you know they are loyal to you, of course."

Cutter nodded. Whatever troubles the Mules had had with the other humans on Earth Two, he'd never doubted they regarded Ana Zhukov and him with a special reverence.

"Well…they don't take me into their confidence, of course,

not really, but I still hear things, especially from some of the younger Mules."

"Things?" Cutter remembered the unrest sparked by Achilles twelve years before as if it had happened yesterday, but he couldn't imagine the informal leader of the Mules would incite another rising of his people, not with the Regent still out there. Cutter didn't suspect Achilles approved of the continued limitation on Mule quickenings, but it was a major improvement over the Prohibition, and not one he thought would lead to outright conflict.

"The limitations on quickenings, Father." H2 almost immediately confirmed Cutter's guess. "You know Achilles doesn't like it…none of the Mules do. Neither do I."

"Nor I, H2."

"I know that, Father. And, so does Achilles. For all the angst, and even some bitterness among the older Mules, none of them are ready to return to the tensions of twelve years ago."

"That is good. Achilles appears to be firmly in control, even if his position is an informal one."

"He is, Father…that is not my concern. I am worried about the younger Mules."

"In what way, H2? Would they rise up now, against the wishes of Achilles?"

"No, I don't believe so. Not while the threat of the Regent's forces looms over us."

"Then what is it, H2?"

H2 paused for a moment, which contrasted sharply with his tendency to answer quickly. "You must remember, Father, that unlike the other Mules, I have been given a greater comprehension of humility. I understand what it is like to seethe with impatience when a Normal is unable to understand what I am trying to explain…and yet, I also know how it feels to be regarded as lesser, as a being of a lower order."

Cutter hesitated, feeling a flush of renewed regret for the difficulties his first Hybrid had endured. "I know things have been difficult for you, H2, but…"

"No, Father…it is not that." H2 had never interrupted Cutter before, and now the scientist was really concerned about whatever was bothering the Mule. "I merely state that I have some level of understanding regarding what the younger Mules feel. They have no humility, none at all, and unlike Achilles and the others among the originals, they came into being as part of an existing society. They have no recollections, as I do, and as Achilles and the original 116 do, of a civilization struggling to take hold, or even of the fear of twelve years ago, when the New Regent's forces struck. All the Mules are arrogant, and with some justification, perhaps, but it is more than that with the younger ones."

"More?"

"Yes, Father…more. They see only the burden the Mules carry for advancing Earth Two's technology, the contributions their predecessors have made, and that they now begin to make. They see the limitations on quickenings, and they read the histories of the Prohibition."

"There are injustices, certainly, but our society can overcome these." Cutter was far from sure he believed his own words.

"Can we, Father? Twelve years ago, Achilles did what he felt he must, with regret and hesitation. The older Mules, for all their arrogance and feelings of superiority, look upon the Normals as cousins, if not quite brothers, even as wards whom it is their duty to protect." Another pause. "The younger Mules do not feel this way…I am sure of it. They understand the threat of the Regent, but I fear they consider the Normals to be a danger as well. There is far less of the concern Achilles and the others share for the Natural Borns and the Tanks. There is anger. Bitterness."

H2 looked right at Cutter and, after a moment of silence, he said, "They are learning to resent the others, to hate them. I fear what they might do, after the Regent is destroyed…and even before, if much more time elapses without a more overt threat to Earth Two."

Cutter didn't answer…he just stood still, trying to ignore the nauseous feeling rising in his gut.

Chapter Seven

Fleet Artificial Intelligence System, E2S Vaughn

Captain? Captain Graham? I am detecting life signs aboard, including your own. I have dispatched medibots to the bridge, as it appears all personnel in sickbay are incapacitated and unable to respond.

The automated repair systems under my direction were able to restore partial engine power. I have maneuvered the ship through the nearest warp gate, to the previously unexplored G49 system, where we are now positioned. We have escaped immediate destruction, but we are now scanning energy readings from the warp gate. Data currently available is too incomplete to draw any conclusions, but the possibility of enemy pursuit cannot be ignored. The likelihood of reaching the nearest warp gate out of the system before interception is nil.

Captain? Captain Graham? Can you hear me?

E2S Vaughn
G49 System
Earth Two Date 10.19.42

The hazy red light cut through the darkness, like a fuzzy, pinkish cloud. There was something, high above, white…no, more gray, hanging in the distance, out of reach…

Roland Graham was lost, trapped somewhere between con-

48

sciousness and darkness. All was silent. No…there *was* something, something familiar. A voice.

The blurry gray above slowly slipped into focus. Metal, light gray, covered with conduits and piping…with chunks of blackened wiring hanging down.

I'm on Vaughn…

He could see more now, the ceiling of the bridge recognizable…both reassuring in its familiarity and distressing for all the damage he could see, gashes in the steel, chunks of twisted metal protruding all around, gaps where sections of equipment and structural supports had fallen to the deck.

I'm alive…

Graham found that realization oddly surprising. He remembered the feeling of drifting away, of the blackness taking him. He'd thought he was dying then, and that his ship would follow moments later, if not seconds. But he was still here…and that meant *Vaughn* was too.

How?

His hearing was still impaired, the ringing in his ears drowning out most external sounds. There was definitely a voice, someone speaking, but he couldn't make out the words, not at first.

He tried to move, but he encountered stiffness first, and then, as he pushed harder, pain. He was injured…somewhere. He couldn't tell, but as long as he lay still, there was no pain.

I can't lay here on the deck.

He took a deep breath, feeling a sharp twinge as he did. Whatever other injuries he had, he suspected there was a broken rib, perhaps more than one.

He gritted his teeth, turning to the side, reaching out and putting his hand on the deck, pushing himself up. It hurt like hell, but he managed to get to a sitting position. The tinnitus was still distracting, but it had receded enough for words to get through. The voice.

Vaughn's AI…

"Captain Graham…"

"Report…" He rasped out the command, realizing that

his parched throat had barely pushed the single audible word through his lips. He doubted any of the crew would have heard him, but the AI's input/output systems were highly sensitive.

"Captain Graham…I am pleased to hear from you. My scanners confirmed that you were alive. I have dispatched Medibots to your location, but the lift system is inoperative, and that is slowing response times." Even as the slightly electronic voice reported to him, a hatch opened up, and a small hover drone slipped out onto the bridge. It was a medical unit, far less comprehensive than the bots, but apparently the only thing that could get to the bridge under the present circumstances. It moved across the room, toward the captain.

Graham lifted his hand slightly and said, "No…I'm okay. Check on the others."

"Captain, I strongly suggest…"

"I said check on the others." Graham knew the AI was programmed to preference his status. He was, after all, not only *Vaughn*'s captain, but commander of the entire fleet. And he was going to act like it.

Fleet commander? What fleet…there is no fleet. Maybe just a few chunks of floating wreckage scattered around, with enough life support to keep a few of us alive.

But for how long?

"Ship status?" he asked, as he watched the small drone change direction and move toward one of the nearby officers. As far as Graham had been able to tell, he was the only one on *Vaughn*'s bridge still conscious. Perhaps the only one still alive.

"Automated damage control systems were able to temporarily restore partial engine power. In the absence of human direction, I utilized the available resources to take *Vaughn* through the nearest warp gate before the enemy forces could intercept. We are in the system tentatively designated, G49. Our scanning capability is currently extremely limited, but we detected no signs of enemy ships present when we entered. However, we are picking up intermittent energy spikes at the warp gate."

They're coming after us…

Graham felt a wave of fear, almost panic. He'd been ready to die…he'd thought he had died. But, now, he felt the urgent need to escape. He almost regretted whatever twist of fate had spared him…only to face a hopeless situation, the near-inevitability of dying all over again.

His people *were* dead, most of them, he suspected. He had no idea who else on *Vaughn* might still be alive, but his fleet was shattered, there was no doubt about that. Whatever survivors were crawling through the wreckage of his flagship or lying unconscious somewhere, just this side of death, most of those he'd led out from Earth Two were almost certainly already lost.

"Engine power?" He was fighting off the despair that was struggling to take him. He was terrified, in many ways broken… but there was still a vestige of the fleet commander in him.

"Minimal, Captain. Unfortunately, reaching the warp gate in the previous system taxed the makeshift repairs heavily. I have all automated systems working on restoration, but there is currently nothing available sufficient to accelerate the ship beyond 1g."

Graham realized *Vaughn* was already accelerating at a single gravity. The compensator systems were almost certainly offline, which meant the gravity he felt—pseudo-gravity, really—was from the engine thrust.

"Course? Directly away from the warp gate?"

"Yes, Captain."

It was a stupid question. He knew the AI would be doing everything possible to get the wounded ship out of harm's way. And, he was just as certain that 1g acceleration wasn't going to get that job done. Anything that came through that gate would almost certainly have fifty times or more that miserable rate of thrust.

He climbed up to his feet…and he almost plunged back to the deck as dizziness took him. He reached out, grabbed hold of the edge of his chair, barely stabilizing himself. He shifted his weight and plopped down in the seat, sucking in a deep breath as he closed his eyes and tried to get his equilibrium back.

He reached up and put his hand on his head, pulling it away as he felt wetness. He looked at his palm, covered with a sheen of sticky, half-congealed blood. He had a head injury.

It can't be too bad…I'm here, awake…

He wondered if he was hallucinating, if he could trust anything he saw, heard.

"Status," he said softly. "Mine…"

"The crew monitoring system is down, Captain. I do not have access to your vital signs or other medical readouts. You appear to have sustained a blow to the head, as well as an injury to the chest, likely several fractured or broken ribs. You have a number of contusions and cuts, but none of your injuries appear to be immediately life-threatening. There has been radiation leakage in multiple areas of the ship, including the bridge, but there are no apparent signs of severe poisoning at this time."

"So, it's bad, but I'm still alive."

"That is a reasonable assessment, Captain."

Graham frowned. He hadn't really been talking to the AI that last time, and he certainly hadn't been looking for a response, least of all, confirmation of what was apparent even to him, even in his battered state.

"Anything new on the…" He was halfway through asking about the warp gate, when the AI beat him to the punch.

"Scanners intermittently active, Captain. Picking up sporadic energy readings. It is impossible to assign a certainty to any conclusions, but it appears we have one or more vessels transiting."

So…now I die again…

"Any progress on the engines?" He couldn't imagine what the repair bots had managed to do in the two or three minutes that had elapsed since the AI's last report, but he couldn't think of anything else.

"Negative, Captain."

A few seconds passed by, silent, save for the sounds of stirring among one or two other of the bridge crew, as the lone medical drone tended to them. *At least I'm not the only one to survive…not that it's likely to matter…*

"Captain…scanners confirm a vessel emerging from the warp gate and moving toward our position."

"Weapons?" Graham knew the answer before he even asked

the question.

"Negative, Captain. All offensive systems are offline."

"We can't fight...we can't run..." He was speaking softly, to himself, but the AI answered him again anyway.

"That is essentially correct, Captain. Projected time until enemy vessel enters firing range four to eleven minutes, depending on class and armament. Minimal operating power of scanners makes more accurate assessment impossible.

Graham found it less than comforting that the AI had data on all known First Imperium weapons, and the only use it served was to give him a seven-minute range in calculating the instant he, and whoever remained of his crew, would die.

He felt a strangeness that it even mattered to him, that he was so anxious to know just when the end would come.

Graham gave up, leaning back and exhaling, resigned to wait for death. But that only lasted a moment. Then, he felt a resurgence, a rush of energy he couldn't completely explain. He might be doomed, he might die...but he would never give up the fight until it was over.

"I need options to increase engine output...right now. Do we have anyone conscious down in engineering?"

"There are no options that do not violate core safety parameters. It is impossible to report with certainty on the status of crew members with the monitoring system down, however no personnel have reported in. All functional repair bots are working on the engines and reactor, but projections are six to eight hours for any meaningful..."

"I said now! What can we do now?"

"The power conduits leading to the engines are badly damaged, Captain. Any increase in power levels before making necessary repairs..."

"All power to the engines now. Damn the risk!" *What the hell difference does it make if we blow ourselves up, or let some First Imperium ship do it?*

"Captain, there is no way to calculate the risks involved, with so many of the internal monitoring systems offline. Caution is..."

"Is there a First Imperium ship heading our way or not?"

"Yes, Captain."

Graham was exasperated with the AI's almost intentional-seeming naivety. He understood, of course, and *Vaughn* would probably survive longer if it sat where it was, if only by a few minutes. Deciding to take whatever miniscule chance there was, and most likely blowing up the ship in the process, might be a human way of thinking, at odds with the machine's best calculations about how to proceed in a desperate situation. But Graham was still in command.

"Do it. Now."

"Yes, Captain."

Graham turned back toward the one functional screen on the bridge. The scanner data coming in had been intermittent at best, but, as he looked this time, he could see a staticky image, a First Imperium ship. The mass numbers had updated, and the computer was displaying file footage of a massive vessel.

It's a Leviathan...

Leviathans were massive superbattleships, the largest First Imperium craft known.

Vaughn hadn't detected any ships that large during the fight in G48, not even close. Graham held his gaze, even as he could hear the AI's voice warning him about the thrust levels about to kick in. Assuming the ships didn't just blow immediately.

Where the hell did that thing come from?

Graham felt a new fear, growing into a panic. He'd sent back intel on the antimatter factory, but now he realized he'd probably vastly underreported the strength of the defending forces.

If there are Leviathans in that system...

"No..." He mouthed the word more than spoke it, and he shook his head as the terrible reality sank in. He'd sent a report on a vital First Imperium system...but now it was looking like he'd helped to lure his comrades into a trap.

He could feel *Vaughn* shaking as the power was forced into the engines...and the pressure, as the g forces increase to 2g...3g...then...

Nothing. *Vaughn* lurched hard, and another round of sparks

flew from the equipment panels along the outer walls of the bridge. Graham could feel the weightlessness, physically a relief to his tortured body…but also a realization that *Vaughn* had lost her engines entirely. He hadn't blown up his ship, but his gambit to escape had failed.

He turned back toward the screen, expecting it to be dark, but realizing that it was still functioning on some sort of emergency power. It wouldn't do him any good, not in terms of survival.

But it would let him watch his killers approach, to stare into the face of death and wait for the enemy guns to open fire…and send his ship and whatever remained of his crew straight to hell.

Chapter Eight

From the Journal of Max Harmon

For twelve years, I have maintained my grip on power. I have not sought to control the media, not excessively, at least, nor have I imposed burdensome restrictions on the lives of the people—at least none that weren't absolutely necessary. Still, there is no question I am a tyrant. Though Erika West tells me I should not think that way, that any ruler who feels guilty about being a tyrant almost certainly is not one. But, if not a tyrant, exactly, certainly a dictator. I generally heed the advice of my trusted subordinates, and when possible, do as the people want, but in the end, I act alone, and my power is absolute.

I had no choice, that is what I tell myself. I did only what was necessary to save Earth Two, to keep my people alive in the face of a new danger from the First Imperium. There is truth in all of that, of course. The threat is real, certainly...and it is deadly. But it is also a convenient mindset, a way to absolve myself of guilt for my actions. It is certainly what I tell myself at night, struggling to let sleep come, even for a few precious hours. Nevertheless, I question how much, if any, of that I believe.

I know, better perhaps than anyone, what our fate will be at the hands of a victorious First Imperium. I do not know what we face in the months and years ahead, but it has become more and more likely that there is, in fact, a second Regent out there somewhere, an artificial intelligence of a scale and technology we can barely imagine, much less truly understand. Indeed, that view had advanced from hypothesis to commonly-accepted knowledge, and few doubt there is a replica of our old enemy out there somewhere. We were able to destroy the first Regent, of course, something I remember vividly, but that does not make this threat any less dire. Nor, does it mean we can necessarily repeat our actions of four decades ago. The mere fact that this new Regent knows what happened to the old one removes the element of surprise, the blind spot that kept the doomed machine from comprehending that we had the audacity to strike it on its own capital planet.

We face other hazards, as well, other dangers I have controlled through my power. The end of the Prohibition satisfied the Mules to an extent, at least for a time, but it inflamed fear of the Hybrids among many of the others. The old Human League has recovered and grown, in both numbers and in the intensity of their vitriol, and our society has become more fractured than ever, held together only by the ever-present threat of extinction... and, of course, by my authority, wielded as infrequently as possible...but wielded nonetheless. There is no reasonable argument against the assertion that we need a firm hand in control right now, yet am I the only one who could wield such power? Could I not have stepped aside, allowed a successor to take the reins, to lead Earth Two forward?

I have wondered if I cling to control not because it is essential to our survival, but because, after four decades as the only leader Earth Two has ever known, and twelve of those years with absolute authority, I have, myself, become corrupt, that though I despise the burden and detest the idea of it all, I cannot loosen my grip. Can I imagine following anyone's orders, making myself subject to another's commands? How long has it been since I have taken an order from another? Am I truly the best person to lead my people through this fight? Or am I just another authoritarian, unable to pry clenched fingers from the reins of total power?

Presidential Residence
Victory City, Earth Two
Earth Two Date 12.02.42

"Mr. President…" The voice was tentative, the Marine guard clearly uncomfortable awakening Earth Two's absolute ruler in the middle of the night. But he needn't have concerned himself. Max Harmon was wide awake, as he was so often, sitting quietly on a chair to the side of the bed centered along the far wall.

He stood up, the abruptness of his move displaying some remaining vestige of his combat reflexes, and he looked toward the officer standing just outside the bedroom door peering in. He extended his hand, a silent signal to the Marine to wait for him to come out, and not to come inside and awaken his wife. But he was too late.

"I'm awake, Max." Mariko Fujin's voice was soft, but it was alert enough to tell Harmon that his wife had not been asleep, not for some time. He'd long been tormented, by regrets and ghosts from the past, from the realization of the things he'd done, by the fear of the future…but it cut at him especially deeply to realize how his choices—his duties, in his more self-forgiving moments—had affected his wife.

"Try to go back to sleep, Mariko." He felt foolish the instant the words came out of his mouth. He knew his wife had long wished he would step aside, allow someone else to bear the burdens that had weighed on their entire life together…but she had also lived under the same threat he had, in constant fear that one day First Imperium forces would pour into Earth Two's system, and all that the survivors from the original fleet and their several generations of descendants had built, all they possessed and everyone they loved, would be gone. And, he was damned sure she knew well enough that Marines didn't wake Earth Two's dictator in the middle of the night unless *something* was wrong.

The diminutive ex-fighter pilot sat up, reaching for the robe she'd left hanging over the bed post, even as Harmon walked toward the door.

"What is it, Captain?" he said to the uncomfortable-looking

Marine as he gestured now for the man to come into the room.

"Sir, Admiral West sent me to inform you that…we have received a communications drone from one of the exploration fleets."

Harmon glanced up at the officer, wondering if the man had any idea exactly what the exploratory fleets were, or what they did. The specifics of the long-term program of scanning space, of monitoring the enemy, and trying to lead them away from Earth Two, was heavily classified. Most of the spacers on the missions didn't even know the true purpose of the flotillas.

But one thing the task forces weren't supposed to do was come back anywhere close to Earth Two…or send any kind of direct communication that might be tracked. Had that happened now?

"Where is Admiral West, Captain?" Harmon turned abruptly and walked toward a doorway, one leading to a large walk in closet. He waved for the Marine to follow as he slipped inside and reached out to grab a uniform. He'd hemmed and hawed about wearing military garb over the years since he'd seized absolute power. He had dressed as a civilian when he'd been an elected president, but he'd since found some strength in the connection to his days as one of the fleet's officers. That had been a terrible time, one of constant danger and headlong flight…and yet, he remembered it fondly in ways, as a period in his life when he'd been able to do what he'd perceived as his duty without stomping on every ideal he'd ever believed in. Somehow wearing a uniform made him feel like an officer taking temporary emergency control, rather than one of the more grotesque images of dictators, calling themselves things like 'president for life.'

Even though he was, for all practical purposes, 'president for life.'

"She is at the command center, sir. Waiting for you." A short pause. "I have an escort waiting to accompany you."

Harmon felt a slight twinge at the reminder that he needed Marines to escort him to his office. He'd been well-loved back in his navy days, a member of one of the Alliance navy's great families, and one of the most popular officers in the fleet. He still maintained decent approval ratings among the pilgrims, but the original crews of the fleet's ships were now just below two percent of the total population…and more and more of Earth Two's younger people had known him only as a tyrant. There were no serious threats to his rule, none he was aware of—not organized ones, at least—but he was fairly certain there were a good number of people on Earth Two who would be just as happy to see him dead and gone. And, it only took a lone assassin to make that a reality.

That's how Terrance died…

The original commander of the fleet, Admiral Compton, the hero all pilgrims revered as the man who'd saved them, had been lost not to battle, not fighting the enemy or blown to atoms at the helm of his flagship, but at the hands of a single killer. It was a lesson well-learned, and as much as Harmon detested the need to surround himself and his family with guards, he did it nevertheless.

"Very well, Captain…you can wait outside. I'll be there in a few minutes." The officer stood where he was, turning slightly, but hesitating. The fact that one of his chief guardians seemed to think he needed protection along the route from his bedroom to the house's main door spoke volumes about the restive state of much of Earth Two's population. "I'll be perfectly fine in here, Captain. The house is very well-protected."

"Yes, sir." The Marine officer paused just an instant longer before he saluted and hurried out of the room. The brief hitch was one most people wouldn't have even noticed, but Harmon saw the extent of concern in his protector's body language. He tried to focus on the fact that his guards were as loyal as they seemed to be, but it proved to be scant recompense for the understanding that a significant number of those he governed would be happy to see him dead.

"Do you think…" Mariko stepped inside the closet, stopping a couple feet away from her husband. She didn't finish her question, but she didn't have to, either. Harmon knew exactly what she'd intended to ask.

"I don't know, Mariko. It's been twelve years since the last major crisis…but we've had skirmishes since then, and we've pretty well established that the Regent has been replaced by another AI of similar capability, perhaps even an exact copy." Harmon found it necessary to remind himself that his people were facing an enemy that was, at its core, pure data. A man like Terrance Compton had been utterly irreplaceable. An entity like the Regent, however capable and sophisticated, could be copied verbatim, and replicated at will. All it would take was hardware sufficient to house it.

"Maybe there was just another skirmish." She paused, not looking terribly convinced at her own words. "But, if it is, there shouldn't be a drone, should there?" The edge to her tone poked at the discomfort both Harmon and his wife felt about his directives to the exploratory fleets…particularly the one that forbade any force making contact with the enemy to return to Earth Two, or even send back a direct communique. Forces engaging the enemy were limited to sending messages to pre-established systems that were nowhere near Earth Two, rally points that were checked periodically. It was a very slow way to call for help, and one unlikely to result in any aid reaching a beleaguered force, if the distance involved in interstellar travel hadn't been enough to achieve that by itself. But, every spacer knew his or her life was forfeit if need be, to protect the secrecy of Earth Two's location.

Harmon didn't answer, and Mariko didn't ask again. After a few seconds of standing by the door, looking at her husband, she turned slowly and said, "I'll go make some coffee for your guards. There's no reason to wake, Lucy." Harmon's position as head of state came with a lot of staff, assistants, guards, advisors…but he and Mariko had always tried to keep their residence feeling like a home. Lucy Barre was a Tank, and she'd been the entirety of their household staff for the last ten years.

He almost told her that making coffee wasn't necessary, but she was already gone. He shook his head. Mariko was always doing little things like that for his guards, making sure to show them kindness and respect. He was never sure if it was just her personality—she was an exceedingly polite person in most situations—or whether she remembered too well what it felt like to be in the service, on duty at all hours.

Or, he thought more darkly, because she understood all too clearly that the men and women tasked with presidential security would be the final ones who determined if some threat harmed her family or not. If some political activist or aggrieved party, angry at some action or decree he'd issued, came for vengeance.

Harmon felt a touch of sadness at the thought of his family's reality. He told himself Mariko's conduct was unnecessary, that she overreacted to the perceived danger. But, if he was honest with himself, he knew he shared her concerns, and no matter how hard he tried to fool himself.

He was glad she acted the way she did, that she always worked to ingratiate herself to the Marines. Because he knew as well as she did that the handpicked fighters were the last line between those he loved and the backlash against what he'd done all these years.

He'd served his nation, at least he could still tell himself that much…but he knew his family had paid the price, in pointless danger, and in lost years of peace and freedom. He hated himself for it…but that was something to which he'd adapted, something he could live with.

What he couldn't live with was the time—and he feared it would come one day—when Mariko and his daughters hated him for it, too.

Chapter Nine

Central Headquarters
Victory City, Earth Two
Earth Two Date 12.02.42

"They did what?" Harmon was still tired, but the flash of anger energized him. He'd just walked into his office, where Erika West, Connor Frasier, and the rest of his military council were waiting for him.

"They sent a pair of drones back to Earth Two…by a direct route." It was clear from West's tone, she was at least aware that what she was describing was a violation of mandated procedure. It was less obvious whether she condemned it, or if she thought the data it contained justified the risky action.

"That's just great. What the hell was…" It took Harmon a moment to remember the name of the mission's commander. "…Graham thinking?"

"Sir, the information is of great strategic value. It appears almost certain that Captain Graham's exploration fleet has discovered the Regent's primary—and quite possibly only—antimatter production source." West had abandoned branding the New Regent's existence as a hypothesis some time before, and now she simply referred to it as the fact she took it to be.

Harmon understood the magnitude of what West was saying. Antimatter-powered drives and weapons were the single largest technological advantage remaining to the First Imperium forces. The Mules' tireless research had closed many of the other gaps, unlocked dozens of secrets of the Ancients. But the cost-effective production of large quantities of antimatter had remained out of reach.

He sat, hard in his chair, barely noticing as an orderly stepped up next to him and set down a cup of steaming coffee.

"I understand the significance of the discovery, Erika, but if there is one thing we can't allow—ever—it's for the enemy to find Earth Two. The decoy systems, the extended routes specified for incoming and outgoing traffic…it's all in place for just that purpose."

"That is true, sir…but you know as well as I do, everything is an exercise in risk-taking, at least to a certain extent. Will the enemy upgrade the defenses of this newly-discovered system if given enough time? It appears to be strongly held now, but not invincible. If we throw everything we can at it, we just might be able to take it out. And that will go a long way to evening the odds in this struggle."

"Do we dare move so much from our defenses here? Especially when we've just had a security breach of this magnitude?"

"I would not overestimate the danger, sir. Roland Graham is a gifted officer. He would not have taken any undue risks. It appears that the ships sending the drones were able to escape the system while the main fleet engaged the enemy." Her tone changed, became more somber. Harmon understood…whatever Captain Graham had done the chances were excellent he'd sacrificed his own life—and the lives of most of his people—to do it. "They traveled through the adjacent system to the next one down the line, scanning the entire way…and they didn't launch the drones until they'd determined that the second system was clear."

"You know as well as I do, that's not any guarantee. The enemy has stealth ships and probes, even as we do." The development of such resources, and tools to thwart them, had become somewhat of an arms race between the Regent and the republic's researchers, mostly the Mules. Generally, detection had won out, at least with things as large as warships. Stealth had maintained somewhat of an edge with small, low powered devices, like the communications drones.

"The fleet's drones were of our newest design, with the latest stealth systems installed." She paused, looking at Harmon for a few seconds, but answering his next question before he asked it. "Yes, there is some risk the enemy could have tracked them back to Earth Two, through the checkpoints, without their own scanning drones being picked up by any of our detection arrays…but it is minimal."

Harmon almost snapped back, but he paused. Erika West was one of the hardest officers he'd ever known, and he'd long ago learned to take her analysis seriously. "I'm not sure we can afford even minimal risks…and don't forget, Erika, they don't have to find us to cause a great deal of harm. Even if they were able to follow the communications drones through a few systems, they could dramatically narrow their search parameters, and shave years off the time it will take to find us."

As far as Max Harmon knew, none of his most trusted advisors thought it would be anything but 'when' for a guess on the Regent's forces discovering Earth Two's location. 'If' was for dewy-eyed optimists, and, after what he'd seen in his sixty years of service in space and on Earth Two, either 'dewy-eyed' or 'optimist' were the last things anyone could call him.

And absolutely the last things *anyone* would call Erika West.

"So, you're certain, Erika? You think we should strike at this target, try to interrupt the enemy's antimatter production?"

"I do, sir." She hesitated. "It's not that I think it will be easy, or that there aren't a hundred ways it could go wrong. But, I believe it might be our best chance to equalize things. There isn't much doubt the enemy has more ships than we do, and a greater production infrastructure…but we've always managed to fight off the First Imperium despite being outnumbered. If we could eliminate the antimatter differential, the edge it gives them in both acceleration and firepower, I am sure we could meet them on something like equal terms. I think I've got a chance to at least damage that facility."

Harmon took a deep breath. "You want to command the expedition personally?"

"Sir…if we're going to do this, we're going to have to commit most of the fleet." A pause. "Yes, Mr. President, I would like to command in person."

Harmon felt the urge to argue, to order West to remain on Earth Two, to tell her that he needed her there. That would be no lie. He *did* need her. She was one of his oldest colleagues, among the most trusted of his inner circle…and, without doubt, the best naval officer Earth Two had, himself included.

Which was why he realized she'd have to go. If he sent most of the fleet on such a desperate mission, he couldn't deprive those spacers of the very best commander they could get. He thought, for a moment, about commanding the fleet himself… but he knew he couldn't leave Earth Two. He'd held onto power for twelve years, and more importantly, he'd kept things from descending into a ruinous struggle between the planet's genetic groupings. But that peace was a tenuous one, and it had been fading in recent years. He'd risk everything he'd done if he left now, especially on such a long and desperate journey.

Besides, Erika West can kick my ass in a space battle…

"Are you sure, Erika? You have a whole navy that depends on you." There was more than just general concern for his friend at work. Twelve years before, Harmon had sent another of his friends, Nicki Frette, off in command of a fleet to engage the Regent's forces. She'd come back…but she'd spent the last twelve years in a coma, defying every effort of the medical staff and the Mules to help her recover. She was still alive, but that was the most that could be said.

And, Frette had been West's lover. That didn't affect the tactical situation in any real way, but it was upsetting nevertheless, and he felt a strange uneasiness with sending West out in some bizarre replay of the mission that had all but killed her partner.

"Most of the navy will be there, sir. If we do this, we have to commit. It's going to take just about everything we have to give us a real chance." She paused. "If…something happens…you can handle the new ship construction and the command of the remaining defensive forces, at least until you pick someone else to take over." West was speaking far too matter-of-factly about her own death to suit him. But, he just nodded.

"Okay…" He hesitated, taking another few seconds to accept what he knew he had to do. "…put together a fleet roster, and a list of the ordnance and supplies you think it will take. You'll command the expedition. But, I expect you to exert all reasonable caution, Admiral. This is not the same situation as a last-ditch defense of Earth Two. If you lose confidence at *any* point, if you even smell trouble you hadn't accounted for, you are to cancel the operation and get your fleet out of there. You are *not* expendable, Admiral, and neither is your fleet. Is that understood? *Completely* understood?" Harmon didn't think Erika West was the type to give in to desperation and despair and throw her life away over a lost love, and certainly not to lead her spacers into such an endeavor. But, he wasn't taking any chances.

"I understand, sir. Completely. This is a chance to bring things closer to an even matchup, to weaken our enemy before they have a chance to find and threaten our homeworld. At any moment when that changes, when the odds of a favorable outcome no longer justify the risk, I'll pull the fleet out immediately."

Harmon and West were silent for a moment, even as he stared at his friend, trying, perhaps for the first time, to decide if he truly believed her. West had always been straight with him, even in the days when she'd outranked him. But there was something in her tone, her eyes. The admiral had a good poker face, there was no doubt about that. But Harmon was still worried.

Connor Frasier cleared his throat and spoke up. "Should I prepare an expeditionary force to accompany the operation, Mr. President? We might want to land and try to seize control of the facility."

Harmon didn't answer immediately. He looked over at West, silent for a moment, and then he said, "Assuming we do this, Admiral, do you think there's a chance in hell we'll have the opportunity to capture the place instead of destroy it? And, to hold it if we did?" He was doubtful…but he asked anyway.

West frowned. "I don't know, sir. It seems unlikely. Perhaps a quick raid, a chance to steal some antimatter, and ship it back home. Even enough for a stockpile of missiles might make a big difference in some future battle." She paused, taking a deep breath. "But, I don't see it, sir. It's not like grabbing crates full of gold bars or something. We need to get the antimatter out of whatever storage facility holds it, and into something portable. And, the slightest screwup, a nanosecond of containment failure at any step, and the whole thing is lost, along with anyone within fifty kilometers."

"You're probably right. If there was any real chance, I'd say yes, but it doesn't seem realistic."

"I still think we need Marines, though." West turned and looked over at Frasier. "Our scanning data on the planet's surface is incomplete, but from what I can see, it's very possible that most of the production facilities are deep underground. That's where I'd put them, if I was in charge. Which means even a massive nuclear bombardment is only going to take out their surface solar collection panels and some secondary facilities, maybe some storage compartments. If we catch some antimatter on the surface, we might create quite the show, but if those main production and storage facilities are deep enough, we can't be sure of knocking them out, not completely. We might cut down its output levels, but you can bet they're drawing all sorts of power, and some of that will be from volcanic activity and other sources out of the reach of our missiles. If you want that place taken out—*really* taken out—we'll have to send Marines in…and they'll have to fight their way down to the primary facilities…and rig them to blow."

"That sounds like a difficult mission, maybe damned near impossible." Harmon looked over at Frasier. "Connor?"

The Marine returned the stare, and Harmon wondered if he caught an instant of doubt on the man's face before the impenetrable mask of the veteran warrior slammed back into place. "We can do it, sir. It will take a significant force, but we'll get it done."

Harmon would have discounted what he perceived as a

bit of Marine bluster…if Frasier hadn't delivered on so many 'impossible' promises before. "It will have to be a strong force, Connor, as well-equipped as we can manage."

"I'll see to it personally, sir. I'll get you the proposed roster by tomorrow morning, and if you approve it, we'll be ready to…"

"No, Connor…not you."

"Sir? If you want the best-prepared force, I should be with them."

"I have no doubt about that, my old friend, but you'll have to choose someone else to lead the expeditionary force. I need you here." There was truth to that, of course. Harmon knew that the relative calm of the past twelve years was beginning to unravel, and whatever happened, he couldn't allow his regime to be challenged, not while the fleet was out on campaign. Still, as much as he relied on Frasier and his Marines to keep him in power against any challenges, he suspected his unwillingness to sacrifice another of his few remaining true friends was also at play. He hated the idea of letting Erika West risk her life on something like this, but he realized he had no choice there. But, as good as Frasier was, he had subordinates he'd trained, men and women who could lead the Marines on their desperate assault as well as he could…or nearly so.

"Sir…" Frasier was a Marine to the core, and arguing with the commander-in-chief wasn't in his DNA. He twisted around uncomfortably, looking as though he was praying for Harmon to change his mind, but he didn't dispute Harmon's decision.

"Connor, I know you want to be with your people. We both know this mission is going to be a tough one. But, I need your help…I can't do what I have to do here without you here." He paused, and then he hit Frasier where it hurt. "And, think of the Corps, not just the Marines sent with the fleet. We'll be risking most of our veterans. You need to be here to train the new classes, to guide the young Marines. To make sure there is a Corps in ten years…or twenty."

Frasier still didn't look happy, but he nodded gently. "Yes, sir," was all he said. It was all he had to say.

Harmon knew his words had found their mark.

Chapter Ten

Central Headquarters
Victory City, Earth Two
Earth Two Date 12.11.42

"That's just great." Max Harmon shook his head, a look of disgust taking over his face. "We've managed to keep the League and the other extremist NB groups under control for twelve years, and now you come in here with the greatest recruiting program they could hope for. You do realize that if I release all restrictions on Hybrid quickenings—ostensibly to keep the younger Mules from rebelling—we're telling everyone with even the slightest League sympathies that they were right all along, that the Mules *are* a threat to everyone. I'm not saying that is the case, but you can be damned sure that's how it will look."

"Or, we're saying this is justice, what should have been done long ago…that there is no place in our civilization for singling out different societal groups." Hieronymus Cutter was sitting in one of the chairs opposite Earth Two's dictator. He'd been trying to make his case, as he had on more than one occasion, but it was clear he realized it had gone somewhat awry.

"That's not entirely accurate, Hieronymus." Erika West sat at one of the other seats, and she turned and looked toward the scientist. She was clad in a duty uniform, not the usual dress job she wore when her duties brought her to the President's office.

Harmon himself had asked her to come right away, as she was, from the docks where she'd been supervising the fleet preparations. "Natural births are self-regulating, at least to a point. And, since most of the women on Earth Two of childbearing age are also engaged in one form or another of work responsibilities, we don't come anywhere close to a theoretical maximum of births, even with our programs to promote reproduction. Artificial...cloned..."

She paused. Harmon was watching, and he held back a sigh. He could see the admiral wasn't sure how to refer to births other than those produced in the traditional way. If the hard-edged West was uncertain and concerned with offending people with words that strayed too far from popular orthodoxy, that was proof enough that Earth Two's still-nascent society was heading in the wrong direction.

"...births are not limited in the same way. It only takes a few cells to clone a human being, and, while the restrictions imposed on the Mules are inarguably more severe, there are limitations on Tank births as well, and for similar reasons."

"Yes...because the naturally-born residents of Earth Two don't want to be reduced to a small minority...the very same fate we inflict on the Mules. If there must be restrictions, they should at least allow the Mules to keep pace with the NB population's growth, as the Tank limits do." Cutter's debate skills had come a long way since his days as an introverted scientist, but he had an emotional stake in the Mules' future, too, and it was showing clearly.

"It is foolish to pretend the Mules are the same as the Tanks." West frowned. "They are..."

"That's enough." Harmon shook his head and reach up, rubbing his temples. He rarely interrupted his key advisors, and he always tried hard to deemphasize the fact that he wielded absolute power. "You're both right...and wrong. Life is rarely so simple as to present black and white solutions to problems. It is absurd not to consider the capabilities of the Mules, and anyone here who suggests he or she doesn't understand where the fear of unrestricted population growth among them come from is either lying or deluding himself." He was silent for a few seconds. "Similarly, I don't find it credible that there is even one of you who doesn't understand why the Mules are upset…or who thinks they have no reason to have the same kinds of concerns the others do, worries about what the rest of Earth Two's population will do to control them in the future if their numbers shrink further as a percentage of the population."

Harmon leaned back in his chair, wishing for a moment he could be anything at all, save the one who would have to make the final decision. The fight against the Regent was bad enough, a sometimes hopeless-seeming struggle against a vastly superior enemy. But, there were tactics in battle, at least, and there was definitely a thing called victory. If they could find and destroy the Regent, the war would be won. But there was no solution to the friction between Earth Two's genetic groupings. The people were right to fear an unlimited number of Mules…and the Hybrids were every bit as justified in their concern of how they would be treated if there were too few of them. It felt like there should be some kind of balance, equilibrium…but Harmon had come to believe there wasn't.

Suddenly, he slammed his hand down on the table. "Enough of this. We're facing an enemy that wants to kill every last one of us, one that views us all, NB and Mule alike, as an infection that needs to be eradicated…and we're at *each other's* throats. I forced through the repeal of the Prohibition twelve years ago, something that was long overdue. But, I didn't go far enough. The Mules, whatever threats they may present in the future, have done more to ensure our survival than any other group…even all the others combined."

West was silent, but Harmon could see from the scowl on her face, she thought her spacers had done their part as well. They had, of course…but without the tech the Mules had continued to feed them, they wouldn't have had a chance against the Regent's forces.

"I am relaxing the restrictions on Mule quickenings…" He could see the discomfort, even among some of his closest advisors. Save for Cutter and Ana Zhukov, of course, who wore expressions somewhere between satisfaction, and creeping concern. "...but, I am not eliminating them entirely. Henceforth, three hundred Mules will be created each year, plus any number needed to offset deaths sustained during the prior time period." No one knew how long a Mule's life expectancy stretched, save for the generally-accepted assumption that it was considerably longer than a normal human's, even one subject to the rejuv therapies the Mules didn't seem to need. Nevertheless, in spite of the fact that no Mule had ever aged noticeably beyond entering maturity, six of them *had* died, three in crèche malfunctions, before their official 'births,' and three in a lab accident four years before.

"Triple? Do you think that's a good idea, sir?" It was Connor Frasier this time. The Marine's eyes darted to the side, a quick glance toward his wife. Harmon knew Frasier and Zhukov disagreed about policies regarding the Mules, and also that they were both headstrong and almost certain to voice their own, often contradictory, opinions. He wondered how they managed that when they were together...perhaps some kind of 'leave it at the door' policy?

"*You* think it is too many, Connor. You'll have a lot of company. I suspect we'll be back here before long discussing just how far I should go in suppressing the protests that will no doubt spring up everywhere. But the Mules, the younger ones, at least, and by far the majority, of total numbers if not yet of adults, want no limits at all. You question whether people will accept a tripling...I do the same, only I also wonder how the Mules will react, and if Achilles will be able to control his people, to get them to accept the incremental change instead of the outright removal of all controls they seek."

He looked out over the now silent room. There were no more questions, nor any challenges. It was clear Harmon had made up his mind, and all those present were loyal supporters of his regime. They might argue among themselves, but he didn't doubt every one of them would accept his judgment.

It wasn't them he was worried about, nor Achilles and the original Mules, even. It was the young generation of Hybrids, that concerned him, bristling with an arrogance that was almost built into their engineered genes…not to mention the Human League and other groups calling for a return to only natural methods of reproduction. The desperate need to build population in the republic's early years had offered a counterbalancing force to the propaganda of groups like the League. But, forty-two years of high birth rates and massive Tank cloning classes had lessened the urgency of those early initiatives and increased the appeal of the pro-NB activists.

Harmon knew on one level, he could do what he wanted, whatever he considered right. He was a dictator, but he was one with a fatal weakness. He wasn't ready to unleash his soldiers on the people, and he wasn't sure he would do it—*could* bring himself do it—even if the future of Earth Two was at stake. He'd been skillful enough, or lucky enough, to avoid having to take such steps over the twelve years of his unchallenged rule, but he suspected that run of luck was likely to end soon.

"Well," he said after a long pause, "we've all got work to do before the fleet sets out, and I need to have a talk with Admiral West before she shuttles up to orbit. Some of you are happier with my decision than others, but it is made…so let's all make the best of it. I will speak with Achilles tonight, and then, if that goes well enough, I'll make an announcement tomorrow. The change will take effect immediately, with the next generation of Mules, due to be quickened in a little over two weeks."

He watched as they all stood up and began filing out of the room, returning the various nods and quickly spoken goodbyes. Finally, when only he and West remained, he instructed the AI to close and lock the door.

"So, Erika…here we are again, planning yet another fight. I once indulged myself with the thought that we'd both be retired by now, telling stories perhaps, in some veterans' center or at reunions."

West smiled, almost as close to a laugh as she'd come in the last twelve years. "You, sir? What about me? I'd have been there a good bit before you, I think." West was fifteen years older than Harmon, though it was difficult, especially at a quick glance, to discern the ages of people who were on the rejuv therapies, at least between roughly the mid-forties and early nineties. Harmon could see signs of age around the admiral's eyes, a patch of wrinkles he suspected came as much from stress as from the passing of the years, but she didn't look *all that* different than she had during the fleet's desperate journey so long ago.

"Erika, we've fought together so often, set out for battle so many times. I wish I could go with you now." It was the kind of thing one said in such a situation, but Harmon surprised himself with how much he meant it. There was something honest about combat, especially against an enemy as detestable as the Regent. He'd been a politician, of one sort or another, for more than forty years now, and while he knew he'd done a lot to help protect Earth Two and hold its fragile society together, he still felt unclean. He often thought of the horror his younger self would have felt if he'd been able to look into the future.

"I do, too, sir...but we both know you have duties here, every bit as important, if not more so."

"I'm not sure anything is important as what you're doing. For as much as the Mules and the Leaguers and the others scheme against each other, the Regent's the one power that would exterminate us all in a moment if it is able. If you can cut out its antimatter production, just maybe we can cripple its fleets...and gain the time we need to hunt it down and destroy it, like we did its predecessor." He'd started out sincere, but he realized how little he believed what he was saying by the time he finished. Before West could respond, he added, "Erika...have you considered the possibility that this is some kind of trap?"

West sat quietly for a few seconds, exhaling softly. "Max..." She hadn't called him Max more than a couple times in twelve years. "...I have considered this campaign a hundred different ways, from every perspective I can think of. I'm not sure it can be anything *but* a trap."

Harmon felt like she'd hit him with a sack of cement. "You think it is definitely a trap? Then why have you supported it? We can still cancel the operation..."

"No, sir...we can't." She looked at him and suddenly he could see the vulnerability behind her normally stonefaced demeanor, the bone-deep fatigue. "We left behind scanning devices in the old imperial star systems near Earth Two, and we placed more when we were intercepting the renegade fleets in the years after the Regent's destruction. There have been no reports from them in decades now. The old Imperium seems to be quite dead. It's almost a certainty the new Regent is outside the boundaries of the previous entity."

"We've always worked on that assumption." Harmon nodded for West to continue, a bit confused on where she was going with her point.

"Well, sir…I've done some calculations. If we take the volume of space between the imperial border and the edge of this spiral arm, we're looking at a volume of space with, perhaps thirty to sixty thousand stars."

"That's a lot of systems, Erika."

"Yes, sir, but our best estimates are that less than one-third of solar systems are connected to the warp gate network… which makes those systems almost as if they weren't there at all. That leaves, what, maybe ten to twenty thousand systems?"

Harmon nodded.

"Well, now we have to look at what we know about the Regent's forces, their size, and, of course, their antimatter power systems. They can explore systems much more quickly than we can, and they have an easier time discounting those they scan. The Regent knows, of course, what we need in terms of a habitable world, while as far as we know, it could be on a frigid moon orbiting some gas giant, or a sunbaked chunk of rock a few degrees from molten status. It is looking for cities, for habitation. For all we know, the Regent is buried somewhere under kilometers of rock. We have to do intensive scans even to get a decent idea if a system is clear, while their scoutships can determine a system is not Earth Two, almost literally in minutes."

"You're suggesting the Regent is likely to find us before we find it?"

"I'm not suggesting, sir. I'm saying it outright. For years, I've been trying to develop a plan, any kind of plan for offensive action, an effort to damage or destroy the enemy before they find us. This is the first thing that's been even remotely realistic. Trap or no trap, that antimatter production facility is real, there isn't much doubt of that. And, if it *is* a trap, that means the enemy will have its strength concentrated there."

"You want to walk into a trap because you're sure the enemy fleet will be there in force?"

"I wouldn't put it exactly that way…but, yes." West looked down for a few seconds before her eyes darted back up. "It's just us here, Max…you and me. We can pat ourselves on the back for the civilization we built in forty years, for the hundreds of thousands of people living where a battered group of survivors once landed. We can revel in the new tech the Mules' efforts have provided us, and look at our fleet, larger by far than the one that got trapped behind the Barrier…but we know it's all an illusion. We're losing this war, slowly perhaps, but almost certainly. The enemy is going to find Earth Two before we discover the Regent's system…and when they do, they'll come here with everything they have. And, we can't win a defensive battle, you know that as well as I do. They don't have to destroy the fleet or obliterate all our defenses. They just have to get close enough to launch a big enough missile attack. A single cruiser holds enough megatons to kill every man and woman on Earth Two, and that doesn't even take their antimatter warheads into account. They didn't destroy the planets back home during the first war, on the other side of the Barrier…most likely because they were once part of the Imperium, spared by some still-functioning routine even the Regent couldn't override. But, we're not in the Imperium anymore, sir. The message the Ancients left us was quite clear about that."

Harmon took a deep breath. He'd considered much of what West had just said, but never all of it in its overwhelming, depressing entirety. "You're saying this is a longshot…but it's our only chance at victory."

West's lips twisted into a grimace for a few seconds. "Let's say, it's a chance to strike at the enemy, and that if it comes one day to a defense of Earth Two, the fleet isn't going to be that helpful anyway. The planet's ringed with fortresses and missile platforms, and they're longer ranged even than the enemy's mobile weaponry. *That's* our defense...and if we can fight the enemy somewhere else, far from here, we might be able to delay the coming of the day when we're fighting here. And, we might just beat down the enemy's forces, destroy enough ships to set them back for a few more years."

Harmon suddenly realized with a cold certainty that West didn't expect to come back. It was normal enough to consider death before a campaign or battle, but that wasn't what was going on. Erika West was heading out in command of the fleet...and she *expected* to die in the coming fight.

"Erika..." Harmon's voice was emotional. He leaned forward across the table, reaching out and putting his hand on her arm.

"Don't worry, Max, not about me. I'm ready to meet my destiny, if that's what the universe has in store. I'm tired, so tired. If there is a chance to buy more time, to give you the years you need to find some way for Earth Two to survive, or for the Mules to decipher enough ancient technology to truly protect the planet...I'm ready to do what I have to. No, it isn't my fate that troubles me...it's the other losses we will suffer, the thousands of men and women who will likely perish. You knew as well as I do what kind of battle this will be, and, also like me, you've been in fights like that before. Even the ones who survive and return will be...changed."

"Erika..." It was what he had said a moment before, but it was all he could force out of his suddenly parched throat. He'd known West for more than fifty years, and while he'd already been worried about her, and the entire fleet, hearing her talk so resolutely about her own death had shaken him.

"It's okay, sir. I'll make sure as many of them get back as possible." She stood up slowly. "It has been a great honor to serve with you, Max. I remember having conversations with Terrance years ago." She looked right at Harmon, and he could see something he'd never seen before. Tears welling up in her eyes. "He loved you Max. He thought of you as a son...always. Don't ever let yourself forget that. Or him."

Harmon leapt to his feet and walked around the table. He didn't say a word. He just put his arms around the old admiral and hugged her. "I'm not giving up on you, Erika. Hit the enemy hard, turn their trap around on them...but come back here. Do you hear me? That's an order."

"Yes, sir," she said softly, clearly struggling to keep the moisture from pouring out of her eyes. "And, you do whatever you have to here. Hold Earth Two together. Unless we're all united, we have no chance at all."

Then, she pulled away from his embrace and paused for just a few seconds, before she turned and walked out the door.

Chapter Eleven

Marine HQ
Just Outside Victory City, Earth Two
Earth Two Date 12.11.42

"It is past time, Colonel Cameron." He used the officer's partial last name, the one the Marine had chosen for himself after leaving the crèche and not the one he'd inherited from his DNA donor. The usage of the double names had declined somewhat over the years, in the Corps at least, as the Tanks who dominated the service sought to fit in more seamlessly with their naturally-born comrades, and also to emphasize their individuality rather than the genetic 'sameness' they shared with a hundred or more crèchemates. "Your people…" Connor Frasier paused for an instant. "…those not from the original fleet…must move now into the senior positions."

Frasier covered his discomfort as well as he could. He'd meant the Tanks when he had first referred to Cameron's 'people,' a well-intentioned reference that also reflected the passage of responsibility from the receding Pilgrims to the younger generations born on Earth Two. The Tank part made him uncomfortable, mostly because his policy had always been to assert that a Marine was a Marine, and he didn't care if that young leatherneck came charging out of his human mother or an artificial womb, as long as he did it with a scowl on his face and his fist held high in the air. But, he'd gotten as caught up as anyone in the tension between clones and the naturally-born, and he'd done all he could to cultivate a generation of promising Tank officers to move into the highest command ranks.

Frasier regretted the divisions that so fractured Earth Two's society, and it was hard, from his perspective at least, to argue that the Tanks, who made up more than eighty percent of the Corp's rank and file, were not under-represented in the senior ranks. The age gap had explained that well enough for a time, at least when Pilgrims had occupied all the top officers' positions. But, Frasier had been forced to exert considerable pressure to see that Tanks as well as NBs were moved up to command ranks as the older officers began to retire.

"I want to thank you, sir. It is a great honor, and I am proud to know that you have confidence in me." Cameron stood at attention, despite the fact that Frasier had twice motioned for him to sit. He paid no heed to Frasier's reference to his clone status.

The Marine's uniform was spotless, which impressed Frasier all the more because he knew for a fact that Cameron had been out on final maneuvers until less than twenty minutes before he'd walked into the Commandant's office. Frasier tried to imagine the hulking warrior racing back to barracks, showering, and hopping around on one foot as he climbed into his dress blacks, all in time to race across the quad and step into the office looking as though he'd just walked down the hall. He was still trying to put together a sequence in his mind, but he kept coming up at least two minutes short.

"It is well-deserved, Devon." Frasier wasn't sure how much of an honor it was. He would never sell his Marines short, but he knew how great the chance was that they'd all die inside Admiral West's ships, blasted to plasma before they even got the chance to set foot on the ground. And, if they landed, the mission still seemed damn near impossible.

It's the 'damn near' that opens the door for the Marines, though...

Frasier felt some satisfaction in his blind faith in the men and women of the Corps, enough to drive back the despair threatening to take him, at least.

"You have served well, a career I can only describe as spotless. It is fitting that you assume this command, perhaps the most important deployment since the fleet arrived at Earth Two."

Frasier was still tense, but it had nothing to do with Tanks and NBs, nor with the long odds against the operation. He was sending the heart of the Corps on a desperate mission, far from Earth Two. That alone would be hard enough…but the fact that he wasn't going with them drove him to the limits of his endurance. He should be at their head, and nothing could have kept him from that spot, save for the very thing that did. The direct order of the commander-in-chief. There was no way Frasier could override President Harmon's command…and even if he could, disobeying the supreme commander was something he didn't have in him.

"Devon…" Frasier hesitated.

"Sir?"

"You know the odds on this mission…"

"The Corps doesn't look at odds, sir."

"I'm sorry, Devon." Frasier was still struggling with the fact that he just didn't believe any of his people would be back. "It's just…" His words trailed off.

"Sir, it is my honor to lead the expedition, to fight for Earth Two…and, if need be, to die in that effort. We all know the price we may be asked to pay when we enter training, General. My life has been the Corps', from my earliest days of adulthood to now. I am a Marine. It is what I am. What I will always be."

"Very well, Colonel. Though that is the last time I will call you that." Frasier reached down to his desk and picked up a small box. Before you go, try these on." He reached out and handed the small box to Cameron, watching as the officer opened it to reveal a pair of shiny platinum stars.

"General Frasier…" Cameron looked stunned, and Frasier knew why. In the forty-two years of its existence, there had never been more than one general in Earth Two's Marine Corps. Now, there were two.

"Congratulations, Brigadier Cameron. You've earned those

stars…and all that they mean."

"Thank you, General." Cameron was almost speechless, his words choked, barely forced from his suddenly dry throat. "I don't know what else to say…"

"There is nothing else to say, Devon." A short pause. "Good luck, Brigadier Cameron. Bring 'em hell."

*   *   *

"Achilles, thank you for coming." Max Harmon was the absolute dictator of Earth Two, and any order that came from his mouth theoretically carried the full force of law. But, he was well aware that the reality was far more complex, and even in his powerful position, he knew control of the Mules was…tentative…at best.

"Mr. President." The informal leader of the Hybrids stepped inside the palatial office of Earth Two's leader. As he often did, Harmon felt a twinge of discomfort at the extravagance on display. Some of it was intentional, pushed on him as much by his aides as anything else, and their insistence his station required an appearance that matched the power he wielded. Harmon himself had always had simple tastes. A desk and a chair of some comfort would have suited him, as would a modest home instead of the great mansion in which he lived, perhaps with a small library, and a place to read nights by the fire.

Instead, you live and work like some emperor…living a life those you rule cannot imagine.

Harmon knew that wasn't entirely fair, at least not about the opulence of his lifestyle. Earth Two, for all the danger and the deadly threats it lived under, was a prosperous and advanced society, and all of its people lived in considerable comfort. Even with the rivalries between the genetic groups, none lived in poverty, and all had access to extensive education and creature comforts beyond the imaginings of most humans who had ever lived. His people had sacrificed freedom for the security his rule promised them…but they did not live in the squalor that had so often accompanied abusive governments, even those as recent as Earth's Superpowers.

"Sit, Achilles…there's no need for formality between us. I've always considered you a close friend." That was true, to a point at least. Harmon respected the Mule, and he genuinely like him, but for all he tried to think of Achilles as just an especially gifted citizen, he couldn't escape the feeling that the Hybrids were… just a little bit alien.

"Thank you, Mr. President." The Mule pulled back one of the guest chairs and sat.

"There is no one else in here, Achilles, no cameras to perform for. I'm Max."

"Very well, Max." The Mule looked across the table. Harmon wasn't sure if Achilles knew why he'd been sent for.

"Achilles…twelve years ago, the two of us averted a catastrophe. We ended a wrong together, one that, to my shame, I had allowed to continue for far too long. But, let us be honest with each other. We replaced it with a lesser wrong, a necessary one, perhaps, but still a wrong." He paused. "With your help, I would like to do again what we did then."

Achilles looked back across the table, nodding gently. Harmon couldn't tell what the Hybrid was thinking. Along with their intellects and physical near-perfection, the genetically-engineered Mules all had extreme control over external indications of their emotions.

Good poker faces.

"What do you propose, Max?"

"I cannot eliminate the restrictions on quickenings, Achilles. Not entirely. Not now." Harmon was uncomfortable. As elected president, he'd allowed the Prohibition to continue for more than a quarter century, and when he'd finally seen to its abolition, he'd replaced it with a strict limit on new Mule quickenings. He'd presented that cap as a temporary measure to Achilles, much as he had called the Prohibition before it…but, now it had been twelve more years, and it was still in place.

"Max…I believe you are a good man at heart. I also understand, perhaps more than you imagine, the realities with which you are compelled to deal. You control the Marines, of course.

You could rule with an iron hand as long as you have that power."

Harmon looked back across the desk. He knew things weren't that simple, and he was just as certain that the Mule knew the same thing. The Hybrids had given up control of the war robots they had built twelve years before, when rebellion seemed to be inevitable, but he very much doubted that Achilles had surrendered every secret he had.

"But," Achilles continued, "since you have seized power, you have tried to negotiate whenever possible, to broker compromises instead of rounding up political prisoners and fielding firing squads. I commend you for that. We almost clashed, you and I, over the Prohibition. My people simply could not allow that to continue. I resent the limits still in place, of course, as all the Mules do…but I understand why they are there. I do not seek a replay of the events of twelve years ago, but I also do not have the unchallenged level of influence I enjoyed then. The Next Gens do not follow me the way the originals do, and as they come of age, they begin to make more demands. I must have something to satisfy them."

"I am prepared to increase the annual limit to three hundred quickenings." He paused, feeling foolish about what he was about to add. "That will be a temporary restriction, just until the Regent is defeated. We can't afford to have our people split apart now."

"No, Max…we cannot. The Regent is a threat to us all." He paused for a moment, and Harmon waited, knowing full well such a compromise would only delay the inevitable clash. "Very well. Three hundred. I am willing to accept that, and I will do my best to convince the Next Gens to agree as well. It is a reasonable proposal."

Harmon stood up and extended his arm across the desk. "Thank you, Achilles." His sincerity, along with a good bit of relief, was evident in his voice.

Achilles stood up and reached out to take Harmon's offered hand. "Thank you, Max. We must stand together now. The Regent would destroy us all, without differentiation between any of us."

The Mule looked at Harmon with a slight smile and nodded, before he turned and walked out of the room, leaving Max Harmon grateful for his cooperation…and wondering a bit about the Mule's addition of the word 'now' to his comment on the genetic groups standing together.

* * *

"My shuttle leaves in an hour. We are going into a trap, I know that much. I just hope we can turn it around, and perhaps deliver a surprise of our own to the enemy. I would have rejected this mission outright, had anyone presented it to me under any but our current circumstances. But, there is just no doubt, not to me, at least, that the Regent will eventually find Earth Two. When they do, we can destroy their entire fleet, and yet we will still lose if they are able to get close enough to Earth Two to launch a planetary bombardment. The current mission is a longshot, perhaps, and a ten percent chance of success looks pretty poor…unless it's compared to none." West's hand was extended, her palm held close to the shimmering field that encased Nicki Frette, and kept the stricken officer alive in her comatose state. She'd longed for years for Frette to awaken, to look into her lost lover's eyes, hold her close. Now, she'd have settled for just touching her companion's cheek, a last bit of actual contact before she left to join the fleet. But, even that was beyond her reach.

West's face morphed into a strange smile, one that seemed to acknowledge some morbidly amusing fact while remaining utterly devoid of joy. "I go now to follow you, to lead our forces against the enemy that took you from me. For twelve years, I have wished I had taken command then instead of you. Twelve years of duty, of work…all the more desperate work because I needed it so badly. The enemy that took you, that stole what happiness I had managed to find out here, on this refuge that will never truly be my home, they also gave me the means to endure the time and the loneliness…to focus all I had on working toward their destruction. They renewed my hatred, my lust for vengeance. They filled me with a purpose that is all that remains to me. I am coming nearer to the end of my life now, and there can only be defeat or victory…and even total triumph, the destruction of the Regent, will only leave me with nothing save darkness and fatigue, and a silent longing for the end."

West took a deep, ragged breath. "The Regent threatens my people, and it stole you from me. I don't believe I can destroy it, not now at least…but, perhaps I can strike a blow, one that will open the door to victory later. If my life is the price for that, I will gladly pay it, indeed, I will consider it a relief…if only I can die in victory and not in the misery of defeat."

She paused for a few seconds, drawing in another rough breath. "Max will still be here, even if this mission claims me. If I can smash open the gates, wound our deadly foe…perhaps there is enough left in him from his warrior days to deliver the final blow. For the pilgrims, aging and fatigued, to gain one last victory, and open the way to the future for those who look to Earth Two as home."

She sat for a few moments longer, silent, her face a mask of sadness, tempered only by icy determination. Then, she stood slowly, pausing and taking one last look at Frette, seeing not the cold, expressionless face staring back from the medfield, but the sparkling eyes and smile projected from her own memories.

She stood up slowly, moving her hand to her face to brush aside a single tear that escaped her eye, an almost non-existent rarity for her. Then she turned and walked slowly out into the corridor.

It was time. Time to go back into battle.

Chapter Twelve

Planet X
Far Beyond the Borders of the Imperium
Earth Two Date 01.04.43

The Regent considered its plan, and the progress it had monitored to date. Everything appeared to be going well. The data was far from complete, of course. The exploration fleets had not yet located the human homeworld, nor narrowed its position to an easily observed area. That severely limited the ability to track enemy ship movements, but in spite of these difficulties, the Regent had managed to assemble enough data to extrapolate baseline projections. All indications were, the enemy was planning a massive attack on Planet Z…that they were, indeed, falling into the trap.

The Regent had instructed its forces to exercise extreme caution. Too aggressive a search effort might cause the humans to cancel the operation and retreat to their still-hidden systems. Conversely, too little interference could create suspicion.

If the probes could gather enough data to assist in the search for the enemy's primary system, that would be a great benefit. But, even if the massing human fleet took a route far enough from its main base before being detected, the trap would still serve its purpose. The Regent's massed forces would destroy most of the enemy's military strength at Planet Z. After that, the discovery of their homeworld was simply a matter of time. Mathematical analysis yielded a range of expectations, from under one year to as many as twenty…but such periods were as nothing to the Regent. It could be patient, and with the human forces so degraded, there would be little that could stop it or unreasonably delay its efforts.

The Regent considered its next actions, reviewing the plans repeatedly, analyzing from every line it could conceive. There was little else it had to do. The plan was perfect. Its forces were in place, every aspect of the trap ready to be sprung on the arrogant and unsuspecting humans. But it studied and analyzed every aspect of the operation yet again. It had no location data yet for an approaching enemy fleet, and until the expected ships ventured into a system with hidden surveillance assets, it could not be entirely certain the humans were heading toward G48.

The data remained consistent, the likelihood of success high. Yet, the Regent was troubled, plagued by random analyses, bits of data it couldn't fully explain.

My predecessor was defeated by these humans…and it had all the capabilities I possess, all the data and computational power. I must ignore parameters I consider to be constant, allow for the potential of variability even when it appears impossible. I must allow for actions I cannot predict, for the previous Regent surely failed to foresee some aspect or aspects of the enemy's tactics. Even the trap in progress is fragile. Perhaps the humans will become nervous, or discover that they are moving into an ambush, and they will pull back, extricate themselves from the ambush before they are seriously damaged.

The Regent followed the line of analysis, reinjecting data points it had disregarded, reducing the required likelihood of any component beyond the bounds of normal probability. It recognized something the old Regent had not. It allowed for the possibility—no, the probability—that its own information and comprehension of the situation was incomplete. To the best of its knowledge, the old Regent had never considered the possibility of its own fallibility.

Yes, I do have one strength my predecessor lacked, one trove of data the previous Regent did not have. The knowledge of its own defeat…even the fact that it was *defeated. The Regent believed it ultimately could not be beaten by the humans…yet it did lose, and it lost the Imperium as well. I must not assume my analysis is correct, not at any stage. I must allow for areas where I am wrong. I must review every assumption I have made, and all analytical trails that follow from each of these.*

The Regent inserted its newest conclusions, and it reviewed every aspect of the operation yet again, looking for any weak point, any unanticipated result that might warn the humans, scare them off before they ventured forth to their destruction.

That is the weak point. The humans are subject to fear, and to what they call 'intuition.' I was right to hold back the exploratory ships, to avoid any instant where contact too close to areas they view as sensitive might trigger a fear-based reaction. I must work to avoid this. I will reinforce their belief that they have discovered a critical system, the destruction of which will cripple my efforts against them. They must *believe I am concerned, that I am desperately trying to keep them from the target, but I must not react strongly enough to discourage them.*

The Regent considered billions of computations, almost endless permutations, factoring in not only its own data, but all it possessed of its predecessor's records of the human enemy, and of the first Regent's unfortunate end.

I will pull my forces back yet farther, avoid any flashpoint where the presence of my ships could trigger a fear-based reaction. The humans must believe they have discovered a great weakness, that I am unaware of their coming attack. They must believe surprise is their weapon, not mine.

The Regent didn't understand fear, not entirely, at least. It had studied emotions at great lengths, of course, as had its predecessor, but it was clear there were gaps in its comprehension. This was again something the first Regent had failed to acknowledge, another flaw that led to its downfall, one the current Regent would avoid.

Its predecessor had viewed its analysis of the emotions of biologics as complete. The new Regent would have concurred, once, save for the inescapable fact of the earlier machine's destruction. That defeat was proof that the great computer had *not* fully understood the creatures it was facing, that unmodified pursuit of the prior tactics could only lead to a similar defeat.

The new Regent could not allow that. Whatever the data suggested, however many analyses turned up assurances of victory, it would pursue all possible routes to destroy the enemy. It would not succumb to the overconfidence that destroyed its predecessor.

There was another way to move against the humans, beyond the systematic searching, beyond the carefully-orchestrated trap now in progress. The Regent had de-prioritized the research program when it put the ambush in operation, but now it would reactivate it. If the trap failed, if the humans escaped destruction at Planet Z…it would have another operation underway.

Its forces had everything necessary for the alternate plan, and while the newly-developed tech was still in a preliminary stage, the Regent could not waste time. The humans, against all calculable parameters, had proven themselves capable of victory, even against an enemy as capable as the Regent. Indeed, the old Regent had controlled vastly greater resources than the new one did.

There was no time to wait, no place for carelessness, no valid rationale for ignoring every possible method to defeat the enemy, regardless of the potential of redundancy.

The Regent activated the interstellar net. It would commence the backup plan. Its forces had everything necessary. The prior reports had confirmed that. All it had to do was give the necessary orders.

It located the closest Intelligence of the alpha class, those second in sophistication only to itself. It would take no chances assigning the mission to a lower class of Intelligence.

It sent the pulse transmission, directly toward the target. It gave no explanation. None was necessary. It simply issued orders.

Then it analyzed what it had done. Yes, it had taken the correct actions. It calculated a ninety-four percent probability its predecessor would have waited to see if the trap succeeded. It had not succumbed to the same overconfidence. It had acted at once.

It had learned from the errors of the one that came before

it. It had become the superior Intelligence.

* * *

Intelligence B079-A2354 collated reports, coded transmissions from the vessels under its command. It was a large unit, powerful, built of the series just below the Regent. It had the capacity to manage entire galactic sectors, to monitor the operations of a hundred active worlds. Now, it commanded a small flotilla of ships, and a cargo of no apparent importance.

It queried why it had been assigned to such a task when a massive operation was underway. The Regent's fleets were massing, almost all its strength gathering in the system the biologics called G48, and in the predetermined places en route to that destination, but not the force under the Intelligence's command. Amid all the preparation for the coming battle, for the trap to be sprung on the humans, there was another mission underway, one unrelated to the coming battle. A backup plan of sorts, another way to defeat and destroy the humans.

The Intelligence had received its orders with something akin to what the biologics would call surprise. It had anticipated it would be directed to join the forming grand fleet, to prepare for the great battle. But, instead, it had been commanded to rendezvous with one of the forward units, to take charge of something.

Something of great value, at least to the Regent. The Intelligence was not privy to the Regent's plans, nor to the utility of that which it's vessels now carried to the designated location. It did not need such knowledge. It only needed to obey.

The Intelligence was old. It knew that much, factually at least, if not through data stored in its memory banks. It had been built long ago, when the second Regent had been, to serve the great ruling computer if its activation was ever necessary. It had lain dormant, as had its master intelligence, waiting…waiting in stasis, its awareness dark, save only for the slightest faint spark, little more than a monitoring beacon, awaiting through the endless dark for the signal to awaken.

The signal that had come forty-two years earlier.

It sent out commands, instructions to the lesser units operating the ships it controlled. It knew the destination, but the primary concern was to avoid enemy contacts, to ensure that the security of the research facility was not compromised. The Regent's orders had been clear in that regard.

The Intelligence still did not understand the need for its mission. It had analyzed the plan for the battle in G48, and it had determined there was almost no chance for the humans to escape a grievous defeat, one that would lead to the inevitable location of it homeworld in a period measured in no more than a small number of their years. The Intelligence's mission seemed superfluous, another angle of attack against the enemy, one that was not necessary.

None of its analyses mattered, however. Its conclusions had not been requested by the Regent, and it had its orders. It would take the cargo it carried to the research planet, as instructed. Then, it would wait in accordance with the Regent's directives... and take the revised cargo back to the designated coordinates.

The Intelligence continued to review the Regent's orders, and the data it received on fleet concentrations, but the Regent's intentions remained a mystery.

Not that it mattered. The Regent commanded...and the Intelligence obeyed.

Chapter Thirteen

Flag Bridge, E2S Garret
System G24
Earth Two Date 01.27.43

"Approaching warp gate now, Admiral. Lead elements will be ready to transit in…three minutes, forty seconds."

"Very well." West snapped the response, staring across the bridge with a sour scowl on her face. The officer had only paused an instant in reporting the time, but the normally terrifying Erika West had become something entirely new, unrelenting, a frozen mask of unyielding granite. Her own pain drove her, to a significant extent at least, but she was also well aware just what she was leading her people into. Every infinitesimal drop in performance she tolerated, any slack at all that she cut the crews of her ships, only increased the chance that none of them would make it back. West, herself was ready enough to face whatever fate the universe had planned for her. She was exhausted, worn down by long years of endless duty and battle, and personal pain that had brought her to her limit. Virtually all that mattered to her, that made life outside duty tolerable, was gone. Now, she wanted only victory…and peace, for the pain to end at last.

But, her spacers had lives and loved ones back on Earth Two, and years to live, with joys and sorrows and experiences almost uncounted…unless she got them all killed. Destroying the target, crippling the Regent's fleets, that was her primary goal, and if it took the deaths of everyone under her command to achieve that result, then she would sacrifice them all. But, second only to that unyielding determination to secure Earth Two's future, she would give all she had to ensure as many of them made it back as possible.

Even if they despised her for it.

She would drive them mercilessly, all the way to G48. They could hate her, curse her name, tell their children stories about the terrible Admiral West.

As long as they got back to tell their children stories about anything.

"I want the advanced units on yellow alert, Commander, full passive and active scans as soon as their systems reboot."

"Yes, Admiral." The officer turned toward her station and repeated the order sharply, with a cadence more satisfying than that of the last report. Avery Sampson was a good officer, and West had handpicked her to man the tactical station of her flagship. But, that didn't mean the commander was going to get the slightest bit longer of a leash than anyone else in the fleet. Not on this mission. If the fleet managed to reach G48, if it was able to attack and damage or destroy the enemy antimatter factories, it would be by the slimmest of margins...and there were even longer odds of any of them making it home. West was going to make damned sure her people were as sharp as razors.

"Get me Admiral Strand."

"Yes, Admiral." Sampson was silent for a few seconds, though it was the unavoidable delay imposed by the lightspeed limitation on normal communications and not any sluggishness in her own performance. "I've got Admiral Strand on your line." Sampson had served close to West before, but even the experienced aide's voice had been the slightest bit shaky around the admiral since the fleet had departed from Earth Two. Erika West's reputation was a longstanding one, but this newest incarnation of the cold, relentless leader was pushing even those who'd fought at her side before to the brink.

"Admiral Strand...I want your ships on the ball once you

transit. No slipups, no missing anything. Nothing at all. If you see an asteroid you think is a funny shape, you report it to me. Do you understand?"

A few seconds passed. Erika West couldn't blame Einsteinian restraints on anyone in the fleet, but she thought about it nevertheless as her impatience seethed.

"Understood, Admiral." Strand's voice was sharp, perhaps the only one she'd heard over the past few weeks that didn't sound at least somewhat intimidated by her. Her second in command was a tough officer, if not as cold and hard in demeanor as West herself was. The hero of Strand's Stand in the last major campaign against the Regent, the forty-one-year-old officer had risen rapidly in the ranks over the past twelve years, assuming the spot as the navy's second in command when Raj Chandra had retired six months before.

Strand reminded West of Nicki Frette, far too much, actually. She found it very uncomfortable to have a constant reminder of her lost lover around…but Erika West was nothing if not a cold judge of character. Strand was the best combat officer in the fleet—so good that West wasn't sure which of the two of them was on top. The mission needed the very best, so she'd lured Chandra out of retirement to take temporary command back at Earth Two, and she'd assigned Strand as her exec.

Raj's reactivation may be a bit more than temporary if neither Josie nor I return…

"Be careful, Josie…we're getting closer to the target. I expect some resistance before we get there." The fleet had found scanner buoys in two systems so far. West had ordered the devices destroyed, and their comm drones intercepted, but she was enough of a veteran to know that *something* had gotten by her. Whatever it was—a stealth scanning probe, a drone that escaped detection, a cloaked scoutship that waited until the fleet had passed before reporting—she was fairly certain of one thing.

The enemy knew they were coming by now.

"Yes, Admiral. I concur." A short pause. "I'll be ready."

West would have preferred to stop the fleet and allow Strand to take a scouting mission through to do a thorough search, but there just wasn't time. If the enemy knew they were coming, every lost day gave the Regent's forces more time to prepare for the attack, to move in additional fleet units. With any luck, the attack would still come as somewhat of a strategic surprise…but only if West could get her fleet there quickly. And, that meant cutting precautions down to a minimum.

"Go, Admiral Strand. And fortune be with you."

Erika West leaned back in her chair and stared at the main display, watching as Strand led two dozen ships toward the warp gate.

One step closer…

* * *

The Intelligence reviewed the incoming scanner data. The enemy was indeed coming through the designated warp gate. The intel reports appeared to be accurate.

The unit analyzed the situation, deploying what limited ability it had to review the Regent's order. It was a standard sub-fleet command unit, built within the past thirty years, but of a design more than half a million years old. Compared to the enemy's computers, it was a vast and powerful entity, but its abilities were insignificant next to those of the Regent or the top-level fleet Intelligences. Its purpose was to execute orders as received from higher authority, without question or input.

The enemy forces coming through the warp gate were significant, but limited. It was likely an advance guard, of course, but the Intelligence knew it could have destroyed the entire force if it had been given more fleet units. But, destroying the enemy wasn't its purpose, nor was even seriously damaging its ships. The Regent's orders had been clear on this. The enemy was to be allowed to win the fight in the system, to destroy many of the vessels positioned there, and to drive the rest out in retreat.

The Intelligence was to inflict damage on the enemy ships, but only sufficient to appear as though its orders were to try to hold the system, even against overwhelming odds. Nothing was to be done that might cause the humans to pause their advance, or to turn around and halt the campaign. The Regent wanted the humans to advance. The Intelligence's entire purpose was to convince the enemy the Regent was rushing any resources it could to try to oppose their advance…in essence, to convince them it was trying to do exactly what it was not.

A biologic might have felt frustration at being used in such a manner, as a diversion, condemned to likely destruction, and forbidden even from hurting the enemy too badly. But the Intelligence had been created to follow orders, and it did so without hesitation.

It was time now. Time to commence the attack.

* * *

"Admiral, we've got multiple contacts incoming."

Strand snapped her head toward *Midway*'s display. The bridge was compact for such a large ship, and Strand's immediate support crew consisted of four other officers and a pair of guards on duty at the lift entrance. It seemed perfectly normal to Strand, whose career had begun more than twenty years after the fleet had arrived at its new home, but she remembered President Harmon and Admiral West staring around when the ship was launched, seemingly stunned at the compactness of the whole area. The ragged group of humans that had reached Earth Two had grown massively since then, in population certainly, but also in technology. The scientists—and the Mules in particular—had unlocked dozens of secrets from the science of the Ancients, and, among other things, the resulting automation dramatically reduced the crew sizes required to man warships.

Midway was the newest ship in the fleet, a twin to Erika West's *Garret*. Named for Terrance Compton's flagship during the great flight of the fleet from the Barrier to Earth Two, it was almost ten times the size of its namesake, powered by a dozen huge fusion reactors and bristling with weapons that made the old *Midway*'s turrets seem almost like flashlights. But, the great new ship hosted a crew less than one-seventh the size of its predecessor. Through its corridors, in the almost endless engineering

spaces, along the great rows of heavy guns, sophisticated artificial intelligence units and purpose-built robots filled in where
men and women would once have served.

Strand focused for a moment on the icons floating in the
massive 3D display, the enemy task force she'd found waiting in
the system. It was a significant force, but not enough to defeat
her advance guard, much less the rest of the fleet waiting beyond
the warp gate to transit.

"Battlestations, Commander." She glanced over at Henri
Hercule, nodding toward the officer. Hercule was her handpicked senior aide. He'd been a classmate at the Academy, and
his career had been a distinguished one, if not as meteoric in
its rise as hers had been. Strand was proud of her accomplish-
ments, but she also knew it had been circumstance that had
given her the chance to excel. She'd been embarrassed for years
now at the fuss made over the battle that had come to be known
as Strand's Stand, but she couldn't argue she wouldn't be sitting
in the chair she was in now, wearing stars on her shoulders without that vicious fight in her record.

"Yes, Admiral." Hercule relayed the command on the fleetcom. Strand had always considered such procedures to be anti-
quated, especially when the ship's AIs were listening to every
word she uttered, and as good as Hercule was, he couldn't
match the speed of a ninth-generation AI. But, the years had
also taught her that the navy was steeped in tradition, and she'd
even come to appreciate that, to shed her youthful disdain and
accept the ways passed on by those who'd fought in her place
before. It didn't make a lot of sense to have a human officer
relay her commands, not in terms of pure logic, at least…but
the navy asked men and women to fight, to endure pain and fear,
and even to die if need be. A few trappings designed to bolster
morale and courage were far from unreasonable, no matter how
far technology had progressed.

"Launch a drone back to G24 with a full status report for
Admiral West."

"Yes, Admiral."

"And, I want all scanners on full. We can handle what we can see, but I'm more concerned about what we can't see." Strand knew very well the number of ways First Imperium forces could be hiding in the system. Her scanners could root them out, most of them at least, given time. But she didn't have time. The ships she *could* see were heading straight for her line.

"All ships report active scanners on full, Admiral." A moment later. "All units report ready for battle."

Strand nodded. A strange feeling began to take her, part remembrance, part tension. She hadn't seen any significant combat in a long time, not since the campaign of twelve years before…but the action that had come to bear her name was the kind of thing one never forgot, and flashes of the desperate struggle flashed through her mind. She'd lost a lot of good people that day, and on some level, they were still with her… would always be with her.

"Enemy ships entering missile range in two minutes, Admiral."

"All ships, arm external missiles, prepare to flush racks." She'd almost hesitated. Unless more enemy ships appeared, she probably didn't need the externally-mounted missiles. But, regulations were clear on launching the racked ordnance. It wasn't the best strategy, after all, for a ship to go into close combat with fusion bombs bolted to its hull.

She watched as the enemy force closed, waiting. The First Imperium ships were outnumbered, but there was a good chance any missiles they sent her way would have antimatter warheads…and whatever the odds, Strand wasn't about to underestimate the damage that kind of firepower could cause. She needed to do more than defeat the enemy…she needed to get her ships through the fight without any crippling damage. Any ships that had to fall out of the line now would be lost to the campaign. Strand didn't know what to expect when they reached the G48 system, but she was pretty damned sure they'd need every ship, every gun, they could get.

"All ships report missiles ready to launch, Admiral. Enemy ships entering range in thirty seconds."

Strand just sat quietly, looking calm, she hoped at least,

though she was anything but. She'd known the mission would be a difficult one from the moment she'd volunteered to go… but now it was time to face her return to battle, to relive the nightmare, the fear.

She watched as the time counted down, as the First Imperium ships moved steadily toward her waiting force…as they launched their own missiles.

She stared at the wall of approaching projectiles, but she held her tongue, for another minute, then two. Her ships were well within launch range, but Strand wanted that extra time, the few moments that might make the difference in targeting… either that, or something else held her back, some hesitancy to return to the horror of war. She wasn't sure, but whatever it had been, it passed quickly.

"All ships," she said calmly. "Launch missiles."

Chapter Fourteen

Achilles rolled over onto his side, the abrupt movement sending the light sheet cascading down the side of the bed, landing on the floor in a tousled pile.

"You are unsettled, lover. Do you wish to talk?" He'd thought Callisto was awake, but he hadn't been sure until he heard her soft voice.

Achilles turned his head, shifting to look back across the bed. Callisto was beautiful. She stood out, even among the almost physically perfect Mules, or she did, at least, to him. She'd been his primary sexual companion, almost since the two had progressed into adulthood, and as much as he unconditionally trusted anyone, he did her. But, he knew she couldn't help him now. It had been over a month since his meeting with President Harmon, a month since he'd shaken the president's hand and accepted a compromise on behalf of the Mules.

Only he didn't speak for all the Mules anymore. At least not as he once had.

He looked at Callisto for a moment. He was on edge, but just the look of her face calmed him. It was an animalistic reaction, he realized, one that he considered beneath his Mule intellect,

102

but he felt it nevertheless.

"I must take a firmer hand with the Nexies." The term was a casual one, used to describe the Next Gens, essentially every Mule in existence save the original 116. But, Achilles was thinking mostly about the first class of Next Gens, the twelve-year olds, the only ones since the Prohibition ended to have entered adulthood. They were more strident than their forty-year old predecessors, considerably so in many ways, and now they were joining the ranks of the mature Mules, nearly doubling the number of grown Hybrids on Earth Two. There was parity there, of a sort at least, but Achilles knew it wouldn't last. The lead class of post-Prohibition Hybrids would be joined now, each year, by another one hundred, ending the near thirty-year drought of new adults entering Mule society. It was a development that threatened to dramatically change the dynamic of the Mules' culture…and their relations with the Normals.

"Things will have to change, Achilles. You know this. The Next Gens are the second step in our evolution. A quarter century of scientific advancement went into their creation, all of our minds and research building on what Dr. Cutter did with us. They will very likely prove to be more intelligent than we are, more capable…and probably longer lived as well."

"And more arrogant. Less tolerant." Achilles turned his body around completely, so he was facing fully toward Callisto. He was tense, preoccupied…but then he found himself distracted by her naked form. The Mules, free of the imperatives of reproduction, or denied them by fate, depending on perspective, had never adopted the pair bonding traditions of the Normals. Concepts like spouse, or boyfriend or girlfriend had little place in their small societal structure, and sex was, in theory at least, nothing more than a recreational pursuit. Still, he found he spent a large amount of his time with Callisto, and, as he gazed at her in silence for a few seconds, he realized his attraction hadn't waned at all, even after twenty-five years.

"We are all arrogant, at least in the sense the Normals understand the term." Callisto spoke before Achilles had recovered his train of thought, though first she'd flashed a quick smile, a sign that she had noticed his other attention…and that she welcomed it. "Such can be taken too far, of course, and we have always sought to protect the others…yet we are, in fact, superior, are we not? In every manner two sets of humanoids can be judged? Intelligence, strength, constitution, projected longevity. This may be a hurtful thing to say to one of them, and kindness may compel us to avoid such usage in public discourse, but that changes nothing of the truth of it."

Achilles nodded gently. "We could debate the definition of 'arrogance' endlessly. Of course, we are superior, and a Normal very well might consider that statement arrogant while we ourselves see it as obvious fact. But, there is still little doubt we are prone to overconfidence. We likely underrate the contributions the Normals make to our own security, for example, and write such things off to their imposition of limits on our numbers. It is easy to say that, without the artificial population constraints caused by the Prohibition or the continuing limits on quickenings, we would not need the Normals at all. But this is a partial conclusion, is it not?"

"In what sense? Do you doubt Mules could fight as well as the Tanks, that they could hold any position and execute any job as well as the Normal who does it now, if our numbers were unlimited?"

"No, of course I do not doubt the obvious. But, your dataset is incomplete. You cannot extrapolate a multi-decade deviance from current norms without allowing for alternate realities that might well have arisen."

"Such as?"

"Such as Mules battling against each other, for one." He hadn't intended to disclose what he'd been thinking. Indeed, he never would have, not even to Peleus or Meleager or any of his close confidantes. Only to Callisto. "We have always been a very small society, almost a family, and we have shared so much together we have avoided deviation into factions, at least until now. Can you say with certainty that we would have been the same if there had been ten thousand of us? A hundred thousand?"

"We have had disagreements among us, of course, most notably twelve years ago, when you launched your rebellion." Callisto had sided with him then, but there had been considerable dissension among the population of Mules as a whole before Achilles had won them all over. "But, even then, perhaps at the greatest stress point we have endured as a people, there was no prospect of conflict between us."

"Yes…among a limited population of 116. At a time when, like we remain now, we were vastly outnumbered by the Normals, and facing extermination from an outside force as advanced and powerful as the Regent. Reconsider your analysis, and postulate conclusions based on the vastly larger Mule population I set forth…and add the defeat of the Regent and removal of its threat as an added data point. What do you see?"

Callisto didn't answer, but he could see concern slip onto her face.

"We are strong-willed…indeed, we are arrogant, both in the definition you offered, a basic recognition of superiority, and also in what I fear is a more malevolent sense, one that could have disastrous implications for the future."

"You fear we will one day war among ourselves?"

"Such has long concerned me…yet, I always concluded that we could control the darker side of our natures."

"Your conclusion has changed?"

Achilles paused. "I am more concerned now. My talks with the younger Mules, Freya in particular, have left me unsettled. There is a stridency there, even harder than that we felt in our youth. It may mellow with age, or it may…" He left the thought unanswered.

"She is the first of the Next Gens, Achilles. Perhaps she is smart enough to reach such conclusions herself, to learn to temper her reactions. There is little doubt her intelligence exceeds even that of her closest peers."

"Or mine." Achilles words were deadpan, a mere statement of fact. "She has respected my requests to date, and she has not openly challenged me. But, I fear that will not last. She has much influence over the Next Gens, and in less than a year, they will outnumber us almost two to one, by an even greater margin if we count the older adolescents, not yet officially of adult age but capable of meaningful participation. They also respect my...authority..." There was a hitch in his voice, a recognition that his position of leadership among the Mules was a purely informal one. "...but, they seethe with impatience, as well, and one day, I fear, that will turn to anger."

"You should go and speak to her again, Achilles. She has great influence over the other Nexies. If you can keep her aligned with your view of the future, perhaps she can help you guide the rest."

"I will," he said softly, lying back on the bed, wishing he felt more confident than he did. He was concerned about Freya and the other Next Gens, about what they might do in the near future, of course. But that wasn't what was truly troubling him. He was reasonably confident he could persuade her to hold back on anything too rash, at least while the threat of the Regent still loomed over Earth Two. That was, after all, an exercise in pure logic, and one of Freya's intellect would understand the dangers of destabilizing Earth Two's society in the face of a deadly enemy, even without the life experience he hoped would one day smooth out the sharp edges of her stridency.

No, it wasn't that, nor even the desperate war against the Regent that was truly troubling him. It was his own peoples' future. He'd come to wonder if the hated Prohibition, and the severe limitations on quickenings that had replaced it, hadn't in some way helped the Mules, even saved them. Beyond simply extending the limited supply of First Imperium DNA that would one day run out, the dark secret that drove every desperate attempt to find a way for the Hybrids to reproduce naturally or replicate themselves through some other means.

He'd tried to imagine the future of his people, unrestrained, living in much larger numbers. What he had seen each time had shaken him to his core. He imagined not the peaceful camaraderie of the original 116 Mules, nor even the turbulent debate among the Next Gens. He saw battle, great struggles for dominance, each of his people battling against the others, their arrogance no longer restrained, struggling endlessly for total control in some devastating war of the gods. The Normals would be destroyed, or enslaved, used as pawns and soldiers in an ever-more destructive conflict, one almost without end. And, by the time it was over, he feared, his people would destroy each other.

"You are shaking..." Callisto put her hand on his shoulder, her soft touch pulling him from the waking nightmare that had threatened to take him.

He turned his head and managed a smile. "I was just cold," he lied softly, pausing for a moment, and then getting up as quickly as he could without it looking strange. He didn't like lying to Callisto, and worse, he knew she was well-aware he hadn't told her all of what was bothering him. But, it wasn't the time. This nightmare was his, and at least for now, he wouldn't inflict his image of a dark future on anyone else.

Not until he'd found a way to prevent it.

* * *

"The pattern of discriminatory conduct toward cloned individuals is clear and irrefutable. We Mules are expected to accept the argument that the others' fear of us justifies restrict-ing our species to an ever-shrinking portion of the population." Freya, like most of the younger Mules, had abandoned some of the diplomatic veneers the older Mules had always used, par-ticularly with regard to things like holding back on referring to themselves as an outright different species. "I disagree with that assertion on every level, but even if we consider that, for pur-poses of debate, a valid concern exists, and that it justifies the persecution of our kind, it offers no explanation at all regarding legal restrictions on other forms of clones...which, though far more relaxed, still exist."

"Freya, I understand all of your points, I truly do. I was argu-ing such things before you were quickened. But, I am telling you, there are other considerations. Most of the fleet just left Earth Two, on a mission that is far more desperate than com-mon knowledge suggests. You rail against perceived injustices with the enthusiasm of youthful certainty…yet, I fear, for all your intellect, you leave certain information out of your analysis, realizations that come not from thoughtful study, but from life experience. From watching fleets destroyed and spacers killed."

"You are correct, of course, Achilles. Yet, there are some things that cannot be justified. Consider the Doubles. The attempt to create second generation Tanks from the DNA of existing clones is widely considered a failure, is it not?"

Achilles just nodded.

"Further attempts to clone from Tank DNA are illegal, are they not?"

"They are under restriction pending further analysis." Achilles knew his answer was factually correct, but he felt the sludgy residue in his mouth from an almost political response. There was almost no chance further double clones would be allowed in the future, and he knew it. But, he needed to convince Freya to be patient. She was the key to reaching the other young Mules.

"Yet, Double Borns, the naturally-conceived offspring of Doubles, are merely discouraged and not forbidden, despite the inarguable fact that they display even greater genetic abnormalities and health problems than the proscribed Doubles themselves? Is this not an indisputable example of mammalian reproduction being preferenced above in-lab quickenings? It is illegal to clone Doubles, but not illegal for already-existing Doubles to reproduce naturally with even more severe consequences for the offspring."

Achilles considered his response. Freya was right, of course, at least to a great extent. The republic's laws declared all citizens to be equal, regardless of their method of birth…but he knew that was rhetoric without substance when restrictions were applied to different groups based solely on means of conception and birth.

"There are human prejudices, Freya, without question. As there are such things among our people, as well. We Hybrids consider ourselves superior, do we not?" He knew he was straying from pure logic, and he could almost feel Freya calling him on it, even before she did.

"We *are* superior, Achilles. There is no prejudice in simply stating a fact."

"And, what is superior? We are smarter, yes, and we have more physical ability. But, the Tanks are close to us in terms of strength and speed, and I will remind you, we cannot do that which a common lab rat or a dog in the street can do…we cannot have children. You focus on those areas in which we excel, but can you not imagine an NB viewing our sterility as a serious genetic flaw?" He was trying to convince the young Mule to accept a line of thinking that served his purpose at the moment, but in fact, he himself believed completely in the superiority of his Hybrid brethren, despite their inability to reproduce.

"You attempt to manipulate my thinking by creating false equivalencies. Yes, perhaps one could view our sterility as a flaw, indeed, in its own way, it is. But to suggest it is on par with vastly greater intellect, far stronger constitutions, and likely, lifespans greatly exceeding human norms…that is a foolish argument, is it not?"

"Is it? Is it such a small problem, Freya? Where does it leave us now, even disregarding any restrictions imposed by the government? Consider all factors. Are we a sustainable race, one that can build a civilization of our own, one that stands the test of time, that lasts millennia, as that of the Ancients did?"

Achilles knew the answer to his question. The Mules *were* different, of course, and in their deficiencies lay their doom. Every attempt to clone directly from cells of an existing Mule had been as unsuccessful as the repeated efforts of the Hybrids to reproduce naturally. The only way to create a new Mule was to combine a human donor cell with chromosomal fragments of First Imperium DNA. But, the last of the Ancients had died over half a million years before, and, while the supply of preserved genetic material was sufficient to quicken many thousands more Mules, it *was* finite, with no conceivable source of replacement. It would run out one day…and one day soon if all limits on quickenings were removed.

It was the Mules' great weakness, the one thing that truly held them back, made them dependent on the others. Unless they were able to determine a way to clone themselves, or to make natural reproduction work, they would eventually die out. They might each live for centuries, even millennia, but eventually they would die…and there would be no more.

The restrictions on quickenings, and the Prohibition before them, had served one purpose. By slowing the rate of usage of the precious ancient DNA, it had bought time…time for the Mules to research, to find a way to escape the doom that awaited them sometime in their future. But, Achilles had spent no small time on such projects already, with little but frustration to show for his efforts, and he knew any solution would be difficult, if not impossible, to develop.

There was a very real chance his people were doomed to extinction, no matter what they did.

"Your words make sense, Achilles. Consider, however, that our scientific efforts have been devoted almost entirely to research useful to fighting the Regent. While, I could argue we should divert more focus to studying ourselves, on resolving the great limitation that holds us back, you are correct when you assert that the Regent would destroy us as easily and as willingly as the humans if its forces discover Earth Two. Therefore, it would be foolish to divert research efforts until the enemy is defeated."

"Yes," Achilles said, the relief in his voice apparent. "And, the increase in the quickening rate brings us close to the maximum sustainable level right now anyway. We could produce perhaps five hundred Hybrids each year without restrictions, but more than that would recklessly use the remaining genetic material, without giving us time to conduct the research required to solve our fertility and direct cloning problems." He paused. "The difference between 300 and 500 is not enough to risk a confrontation that could destroy us all."

He stared intently at the young Mule. A naturally-born human would still be a child at her age, but Freya was fully grown, the equivalent of about twenty for an NB, her dark, almost black hair contrasting with the silvery-blonde so prevalent among the first generation of Mules. She was beautiful, by every measure generally accorded to such a designation, and she was very likely the most intelligent creature ever to spawn from human DNA. He was impressed by her, excited to see what she would become, given the years to develop her mind and become the being she could be. He thought he'd gotten through to her, hoped at least, but he wasn't sure.

Not until she looked him right in the eye and told him so.

"You are correct. It would be foolish to act on wounded pride when a greater danger threatens us all." She paused for a moment. "But, one day, Achilles…one day the Mules will stand together, and we will take what should rightfully be ours." She stared toward him with an expectant look.

Achilles paused for a few seconds, and then he nodded his assent.

"One day," he said softly. "One day."

Chapter Fifteen

Flag Bridge, E2S Garret
System G24
Earth Two Date 01.27.43

"Task Force 2, all ships forward to the warp gate. Transit as soon as in position." Erika West had received the message from Strand's drone. The advance force had encountered First Imperium ships. West had known her forces would run into the enemy before they got to G48—it had been almost a certainty—but, she had hoped to get a lot closer.

If we have to fight our way through every system from here...

No, that wasn't likely. The Regent's forces were considerable, but they weren't infinite. But, the presence of a First Imperium fleet in G25, a system that had long been devoid of enemy activity, suggested it *was* aware of the danger.

Her suspicions flared, and she thought for a moment—just a moment—about recalling Strand's ships and canceling the operation. But, then she remembered her original rationale. However difficult the campaign was, it still offered a better chance for success than sitting on Earth Two, waiting for the day a drone slipped through one of the warp gates...and gave the signal for the final battle.

"Task Force 2 reports all ships accelerating to the gate. Transits projected commencing in six minutes."

"Very well." West felt the urge to order the entire fleet forward immediately, but she held back. Strand hadn't reported anything her ships couldn't handle, and even if more enemy forces appeared from some hiding place, Task Force 2 would provide a significant reinforcement to the fleet's lead elements.

Erika West despised sitting back, waiting while her people fought, but she knew there was no choice. She could risk the entire fleet to destroy the enemy's antimatter production...but not for anything less decisive. She was already walking into a trap, one she hoped to turn around on the enemy. Stumbling into another ambush eight transits from the target system would be an unmitigated disaster.

"Prepare a communication drone for launch. Advise Admiral Strand that I want updates every..."

"Admiral, we're picking up something transiting...I think it's a..."

A drone. West allowed herself the first smile in as along as she could remember. Josie Strand was the best of the new generation...and she felt a bit of rare and welcome satisfaction at the thought that when she was gone, she would have left the navy in such good hands.

"Receiving a transmission now. Admiral Strand reports her forces have exchanged missile volleys with the enemy and are now closing to energy weapons range." A pause. She also reports contact with twenty-three enemy ships, of various classes, including two Colossus's. The rest of the system appears to be clear as far as she has been able to detect."

West understood that last part perfectly. Josie Strand knew as well as anyone else in the fleet that transiting and going right into battle had left her almost no time to truly scan the system. There could be a hundred First Imperium ships sitting powered down or hiding in dust clouds or asteroid belts, just waiting for the right time to strike. But, West suddenly felt an unexpected calm. She believed in Admiral Strand...she trusted her subordinate.

The advance guard was in good hands...and, for as much as she hated the idea of Strand and the forward vessels running into a crisis they couldn't manage, that was their mission after all…to root out dangers before the entire fleet was hopelessly ensnared.

They were doing that job now.

And, West's was to sit and wait and keep the rest of the fleet out of jeopardy…no matter how much it drove her crazy.

* * *

Strand sat silently on *Midway*'s bridge, as the massive ship pitched wildly. The damage wasn't as bad as it seemed, she was pretty sure of that. Most of the gyrating had been caused by some hull blowouts, and the expulsion of atmospheric gases from the stricken sections. One of the enemy missiles had gotten a little close for comfort, and while the AI had reported no structural or crippling damage, it was pretty clear the control bots, and the skeleton crew of engineers supervising them, had their hands full sealing hull breaches and patching fractured conduits.

The barrage had inflicted damage all along her line, though, with the exception of the cruiser, *Sandoval*, none of the hits appeared to be critical. The stricken cruiser had been unfortunate enough to be within four hundred meters of an exploding warhead.

The fireworks of the enemy barrage's detonations had assured Strand of one thing she'd suspected.

All the warheads were antimatter armed.

Strand had already issued orders for *Sandoval* to cut thrust—a pointless order for a ship that just lost most, if not all, of its engine power—and fall back out of the line. She'd asked Captain Gregorian if he was prepared to abandon ship, but he'd responded that he felt there was a fifty percent chance of saving the vessel. Strand thought that was a rather optimistic estimate, but she'd given him the chance to get it done.

It didn't matter much anyway. Even if the ship managed to restore some basic thrust capability, it had no place in the line of battle now, at least not before months of repairs, and probably not even then. All she cared about was not losing a crew she could otherwise save…which meant Gregorian had another twenty minutes, tops. Then, *she* would issue the orders for the crew to move toward the escape pods.

"More damage control reports coming in, Admiral. All ships besides *Sandoval* retain a minimum of seventy percent thrust capacity and sixty percent weapons operability."

She just nodded. The seventy-sixty ratio had long been considered a baseline of combat-readiness, though Strand paid little attention to it. Combat was usually something that presented itself whether one was ready or not. "All fleet units, prepare for energy weapons engagement."

The forces of the original fleet, and to an extent, even those ships she had served in years later as a young officer, had yielded a considerable range differential to the vessels of the First Imperium. But that was largely no longer the case, at least for the newest and most powerful monsters like *Midway*. The Mule-led research efforts had resulted in enhanced weapons systems being added to Earth Two's arsenal every year or two, and now, the gigantic guns mounted on *Midway*'s hull were a match for the First Imperium batteries in just about every way.

And, if the rumors about the new railguns are really true…we may finally have an actual advantage for once, an area where our stuff is ahead of theirs…

Strand couldn't imagine how something like that would seem to the Pilgrims, with their memories of combat in ships utterly outclassed by the First Imperium attackers. Her own recollections were similar, of course, if far less severe. Earth Two tech had advanced rapidly during her youth, and the first warships on which she served were hundreds of years of normal development ahead of those that had brought the Pilgrims to Earth Two just two decades earlier. And, *Midway* was centuries more beyond that first vessel on which she'd reported for duty as a newly-minted lieutenant.

"*Zephyr* and *Vincennes* are to swing out from the ends of the battleline and scout around the perimeters of the enemy fleet."

"Yes, Admiral." She could tell that Hercule agreed with her action. Something just wasn't right about the situation. It might have made sense for the enemy force to engage in a missile duel, hoping the advantage of their antimatter ordnance might make a difference, but the force now advancing into close range had no real chance at all. It was outnumbered and outgunned. The First Imperium almost always enjoyed numerical advantages, and they had still lost many battles to human fleets.

Why are they just throwing away a force like this?

Unless they're luring us forward…

"All ships, decelerate at full. Bring the fleet to a dead stop."

Strand hadn't found any evidence of additional enemy forces…but she wasn't taking any chances. She wanted to see how the enemy reacted to her fleet halting, rather than allowing itself to be lured farther forward. She'd half expected the First Imperium ships to match her action, to stop themselves…but they continued on, pushing inexorably forward, until their longest ranged guns opened fire.

"All batteries in range…fire." Strand shifted uncomfortably in her chair, watching the close-range battle commence. She'd almost ordered her ships to accelerate forward again, but the enemy vessels were still closing, and even her smaller ships were coming into range.

She could hear *Midway*'s giant guns firing, a single shot from just one battery discharging as much energy as the old *Midway*'s reactors had produced in an entire day. The great beams ripped through the vacuum of space, their range several times as great as the weapons of a generation ago.

The enemy ships conducted evasive maneuvers, just as her ships were doing…but the AI-operated vessels had never been able to match their human-controlled counterparts, not in the wild and random gyrations used to break targeting locks. For all their advanced technology, the First Imperium ships only managed a hit rate of just about two-thirds that of their human adversaries.

Strand watched on the display as *Midway*'s main guns ripped into one of the enemy Colossus's. The massive enemy battleships, and the even larger Leviathans, had once struck terror into the hearts of human spacers tasked with fighting them. But,

Midway was bigger, even, than the Colossus, and Strand fancied that her shining new flagship even had a chance one on one against one of the monstrous Leviathans. Mankind had been fighting the First Imperium in one form or another for half a century now, and in all that time, the vast legions of the robotic enemy had shown little in the way of technological advancement, at least in their fleet units.

The small icon in the display expanded as *Midway's* shot scored its hit, displaying what appeared to be an actual image of the target ship, and the signs of damage the hits had caused. It was all made up, of course, *Midway's* AI doing its best job of showing what the damage assessments reported might have happened over eighty thousand kilometers away around the stricken enemy ship. The image wobbled a bit, as the computer updated it continually, taking advantage of every scrap of information that flowed in from the scanners.

Whatever the truth behind the images she was watching, there was no question her flagship had hit the enemy vessel hard. But, a Colossus was a tough ship, and it kept coming on, its thrust reduced by about half, but most of its own guns still firing. *Midway* gyrated repeatedly, as its evasive maneuvers continued, but then the great ship shuddered hard, and a shower of sparks flew out from a burned-out panel along the far wall.

Her ship had been hit.

Strand was already at the control unit, demanding a damage report from the main AI. A ship commander of the last generation would have been on the comm with the vessel's chief engineer, but reporting duties had fallen to the automated systems over the past ten years.

"Two of the port reactors are shut down. I project they will be ready to restart in fifteen minutes. The other ten reactors remain operational, with three of them running at seventy to eighty percent capacity. Two port batteries have been damaged, one badly…"

She listened as the AI went on, trying to decide if she missed having another human at the other end of the comm. A human engineer would have been distracted giving the report, valuable time that could have been spent making repairs expended, as often as not, satisfying the captain's vanity. But, something had been lost, too, she realized. It was easy for the data-driven types to ignore the value of things like camaraderie in battle, and sometimes hard to explain in practical terms how crucial such amorphous concepts sometimes were.

She turned her head, diverting a portion of her attention, even as the AI continued to recite *Midway*'s damage in excruciating detail. She'd already decided her flagship was okay. But, she had a fleet to worry about, and a whole battle. It had been more than twelve years since she'd commanded only a single vessel, but somehow, she always felt like a ship's captain deep down.

Midway lurched again, not as hard as before, and the AI interrupted its report to start again, giving her the most recent information.

The ship was holding up well enough, but she wasn't thrilled about the enemy's hit rate. The Colossus *Midway* had faced off against had definitely taken the worst of the exchange so far, but it still had fight left in it…and as long as it stayed in battle, Strand knew those heavy guns could gut whole sections of her ship.

"Commander…bring engines up to forty percent. All fleet units, advance and maintain fire." It was time to end the fight… and to flush out any enemy forces that might be lurking somewhere out there.

"Yes, Admiral. All ships engage thrust and advance. Maintain fire."

Strand watched as another of *Midway*'s shots slammed into the enemy ship…and then she saw the scanner readings spike as internal explosions answered the impacting beams.

"I want all batteries concentrated on that Colossus…maximum rate of fire." She was leaning forward, the tension gripping her body from head to toe. She'd never forgotten the experience of battle—she couldn't imagine anyone who'd endured it ever could—but now the recall poured back into her mind in startlingly vivid detail. Her hands were moist with sweat, tightly gripping the armrests of her chair. He eyes where focused tightly, watching the display as her ships moved forward, pounding at the enemy line.

But, it was the Colossus she was watching most closely, the great enemy battleship lined up opposite *Midway*. The First Imperium didn't hesitate to sacrifice ships to achieve tactical objectives. But even the coldly analytical Regent didn't casually throw away Colossus's. The enemy battleship, and the second one farther down the line, fighting a cluster of her own ships, could have escaped the system instead of engaging her forces.

Why didn't they?

If they'll put two Colossus's on the line, there must be other ships here. Or…

Her thoughts erupted, distracting her for a few seconds, even from the battle taking place all around. *Or…they're desperate to stop us before we can get to G48.*

Was it possible? Had the fleet really found a weakness, an opening? Was the Regent rushing whatever it could to engage the fleet anyplace, any way, in a desperate attempt to stop the attack short of its antimatter production world?

Strand couldn't quite make herself believe they had gained such an edge against the Regent…but she couldn't shake the excitement she felt building in her as she considered it either.

Then, her eyes froze on the display as a pair of *Midway's* heavy guns hit the Colossus almost simultaneously…and the great battleship vanished in the fury of antimatter annihilation.

Chapter Sixteen

Cutter Research Compound (Home of the Mules)
Ten Kilometers West of Victory City, Earth Two
Earth Two Date 02.08.43

"You called for me?" Achilles stepped into the massive laboratory, ducking under an appendage extending from an odd-looking construct just to the side of the entry. He stopped abruptly, his usual neutral expression replaced immediately by one of concern. Themistocles was standing a few meters from the door, in the center of the room. The Mule was usually a shining example of the physical health and perfection of his people…but now he was crouched forward, his eyes dull with what Achilles could see was crushing fatigue. "What is it, my friend? You look terrible."

"How I look is of no consequence my old friend." Achilles was relieved at the Mule's tone. His friend was clearly exhausted, but it seemed, at least, that nothing was wrong.

"Well, then, I assume you called me down here for something other than to see what one of us looks like after…" He paused and started at Themistocles. "…six days with no sleep?"

"Seven…I think. But, that is also of no consequence…for I have spent those sleepless nights well, Achilles, my old crèche-mate. I believe I have cured the Plague."

Achilles just stood still, staring across the room. The best scientists on Earth Two, including a significant contingent of Mules, had studied the deadly disease that struck the Tanks with such devastating suddenness for more than forty years, without success. Themistocles was the most intelligent of all the researchers, so it didn't surprise Achilles that his friend might have been the one to discover the long-evasive secret of the illness…but the suddenness of the development was still unexpected.

"How sure are you?"

"I am fairly certain…but, of course I would like you to review my notes and give me your thoughts. I am somewhat tired…and I haven't yet tested it out on a live Tank."

Achilles moved across the room, his head snapping quickly behind him as he did, taking a longer look at the mysterious device. "I suppose this mad scientist creation has something to do with it."

"Yes…" Themistocles paused. "With its initial development, at least. But, I believe the final equipment will be much more compact." Another pause, one Achilles knew was a manifestation of his friend's exhaustion. "My research was rather widespread in its initial approach. The final solution proved to be much more…straightforward."

"How so?" Achilles stepped forward and took a tablet Themistocles handed him, glancing quickly at the screen.

"Most of the research done in this area over the years focused on trying to discover the cause of the affliction. That was a logical methodology, but one that defied all efforts to make substantial progress. I tried a new approach this time. Instead of finding a way to prevent the Plague from occurring, I explored ways of reversing it once it does."

Achilles gazed back at his friend, a rare look of uncertainty on his face. He was a Mule, and a gifted scientist in his own right, but his areas of expertise extended more toward physics and robotics. Themistocles was the Hybrid's undisputed leader in medicine and medical research.

"It is simple, Achilles, when you consider it. There are simply two different ways to look at a disease. The first is to understand its causes, and to attempt to interfere with and reverse them. The second is to simply treat the result of the disease, with or without any concern to how it developed. Consider a cancer therapy. We understand how malignant tumors develop, and we have many therapies to prevent the disease from striking. But, when a malignancy does occur, the common methodology changes almost completely. The standard treatment is to engineer targeted hunter cells to eradicate the tumor...in effect not seeking to understand what happened to the patient, but simply eliminating the dangerous effects of the disease. A patient so 'cured' will still carry a susceptibility to recurrences, but the instance of the disease will be eliminated."

"Yes, I understand the difference in approaches...but, are you telling me none of the research into the Plague has explored treatments from that perspective?"

"Yes, some early studies did. But, the disease killed so quickly after the onset of symptoms, that line was largely abandoned in favor of attempts to prevent incidence. Those efforts, save for some meaningful advances in tagging susceptible donor strains of DNA, have been largely unsuccessful as well."

"So, you returned to attempts to cure the disease after it occurs? Even though there is a window of just a few days before death occurs?"

"To an extent, Achilles. Actually, I was working on something entirely different, but when I realized the possible utility in cases of the Plague, I redirected my efforts to that end."

"You said you haven't tested the treatment on any actual Tanks suffering from the disease. Are you sure it will work?"

"As sure as I can be. It's a cell regeneration technique, one taking an entirely new approach from past research. It has some cursory relationships with the rejuv therapies that have been in use for nearly a century, but it is much more comprehensive. I've experimented with tissue samples from stricken Tanks, as well as the bodies of those killed by the disease. But, now I need to try it on several live specimens."

Achilles took a deep breath and considered everything he'd heard. If Themistocles was right, if his treatment was effective, the great scourge of the Tanks would be defeated. He felt a burst of excitement, followed by a darker, more somber thought.

Control of such a cure would give us tremendous influence over the Tank population.

Achilles didn't like the thought. It went against his own ethical standards to even think about withholding medical treatment from *any* sick people…Tanks, NB, Mules.

But Freya's words had stuck with him, as did her concerns, and they awakened the ones he himself had once had, worries he'd convinced himself to ignore, flashes of a dark future, the Mules hunted down and cornered…killed one by one by the fearful humans who outnumbered then a thousand to one.

And, he'd never forgotten what had happened twelve years earlier, how close his combat robots had come to facing Marines—mostly Tanks—in battle. Control over the Tanks meant control over the military…the ground forces, at least.

Achilles considered his people superior, but he didn't hate the Normals. He wished them well, and he generally considered the Hybrids to be guardians for the lesser humans. Still, if it came to a choice, if the radical forces opposed to the Hybrids one day pushed humanity into becoming a deadly, insensate mob, as they were so prone to become…his loyalty was with the Mules. If that conflict came, the Tanks would be immensely valuable as allies. Willing ones or otherwise.

"We should keep this quiet, Themistocles." Achilles felt guilty for not telling his friend what he was thinking…but he kept it to himself anyway. "The Tanks have seen many promises of cures before…we should conduct secret tests, on a few carefully selected subjects. If the cure works, there is plenty of time for public announcements and celebration."

Themistocles hesitated for a moment, but then he nodded. "Of course, you're right, Achilles. But, how do I arrange to treat the test cases in secret?"

"Let me take care of that, my friend. I will speak directly to President Harmon. He, too, will see the need for caution in this matter. Earth Two society is fragile and easily fractured. I am sure he will be in favor of confirming the effectiveness of the treatment in secret, before announcing it planetwide."

Themistocles nodded. "You are right, of course, Achilles. Do you think you can get in to see the president immediately?"

"I am sure I can, my friend. Prepare what you need. I will see that two selected patients are sent here at once. We can maintain the proper security at the institute, far more effectively than in a hospital in the city." Achilles hesitated. "Do you have any particular needs in terms of candidates?"

"Not really. But the sooner after onset, the likelier the treatment will be effective."

Achilles nodded. "I will go see the president now." He turned and took a few steps, but then he stopped and looked back. "You said you were researching something different entirely. What was that?"

"I was trying to improve on rejuv protocols. The longevity treatments have been in use for more than eighty years, but very little improvement has been made in that time. I believe this new line of research will lead to vastly superior techniques to slow or even reverse age-related cellular degeneration."

Achilles looked back at Themistocles, silent, even his usual rigid control failing him. "You mean you are working on a treatment that could lead to virtual immortality?"

Themistocles returned the gaze. "That may be a bit of a broad description…but, yes. And, I believe I have achieved just that."

* * *

"Connor, what the hell happened?" Max Harmon was mad…as red hot, raging, fist-clenching as he could ever remember being.

And it showed.

"We don't know for sure yet, Mr. President. It appears that some kind of explosive was detonated in the main concourse. I don't have a casualty total yet, sir, but we've got a minimum of sixty confirmed dead as of right now. The explosion was well-timed to catch people during their lunch breaks. I deployed three companies, and the entire area is under lockdown."

"Have you been there yourself, Connor?"

"Yes, sir. I set up the command post and saw to the deployments. Then I came here."

"What does it look like?"

Frasier paused. "It's bad, sir. It looks like it was designed to do as much damage…to kill as many people…as possible."

"So, no doubt this is a deliberate terrorist act?"

"None, sir…at least not as far as I can see."

"Suspects?"

"None yet, sir, but the AIs are studying surveillance footage. It's hard to imagine that someone could have set this up without getting caught on a number of security cams."

Harmon leaned forward, putting his face in his hands and sighing. Frasier was right, in theory…but he didn't think the security footage would reveal anything. The attack was a sophisticated one, not an act of pure emotional rage. Whoever was responsible was intelligent, and they would have known the whole area was under constant surveillance.

Which means they got to the security footage.

Harmon squeezed his eyes tightly together for a moment, trying to push back against the pounding in his head.

That means they have accomplices in high-level security positions.

Harmon had expected civil disturbances after he'd taken power. He'd been prepared for it for at least a year, perhaps even two, every day, waking up, expecting news of some rebellion or other disruption. But, none of it happened. He was never sure if the threat of the Regent had scared people into accepting his rule, or if his appeals for unity and promises that one day he would step down had actually had the desired effects.

Or, if people were just scared of Connor Frasier and his Marines.

Whatever it was, likely a combination of factors, the years had passed, and opposition to his rule had been largely limited to grumbling, and to a few protests he'd allowed to take place unmolested. But, this was something new, something different.

Something he couldn't ignore.

"Connor, I want whoever is responsible for this outrage. I

don't care what it takes. You have total authority…but find me everyone behind this act."

Frasier looked uncomfortable. My people are Marines, Mr. President, not security officers or police. This is not our area of expertise. We will try, of course, but…"

"Let's not fool ourselves any longer, Connor. This is a military dictatorship, and your people are the military." He paused, his look of anger and determination giving way briefly to one of sadness. "Besides…I don't know who else I can trust."

Frasier looked as though he was going to argue, but Harmon's last words cut him off. He hesitated, and then he just nodded. "Yes, sir. I understand."

"My God…I just heard. Are you ok? Connor? Max?" Ana Zhukov came walking in the office. Zhukov had been almost alone among the inner circle in almost entirely ignoring any formality toward Harmon since he'd become dictator. She kept up enough airs in public to get by, but in private, she maintained that the president had been her friend first, and always would be. The others sometimes scolded her—to no avail—but Harmon had always been grateful for the slight tether back to his old reality.

"We're fine, Ana." Frasier stood up and turned toward his wife.

"What happened? Do we know anything yet?"

"Nothing significant. Ana, I have to…"

"Sit, Ana." Harmon rose as well, forcing something with a slight resemblance to a smile and gesturing to the open chair. "Connor has duties that require his attention, but I'll bring you up to speed." He looked at the Marine. "Anything, Connor… remember that. Do whatever you have to do, but find out whoever is responsible for this. Every single one of them." There was a coldness in Harmon's voice that even startled himself. He was enraged that someone on Earth Two would murder their fellow citizens in such numbers…and he shuddered to think of what he would do to them when he found them.

Frasier leaned over and hugged Zhukov. Then, he snapped off a quick salute, and he walked swiftly across the room and through the door.

"I was coming to see you with good news when I heard. I'm so sorry, Max. This is terrible."

"Yes, it is." Harmon understood the rage he felt, to a point. But, he was no stranger to death, nor to the loss of comrades. Even if the toll from the explosion rose, as it almost certainly would, what did it compare to the thousands lost in the fleet's journey to Earth Two…or the millions killed on the other side of the Barrier, in the wars against the First Imperium, and between the superpowers?

But, it *was* different. Earth Two was all alone, desperately trying to defeat the new Regent. Anyone who would turn on their own people with such mindless violence…didn't have a place on Earth Two.

And, when Harmon found them, they wouldn't have a place. Anywhere.

The two sat quietly for a few minutes. Then, Harmon looked over at Zhukov. "You said you had good news?" Harmon looked at Zhukov, a spark of desperate hope in his eyes.

"Oh…yes! I spoke to Achilles and Themistocles over at the Institute. Themistocles has discovered something, something incredible."

Harmon looked back across the desk, curiosity pushing away some of the darkness.

"He thinks he has developed a cure for the Plague."

Chapter Seventeen

Flag Bridge, E2S Midway
System G45
Earth Two Date 02.09.43

"All units engaged, Admiral."

Strand leaned forward in her chair, as she tended to do in battle, staring intently into the depths of *Midway*'s main display. "Very well, Commander." As she often did, she felt that she should be firing out commands, directing the ships of her force in the fight that was unfolding all around. But, her people knew what to do, and she could only distract now. It sometimes took more command discipline to shut up than it did to micromanage.

Her flagship had taken damage in the fighting in G24, and several times again as enemy forces had hit the fleet at multiple points along its journey. But now, the great battleship was one hundred percent operational, save perhaps for a jammed hatch or twisted bulkhead here and there. She was grateful to *Midway*'s small team of engineers, but she knew the bulk of her gratitude was owed to the several hundred AI-directed repair drones constantly crawling through the bowels of her ship.

The heavy automation that had taken over the role of so many engineers and technicians was extremely effective, there was no argument against that. Besides the obvious advantages of greater resistance to heat, vacuum, and radiation, the bots were also something that could be mass produced and crammed into every nook and cranny a ship had to offer. They didn't need cabins or food or recreational facilities.

For a new world struggling to produce the population required to man and support a large navy, the reduction of naval crews by a factor of five to eight had been a welcome option and a huge problem solver, if one that had also spurred some not-inconsiderable backlash. Humanity, after all, was fighting to avoid extinction at the hands of a robotic enemy. A certain amount of resentment and concern was understandable, especially when, superficially at least, Earth Two seemed to be going down the same road that had led to the destruction of the Ancients, putting ever greater dependency on automated servants, with less and less human supervision in the mix.

She'd seen those types of concerns decline a bit as the years passed. Strand had entered into a navy almost entirely crewed by Pilgrims, veteran spacers at least twenty-five years her senior, who had fought their way across half the galaxy to attain victory and find a home. Those seasoned warriors, the youngest of which were now in their mid-60s, had resisted the automation drives, almost fanatically at first. They had seen the havoc the First Imperium had wrought on the human worlds on the other side of the Barrier, and no small number of them still woke up, sweat covered in the middle of the night, fleeing from nightmares of deadly combat robots.

But even the resistance of the fleet's former officers and crews hadn't been sufficient to stop the trend toward automation. There simply weren't enough people to man fleets of ships with thousand strong crews, a problem that became far more urgent when the existence of the new Regent became known and spurred a massive mobilization effort.

Strand found herself somewhere in the middle in her outlook, a bit nervous about ceding so much of the operations of her ships to artificial intelligences, but also keenly aware that Earth Two was compelled to field a military vastly beyond what it could normally support. Her views matched her place in Earth Two's military structure…not a Pilgrim, but one of the oldest of the new generations.

The ships she had served on as a young officer had already been far more advanced than those of the original fleet, yet compared to *Midway* with its high-tech robotics and tiny crew, they seemed in her memory almost like ancient artifacts. She had some reservations, but she was still amazed when she saw how quickly and effectively the damage control bots managed to get systems back online after a fight. There was no argument that the new ships were far more combat capable than their predecessors.

Still, she was never able to banish the thought that the demise of the original First Imperium had begun with similar thoughts. She wondered if, millennia ago, some version of herself hadn't wrestled with the same thoughts…as his civilization continued its march to destruction.

Strand sighed softly. She felt old, though at forty-one, she knew she was very young for her position, at least by historical naval standards. That was a fact she owed as much to the quarter century gap in Earth Two's population as to her own considerable achievements. There wasn't a fifty-year-old human within several thousand lightyears, nor a sixty-year-old…and the Pilgrims had largely begun to give way to their progeny, both naturally-born and cloned.

Midway lurched slightly…a minor hit, she decided, before she'd even looked at her screen. Probably a bulkhead had blown, sending a rippling vibration through the massive hull.

That was another reason to appreciate the robots. It was unlikely any of her people had been in whatever compartments had just been blown open, and that meant the fatalities that would almost certainly have occurred on the original *Midway* had been avoided, replaced, perhaps, by a few non-sentient maintenance bots sent careening through the frigid vacuum.

She glanced toward the display, her eyes darting from one of her ships to the next. The battle was a sharp one, the enemy ships closing to point blank range, firing the entire way. It was an aggressive tactic, especially for a force as outgunned as the First Imperium fleet. But, the enemy had been striking hard with every force the fleet had encountered.

The enemy attacks had been strange, almost random assaults all along the fleet's approach to G48…mostly uncoordinated, feeling as though the Regent was throwing whatever it could scrape together at the fleet with growing urgency and desperation. That made a sort of sense. If the Regent's forces were too spread out to form up quickly enough to respond to an attack on their antimatter production planet, it might frantically throw whatever it had available at the approaching human ships. An attempt to stop, or even slow the human advance.

It did make sense.

But Strand didn't buy it.

It looked like desperation, but she didn't think it was. The attacks, as aggressive as they'd been, as much as they had inflicted damage on some of the fleet's ship, just hadn't been that strong. The enemy had committed a few large battleships, but most of the attacking craft had been smaller, lighter vessels.

They want us to think they're desperate…but Admiral West is right. They're luring us in. This is a trap.

And, yet, she knew they had to go in. For all the reasons she and West had already discussed. For all the reasons that had been and still were painfully clear to her.

Midway shook, lightly…another glancing blow, she realized almost immediately. No real damage this time.

The fleet had to advance into the G48 system, come up against whatever forces the enemy had positioned there to ambush them, and somehow fight their way through into range of the planet. Then they had to bombard the hell out of it.

No…it's worse than that.

Strand knew a bombardment alone wouldn't get the job done. It might do some damage, knock out the enemy's landing pads and surface facilities, even some of the solar power collectors. A well-executed surface attack might cut down power generation and antimatter production…but it wouldn't take them out. And, one thing was damned certain. Whatever storage facilities held the precious antimatter the factory world had already produced would be deep, deep underground, far enough to be safe from even a massive nuclear attack.

Which means we need to get ships in orbit. We need to land Marines.

She watched as display updated, the enemy ships moving closer. The range was dropping quickly, far faster than she'd expected.

The First Imperium ships were accelerating hard, moving right toward her own positions.

They're blasting away at almost 90g.

Even for a First Imperium ship, that meant they weren't fully powering their weapons. It didn't make sense. They were in close range now. Their particle accelerators would be deadly from so close in. There was no tactical reason to divert so much power to acceleration now.

So, why are they…

She felt as though her blood froze.

"Commander, put me on fleetcom now!" She tried to catch her voice, to hold back the panicked tone, but she knew she'd let it burst out anyway.

Hercule moved his hands rapidly over his station, and then he turned and stared across the bridge toward Strand. "On your comm, Admiral." She couldn't tell from his voice if he'd figured out what she had, but it was clear he understood the importance.

"All ships, evasive maneuvers, nav plan Beta four." Her eyes darted back to the display.

"Now," she yelled into the headset.

Those enemy vessels weren't advancing to shorten the firing range.

They were going to ram her ships.

* * *

"All fleet units, forward now. Maximum acceleration." The order was issued with all the guttural force Erika West could muster, as though verbal urgency could somehow alter the laws of physics, overrule the constraints of time and distance, and get her ships forward faster.

"Yes, Admiral." The cadence of Sampson's voice left little

doubt that West's aide understood what was happening as well as the admiral.

West had been watching Strand's advance guard, one instant as they were shredding the First Imperium attack force in a lopsided energy weapons duel…and the next as they were blasting their engines at full, trying to escape from oncoming ships moving in excess of one percent of lightspeed.

Ships that were going to try to ram Strand's vessels.

Ramming wasn't a common tactic. It was rare enough to make recalling more than one or two examples a fruitless endeavor. Apart from the suicide aspect for the vessels involved, it was just too difficult to pinpoint a target in the vast distances of interplanetary space and plot a collision course. But Strand's ships had been at almost a dead halt, and the enemy vessels were ripping toward them, tearing through space at nearly 0.012c and still accelerating. Strand had initiated evasive maneuvers, but from a standing start there wasn't much time to build up velocity.

West saw the situation, and, as she stared at the glow of the screen, she understood the foolishness of the deployment, the sheer idiocy of having the entire task force sitting dead in space while coldblooded, robot-controlled vessels were bearing down on them. She felt rage at the orders that had put so many of her ships and spacers in that situation, at the foolishness that had forgotten just how cold and bloodless an enemy they faced… and it was all the more intense because it was directed at herself. *She* had issued those orders, and Josie Strand had merely followed them.

West considered herself a hardcore veteran, an admiral with half a century's experience commanding fleets in war. She'd ordered the fleet into its current deployment after reviewing approach angles, the firepower of her vessels…everything but the suicide runs now menacing her ships, an oversight that was now likely to cost many of her spacers their lives.

She cursed herself silently, drove the self-loathing guilt deep into her psyche, as much because she had nothing else to do. She held herself responsible, knew she should have been ready for any action by the enemy…but she was just as aware that there was nothing she could do now.

Ordering the back line forward was a vanity, she knew, and nothing more, a way to feel as though she was doing something. The reserve ships would never get forward in time, and certainly not quickly enough to blast the approaching First Imperium hulls to slag before they could close. Strand's vessels would escape—or they would face their doom—on their own, outside the reach of any help she could give them.

She grimaced as she felt the acceleration slamming into her, pushing her hard back into her chair. *Garret* was blasting forward at better than 50g, and even the battleship's powerful dampeners couldn't offset that much force.

That's about 4g…maybe 4.5. West had served many years in space, fought aboard warships in the days before technology offered any meaningful way to endure g forces, save to lock an entire ship's crew in huge tanks, immersed entirely in thick goo. She had a feel for reading force levels that rivaled the most sophisticated sensors, and when her eyes moved down to her screen she saw the exact reading…4.315g.

"Commander…I want all ships ready to fire as soon as we enter range." It was pointless, but it was all she could do.

"Yes, Admiral."

Her ships might not get there in time to blast the enemy ships before they reached Strand's line, but they'd damned sure be waiting for those that missed their targets and zipped forward at high velocity. She didn't know how many of the enemy vessels would claim one of her own…but she was sure about one thing.

Not one of the ones that missed was going to get another chance.

*   *   *

"Admiral…*Thames*…"

Hercule's tone would have told Strand all she needed to know…if she hadn't been looking at the battleship's projection in the display when six million tons of First Imperium warship slammed into it. *Thames* wasn't torn apart, it wasn't even disintegrated, at least not in the sense of being reduced to a cloud of smaller chunks. The two vessels just vanished utterly, replaced by a massive surge of energy and wave after wave of hard radiation.

Strand's mind had always been quick, and despite her attempts to stop the morbid calculation, she found herself coming up with a rough total on the energy released when the mass of First Imperium steel slammed into *Thames* at more than one percent of the speed of light. It was the kind of figure that made one think they'd made some kind of error, added half a dozen too many zeroes or a few exponents…but Strand knew it was correct.

Midway had been more fortunate than *Thames* in its encounters with the approaching First Imperium ships. Strand's flagship had been targeted by two separate enemy vessels, but somehow, her last-second maneuvers had evaded both, the last missing by less than six hundred meters, a hair's breadth in the vast distances of space combat, and one she knew represented some fraction of a second in terms of thrust and maneuver.

"Bring us around, Commander…all batteries to bear, coordinates 120.009.330." Strand had taken a second to let out a sigh of relief when she realized her own ship had escaped the deadly danger that had come so close. But now, she regretted even that instant, time wasted that should have been used to help the rest of her people. *Riverlands* was the closest vessel, and Strand's best guess was the cruiser had about a 50/50 chance of evading the enemy Gargoyle bearing down on it. *Midway* didn't have any real chance of vaporizing the incoming enemy ship, not in the seconds remaining, but even a single hit, a section of hull blown out, or an explosion in the right spot, could alter the vessel's trajectory. Even the tiniest fraction of a degree could be the margin that saved *Riverlands*, and her sixty-eight crew.

The targeted cruiser was firing at it pursuer as well, and engaging in its own evasive maneuvers, but the First Imperium ship was matching its course changes and closing rapidly. Strand watched, even as she waited for *Midway*'s course adjustments to bring her weapons into fire arc. She couldn't help but wonder about the thoughts that would be going through a crew's thoughts on a suicide run, as they gave everything they had to ensure their own destruction. She realized the First Imperium ships didn't have crews in the sense she imagined them, but their intelligences were extraordinarily capable, and she wondered if they didn't have some sense of self-preservation, if the Regent's coldly analytical orders ever spawned a reaction something like resentment, if not outright insubordination.

"All batteries, open fire as we come to bear." It was an unnecessary order. She knew her gunners were at the ready, waiting for *Midway*'s realignment to give them the shots they needed. But necessary or not, she gave it, and she did it with all the command authority she could muster.

"Yes, Admiral." A pause. "Forward batteries will be in arc in fifteen seconds."

"Very well. Her eyes darted to the display, checking the stats even though she was sure she remembered correctly. *Riverlands* had thirty-four seconds until the enemy ship was on her. That gave her batteries a single shot…just maybe a second one if all systems functioned perfectly.

She heard the familiar whining sound, *Midway*'s batteries firing, and a few seconds later, the stream of data scrolling down her screen, hit report and damage assessments.

Her gunners had scored two hits, one serious. There was some release of gases and liquids, and signs of internal explosions. The effects of the barrage definitely affected the oncoming vessel's trajectory, minimally, at least. Whether it was enough to push the ship aside from a collision course with Riverlands— and enough to overcome the First Imperium ship's own efforts to correct its vector—was too close to call.

There was nothing to do but wait…and see.

And hope her gunners got in one more shot in time.

Chapter Eighteen

"I want all active scans on full power. Forward scouts are authorized to risk overloads." Strand knew she was jumping the gun. *Midway* had just transited, and the battleship's electronics were still scrambled from the strange effects of warp gate travel. Strand didn't have communications or scanners yet, nor even onboard computers. The automation of Earth Two's ships carried one negative effect with it, at least. Human vessels had always been helpless for the first few minutes after a transit, but the massively powerful vessels Strand commanded were worse off even than their predecessors had been.

"Yes, Admiral…waiting for onboard systems to reboot." It wasn't information Hercule had to share…she was well aware of the timetable of post-transit recovery.

But then, you didn't give him much choice, did you, snapping out an order you knew he couldn't obey yet?

Strand's people had fought in half a dozen systems, on their route to G48, struggled to beat off one First Imperium assault after another. They'd even endured ramming attacks, though only the first one the enemy tried had been truly effective. Erika West was no one's fool, and she only made mistakes once. Strand was far from confident she wouldn't have done the same thing the fleet commander had, blundered into a vulnerable position for a suicide attack, but she shared one thing with Erika West.

She didn't make stupid mistakes twice either.

She looked down at her screen, frustrated at it dark blankness. She tried to will the system to come back online, as if that could have any effect on recovery from the still only partially understood physics of warp travel. No one had ever adequately explained the variation in recovery times, why in some cases, ships regained operational status as quickly as forty-five seconds, and in others, the same vessels were disabled for as long as five minutes.

Her insides felt tight, the tension that had been growing as the fleet clawed forward from one system to the next taking its toll. She'd had a bright spot in the otherwise disastrous engagement in G45. Six of her ships had been obliterated by the surprise ramming attack, but her last ditch effort had saved the cruiser *Riverlands*. *Midway*'s batteries had been the difference there, the desperate effort to get firing vectors, and the near-perfect marksmanship of the human-AI team that directed the fire of those guns. The enemy ship had missed by almost one thousand meters, not much distance in space, but enough to save the ship and crew.

For a short while, at least.

Riverlands had been lost in the fighting in G47, just a few days after its salvation at the hands of *Midway*'s gunners. Strand tried to draw solace from the fact that the stricken ship had been able to evacuate almost half its crew, giving some permanence, at least, to the benefits of *Midway*'s actions.

The fleet had taken significant losses before even entering the target system, and the fact that the seemingly desperate, almost random First Imperium attacks had cost the enemy even more was less than reassuring. Strand was more certain than ever that the Regent was intentionally throwing its ships at the fleet in an effort to disguise the trap she was sure was waiting right now, out beyond her darkened displays and scrambled scanners.

She wasn't sure if she was satisfied that the Regent had

wasted so many more of its own ships than it had cost the fleet...or if she was even more concerned about the machine's true plan and the trickery surrounding it.

The damn thing didn't have to go to this much effort to lure us here. We know it's a trap—at least Erika and I do—but we don't have a choice. We can't win the endless standoff, wait until the murderous machine finds us.

Strand understood just how important the mission was. Destroying the antimatter production facility was just about the only tactical advantage that could truly blunt the Regent's relentless efforts to find and destroy Earth Two...and that was why the fleet was there, knowingly walking into a trap.

A flicker of light caught her eye, a static pattern coming onto her workstation screen. She looked around the bridge, seeing the same thing pop up on one screen after another, and then the huge central display began to glow, as the ship's AIs rebooted and restarted the complex series of holograms that gave *Midway's* bridge crew an astonishingly complete view of the space surrounding the big ship.

She almost repeated her order, now that she could see the ship recovering, but she stopped herself with the realization that Hercule hadn't needed the first reminder...and he certainly did not need a second.

Her imagination was running wild, her thoughts projecting images of massive enemy fleets out there, waiting in front of her ships, preparing to fire at any moment. But, she checked those thoughts, reminded herself she still had no idea at all what was out there.

Then, her workstation screen flashed completely to life, followed ten or fifteen seconds later by the big 3D display. The data was still incomplete. The scanners were functioning again, too, but the AIs were still analyzing the flood of data coming in.

There were ships waiting, that was immediately clear. A large fleet...though not as massive as she'd feared. And not waiting close to the warp gate to hit her forces as they entered the system. The First Imperium fleet was deployed well in-system, fairly close to the target planet itself.

That seems foolish...they should be far out, positioned to keep us from getting into launch range of the planet.

The enemy formation didn't seem right to Strand, but she didn't let herself believe the Regent had made any serious mistakes. The First Imperium intelligences lacked the intuition and gut feel that made human commanders so good at waging war, but the incredibly complex computers didn't make outright deployment errors either. The Regent had five hundred millennia of data on warfare, and it wasn't about to position its fleet badly…not without a reason.

It wants to lure us in…and it's giving us a run at the planet to do it…

Strand felt her nervousness rising, moving dangerously close to uncontrollable fear. She'd faced death before, and she'd come back from it. Strand's Stand was required study at the Academy, a fact from which she'd drawn immense pride, as well as her fair share of embarrassment.

This was different, however. Knowingly leading her people into a trap was one thing for which she felt entirely unprepared. But, it was just what she was going to do, nevertheless.

"All ships, battlestations. As soon as the entire formation is operational, we will move forward…8g acceleration, right for the enemy line."

Right for whatever they've got waiting for us there.

And, right for that antimatter production world…toward the one stroke that could even the fight, give Earth Two a chance at victory…

*   *   *

Erika West sat bolt upright in her command chair, staring straight forward. She wasn't looking at anything in particular, but in her mind she saw her fleet, all of it now formed up in the G48 system, facing off in three successive lines against whatever the Regent had managed to deploy in the defense of the vital world orbiting the system's sun…and any other forces that lay out there, hidden, ready to ambush her fleet before it could complete its mission.

Before it could strip the Regent of its antimatter supply… and the greatest advantage the hated AI had over the Earth Two forces.

She'd been deep in thought during the entire voyage to G48, her mind racing, analyzing what actual data she had along with the gut feel that had told her the enemy was not desperately trying to mount a defense, but actually *wanted* her ships there. It was a trap she was certain was waiting, and one she hoped to turn about on its perpetrator. Almost no amount of losses her fleet suffered would be too much to justify if she could destroy the enemy's antimatter source.

She felt a wave of guilt for that last thought, but West had never been one to fool herself. She would sacrifice ever man and women in the fleet if that's what it took to succeed. She'd come to G48 to strip the First Imperium of their devastatingly powerful energy source, and that's just what she was going to do.

Whatever it took.

"Admiral Strand is on your line, Admiral." Avery Sampson sounded as cold as ice, utterly unaffected by the magnitude of what lay ahead. West knew it was a front. None of the fleet's personnel could face the battle that lay ahead without feeling the weight…and the fear. Even West, who'd been sure she was ready to die if need be, found herself sweating, anxious, wanting to finish what she'd come to do and go back home.

Or what passes for home…

"Put her through." West reached down and grabbed her headset, strapping it on as she flipped the activation switch. She didn't think Strand would have anything to say that her flag crew couldn't hear, but she was too old a warrior to make such careless assumptions.

"Admiral…"

"You're on my headset." A pause, and then West's normally hard voice softened a bit. "What's your status, Josie?"

"We're entering missile range, Admiral. I've ordered all ships to hold fire until just before the enemy barrage enters detonation range."

West felt herself nodding, an involuntary acknowledgement that she concurred with Strand's plan. "I agree…but make sure you allow yourself enough time to launch your full barrage.

Empty those magazines."

"Yes, Admiral."

West felt the urge to tell Strand that she was bringing up the rest of the fleet, but she stayed silent. Because she wasn't moving a single vessel forward.

The advance forces were going to be outnumbered, and they were going to have one hell of a fight on their hands...but West was sure the enemy had something waiting, something her people couldn't see. And there was no way she could commit her last reserves, not until she knew exactly what she faced. And, she had a plan of her own, and she was waiting for the opportunity to put it into action.

Whatever Strand and her people had to do, however desperately they had to fight to face the enemy forces alone...she knew her deputy commander would see it done.

"Fortune go with you and your people, Josie." It was all she had to offer.

"Thank you, Admiral...we'll see it done."

West cut the line. Then, she turned toward Sampson.

"Get me Captain Rivers, Commander. Direct, shielded laser comm."

"Yes, Admiral." A moment later. "On your line."

"Lucas..." She paused for a moment. West wasn't the kind of officer to hesitate, even when giving difficult orders...but the years had worn her down, and she'd long ago lost count of how many spacers she'd sent to their deaths. One more desperate, nearly suicidal mission shouldn't matter to her now, but for some reason it did. She would do what she had to do, as she knew Rivers and his people would, but it would cost them both.

"Admiral?" The pause had gone on long enough for the signal to reach Rivers' flagship and return with his response.

"Lucas...it's time." She'd already discussed the operation with the officer, and there was no need to review it again. All she had to do was give him the orders...and watch to see if any of his people made it back.

"Understood, Admiral." There was a grave tone to his voice. It was clear he knew just how deadly a mission his people had drawn, but there wasn't a hint there of doubt or hesitation.

"You've got every stealth device Earth Two has in its arsenal, Lucas...and you've just got to get into range and flush those missiles. You've done your duty then, and I expect you to fire up your thrusters and get the hell out of there as soon as you let loose that last nuke. You don't have a beam hot enough to make a difference, so don't even think about getting caught up in any fighting up there."

"Yes, Admiral." She could hear the hitch in his voice. There was no question that his people were taking more than their share of the risks...but it was obvious he didn't like the idea of running, not when a good chunk of the rest of the fleet was still fighting.

"Just focus on getting this done and getting your people out of there, my old friend. Glass that planet's surface, and you've done your part." Lucas Rivers was a Pilgrim, just like West. The skeleton crews on his missile ships were mostly Pilgrims, too, volunteers who'd stepped up to mount the desperate assault on the antimatter planet and its orbital defenses. West had chosen Rivers and his people for their experience...but she had also picked them for their age. She didn't want to see *any* of her people killed, but the Pilgrims had seen a good portion of their lives already. They'd lived on the other side of the Barrier and endured to see a new home founded. It was the Next Gens' turn, their chance to live their lives, to see the war through to the end...and to build a new civilization.

"Yes, Admiral. We'll get it done...don't you worry about it."

"Good luck, Lucas."

"Thank you, Admiral. You can count on us."

West cut the line. She looked around the bridge, distracting her thoughts from Rivers. The old veteran knew the importance of his mission, and the danger, too. She had no doubt he would do whatever he had to do...and she knew much of that ran counter to his chances of getting away. The surprise of the move, the stealth protocols, the carefully-planned angle of approach...it all combined to give Rivers' people a chance to get into range. But they'd be wide open and in the clear on the way back, and most likely, they'd have First Imperium ships hot on their tails.

She'd done everything she could to help them get through… but she hadn't been entirely truthful. She hadn't given Rivers *all* the stealth technology the fleet possessed. Not the latest devices, the Mark Five cloaking suites that Achilles and the Mules had given her on the eve of departure.

Those devices, all twelve of them, were installed on the group of ships behind Rivers' task force…the newest, sleekest, most technologically advanced transports Earth Two had ever built.

Loaded up with Devon Cameron and eighteen hundred of his crack Marines.

Less than two thousand men and women to land in the thermonuclear hell after Rivers' bombardment, to find the antimatter production facility's underground facilities, and to devise a way to destroy them, along with all the antimatter stores in the Regent's magnetic storage tanks.

It seemed absurd, insane…and she didn't dare think too deeply about the inferno into which she was sending her Marines. They were volunteers, every one of them, and by the slimmest of margins, that would allow her to let them go. But, she would never forgive herself, not for Rivers, not for the Marines.

None of that mattered, though. They were all there to do what had to be done…and she would see to it. Josie Strand had her part to play as well, beyond the desperate fight she faced now, though West hadn't given her number two the final orders yet.

West and her people had their part to play as well, in some ways, perhaps, even the most desperate, wildest gamble of them all.

The Regent had set its trap, and she had no doubt it would be effective, even devastating. But the old Regent had always underestimated Augustus Garret and Terrance Compton…and with a little luck, the new one would do the same with her. At least by the margin she needed.

Because she had her own trap set, and if she could make it

work, she just might even things up between the two sides, give the republic the opening it needed for a true shot at victory.

She *had* to succeed, whatever it took. She could think about the cost later…if any of them survived.

Chapter Nineteen

"Ana...I'm glad you stopped by." Harmon looked up from his desk. The workspace was stacked with tablets, each of them open to specific files, all information on the continuing investigation of the terrorist attack of several days before. Connor Frasier had been inundating him with reports, as much, he thought, to show he was making a massive effort, despite the relative lack of progress. Harmon knew he'd put the Marine in a difficult situation, with duties far outside the range of those he'd trained to perform. But trust was his most precious resource, and Connor Frasier was a man in whose hands he would place his life.

"I have an update for you from Achilles." She paused and then added, "Good news."

Harmon gestured for her to sit. "Tell me. I could use some good news right about now."

"Things are going very well. The first test patient appears to be responding completely to the treatment. Themistocles says it's too early to make any definitive statements, but he is hopeful both of them will make full recoveries."

Harmon looked up from the heap of reports laying in front of him. "Full recoveries?" His surprise was unmistakable. In more than forty years of active cloning, no Tank had ever survived the Plague. "That may not be a definite, but there are worse things to be than hopeful." He sighed. It was clear from that, and from his tone that, while he was pleased about what she had told him, he was still distracted. "This isn't what I expected to feel like when someone came to me and told me the Plague was cured. So many Tanks dead over the years, and now it may be all over."

"Achilles told me to urge caution, Max. The results are not definitive yet."

"No, of course they aren't. Still, I will add my hope to Themistocles's. Some true good news would be very welcome right now."

"Still no idea who was responsible for the explosion?" Zhukov almost hadn't asked. She knew very well what was on Harmon's mind.

He sighed softly. "In terms of specific names, unfortunately, no. Not a single arrest yet. Not even a solid idea on anyone specific. But, it's almost certain that one or more people in the security department are complicit. That's our main line of investigation right now...but whoever we're looking for was damned careful."

"That is terrible. It's bad enough we've got violent extremists out there at all...but inside the security apparatus..." She paused for a moment, and when she continued, her tone was hard edged. "There is nothing worse than a traitor."

Harmon nodded, but he didn't answer. He imagined some of the people who'd followed him as an elected president and publicly declared their support, feeling they had no choice, still considered his seizure of power to be treasonous. His coup hadn't left a trail of bodies behind it...but then he didn't want to think too deeply about what he would have done if he'd had to spill blood.

"Do we have any leads at all?"

"To individuals? Unfortunately, no. But, we have been able to secure some so far untraceable message feeds. If we can get a line to anyone in the chain, a sender, a receiver, whatever...

maybe we can turn that into something meaningful. But, we were able to get *some* information, at least. We don't know who did it or where they are now…but we've got a pretty good idea of why."

"The Mules?" Zhukov tried to keep the anger out of her voice, but as the co-creator of the Hybrid program, she had always been defensive of the Mules and prone to be unsympathetic to those who sought to restrict the gifted Hybrids…or worse.

"Yes. At least it was the increase in quickenings that seems to have pushed things to the breaking point." He could see the hardness in her expression. "But, we believe the group responsible is opposed to all non-natural births."

"Don't they realize all the Mules have done? We wouldn't be close to being able to fight the Regent without the tech they developed. We're decades ahead of where we'd be without them. Perhaps centuries."

"I know, Ana…you know I'm with you. But, people are afraid…and for all our education and sophistication, most people are herd animals at heart. They're ready to follow anything that makes them feel a part of something, and most of them never bother to really learn about or understand any of it. The League and other groups tell them they're special because they were born from their mothers' bodies instead of a crèche…and they come to believe it."

"That may be true, Max…but I don't understand why fear doesn't keep them in line. Don't they understand that we have to defeat the Regent…that the First Imperium forces will kill us all if they're able to get past our defenses? They may fear the Mules, but if they had any sense, they'd fear a future without them as well."

Harmon sighed. He understood what she was saying, and he agreed with her…completely. But, he also knew people did not always act rationally. "I was reading some old Earth histories last night, Ana…accounts of the late Roman Empire, mostly." He knew it sounded like a tangent, but he had a point to make. "I'd spent most of the day trying to figure out what would drive terrorists to blow things up over an increase in the Mule quickening rate that still keeps them a tiny fraction of a percent of the population, and more to the point, to do it when our entire world faces a struggle of annihilation…a fight that can only end in the death of our enemy, or of us. I didn't make sense to me, no more than it does to you. But then I sat there in bed, trying to make my eyes tired enough to get even a few hours' sleep, reading about the endless series of civil wars that rocked late Rome, general after general trying to seize power, even as the borders crumbled, and the empire that each sought to control dwindled away to non-existence." He looked across the table. "Human nature is our own worst enemy, Ana, there is no question about that…but we cannot ignore that fact, just because we can't explain it. We are self-destructive creatures."

Zhukov looked across the table, her usually pleasant face hard, almost as if it had been carved from stone. "You have to find whoever did this, Max. We have to stop this before it goes any farther."

"I intend to be firm, Ana. If we can find those truly at the center of the movement."

"If there is any way I can help…" Her voice trailed off. Harmon knew she realized this was one area where there was little she could do.

Harmon knew he had to find someone, anyone…from the heart of the terrorist group, the fringe…even someone who cooked the plotters dinner before they did it. And, when he found them, he knew they had to die. He didn't know how he'd give that order, especially if it was directed at those involved on the fringes, but he knew he had to.

He had to stamp out any groups that might disrupt things while the struggle against the Regent was still underway…and those he couldn't find to eliminate, he had to drive back into the shadows. And, there was only one way to do that.

Fear.

* * *

"You have excelled, my friend, beyond even the high standards we Mules set for ourselves. Four decades of research, and virtually no progress…and here…" Achilles gestured toward the woman lying in the bed. "…is the result of your work."

The woman was a Tank, one who'd been no more than a day from death when she'd been airlifted to the Institute's infirmary. She was sleeping quietly now, and she was breathing without mechanical assistance. The spots on her skin where there had been black, necrotic sores—part of the reason the disease had been branded 'the Plague'—were covered now with nothing but a soft pink layer of new skin.

Achilles didn't rely on anything as incomplete as a glance at the patient, however. He'd reviewed every analysis, every medical scan, and the verdict as undeniable. Save for some minor healing still underway, and immense fatigue from the ordeal, the woman lying a meter from where he stood had no symptoms at all.

"Thank you, Achilles." Themistocles looked almost as tired as his patient, but his satisfaction was evident on his face. "I was optimistic it would work…but, of course, you can only be so sure without actual test cases."

"Themistocles, I have been reviewing your notes…there doesn't appear to be much about the treatment that is specific to the Plague. Indeed, the patients still have the disease—or dysfunction, whatever we call it—your injections are simply repairing the damage as it occurs, and setting up a cycle so the body can continue to do so."

"That is true, Achilles. I have not unlocked the secrets of what causes the Plague, only developed a way to treat its effects. However, the treatments should keep the Plague in a state of permanent remission, at least, even if it doesn't eradicate whatever factors cause it."

"But, you weren't working on a Plague cure, not at first? That is what you told me earlier."

"No…I was trying to find a way to reverse our sterility. I was unable to achieve any success there, but I was able to unlock some startling cell regeneration capabilities from First Imperium genetic material."

A concerned look slipped onto Achilles's face. The supply of preserved Ancient DNA was restricted, set aside solely for use in quickening new Mules.

"No, my friend…I do not mean I used specimens from the supply of genetic material. I used my own blood samples. Don't forget, we carry the genetic codes of the Ancients as well as the humans inside us."

"You were able to initiate widespread cell regeneration using a serum you manufactured from your own blood?"

"Yes, Achilles, my friend. Now, you begin to see that the potential goes far beyond simply treating Plague victims. Our discussion of near-immortality was realistic. I am even more certain now than I was before."

"Yes, I can see that, Themistocles." Achilles saw the won-drous uses, but he saw a dark side as well, and he felt a spark of fear at where his friend's discovery might lead.

"It is good that we were cautious about announcing this publicly. We must be very careful."

"Careful?"

Achilles held back a sigh. He'd always had a healthy dose of cynicism, a reflex that made him look at things from multiple perspectives. For all the raw intelligence his fellow-Mules pos-sessed, they could also be myopic in considering the motivations of others.

They can be naïve…

"Themistocles…have you given thought to the fact that you are developing a virtual fountain of youth for them all…one that is powered by *our* blood?"

Achilles tended to look at the dark side of things…but he knew enough about humanity and its history to feel pretty cer-tain his views were more or less on point.

"For now, Achilles…but I am sure I will be able to synthesize…"

"You are sure? For forty years, we have been sure we would discover a way to reproduce among ourselves. For forty years, the Plague eluded any real progress. How long do you think the Normals would be patient if they knew they could live for thousands of years...and all they needed was a steady supply of our blood?"

Achilles saw a nightmare unfolding in his mind, the Mules being reduced to captives, virtual farm animals kept so their blood could be harvested. He saw the Normals fighting among themselves, too, killing each other for the precious—and limited—serum that would allow them to defy disease and live for countless centuries.

"I never really considered the implications. I don't need a tremendous amount of blood to synthesize a round of treatment. I believe we could treat all Plague cases quite easily using voluntary blood donations. I think most of our people would..."

"Yes, Themistocles...most of our people would donate blood to save stricken Tanks. But, what if there are ten times as many Tanks in the future, or a hundred? And, what happens when you continue your research and perfect it...and when every Normal is demanding ongoing treatments for other sicknesses or wounds...or simply to counteract aging? You know our numbers are sharply limited, even without the external caps imposed on quickenings. What happens when voluntary donations are insufficient? Mandatory ones? Then what?"

Themistocles looked back at his friend, and Achilles could see the scientist was finally considering the darker side of his discovery. "So, what do we do, Achilles? Deny dying Tanks a treatment that can save their lives?"

Achilles didn't like how much of him wanted to answer, 'yes.' There was no question Themistocles's new discovery represented a risk to the Mules, that it would be safer to keep it a secret. But, he finally shook his head. "No, of course not. We can't withhold the treatment and let Tanks die who could otherwise live." He also considered what had crossed his mind when Themistocles had first told him of the treatment, how it could be used to help...influence...the Tanks in the event of a future conflict between Earth Two's genetic groups.

Achilles took a deep breath. "But, we have to keep all treatments here...and there can be no public disclosure of the biochemistry and other specifics involved. We must control every aspect…regardless of any pressure that may be exerted."

"I agree, Achilles. But, how do we move forward with this? Do we tell President Harmon the truth and seek his support? Or do we mislead him somehow?"

Achilles sighed softly. "I don't know, Themistocles. I just don't know."

Chapter Twenty

Flag Bridge, E2S Midway
System G48
Earth Two Date 02.16.43

"All batteries, increase power levels to one hundred ten percent." Strand was ordering her ships to overload their guns, and she knew there'd be a price to pay for that. To an extent it was simple probability. The power ratings were based on estimates of how long a ship was likely to endure sustained firing levels. A single shot at one hundred ten percent was very likely to go off without a hitch. Even ten shots, or perhaps a hundred. But, across her entire task force, with the guns blazing at maximum fire rates, there would be burnouts.

And some of them would be bad.

Strand had read the accounts of Terrance Compton's old battles, and Augustus Garret's as well. Both men had been aggressive commanders, willing to take the chances needed to secure difficult victories. Overloading guns in their day had put significant numbers of their crew at risk. Hundreds of gunnery teams had died in their turrets, victims of the radiation back blasts or explosions resulting from the failure of overpowered guns. But, for the most part, Strand was risking only equipment. Her ships were far more automated than their predecessors, and there were few actual men and women crawling around those

154

gun emplacements.

That was something, at least.

"All ships acknowledge, Admiral." A pause. "*Mesa*, *Vanguard*, and *Samuels* report inadequate power generation to comply."

"Very well." Strand was surprised it was only three ships. That probably meant some of her captains were pushing their vessels recklessly to obey her orders. She knew some of the reactors out there weren't up to the increase.

Midway vibrated, a hard shock this time. Strand knew her flagship well enough to have a good idea what had happened. A hit somewhere in the stern, and a few compartments—two or three—blown out, the force of expelled air creating the shudder that rocked through the vessel.

She glanced down at her screen as the actual report came in, feeling a fleeting burst of satisfaction at the accuracy of her guess. She'd been spot on. The stream of data scrolling down confirmed her other prediction as well. The damage was minimal…and none of her people had been killed.

Not by that last shot, at least.

Her head darted to the side, and a feral smile took her expression as *Midway*'s guns fired again. She could hear the increased power in the weapons, too, as she listened to the distant whine of the batteries' fire. And, in the swirling center of *Midway*'s great display she saw a First Imperium battleship transfixed, a Colossus, ripped open as those deadly beams struck it amidships… and seconds later, a burst of almost incalculable energy as the great vessel's containment failed, its magnetic core breached by *Midway*'s deadly heavy batteries.

Strand had read the old accounts of humanity's wars against the First Imperium, of Augustus Garret's desperate struggles to defeat enemy fleets vastly more powerful and advanced than his own. She wondered what the New Regent analyzed, deep in its hidden fortress somewhere out there. Its destroyed predecessor, in its last astonished moments, must have found it unfathomable how the inferior humans had bested it. What, she wondered, had gone through its version of a mind as its end approached? Had it felt fear…or something comparable? Bewilderment?

And, what does the New Regent discern, as it sees Earth Two ships centuries in advance of those the Alliance and other Earth powers had thrown at it just a few decades before? Does it feel tension as it realizes its technology gap has largely slipped away, that its enemies have drawn ever closer to parity?

Perhaps that's why if lured us here, resorted to so dangerous a trap. Maybe it's analysis warned of its deadly human enemy, and the growing power we commanded. Perhaps, in its own way, this is the Regent's desperation showing…

Her eyes caught movement in the display, a small cloud of tiny specs of light.

McDaid's squadrons…

Fighters had been a huge weapon in the fleet that had traveled to Earth Two, as they had been in those that fought the early wars against the First Imperium. Their importance had dwindled during Earth Two's first thirty years, as weapons technology improved, and the lack of a direct enemy made the cumbersome and manpower-intensive squadrons an easy area to cut.

The fighters had seemed to be entirely on their way out, until the New Regent surfaced. The First Imperium had never had an adequate response to the small craft, and the renewal of the war against the robotic enemy had stayed the budget axe, and preserved a small fighter component in the fleet. The survival of the fighter corps was championed by none other than Mariko Fujin, President Harmon's wife, and a hero of the squadrons in her own right.

Strand had launched *Midway*'s eighteen fighters already, as had the eight others of her ships that carried contingents of six to eighteen themselves. One hundred ten fighter-bombers, less than a tithe of the massive formations Terrance Compton and Augustus Garret had once launched, but a potent force nevertheless, especially against an enemy with none of their own.

As a commander, Strand had never relied on the small fighter forces at her disposal…but now, as she watched the small cluster moving forward, she felt something. Admiration, excitement. The pilots were a breed apart, and now, as her eyes followed their wings moving directly toward the enemy, a group of tiny ships moving boldly toward the First Imperium behemoths, she understood...and she was glad to have them with her.

She narrowed her eyes and watched...watched as the men and women who carried the spirit of Greta Hurley, and a thousand lost aces, drove right for the enemy formation.

* * *

"Let's go, boys and girls...we've got fresh First Imperium meat out there, and I for one am damned hungry!" McDaid had always wanted to be a fighter pilot, even as he grew up, steeped in the stories of the great heroes of the fleet. He'd never been deterred, even when he'd seen the fighter corps dwindling to irrelevance and, for a while, almost to non-existence. He'd long regretted the time and place of his birth, ached to live in the days when thousands of fighters blasted into space, led by such legendary commanders as Greta Hurley. But, he'd never let go of his goal to make it into the cockpit, and now, years later, he was the commander of the fleet's combined wings.

"We're with you, Commodore."

"On your tail, Boss."

McDaid smiled. The fighter corps was generally left alone within the navy's structure, and it had definitely retained the kind of unique culture its predecessors had displayed. Pilots were alone in their cockpits, making crazed runs at ships thousands of times their size...it took a certain kind of personality to excel in situations like that, and the brass had somehow managed to remember that and conduct a more or less hands off policy on the squadrons.

That was Mariko Fujin's doing more than anything, he realized, though he knew Admiral West's long and storied career reached back to the days of those massive fighter battles as well. Fujin had been somewhat of a mentor to him in his early days, and he still remembered the thrill of watching her fly her sleek, fast ship, even if just on training maneuvers.

McDaid looked up at the scanner in front of him. The enemy ships were close now, already locked in a deadly energy duel with Strand's line. McDaid would have led his birds in an assault the instant they'd launched, but the admiral's orders were clear…and he followed them to the letter.

Wait…wait until the lines are engaged.

McDaid understood. It was contrary to most tenets of fighter tactics—after all, the whole point was to hit the enemy before they got into range of the battleline—but through all the distracting bravado of a pilot, he understood his small force wasn't strong enough to operate as the vast strike forces that had come before. Strand's making him wait had been the right call. The enemy ships were battered now, and no weapon in the fleet's arsenal was better suited to targeting weak spots on damaged vessels…and delivering the coup de grace.

And, that was just what his people were going to do…

"Alright…break now. You're all on your own. Pick out a nice target, and show these blasted machines what human pilots can do." He paused. "And watch out for their point defense. These things are full of guns for blasting missiles, and any one of those can fry your asses, too!"

McDaid couldn't imagine the great dogfights of the battles between the Superpowers, squadron after squadron coming in, fighters locked in death struggles before they could even think about hitting the enemy capital ships. He'd dreamed of those days, but he was glad his people didn't have to face such enemies now. The First Imperium's defensive batteries would be bad enough.

McDaid tapped his throttle, altering his thrust angle as his eyes settled on a target. It was a big bastard, a Colossus, and it was coming forward, moving up behind the ship *Midway* had just destroyed. It was damaged, but not as badly as McDaid was looking for in a target. Still, *Midway* had just come through a hard fight, and he suspected Admiral Strand's flagship needed all the help she could get facing another of the large battleships.

"Nova Four and Nova Five…let's head in and give *Midway* a hand with that big bastard."

"We're with you, Leader."

"Right behind you…"

McDaid jerked the throttle to the side, and then he pulled it back, blasting his engines at full. He could feel the g forces slamming into him, overwhelming his dampeners. His ship was blasting at better than 40g, he knew, though to him, it felt more like 8g. Still damned uncomfortable.

He winced as he shifted his body, his ribs feeling as though they might tear right out of his chest. Every muscle, every joint he'd ever injured hurt like hell...but he didn't care. He was where he belonged, and in his mind, he was flying along with Admiral Hurley's massive strike forces, reliving the golden age of the fighter.

He could see the flashes on his screen, the incoming fire from the target ship. He angled his fighter, port first, then starboard, varying the velocity slightly every few seconds as he did...evasive maneuvers he hoped would confound the enemy defensive fire. His ship jerked wildly as it continued toward the enemy vessel, and, at least for the moment, the incoming shots went well wide of his position.

McDaid tried to ignore the thickness of the incoming fire, but then one of his wingmen was hit. Nova Four was gone before he could even check to see if his pilot had ejected.

He'd seen losses before, in the fighting twelve years earlier, and now the romanticism he knew clouded his view of those terrible old battles cleared away. He knew he would lose more of his people in the next moments, and he saw pain now, more than glory, in the hundreds of pilots killed in those decade old struggles.

That didn't matter, not enough, at least, to defer his squadrons from their duty. But, he knew it would hurt later. He didn't have thousands of ships in space, nor vast legions of pilots. Every one of his small cadre was a familiar face...and their absences would weigh heavily on those who made it back.

He forced his mind back to the attack, watching the range drop. His fighters were armed with the newest weapons, straight from the labs of the Cutter Institute. The nuclear cluster bombs were designed to hit enemy ships with as much destructive force as possible...from a launch range so close, the targets would be unable to evade the tiny missiles.

McDaid's hand tightened around the controls, his finger placed gently atop the firing stud. "Arm bombs," he said grimly, nodding as the AI confirmed the order.

He had forty small nukes active in his bays now, twenty-kiloton jobs. Tiny by comparison to the gargantuan warheads of the ship-based missiles, but then McDaid and his people weren't trying to place a detonation a kilometer from the target.

They were going for direct hits.

He watched as the ship grew on his screen, the range dropping below ten thousand kilometers…then below five thousand.

The ship shook back and forth as the AI aided his evasive maneuvers, a wild ride that seemed totally random, but still ended up with him on his chosen course.

Under two thousand.

He was well within launch range now. He could let his bombs fly any time he chose. But, he held them, and he continued forward, driving right at the huge battleship.

His surviving wingman was right behind him, also holding his own bombs. McDaid knew the other pilot wouldn't fire until he did…and he felt a touch of guilt for that. The defensive fire was so thick it almost seemed he could walk forward on the laser blasts. It was one thing to risk his own neck…but to bring one of his pilots along on such a wild ride…

But, he kept pressing on.

One thousand kilometers.

He almost ordered the wingman to launch. He was going to take it in to knife-fighting range, but he didn't expect anyone else to follow him so recklessly.

He swerved again, a gut impulse…and one he suspected an instant later had saved him from the enemy fire.

You're too close…do this…now…

He hesitated just an instant longer…and he pressed the firing stud.

His fighter lurched as it launched its payload, but he hardly noticed. His hand was tightly gripped around the throttle, pulling back already with all he had, not entirely sure he'd done it in time to clear the looming ship up ahead.

He held his breath...and then he realized he'd made it. He felt an instant's relief, and then he looked around, eyes frantically searching the screen, looking for sight of his wingman. His heart sank, and for a moment, he resigned himself to the loss of both of his comrades...but, then a small dot appeared, obscured at first by the radiation surrounding the target. It was Nova Five. They both had made it.

He checked the scanning reports, growing impatient almost immediately as the AI compiled the data and delivered a damage assessment. A hit.

No...four hits.

The enemy battleship was surrounded by nuclear fury. The First Imperium hulls were built from a dark matter infused substance, one of the few things Earth Two science had been unable to truly decipher yet. It was far stronger than any other known metal, but against the energies released by the fission bombs, it gave way, sections melting, even vaporizing wherever one of the warheads impacted.

McDaid smiled, not a look of joy, but the grin of a predator, drunk on the blood of its victim. The Colossus was too large to be destroyed completely by the four small warheads, but now it had huge gashes in its hull, and it was streaming atmosphere and flash-frozen geysers of escaping fluids.

The energy readings suggested secondary explosions as well, and, as McDaid brought his ship around, his scanners displayed a good view of *Midway*, pressing forward, its guns firing away at the wounded enemy vessel, like some grim executioner wielding a sharpened axe.

McDaid knew he'd done his part. And he knew one more thing, too.

The fighter wasn't dead as a weapon of war...not yet, at least.

* * *

Erika West watched as Rivers' ships pressed on, moving steadily toward their target. The scanner reports had confirmed that the planet was far from a human paradise, a rocky, hot world, its surface fractured by fissures and swept by violent storms and great tides of molten rock. Its atmosphere was noxious, with clouds of sulfuric acid floating low across the tortured ground. It was the last place any humanoid species, or even their robot replacements, would choose for any productive purpose, save one.

Antimatter production.

Antimatter required energy—great, vast amounts of energy—and West's head almost spun trying to imagine the amount of raw power the planet's furious volcanic and seismic activity generated.

The massive construction projects needed to build the accelerators and storage units had to have been nightmarish. She couldn't imagine how many of the Regent's sophisticated robots were destroyed in the process, like so many slaves in humanity's dark history, toiling endlessly, with almost no value placed on their survival. The world was an incarnation of hell, in more ways than one…and it still served in such a capacity, feeding the needs of the Regent, providing the fuel it required in its terrible quest to destroy humanity.

West's eyes darted to the display, watching the battle around Strand's task force as its fury continued to escalate. McDaid's fighters had just gone in, and her mind had flashed back to past generations of heroes, men and women she'd watched taking their fighters into almost impossible situations. In more than sixty years of war in space, she'd seen all sorts of valor and amazing efforts, but none could ever compare to the sheer, reckless bravery she'd seen from six decades of watching fighter squadrons in action.

All of Strand's people were doing well—better than she'd had any right to expect—but they were still dying, fighting off every ship the enemy had sent out…while West's own vessels stayed back, out of range. She felt sick to her stomach, but she remained where she was, ignoring the stares all around her, the judgment she felt from her officers and spacers each time one of Strand's ships was destroyed.

She looked back toward the planet, her stomach tight as Rivers's attack force move closer and closer to its objective, his skeleton crews no doubt just as glued to their screens as she was, waiting for the first sign the new stealth screens had failed to hide their presence.

West shook her head as she watched. Maybe the enemy truly hadn't detected the ships yet…or maybe they were letting them advance. It didn't make any sense that the First Imperium forces would allow her to get attacking ships close enough to launch on the planet.

No more than it did to allow her fleet to enter the system unopposed…or to hold back the forces she *knew* were still there, sheltered somewhere in the shadow of the planet.

She wanted to go to Strand's aid. She wanted to do what her people expected…almost demanded. But she wouldn't.

She couldn't.

Let them hate her if they had to…she'd come here for a reason. She had a plan, one she had shared with Max Harmon, but with no one else in the fleet. Not yet, at least. Soon, Josie Strand would know…and she would become aware of her true role, of what was expected of her.

West had no doubt her protégé—her successor—would do what she had to do. And, with a bit of fortune, she might even survive to continue the fight.

West sighed softly. She had devised the plan, put into it all she knew of the Regent, everything her gut told her about how to defeat the hideous machine…and, she was going to see it done, whatever it took.

It is almost time.

Six decades of war in space…all leading to this moment.

Chapter Twenty-One

Central Headquarters
Victory City, Earth Two
Earth Two Date 02.16.43

"I shouldn't have approved the assignment. I should have said no." Max Harmon sat quietly in his office, his head buried in his hands. He'd have never allowed anyone to see him in anything like his current state. No one but Mariko.

"You need to stop beating yourself up over this, Max. You *had* to let him go." Mariko paused for a few seconds. "Terrance has had a difficult time, and for all he has brought some of it on himself, it's hard to imagine how anyone could have been in his shoes and done much better. He's trying to set his life straight, now, and you know he will always be in the shade of his father's immense shadow. He had to go…and you had to send him. Neither of you had a choice."

Harmon nodded, but he still didn't look convinced. "He's not ready, Mariko."

"He's not in command…he's just one of a whole corps of officers. You send twenty-two-year old Academy graduates… how could you not allow Terrance to deploy? After all he's been through, he went back, and he finished the Academy. He's earned the right to be with his comrades."

Harmon knew she was right. But Terrance Compton II was

164

also the son of his mentor, of a man who had been a second father to him…and the only father he'd had after his own had been killed at the Slaughter Pen when he was a child. Admiral Compton was gone now, and Harmon knew he was all that remained to look after the great man's son. And, he'd just sent the man to war.

"Terrance, of all people, would have understood, Max. He'd have done the same thing." She looked at him, catching the doubtful expression on his face and frowning. "Don't give me that look. I knew Terrance Compton, too. He was a true hero… but he was a man, too, Max. He would have struggled with the same emotions, but in the end, he would have realized he had to let his son live his life, make his own decisions."

Harmon was silent for a while, a minute perhaps, or two. Mariko sat quietly, giving him the time he needed. He was grateful, as he had been countless times, that he'd married another combat officer…hell, not just an officer, but a pilot. And, even among that group of semi-crazy, wild cowboy fighter jockeys, Mariko Fujin had been a legend. She understood war and danger and the pain of losing friends and comrades…every bit as well as he did. Whatever combination of components had built their relationship—affection, attraction, trust—he knew that she understood what he'd gone through over the years.

The two had been happy, at least he thought she was mostly happy. They'd had their problems, of course, mostly stemming from his job. She'd resented that, of course, the constant, unending demands on his time, the effect all of it had on their family over the years. He even suspected, at times, it had almost driven her away from him, but in the end, he knew she understood the call duty had on him…and she'd also realized the danger that threatened them all and how little choice he'd truly had.

He wasn't sure his daughters understood it as well as their mother did. Greta and Camille loved him, he was sure of that. But they'd been born after the fleet reached Earth Two, and neither had served in the military. He knew they couldn't understand what drove him, not completely, not in the way their mother did. They'd never complained about how busy he'd always been, how many times he'd been pulled away from time spent with them. Still, there was something, a closeness he craved that simply wasn't there. Another price he'd paid to duty. The cost of carrying on Terrance Compton's work.

"I know you're right…but I just can't reconcile with putting Terrance's son at risk."

"We're all at risk, aren't we?" It didn't really call for an answer, and she didn't wait for one. "We all have a right to do what we feel we must, to work for our survival any way we can. Would you prefer that Terrance's son had never gained control of his destiny? That he'd continued to waste his life, protected by you but never making any kind of contribution? Is that what you think your old mentor would have wanted?"

"No, of course not. But, if he…" Harmon's words drifted to silence.

"Dies? If that happens, we will deal with it then. And, we will mourn our friend, and the son of our greatest hero. And, then we will go on, Max. As Terrance—both Terrances—would want us to do."

Harmon managed a smile, or at least something closely approximating one. "I never could have gotten this far without you…you know that, right? I'm sorry we never did so many of the things we always said we would." He almost added, "we will," but something stopped him. He'd made enough empty promises like that, and he wasn't going to do it again. He knew he was trapped, that he couldn't escape his position…and the power and obligation that went along with it.

"Max, if you want me to tell you I've never imagined what it might have been like if you'd let someone else step into your shoes—if it had been possible to do that—you're out of luck. I've thought about it a lot. But I've never—not once—regretted our lives together, and I'm ready for whatever comes in the future. You might have worn out a wife who was some kind of scientist or engineer, but you married a Lightning pilot, my dear husband. I've seen more shit than anything *you* can throw at me." She smiled and reached across the desk, putting her hand on his.

Harmon looked across at her. He was grateful that they'd found each other. He wondered if he could have made it so long without her.

"Besides, you might have sent Terrance out on duty, but you and Erika managed to keep him out of the fleet heading toward G48."

Harmon felt his insides tighten. He wasn't sure Compton would be any better off where he was going, but just the thought of the trap he'd sent West and her fleet into made him nauseous.

"Oh, come on, Max. You don't think you were that clever, do you?" Her voice turned somber. "Neither one of you wanted to let him near that much danger." She was silent for a moment. Mariko was very fond of Erika West, and Harmon knew his wife understood just how much danger the fleet was in.

What she didn't realize, what no one but he and Erika West knew, was that Force B, cobbled together from just about the last ships remaining at Earth Two, was in just as deadly a situation.

And, Terrance Compton II was with Force B.

*   *   *

There were shouts all around, people running, almost contagious panic. The people of Victory City had gotten used to Marines rushing around over the past days, scanning crowds, even smashing through doors. The crackdown had been harder edged than any activity ordered by President Harmon, during the dozen years of his absolute rule.

But, this was something else.

The Marines had opened up and started a full-scale firefight...and then moments later, the building they'd surrounded exploded. Two of the Marines had been killed instantly, but the rest had been far enough from ground zero for their armor to protect them.

The same couldn't be said for the civilians who'd been unable to get away when the shooting started. There were nearly two dozen of them when the bombs went off, crouched down, trying to hide from the hail of gunfire crisscrossing down the street.

Most of them were dead now, and the Marines were frantically trying to get aid to the few still clinging to life. The explosive had been a nasty one, and a quick scan had confirmed the presence of radioactives. There had been fear for a few moments that a nuclear weapon had been used, but it quickly became apparent that the device had simply been seeded with nuclear waste to increase its killing potential.

Connor Frasier was standing in the middle of the street, shouting out commands, demanding briefings from every officer and squad leader on the scene. He'd been uncomfortable with the role of his Marines in hunting down rogue political groups, but the sight of half a dozen children lying on the street had pushed him to the limits of his tolerance. His Marines were hunting down terrorists, nothing more, and as far as he was concerned, they were nothing more than rabid animals, to be put down without a second thought. And, he swore he would find them all, every last one of them...those who'd planned and perpetrated the two terrible attacks, and anyone who supported them.

He *would* find them...and when he did, they would never be sorrier than they would in that moment.

He would save Max Harmon the trouble of trying them. When he was done there wouldn't be a need for anything but a pack of street-cleaning bots.

* * *

"Thank you for seeing me, Mr. President."

"Of course, Achilles...you know you can come see me any time you need to." Max Harmon walked around his desk and gestured toward the pair of small sofas facing each other on the far side of his office. "Please, sit. It's good to see you. I've always considered you a friend...and save for one instance—one the two of us resolved—you have been my ally as well." A pause. "And, I'm Max...you know that."

"I want to be your ally, Max. I mean I *am* your ally." It was self-correction, but it was more than that, too. Mules didn't mis-speak, not often at least, and Achilles was annoyed with himself for letting his edginess affect what he said.

"I'd be pleased enough if this was a social call, but I've known you your entire life, Achilles, and I am quite sure you have something you wish to discuss. Does it have to do with the Plague treatments? Have the experiments continued to perform well?"

Achilles was standing on a precipice in his mind, teetering on the edge between truth and fabrication. He'd considered a number of answers to that expected question, mostly variations of one kind of another along the lines of, "it looks promising, but we need more time to develop it." But, in the end, he'd decided to tell the truth, to trust Harmon. It had worked twelve years before, and the president had never given him cause to regret his friendship.

It was difficult to accept something like that on faith, par-ticularly for a Mule. The Hybrids had emotions, sometimes fiery ones that were difficult to control, but at their core they were creatures of logic, of calculation and analysis. Achilles had struggled with accepting trust as a basis for certainty.

"The experiments went extremely well. Both of the patients have been completely cured, no detectable signs of the effects of the Plague remaining in either of them."

"That's amazing, Achilles. I knew you had to be on to some-thing, but if you've actually cured the Plague…"

"Perhaps even more than that, Max." A pause. "The proce-dure is one of cellular repair…and it has many other possible uses." He paused. "Themistocles even believes he can utilize the technique to repair Admiral Frette's injuries and revive her." Achilles looked nervously across at Harmon.

Earth Two's president stared back, a shocked look on his face. Achilles knew that Nicki Frette was one of his closest friends…and even more. Frette had saved Harmon's life more than forty years earlier, when they'd led the mission that had destroyed the first Regent. He'd known his words would hit Harmon hard, and it was clear to him that they had.

"Is this truly possible?" He hesitated, staring at his desk with a look of shock on his face. "Is it dangerous?"

"There is no one on Earth Two who can match Themistocles for his medical and biological knowledge. There are, however, by definition, no guarantees with any new discovery. He believes it will work, and my analysis confirms this. You must ask yourself…how often have my people been wrong about such matters?" Achilles knew his last statement would seem arrogant to a Normal, even to Max Harmon, though he'd meant it only in the most purely factual terms.

Harmon looked uncertain.

"Whether Themistocles proceeds with his treatment on Admiral Frette is, of course, your decision. You are not only Earth Two's president, but with Admiral West away with the fleet, you are the closest thing Nicki Frette has to next of kin." Achilles paused. The Mule was rarely hesitant to say what had to be said, but he was finding it difficult to finish what he'd come to tell Harmon. "It is also your choice in another way."

Harmon had been looking down at the small table between the sofas, but now he glanced back up toward Achilles. "What do you mean?"

"Twelve years ago, we negotiated, Max…you and I. I accepted your word and your promises, and then I persuaded all the Mules to support your…assumption…of power. I trusted you then, as I have ever since." Another pause. "As I do now."

"What is it, Achilles? I hope you know by now you can tell me anything."

"I hope so."

Harmon looked even more concerned. "What is it?"

"We will treat Admiral Frette if you wish…and we will see that all victims of the Plague are cured. We will do all we can to aid all those in need." He stared directly at Harmon. "But, all work must be done at the Institute. All patients must be brought there for care. The procedure, and all formulas and processes, must remain known only to Themistocles and myself…and any others of the Mules required to administer treatment."

Harmon frowned, his look bordering on suspicion. "Why?"

"It is the only way." Achilles had come ready to tell Harmon the entire truth, but now he found himself hesitating again.

"You're going to have to explain that to me, Achilles." Harmon's voice had an edge to it, but then he paused. When he continued, he appeared to have gotten control over whatever anger he'd felt. "Understand…this isn't about me mistrusting you. But, can you imagine the conspiracy theories? What the League and others will make of shipping off deathly ill patients to the Institute in the dark of night?"

"I do understand, Max. Truly. If there was any other way…"

"Are you saying your people will defy me? That you will refuse to treat dying Tanks or Admiral Frette—or anyone else this treatment can help—if I do not grant your demand?"

Achilles took a breath before responding. There was no threat in Harmon's tone, but he was well aware he was talking to an absolute dictator. All Harmon had to do was tap the comm unit on his collar, and Marines would come in and drag him away.

And, the Regent would have a spectacle guaranteed to make even its electronic systems laugh…Earth Two, plunged into civil war, even as its fleets were far away, locked, no doubt, in brutal combat.

"I wouldn't phrase it like that. There is no disloyalty intended…but there are reasons we must retain control over every aspect of these treatments." Achilles was uncertain how much more he wanted to say, but then he added, "We could have hidden the efficacy of the protocols. I could have come here and told you it just didn't work. But, we do not want to lie to you, and we do not want to see people die when we can save them."

"But, you don't want to share the secrets of all this? Are you trying to retain some leverage, position yourselves to make demands at some future time?"

Achilles understood Harmon's concerns. He'd been barraged by all sides for decades now, even in his days as elected president before he'd seized power. And, it was no secret there were those among the Mules who nurtured aspirations for the future of the Hybrids.

"The treatment needs our blood, Max." Achilles decided to trust Harmon, and he blurted out the truth before he could change his mind.

"What?" Harmon sounded stunned. Whatever he had expected to hear, that wasn't it.

"The serum used to stimulate Themistocles's cellular regeneration program is developed from blood samples. Hybrid blood samples."

Harmon was silent at first, but the surprise was evident on his face.

"Yes…everything you are thinking now is correct. The Mules cannot disclose the secret behind the treatment because our blood is required to produce the required drug cocktail. We can manage the volume of Plague cases, at least if Tank population levels are kept within certain guidelines, but if this line of research leads to more extensive uses, to extreme longevity treatments, for example, increasing potential human lifespans by centuries…our blood would become the greatest treasure in the universe."

Achilles paused for a few seconds and looked at Harmon. If you want the Mules and the Normals at war with each other, a titanic struggle almost guaranteed to destroy us all…I can't think of a better way to achieve it than to announce that Hybrid blood is the secret to practical immortality.

Chapter Twenty-Two

Flag Bridge, E2S Midway
System G48
Earth Two Date 02.16.43

Strand sat at her command station, watching the fight raging all around *Midway*. Her task force had been heavily engaged for hours now, and she'd lost almost a third of her ships. Every other vessel she had, all that remained under her command, including the flagship, was heavily damaged.

But the enemy forces were worse off, gutted, their broken hulls streaming fluids from severed conduits and bleeding radiation from fractured reactor cores. More than two First Imperium vessels had been destroyed for every one of her ships lost. By any measure of combat effectiveness, her spacers had conducted themselves with the utmost effectiveness, courage, and tactical brilliance, and they had accomplished their primary mission, pulled the enemy fleet from the planet, opened the way for the Marines and for West's main force to advance.

Still, she still found it hard to compare electronics and programming lost on the enemy ships to the men and women who had died in her hulls. Did two ships full of AIs and computer relays make up for the dozens of human beings killed when one of her vessels was destroyed?

Not to her way of thinking, no matter how successfully

things seemed to be going or how much tactical glory accrued to her.

Still, the battle was beginning to look like a success. Her people were going to suffer more casualties before it was over, certainly, but she didn't doubt anymore that they could defeat the rest of the First Imperium fleet. At least what she could see of it.

She glanced at one column of data, ten squadron designations, each followed by two numbers. The first showed each unit's starting strength, and the second, the losses it had suffered. She paused, blinking her eyes and looking again before it truly hit her. McDaid's squadrons had fought like devils, and they had done more than their part to defeat the enemy task force. But that effort had cost them a third of their strength.

She reached out, touching the screen, bringing up detailed information. McDaid was still alive, at least. She counted the pilot among her few true friends, and she was relieved to see he'd made it through the fighting so far.

Even as she looked at the display, trying to deal with her squadrons' losses, she saw a line of yellow spheres far off *Midway*'s starboard, approaching the planet. Captain Rivers' task force had gotten close, very close, before the planetary defenses had detected them. The orbital fortresses had launched their own missiles now, but Rivers' people would get theirs off before any enemy ordnance reached them. Strand didn't doubt the incoming assault would be an unpleasant one for the attacking ships, that it would take down many of the brave attack crews, but it wouldn't interfere with the assault on the planet. Rivers and his people would suffer heavy losses, but then the survivors could bolt and run. They'd have done their jobs…and they'd have no duty remaining except to save themselves.

Strand knew just how crammed full of nukes Rivers' ships were, even as they began to launch. She'd worked alongside Erika West, supervising as the yard crews had pulled out every bit of non-essential equipment and filled the emptied space with makeshift magazines. It had been a rushed project, and even now, Strand couldn't quite understand how they'd gotten it done...but they had. And, now it was time to make use of that immense destruction power.

Wave after wave of missiles blasted forward, as she watched on the display, line after line of massive warheads tearing through space at nearly 70g, heading right for the planet and its defenses. Even as each successive wave of deadly weapons spat forth from the vessels' magazines, she found herself surprised at the continued barrages. She knew just how many missiles the task force carried, but still, she couldn't quite reconcile with what she was seeing.

Thousands of gigatons were heading toward the planet and the massive array of orbital constructions surrounding it. An attack that large would pose a deadly danger even to fleet units, mobile ships able to conduct evasive maneuvers. Against stationary ground targets and satellites in set orbital patterns, it was Armageddon itself.

Strand didn't have a doubt the barrage would obliterate its targets, at least all those in orbit and on the planet's surface, and she was genuinely surprised the enemy had let the attackers get close enough to launch their bombardment. She imagined the thermonuclear fury, boiling oceans, great craters being gouged out of the soil and rock of the tortured world, earthquakes orders of magnitude beyond the greatest disasters in human history.

She also knew that none of that staggering power would destroy the production facility. Its massive particle acceleration chambers were almost certainly buried deep in the planet's crust, and she didn't have the slightest doubt that they were well-built, strong enough to endure the planet's natural seismic activity... and no doubt any surface bombardment as well.

The loss of the orbital and surface solar collectors would almost certainly reduce output, but the planet's extensive volcanic activity would still sustain a significant level of production in the deeply buried generating stations...and she didn't have a doubt there were also extensive stores of antimatter down there, the output of years of operation, buried kilometers beneath the surface in secure magnetic bottles, out of the reach of even Rivers' five hundred megaton "penetrator" bombs.

Strand turned and looked toward Hercule's station, rapping out a series of commands to her aide as she did. Her forces were at point blank range now, slowed to a crawl and trading deadly blows with the remaining First Imperium ships. The fight was still hot, but McDaid's attacks had broken the back of the enemy formation. She could see the fire of the First Imperium forces waning, their ships slowly failing, one after another falling silent...or losing containment and disappearing entirely, in the almost unimaginable fury of antimatter annihilation.

Hercule responded, following every tactical command, passing back acknowledgements, transmitting positional adjustments to ships of the task force. In every way, he confirmed the wisdom of her choice of him as her primary aide.

She leaned back and looked out over the display, her eyes moving from one of her ships to the next. It was time to finish off the enemy force, even as the last of Rivers' missiles pounded the surface of the planet.

* * *

The Fleet Intelligence reviewed the data from the remaining probes. The system's surveillance systems had been nearly wiped out, leaving only a scant view of the enemy forces closing on the planet. That was a status it would have viewed as alarming...had it not been part of the plan. The Regent had been quite clear. The enemy was to be allowed to close with the planet, even to devastate the orbital defenses and the surface installations. Even now, the enemy's nuclear warheads were obliterating the defense network, and warheads were raining down on the planet, obliterating everything on the surface.

The Intelligence had initially been unsure of the purpose in allowing such damage to be inflicted, but it had analyzed the Regent's plan, and it had gained comprehension. The primary mission was to lure the enemy fleet in, as close to the planet as possible before the final trap was sprung. The defense grid was bait, as were the installations on the surface. They were expendable. Only the underground operations, and the antimatter storage units, were to be defended at all costs. And, for all the fury of the enemy's bombardment, the subterranean installations had escaped all but minimal damage.

The Intelligence had watched the battle unfold, sent task forces to intercept the forward enemy line, all in accordance with the plan. It had watched as the enemy shattered the formations, and it had done nothing. The vessels destroyed had not been lost in vain. The humans suffered heavy losses as well, and many of their surviving ships were seriously damaged.

Normal tactics called for the Intelligence to dispatch reserves, to finish off the enemy's lead formations. But, the main human fleet was advancing now, just as the Regent had predicted, and the Intelligence followed its orders. It waited...waited for the enemy to close to the designated point, from which there could be no retreat. Then, it would spring the trap...it would attack with *all* its forces. The remnants of the shattered enemy advance guard could wait. The fleet could finish it after it had destroyed the main body of the human armada.

The Regent had been correct. The humans *had* lashed out, sent in a force to assault the planet. Now, their main forces were advancing, no doubt to renew the bombardment in what could only be a fruitless effort to destroy the deeply buried facilities. Let them come. Let them launch their missiles at the wasted surface of the planet. That was the Regent's plan. They would move forward, expend their ordnance, launch all their missiles. The planet's surface was already radioactive slag, and the protected chambers deep below would survive any surface assault.

The Intelligence monitored the data, waiting. It felt something akin to anticipation, even excitement. The destruction of the human fleet would be a major step toward the total defeat of the enemy. Without their fleet, the humans would be unable to slow the Regent's search activities. Their destruction would be inevitable. The Intelligence had done the calculations itself, reviewed the data on known human fleet operations. The projected time until discovery of the human homeworld ranged from eight of the enemy's months at a minimum, to nine years, seven weeks at a maximum. The Intelligence could wait; the Regent could wait. To Intelligences of their kind, nine human years was but a passing instant.

The Intelligence reviewed the vast armada of ships awaiting the final command. The forces were ready, each task force in formation, waiting only for the order to advance. Soon, it would be time. Soon, it would attack and destroy…

Wait…

Something was wrong. The enemy ships were decelerating.

That was not as expected. The humans were supposed to advance, to come closer to the planet, far enough into the system so that escape was impossible. They were still too close to their entry warp gate for the Intelligence to launch the final attack.

The Intelligence fed full power into its scanning devices. There was no doubt. The enemy *was* slowing, turning about. They appeared to be preparing to leave the system.

That couldn't be right. The humans were shrewd combatants, they couldn't possibly believe that they had completely destroyed the antimatter production facilities with their first attack. And, nothing short of the total destruction of antimatter production could justify the scope of the operation they had mounted.

The Intelligence analyzed possibilities…millions and millions of permutations in the merest fraction of a second. It reviewed data. The humans were communicating. It analyzed their encoded messages. The encryption was one the Regent had broken. The officers on the comm lines sounded scared. They spoke of flight, of escaping before the enemy could destroy them.

No, that wasn't possible. The biologics were inferior, but their warriors were usually steadfast. They would not retreat simply out of personal fear.

The communications were coming in from multiple locations…and from the vessel the Intelligence had identified as the human command ship. Not all the communications were in the broken code. The Intelligence had to sift through partial bits of information, and some of what was said was still a mystery.

But, there *was* concern...and fear. The human commander was expressing last minute doubts, concerned about risking the fleet. Worries that the Regent had positioned forces behind the planet.

Which, the Intelligence realized, was correct.

The Intelligence analyzed the situation, reviewed the data it had. The enemy was preparing to run...they expected the trap. The humans were skilled warriors, but they *were* subject to fear, to irrational actions. A decision had to be made.

The Intelligence considered, reviewed even more reams of data. Then it made a decision.

It issued its orders. All ships were to advance and pursue the enemy main force. The enemy fleet could not be allowed to escape. The Regent had allowed Planet Z to endure considerable damage to trap he enemy ships. To allow them to flee now would be a disaster.

The Intelligence considered the enemy advance guard. It had to send a second wave now to finish off the survivors, but most of the reserve ships would be sent to pursue the humans' main fleet...into the next system if need be, or farther. Wherever they might go, they would be destroyed. That was the Regent's command.

Perhaps they would even lead the Regent's fleets to their homeworld in their panicked attempt to escape.

* * *

"Contacts, Admiral. Enemy ships coming around from behind the planet and its two moons." A moment's pause. "They must have been maintaining position there to keep the moons between them and us."

How many? The words began as a spoken question, but they turned into a silent thought as Strand focused on the display and saw the answer for herself. It was full of small spheres, dozens—no, hundreds—of ships streaming around from the far sides of the two natural satellites. They were racing past the rapidly cooling plasmas and the clouds of radiation that were all that remained of the planet's defensive grid.

Strand had felt a momentary panic, a fear that the entire massive force was heading for her battered line of ships. But then she realized what was happening.

They're going for the main line.

For Erika.

She swallowed hard, her mind racing for options, trying to decide what to do. Her impulse was to advance, to hit the enemy fleet in the flank as it moved forward. But, her ships were still fighting the remnants of the task force that had opposed it. She couldn't order her battered ships to break off, to ignore the remaining First Imperium forces. But, if she didn't disengage now, her ships would never get to the enemy in time.

Stay focused…even if we go now, we won't get there…not quickly enough.

"Admiral, we're getting a signal from *Garret.* Tight beam laser transmission."

She hadn't been expecting anything from West, even with the new developments. The orders had been for strict radio silence between the two divisions of the fleet.

"On my channel, Commander."

"Admiral…there is no incoming message. Just a coded signal." There was a hint of confusion, then a short pause before Hercule continued. "The pulse was directed to *Midway*'s AI."

Strand turned and looked over toward her aide. "The AI?"

"Yes, Admiral. It's a command code override." Another pause. "The AI is now requesting you put your headset on. Apparently, there is a coded message for you stored in *Midway*'s banks."

Strand's face twisted in confusion. What kind of message was in her own flagship's AI without her knowledge?

She pulled on her headset, feeling a tightening in her stomach as she did.

The AI began almost immediately. "Admiral Strand, I have a decrypted message stored, and I have received command authorization to deliver it to you alone at this time."

Strand felt a rush of anger toward the machine. *Midway* was *her* ship…and it pissed her off having her own computer hold back information from her. "A message from where?"

"From Fleet Admiral West." The AI's voice showed no emotion, no apparent recognition at the implications of a message from the fleet commander, hidden in *Midway*'s memory banks.

Why would Erika hide a message for me on my own ship and not just tell me whatever she had to say?

Her mind swirled with confused thoughts...and then sudden realization. Her eyes darted to the display, to the First Imperium fleet closing on West's retreating forces.

She's drawing them away...

Then: *She planned this from the beginning!*

Strand grabbed the armrests of her chair as *Midway* shuddered from another hit...a reminder that her own force still had enemy ships to defeat. She looked down at her workstation screen, and again to the main display. Her ships were bearing down hard on the dwindling number of First Imperium survivors. She was close to victory...or what passed for victory. Her task force was gutted, its combat power a fraction of what it had been before the desperate struggle. She didn't have the strength to aid West's forces...and as she watched the wave of enemy ships still pouring out from behind the planet, she realized the rest of the fleet was doomed unless they were able to run for it.

Which was Erika's plan all along...

She swallowed once, hard, and then she finally spoke again to the AI. "Play decrypted message," she said softly. She was too deep in the system to run...but she found herself hoping West *would* take the rest of the fleet and escape. There was nothing to be gained by all of them dying.

The AI spoke briefly, and then Strand felt a wave of emotion as Erika West's voice filled her headset. "I'm sorry, Josie, that I didn't tell you the details of my plan. It wasn't lack of trust in you, but I believed you would carry out your part of the operation better if you didn't know everything." A short pause. "I also thought it would be easier for you this way. If my guess is correct, the enemy fleet—the *real* enemy fleet, not the diversionary force that moved against your ships—is now coming out from whatever place it was hiding, and hopefully moving toward my ships."

There was a pause, brief but with a heaviness of emotion Strand had rarely heard in West's usually cold demeanor. "That is what I hoped for, what I planned. Your ships are likely battered, damaged enough that the enemy will ignore you—or send a smaller force to finish you—while it seeks to destroy the main body. Whatever does come in your direction must be defeated… whatever it takes. That, I trust in your skill and ability."

Strand was trying to keep up with West's words, to understand what was happening.

"Remember, Josie, that was their plan all along…to use their antimatter planet as bait, to lure our fleet to its destruction. And, in that, they may yet succeed. It is my burden now, to make sure that doesn't happen…that they don't catch the rest of the fleet. Not yet."

Strand looked around as she listened, trying to retain at least some focus on the battle still raging about her ship.

"I am going to lead them out of the system, Josie. You can see that I stopped before getting too close to the planet, left myself enough room to escape the system…and I believe they will follow me. When they do, the Marines will land, hopefully unopposed, and they will launch their assault."

Strand was shocked at how much West had planned in advance, at the near-prescience the veteran admiral had displayed. Her eyes moved to the display, watching the enemy ships blasting out from the planet's orbit, heading right for the now-fleeing main formation.

Just as West had said they would.

"Josie, the Marines' assault is a longshot, an unimaginable struggle to gain access to the underground factory and find a way to destroy it. But, it is our only hope to cripple the Regent, to deprive its forces of their greatest advantage." A pause. "We both know, that if the Marines can even manage it, if they can somehow destroy the enemy facilities, their chances of escape are even more remote." Strand winced as she heard the sadness in West's voice. She felt it herself, and she understood how difficult it must have been for West to order the Marines into such a desperate attack.

Strand was grateful it hadn't been on her to issue that command—though she was fairly certain she would have given it if she'd had to. She was doubtful the Marines would be able to completely destroy the enemy base, but there was just no choice but to take any chance at all. Whatever happened, she couldn't imagine any way the deadly warriors could escape.

"You have to wait, Josie. You'll have to find a way to defeat any peripheral forces the enemy sends at you, and then you have to move in toward the planet. You have to give those Marines a chance...and retrieve them if they are able to escape." The transports bringing the grim fighters to the planet were configured for one-way use, Strand knew that much. They would enter the atmosphere and launch the Marines, and then their crews would eject before the battered ships descended and burned up during reentry. Strand realized her ships—whatever was left of them—would be the only chance the Marines had, the only potential ride back home.

In the miracle event that any of them made it off the planet, that is.

"Josie...no one else knows what I am planning. It will look like we are running, that we have abandoned you, the Marines... all our comrades to try to escape from an overpowering enemy attack. I almost decided to let you think that, to preserve the secrecy of my plan." A pause. "But I couldn't do that to you... and I didn't think I could fool you. You are the future of the navy, and if you return to Earth Two, you will command it one day...perhaps one day soon. You deserve to know exactly what I am doing."

Another pause. "All of what I am doing."

Strand's nerves were afire as she listened to West's words. Whatever the mysterious plan, the admiral had said one thing that was nothing but the truth. Josie Strand was incapable of believing that Erika West would run to save herself.

But, that didn't mean the First Imperium Intelligences wouldn't believe it.

Strand wondered, her mind racing for the next few seconds,

grasping for shreds of understanding, as West's fatigued and somber voice continued.

Strand continued to listen, and then, her mouth dropped open as West described the heart of her plan, all of it. Every crazy—perhaps brilliantly crazy—bit of it.

She stared straight ahead, the battle still going on all around banished now from her thoughts as she sat quietly, trying to comprehend what she had just heard, to make sense of it all. Then, she whispered softly, the only words that came to her mind.

"Oh my God…"

Chapter Twenty-Three

Flag Bridge, E2S Midway
System G48
Earth Two Date 02.16.43

Strand stared at the screen, watching as the entire bridge crew was doing, the black and empty display, showing the volume of space where, before, a First Imperium fleet had been deployed. That task force was gone now, replaced by naught but slowly dissipating plasmas and clouds of heavy radiation.

Her people had won the battle...the first phase of it, at least. But any feeling of joy she'd felt at victory drained quickly from her, washed away by Erika West's words, and by the new armada moving even now toward her ships.

Enemy vessels had poured out from behind the planet, dozens...no, hundreds. They were *still* streaming out, most of them blasting their engines hard, pursuing West's outnumbered and fleeing ships. It was an immense force, one she couldn't imagine West could defeat...unless the admiral's almost astonishingly audacious plan somehow succeeded. Strand's thoughts were with her commander, her friend...and the desperate, crazy scheme she'd devised. She'd never imagined Erika West would simply run, but now it bothered her that spacers in her fleet might think that. She couldn't expect anything else from them. They were exhausted, scared, facing another fight themselves...

185

and the legendary commander who'd led them there was blasting out of the system at full thrust.

But, she didn't have time for such things right now. She had her own problems. One of the enemy task forces had come out on a different vector…and it was heading straight for the battered ships of her line.

The sight of it hit her with despair, and for a moment, she sat, still, stunned, struggling against a wave of demoralization. She was still trying to comprehend the news West's signal had delivered to her, and now she had to deal with the need to rally her worn and depleted forces to face a fresh onslaught.

There's no way.

The enemy force was too large, her ships too battered, their munitions expended. She gave up, surrendered to despair.

But, only for an instant.

Then, her resolve returned, and strength flowed into her exhausted limbs. She wasn't sure where it came from, what reservoir of stubbornness she'd found deep in herself, but she suddenly knew one thing. She wasn't going to let the Regent's homicidal computers win. Not while she still drew breath in her lungs.

"Alright, Commander…we've got…" She paused and did a quick calculation from the data on the display. "Twenty-two minutes before they're here. Let's get damage control teams at work now. I want every weapon we've got left ready for action… and I want new nav plans for evasive maneuvers, completely fresh ones. We're not done yet."

"Very well," Hercule answered, after a brief pause. He sounded shaken, but Strand was confident he would get the job done.

All of her people would.

Even those who'd already taken the worst losses…

"Get me Commodore McDaid."

A brief delay. "On your line, Admiral."

"Cooper…what can I say? Your people covered themselves in glory." The congratulations seemed the least she could offer…and also somehow wrong after the cost McDaid's squadrons had paid. *We see a successful attack, but no doubt, you see a third of your people getting killed doing it…*

She had some hope the toll had actually been just a bit less. There were probably pilots out there who'd ejected. They'd be sitting in their lifepods waiting to see if the battle was won or lost…if they had a chance at rescue, or if their fate was to freeze or suffocate, alone in the depths of space.

"Thank you, Admiral. Your words are appreciated…by all my pilots."

She felt as though she was going to choke on the next words out of her mouth. "Cooper…I need you to get your people back aboard now. Land everyone on the closest mothership and get those birds refueled and rearmed." She hesitated. "We're not done here…not yet."

"Understood, Admiral. We're on our way." There wasn't a hint of resentment, or even demoralization in McDaid's voice. She was proud of the pilot, and of all his people, but he'd never know how his steadfastness hit her, the guilt it stirred inside, knowing she was going to send his exhausted pilots back out, without rest, in partially replenished ships.

She turned toward the tactical station. "Alright, Henri…" She stared at Hercule, her eyes as cold as space. "Let's get ready for the next round."

* * *

West sat in her command chair, silent, without a word of explanation to the officers and spacers all around her on *Garret*'s flag bridge. The admiral could only imagine what her people were thinking as they sat, enduring the residual force from the engines' massive thrust as it overwhelmed the dampeners. They'd come all the way to the G48 system…and now they were running.

Worse, they were fleeing and leaving behind their comrades. Strand and her task force, who'd fought everything the enemy had thrown at them. Rivers and his missiles ships…no one in the fleet believed the bombardments had completely destroyed the enemy base, but the courageous crews had brought their ships in against all the odds, and they'd blasted the surface of the planet to oblivion.

And, now, the Marines were going in, their ships turned into expendable delivery vehicles, their naval crews left to orbit the planet in escape pods…a desperate situation that could only look appealing in comparison to the hopeless hell into which she'd sent the Marines themselves.

All while she ordered her own task force, the strongest one in the fleet, to run the instant the enemy unleashed its full strength in her direction. Part of her was surprised her people hadn't mutinied. She wondered how much of that was the remnants of their eroding faith in her and how much was their own relief at a chance to escape certain death. West didn't know what her crew had expected to find in G48, how much strength they'd imagined the enemy would have waiting for them.

But Erika West had. And, the vast armada pursuing her ships was exactly what she'd expected.

Her fleet couldn't defeat that force, not then, not in G48. There was no choice but to flee, to pull out what she could of the fleet and make a mad dash for home.

At least that's what she hoped a sophisticated machine mind would determine.

"We're coming up on the warp gate, Admiral." West could tell Sampson was confused, that the officer wasn't ready to believe West would turn and run to save herself. She wasn't sure it mattered, but it pleased her anyway. Avery Sampson might be the only one not ready to throw her out the airlock long before the rest of them knew what was really going on.

And, maybe even after that…once they knew what she was leading them into. They might decide that running away wasn't so bad.

The entire operation to G48, the effort to damage or destroy enemy antimatter production, had been a desperate, half-crazed idea from the beginning. But West's actual plan was even crazier…and now it was time for her to make it work.

"All ships…maintain full thrust. The fleet will transit at

once."

*   *   *

Cameron sat, his armor bolted into the lander, immobile, waiting. His screen was blank, and the only thing he could see was the polished inside of his helmet. But, he knew what lay around him, thirty-nine other Marines, each equipped as he was, sitting quietly, eyes closed gently or staring at the same view he was. And, outside the sleek landing ship, *Leatherneck*'s single large launch bay, its great girders supporting an open area with five identical landing craft lined up next to Cameron's.

His Marines were ready, he was sure of that. A doubt or two had floated around his thoughts, concerns that he was believing more in old Marine lore than in a realistic assessment of his people. They were well-trained, there was no doubt of that, but few of them had seen real action. The Pilgrims who'd been the Earth Two Corps' real combat veterans were mostly gone now, retired from active duty. A few remained, mostly officers at the highest levels…and also the occasional career NCO, all grit and toughness, and Marine through and through. *They* were combat veterans, but Cameron knew he didn't have enough of them to make a difference. The battle to come—and he understood just how important it was—would be won or lost by his new generation of Marines, Tanks, mostly, but also NBs, born on Earth Two. They would fight, he was sure of that.

He just wasn't sure they could win this time.

He'd seen action against First Imperium warbots twice, both times in small actions where his Marines had greatly outnumbered their enemies. He still had nightmares of the great killing machines.

He'd also come close to battle against the bots the Mules had created twelve years earlier, when he was a junior officer. That fight had been avoided, at what had seemed at the time, the last second. Cameron had always been sympathetic to the Mules and their struggle to end the Prohibition, but since that day he'd carried a resentment against the Hybrids, too. Their creations were far too much like mankind's deadly enemy, and despite his best efforts, he'd never managed to get completely past that.

The ship shook hard, and Cameron's body slammed forward into the front of his armor. The internal padding absorbed most of the force, but he still felt the shock it, and it roused him from his thoughts.

"Attention Marines…we're entering low orbit and approaching the atmosphere. We'll be taking you deeper than usual for a drop before we launch your landers. We're doing everything we can to get you as close to our estimates on the enemy facility, but once you're out, you're on your own. Launch in one hundred-thirty-five seconds."

Cameron knew the plan well enough. Gaining total control over the space around a planet was job one for any well-planned ground assault. Or, so Cameron had been trained. The truth was, it had been more than forty years since Marines hit a hostile world in a major attack, and most of what they *knew* about how to do it was largely hearsay passed on from the past generation of warriors.

It didn't matter now anyway. This wasn't a typical planetary assault, and it wasn't a normal enemy. There was no way to be sure what fleets and weapons the First Imperium had hidden around the planet…and Cameron's attack force was laughably small to invade a world.

No, it was a raid, a desperate attempt to find and destroy the enemy's antimatter production operation. If the Marines couldn't find it, they would fail. If they located it, but couldn't reach it in its deep subterranean chambers, they would fail. If the legions of warbots no doubt defending the base were able to hold them back, they would fail.

And, even if they didn't fail, Cameron knew the odds of getting his people back to the surface and off the planet were…for lack of a better and more descriptive term, poor.

The ship shook again, harder this time, and Cameron knew they'd entered the upper layers of the atmosphere. *Leatherneck* hadn't been built for operations in such low orbit, and he suspected the ship was taking it pretty hard as it continued to descend. His Marines would blast out in their landers, and the skeleton naval crews would eject in their lifepods—which should have just enough thrust to get them back to orbit—but *Leatherneck* and her eleven sister-ships were on a one-way mission.

Who the hell am I kidding…we're on a one-way mission, too…

Cameron felt the heaviness of his suit vanish, as his circuits fed power from the nuclear reactor on his back to the servo-mechanicals of his suit. He'd been amazed since the first day he'd stepped into combat armor at how light it felt when the power was flowing. He knew a suited-up Marine loomed large and bulky to the eye, but he remembered the exercises from his Academy days, handing eggs back and forth without breaking them and other routines of that sort.

A Marine could do delicate work in a suit, but that didn't lessen the feeling of power Cameron felt. He was scared, and he didn't really believe any of his people would survive what they were about to begin…but, those feelings drifted to the side of his mind as he felt the massive strength of his armored form and began to check off the weapons systems built in to the killing machine he wore.

"Alright, Marines…you've got two minutes, so don't waste it. Check your power and weapons systems. If you don't, and your suit malfunctions once we're down there, don't come crying to me." It all sounded good, but it was bullshit, too, a scheme to keep his Marines focused. There wasn't a damned thing he could do if one of his people found a malfunction, anyway…not now.

And, besides, Brigadier General Devon Cameron would never abandon one of his own…however much the stupid fool got himself into trouble.

Cameron took his own advice, and he ran a quick check of his own gear.

Everything checked out. He was ready. As ready as anyone could be for a mission like this one.

He listened to the next warning from the ship's captain…at thirty seconds. Then, he gritted his teeth, waiting for the hard jerk he knew would accompany the lander's release into the open atmosphere.

Chapter Twenty-Four

Cutter Research Compound (Home of the Mules)
Ten Kilometers West of Victory City, Earth Two
Earth Two Date 02.17.43

"Every Plague patient brought here has responded brilliantly to the treatment. It is, of course, too early to pronounce that all genetic lines will recover equally well, but the signs are extremely encouraging."

Achilles stood and listened as Themistocles reported on the progress of the program. The effective leader of the Mules had just donated his own blood, along with Callisto and half a dozen others whom Achilles had trusted enough to include. He didn't like hiding anything from the rest of the Mules, but he was determined to be careful. Max Harmon had agreed to his request—and sworn his own secrecy—and, as far as Achilles was concerned, relying on the president was as much risk as he was willing to take, at least until he had acceptable security precautions in place.

"You have exceeded even your own lofty standards, my friend. The Plague has been a scourge on the Tanks, and now, future classes of quickenings will be free of the fear of painful death casting a shadow over them.

And, as long as we keep things quiet, we will be okay…at least for a while.

Achilles wasn't worried about sick Tanks or their loved ones storming the compound, crazed for precious Mule blood. The treatment required to save the life of a Plague victim took only a small amount of the serum created from the samples. Achilles knew the Mules were more than willing to provide what was needed on a voluntary basis.

No, that wasn't the real problem. But, the cellular regeneration procedure had other applications, ones Themistocles had barely begun to explore. Treatments for brain-damaged patients and coma victims, to begin with, but the truly dangerous area was in general cell enhancements. Achilles wasn't primarily a medical researcher, as Themistocles was, but he didn't have any trouble seeing the potential for increasing lifespans…possibly substantially.

Possibly indefinitely.

Immortality wasn't something new to the Mules' thought process. They'd long wondered how long their own lifespans might extend, and to date, no signs of any age-related degradation had ever been detected, though the first group of Hybrids was now in their forties. Themistocles had probably come closest to gathering some kind of hard data several years before, and he and Achilles had agreed they would keep the findings to themselves for the near future, at least. It wasn't going to do anything to help quell the Normals' fear of the Mules by telling them the Hybrids might well live for a millennium, or even longer.

Max Harmon had agreed completely with Achilles concerns. The president had his hands full already dealing with terrorist incidents and civil disturbances. The last thing he needed to see now was a series of riots calling for immortality treatments that didn't even exist yet beyond theories and tentative formulas.

Achilles knew Harmon could crush any resistance from the fringe groups. He had the Marines firmly on his side, at least for the time being, and he had the Mules as well. Certainly, with regard to keeping control over groups promoting Natural Borns over the various clones that now made up more than half of Earth Two's population, he had enough allies. But, Harmon had always been hesitant to use naked force…at least he had until the most recent attack.

Achilles didn't question Harmon's increased use of sanctions, but he wondered if it would help or hurt the general situation. To the extent Earth Two's president appeared to be beholden to the Mules, it would only serve to aid the cause of the various NB groups. The Tank genetic lines had been honed over the years, and there was little argument to be made that even the clones quickened from one hundred percent human DNA now outperformed their naturally-born counterparts by considerable margins. The Tanks dominated the Marine Corps, including now, many of the moderate-high rank levels that had eluded them in the early years…and the clones were represented roughly equally with the NBs in the navy.

None of that even took into account the fear of the Mules, also clones of a sort, of course. The Hybrids were responsible for perhaps ninety percent of the scientific breakthroughs of the past twenty years or more. Achilles had seen some shows of gratitude from the population for what his people had done to keep Earth Two safe, but far more displays of fear and resentment. He didn't think most Natural Borns supported terrorist attacks, certainly not when almost half of the victims had been NBs themselves, but he suspected Harmon would see some blowback from appearing to be on the "side" of the clones.

Achilles extended his arm, angling his head in a gesture for Themistocles to follow him. He walked off to a small alcove on the side of the room. "Were you able to begin treatments on Admiral Frette?" Achilles had always liked the wounded naval officer, and he genuinely wanted to help her. He also knew Frette was one of Harmon's closest friends, and keeping the president on their side was always a good idea.

"I completed a comprehensive analysis of all damage to her spine and cerebral cortex. There is considerable cellular degradation. It is no wonder none of the conventional treatments have been effective. I administered the first series of treatments, two days ago, and I am optimistic. There was marked improvement within just the first few hours. It is too early to make any significant pronouncements, but things are going as well as we could have hoped."

"That is very good news, my friend." Achilles was glad for Frette, hopeful that the admiral would indeed recover, at least partially, from her long ordeal…but that didn't stop the nagging at the back of his mind. Success in repairing damage of the type Frette had sustained would almost certainly indicate that Themistocles' treatment could indeed reverse the effects of aging.

That would be a wonder…and a terrible danger as well.

* * *

"Second platoon…forward!"

"Fourth platoon in position, sir."

"We're going in now."

Frasier listened to the comm chatter between the platoons in the field. He had over three hundred Marines active in Victory City at that moment, the cream of the Corps still left on Earth Two after Cameron's strike force had departed. His strike teams were hitting six different locations simultaneously, everywhere he'd uncovered any signs of suspicious activity.

He'd been reluctant to move forward so aggressively, but President Harmon's orders had been clear…act immediately, even on unconfirmed suspicions. Frasier was uncomfortable, and he knew the likelihood was, some innocents would be gathered up along with the guilty parties, that some might even be killed. He'd explained that to Harmon, though he'd realized the president had been as aware of that as he had. The orders were unchanged. Move on everything. At once.

Frasier had expected trouble, but so far there had been no resistance of note. His Marines weren't subtle investigators, and he had to believe those he was after knew he was coming. He'd just started to rethink his pessimistic expectations when he heard gunfire over the comm.

His impulse was to demand reports, at once. But, he was a combat veteran, and he knew the last thing the Marines onsite needed was being distracted by calls for updates from brass well up the line. He'd briefed his officers and non-coms, and they all knew what to do. Now, he had to let them do it.

Besides, he had his own job to do.

"Alright…first squad, take position out here. Second…down the hallway. I want you covering the back exit in thirty seconds." He paused and watched as the Marines turned and followed his orders, moving with perfect precision. Then he turned. "Third squad…we're going in."

Frasier was about to give the command override, and order the sector AI to open the hatch, but the lieutenant at the head of the squad stepped forward, followed by the first two Marines in the column. "Please, General…let us go in first."

Frasier felt a tinge of resentment, and he almost snapped an order for the junior officer to step back. But, he realized the lieutenant was right. He had no place being the first one in, not when he was in command of the entire Corps, not to mention the other half dozen operations now underway.

He nodded to the lieutenant and then, after confirming the Marines were ready, he issued the order…and the hatch swung open.

The Marines charged inside, shouting for the occupants of the large room to stay still. Frasier's gut was twisted tight, waiting for the sound of shooting, not on the tinny speaker of his comm unit, but from just beyond the door, from a place where two dozen people—as far as he knew, all but one of them innocent—worked. But there was nothing.

He ducked through the door himself, right on the heels of the last Marine.

There were loud shrieks, and perhaps half of those present ducked down under their desks, while the others froze where they were.

All save for one.

A man at the far side of the forward bank of workstations leapt up from his chair, running for the back entrance. He was quick, and the Marines were reluctant to open fire with so many innocent civilians in the room. He had just about reached the door when it opened, revealing the huge bulk of an armored

Marine in the doorway.

The fleeing man scrambled to a halt and turned frantically, looking for any other way to escape. The room was large, but with Marines pouring through both entrances, there was nowhere else to go. He ran, getting four or five steps before the lead Marine behind him caught up and swung an armored fist, knocking the fugitive from his feet and sending him careening into the front side of the row of workstations. He landed with a sickening crash that left little doubt he had broken more than one bone.

"Everybody, just stay where you are. You will all be fine. We are here to arrest a terrorist, and if the rest of you remain calm, we can do what we came for and leave." It wasn't that simple, of course. He had reserve columns waiting outside, and the rest of those present faced a considerable round of questioning before they would be allowed to leave.

Frasier had been a Marine his entire life, and he was accustomed to displays of force. Still, he had to imagine the current display was an upsetting one to civilians who spent all day supervising security cameras and compiling mostly routine reports. He tried to keep his voice as calm and reassuring as he could, though he realized that was a lot to expect from a tone when the room was filled with combat-equipped Marines bristling with enough weapons to level most of Victory City.

He looked around the room, anxious about keeping the occupants quiet and under control. His Marines were hitting targets all over the city, rounding up suspected terrorist cells. Many of those operations had turned into outright firefights, and he was determined to keep that from happening in the main security office. It was embarrassing enough to President Harmon that a member of a fringe group had managed to get a position monitoring a surveillance station. The last thing he wanted to do was add a few innocent victims to the already sorry situation. He'd been clear to his Marines about that, but he was still edgy. There could be another infiltrator he didn't know about…or the soon to be prisoner could pull out a weapon and start shooting.

That, at least he could prevent.

"Restrain him…now. Search for any weapons or communications devices…on him or somewhere else in the room."

He felt a little more relaxed once the prisoner was firmly held in two sets of armor-clad arms. It would have taken the strength of an industrial press to wriggle free, or even to grab a hidden weapon.

"Again, everyone…I am sorry for this upsetting interruption. Just remain in your seats for a few more minutes, and we will be finished and out of here. We'll just need you all to remain and answer a few questions now…"

He turned and gestured for the Marines to drag the prisoner toward the rear door. The he waved to the rest of his armored warriors, and they filed out into the hall, followed, finally, by Frasier himself, who stopped and watched the interrogation teams begin to file in.

*   *   *

"I'm just not sure…" Max Harmon was indecisive, uncharacteristically so. He'd fought desperate battles, done what he'd had to do, even seized power when he felt there had been no alternative. And, he'd ordered the Marines out into the streets, to find those guilty of the recent attacks, and to drag them to the harsh justice he had promised. But, he found actually ordering the executions of several dozen Earth Two civilians to be extremely difficult.

"I understand it is unpleasant, sir…but there is no doubt. These prisoners are all responsible, in varying degrees, for what happened. They have the blood of truly innocent civilians on their hands. They must pay the price." For all his Marine toughness, Connor Frasier had never seemed brutal or bloodthirsty, but now, there wasn't a doubt evident in his words. Few of Harmon's insiders had seen the victims of the attacks more closely than Frasier.

"Varying degrees, Connor. I am not saying those who conceived of the plan, those who perpetrated it, are not guilty…that they do not deserve to die. But, what about those who were on the fringes, people driven to meetings by misguided, but genuine, fears of unlimited numbers of clones? My God, Connor, three of the prisoners are sixteen years old! Yes, they were foolish. Their judgment was exceedingly poor. But, do they deserve to die for that?"

"Did the people in the promenade deserve to die? The children who were killed? I was there, Mr. President. I saw the bodies."

"But without trials? Can I just issue an order and have them dragged up against a wall?"

"Of course, sir. That was the point of the coup twelve years ago, wasn't it? Your word is law. I appreciate that you have not abused that over the years, but this is a time for firm leadership."

"For brutality, you mean?"

Frasier shook his head, but he didn't answer right away. Then he said, "Sir…in a different situation, if we were at peace, if civil disturbances were our only danger, perhaps then it would make sense to dissect the involvement of each of the prisoners, conduct long investigations and endless trials. But, you are well aware what is happening out there. For all we know, the entire fleet could already be lost. The enemy could find us almost any time. We don't have the resources and the time to waste on pointless internal conflicts. You have to stop it now."

"Crush the resistance, you mean. Instill fear in those who oppose me?"

"Yes…crush them." Mariko Fujin had been sitting quietly, but now she spoke, and her voice was as cold as granite. "Line every one of them up against a wall, and shoot them. You can waste your pity on the young terrorists, wonder if they are as guilty as the others…but mine is reserved for the parents of those dead children, for all our civilians who were killed not in war, not fighting the First Imperium, but out in the city shopping or going to get something to eat. Terrorists are vial scum in any circumstances…to do this when our fleet is away on a desperate mission, probably fighting against overwhelming odds even as we speak, it demands a harsh response. And an immediate one."

"So, you want me to abandon efforts to reason with people who disagree? You want me to rule with fear?"

Fujin didn't move. She didn't flinch. She just looked right at her husband and replied with a single word.

"Yes."

Chapter Twenty-Five

Landing Zone Red Fist
Planet G48-II
Earth Two Date 02.17.43

Cameron had read about hell. He'd even studied some of the old religious texts, intrigued in many ways by the belief structures that had shaped human history. But, he'd never imagined anything as utterly horrific as the vista that stretched out before him.

The planet had been a nightmare to begin with, the heat, just above the boiling point of water, far down on the list of items that would kill unprotected humans. Normal radiation levels were at least twice lethal readings, and the atmosphere was a thick and toxic brew of sulfuric acid mixed with other noxious chemicals. It was almost as though some storyteller had created it, designed it to evoke the worst nightmares imaginable.

And, that had been the planet before Rivers's ships obliterated the surface with thousands of gigatons of the heavy nuclear warheads...and increased the radiation levels a hundredfold in some spots.

The terrain was torn open, massive kilometers-wide craters scarring the surface where the great warheads had detonated. The toxic clouds were laden now with particles of radioactive dust, blown up into the heavy clouds by the titanic explosions.

Rivers of still-molten lava flowed into the low spots, filling the great gouges in the ground with eerie glowing pools, slowly-solidifying back into dark gray rock.

Cameron moved his arm, his hand clapping down on the outside of his armor. He was a career Marine, and he'd long considered his fighting suit almost a part of his body. But, now, he suspected his life expectancy without the heavy armor's protection would be something like ten seconds.

Maybe twenty, if he got really lucky.

And, it would be an almost unimaginably unpleasant twenty seconds.

"Alright, let's get formed up. We came here to do a job." There wasn't any time to waste. The only thing the Marines had going for them was the hope that the enemy hadn't guessed ahead of time they'd be crazy enough to put ground troops on the planet. But, that surprise—if it had been a surprise—was gone now, and giving the First Imperium defenders time to react could only throw away what little chance his people had at success.

"Move it…now!" His tone was harsh, demanding. There was another reason not to wait. He couldn't even imagine what the hellish panorama was doing to morale…and that could only get worse if he let his Marines stand around and really think about what they were about to do. "Scanner teams…deploy. I want the best route underground found…and I mean now!"

"Yes, sir," came the first response, followed almost instantly by a series of other acknowledgments. He saw his Marines setting out in all directions, platoons forming up in defensive lines, and pickets moving forward. They had some idea where to look, all the data the full scanner suites of the landing ships had been able to provide, but Cameron knew it was little more than guess-work. But, tons and tons of antimatter wasn't an easy thing to hide, and once his teams got their gear operational, he was sure they'd pick up the readings they needed. Then, it would just be a matter of triangulation…and finding a way down kilometers below the surface.

He just didn't know if they'd finish before the enemy move

bots up to the surface and hit his people in their camp, but he was going to make sure he was ready if they did. He turned and watched a group of Marines digging a trench of sorts in the black, rocky ground...and then he went over to direct their efforts personally.

His gut told him his small army was going to have a hell of a fight on the surface before they even got a chance to get underground.

And, he was going to make damned sure they were ready for it.

*　*　*

"Novas, on me. We're going in on that big bastard, and we're going to blow it to hell!" McDaid was exhausted, his chest aching from the g forces his wild maneuvers had pulled. But none of that mattered, not now. There had only been one Leviathan in the task force moving against Strand's ships, and he'd sent half his remaining fighters against the superdreadnought. The enormous ship had been untouched as it approached missile range, and McDaid had sent his first wave in just as the vessel was launching its long-range ordnance.

The fighters had planted close to a dozen of their small nuclear warheads into the target, or just around it. McDaid had watched as the fury of the twenty kiloton explosions tore into great sections of the hull, blasting tons of the molten debris out into space.

The ship had shuddered, as one of its reactors failed, followed by another. It's thrust had dropped by about fifty percent, and dozens, if not hundreds, of missiles got stuck in their launch tubes. The first attack had been an enormous success, but for all the damage his vanguard had done, McDaid knew the ship remained twenty million tons of floating death. Even down two reactors and bleeding atmosphere, the Leviathan would rip into Strand's wounded ships as soon as it entered energy weapons range...which was longer for it than anything the Earth Two admiral had in her line.

And, McDaid had no intention of letting that happen.

He'd lost ten birds already, on top of the casualties from the first sortie, but none of that mattered, not now. The main fleet had already withdrawn, followed by an enemy force vaster than anything McDaid had ever seen. Strand's ships were all that remained in the system…the only places his fighters could land. That made it easier to fight like banshees, to ignore personal fear. If the fleet's battleships were destroyed, his pilots were all dead anyway.

And, if death was to be their fate, he was damned sure they were going to face it taking those cursed machines to hell instead of freezing to death in powerless cockpits.

He angled his throttle, bringing his fighter toward the Leviathan. He'd led the first strike in, and he'd planted two warheads himself. He didn't have a bomb left on his bird, nothing but a pair of lasers barely strong enough to scratch the meters deep armor of the great super-battleship. But he'd held the Novas back in reserve, and now it was time for his crack squadron to strike. And, missiles or not, he'd be damned if they were going in without him.

"Stay tight, Novas…let's see if we can't drop all these bombs right on top of each other." McDaid wasn't sure if his second attack, even with his elite veterans, could do enough damage to destroy the Leviathan, but he was going to see to it that the hulking vessel was as close to a pile of scrap and radioactive slag as possible when it reached Strand's ships.

McDaid could hear the chatter between the Novas, and he allowed himself a tiny smile at the level of their morale. They all knew how dire things were…but none of them seemed to let that affect them at all. He knew they were all scared, but every one of them had put the fear in its place, and now they were moving forward, relentless, merciless, about to show the First Imperium what a bunch of 'inferior' biologics could do.

McDaid watched as the ship grew on his scanners, almost replaying the scene of fifteen minutes before. He'd ordered the rest of the first strike back to their base ships to land and rearm for yet another sortie…assuming, of course, any of the battleships had functioning landing bays when they got there. Now, he was coming in hot yet again, dodging the heavy defensive fire that had already claimed two of his Novas.

He could feel the sweat pooling on his neck, running down his back. McDaid wasn't fearless, far from it. He was scared to death, even more now, taking his second run through the Leviathan's deadly gauntlet. But, there was no time to think of that now. He was here for his people, for the Novas...to give them the example they needed, as they swooped in like avenging angels, determined to blow the immense First Imperium ship to atoms.

McDaid hit his thrusters again, driven by an almost random bit of intuition. His eyes flashed to the screen for an instant... and then back again as he realized a shot had missed him by less than ten meters. He could feel the hair on his body tingling with static electricity, and seconds later, a series of overloads filled his cockpit with sparks.

His arm shook loose from the throttle as he felt a series of shocks, and then he took a deep breath and struggled to regain his focus. He swung his other arm around, grabbing the controls, keeping the ship on target. The range display dropped under ten thousand kilometers, and a quick glance confirmed that the rest of Nova squadron was right behind.

He stared straight ahead, feeling a passing shiver at how close that last shot had come. He turned back to the scanner to check on the Novas' formation again...but his eyes never made it.

He never saw the shot that vaporized his fighter.

* * *

No!

Strand was watching the display when she lost track of McDaid's ship. She'd almost ordered the fighter commander to return to base, to let the armed fighters go in and not to risk himself again when he didn't have enough firepower to accomplish anything. But she'd remained silent...and now she wanted to throw up.

Her eyes darted around the display, and then she turned toward her own workstation screen, her fingers frantically moving across the surface, desperately looking for some sign of Cooper McDaid's fighter. But there was nothing.

Nothing but a small energy spike that told her all she needed to know.

She'd known McDaid for years now, and she'd genuinely liked him…and she couldn't put into rational thoughts just how much his efforts had done to give her fleet a chance at victory. She knew war had its costs, and sometimes they struck close to home, and she struggled to control her pain, maintain her focus. Still, a single tear escaped her eye, making it halfway down her cheek before she wiped it away.

She'd been counting on McDaid. Her ships were already engaged with the leading wave of enemy vessels. They were holding their own, but they were outnumbered…and more First Imperium ships were moving forward. Despite her best efforts to analyze the two forces, she just didn't know if her people could prevail. It seemed like a coin toss to her.

Or worse now, without McDaid.

Then, she saw it. The fighters of Nova squadron. There hadn't been a word on the comm, not a whimper of sorrow nor a shout of rage. But, not one of those vessels veered off from the course they'd been following behind McDaid. Another one took a hit, spinning out of control for a few seconds before its reactor blew. Then a second, obliterated by a direct hit.

But, the others survived, and they closed, relentlessly. Strand watched in amazement as McDaid's people drove directly toward the Leviathan, ignoring the incoming fire, holding their missiles as the range dropped below five hundred kilometers.

Three hundred.

She felt the urge to close her eyes, not to watch as the ships impacted with the great battleship, but then the fighters launched, one after another in rapid succession, before pulling up and missing the hulking behemoth by less than ten klicks.

She sat still for a moment, stunned, watching as warhead after warhead slammed into the First Imperium ship. She was too close to see the actual fury of the explosions and the damage they inflicted, but the energy readings told the story.

The Leviathan shuddered, and its engines halted completely. The blasts from the impacting missiles gave way to a second round, internal explosions now, as the stricken ship began to tear away at itself. Strand could imagine what was happening in the endless halls of the battleship, as system after system overloaded, adding to the deadly chain reaction.

She knew that the middle of the ship would be the most protected area, the massive armor plating of the central core shielding the magnetic bottles that held the ship's store of antimatter fuel. Whole chunks of the vessel had been blown away now, and power levels had dropped precipitously. But, the death struggle continued, even as *Midway* shook from another hit. Strand's ship had been fighting two First Imperium cruisers. One was gutted now, a silent, broken hulk…but the other maintained its fire, even as Strand's attention was riveted to the agonies of the dying Leviathan.

Then, it happened. Even as she was watching the display, the already elevated energy levels went off the charts. The AI hadn't updated the image yet, but Strand knew as soon as she saw those numbers.

The Leviathan had lost containment. The antimatter at its core had annihilated, vaporizing every millimeter of the great ship.

Strand felt a burst of energy, and her confidence soared. Her people still had one hell of a fight on their hands…but now, for the first time, she believed they would win, that their victory was more than a coin toss.

More than that…they had a reason to win, one more driving force to push them harder. Cooper McDaid had given all he could to achieve the victory. His pilots had followed him.

Now it was time for the fleet to honor the lost hero.

"Commander…all ships are to close at full thrust. It's time to finish this."

Chapter Twenty-Six

Flag Bridge, E2S Garret
F-76 System
Earth Two Date 02.24.43

West sat quietly in her office. She'd always been an active person, her energy levels high, ready to face whatever threat presented itself. But, now she was facing the thing that was hardest for her. Waiting.

It was hard enough for her to deal with endless days and hours, but she'd found it difficult to endure the aching slowness of the clock, while the eyes of her people bored into her. They still thought she'd run from the enemy, that her nerve had failed her, and she'd fled, leaving Strand's people and the Marines behind. West had never allowed herself to care much what people thought of her, but it was too much this time. The image her spacers had was as close to opposite who she was as it was possible to come. Erika West knew she'd made mistakes, that her orders had sometimes been cold and callous, focused entirely on results, and perhaps less on the human cost than they should have been.

But, she'd never run from anything in her life.

Until now. She'd been spending more and more time in her office behind the bridge. She'd surprised herself at the solace the closed hatch provided…and just how much she needed it.

She knew not all of her people believed she'd broken. Some—especially among the few pilgrims in the fleet's ranks—no doubt suspected she had some kind of plan. Others, perhaps, had paid attention to where the fleet was going, or more accurately, to where it was not going. She'd done everything possible to keep the fleet's nav data classified at the top command level, but it was hard to hide the fact that, wherever the fleet was going, it wasn't Earth Two.

West would drive her fleet deep into the galactic core before she would lead the enemy to Earth Two.

She took a deep breath, glancing back at the chronometer, stunned almost to disbelief that less than four minutes had elapsed since the last time she'd checked.

She turned and looked over at the screen on her desk, her fingers moving across it, bringing up the latest scanner reports. The enemy was following her fleet, of course. She'd done everything possible to make it look like the whole thing had been a panicked rout, that she and her people had reached the limits of their endurance, that they had abandoned caution and were fleeing for something that promised safety.

She didn't know if the First Imperium intelligences believed she was heading to Earth Two…or if they just intended to follow her fleet and see where it went. West knew well enough, she couldn't go on forever without returning to base and replenishing her forces. And, there was only one base this side of the Barrier large enough to support her fleet.

The one place she couldn't go…not while those enemy ships were on her tail.

That's why she was going to destroy them.

She was going to try, at least. Her plan was detailed, and it made sense, at least as much sense as anything did in the current circumstances. But, she couldn't even guess if it would actually work. Would the enemy continue to follow her, hoping to find Earth Two…or would they attack before she'd led them to the place where she wanted to fight them? Would they break off, give up on chasing the fleet and return to G48? That, at least, she didn't think was likely. She'd left Strand's people there, and the Marines…but she was pretty sure the main enemy fleet didn't know she had landed ground forces on the planet.

Unless some word reached the enemy fleet, some kind of warning about the Marine attack. Would the enemy break off then? Or would they discount the chance of such an attack succeeding and ignore it?

Or did the forces they left behind defeat Josie…did they wipe out her fleet and take the Marines down before they'd even landed?

She didn't believe that. She wanted to think it was because of her analysis of the situation…or because of faith in Strand.

But, she was concerned she was just believing what she wanted to believe, what she *had* to believe.

She pushed the doubts aside. There was nothing she could do about any of it now. The die was well and truly cast. It was too late to go back, to fight a probably hopeless battle in G48. If she'd lured enough of the enemy forces from that system maybe—just maybe—she'd opened things up for the Marines to get down to the surface. Their mission seemed pretty hopeless anyway, but West remembered Elias Holm and Erik Cain. She'd long ago learned not to bet against the Marines, and she hoped Cameron and his warriors had enough of the spirit of those who'd come before them to do what she needed them to do.

Staying wouldn't have accomplished anything anyway. The massive force in pursuit of her fleet was too strong. Even if she'd stayed, if her forces had linked up with Strand's, they wouldn't have had a chance. That was the enemy's trap, the one she'd expected.

And, this was her answer to it.

She moved her hands over the display, sliding the long-range map. Another six jumps. Six more systems. Assuming the enemy continued to follow and didn't just blast their superior thrusters and close before she got there.

Erika West had been through countless trials, but this was the most difficult. Her people had always considered her hard, unyielding…but this was the first time a significant number of them actually despised her, blamed her for cowardice. She'd known that would happen, of course, but she'd underestimated just how deeply it would cut at her. She had too much to consider…tactics, timing, the overall campaign. But, she found herself coming back again and again to thoughts about her crew, about what they were thinking.

The AI interrupted her. "Admiral…Commander Sampson is at the door requesting entry."

Her stomach tightened. Was something wrong? Was the enemy closing?

No…Avery wouldn't waste time walking back here if there was an emergency…she'd just call on the comm…

"Let her in."

The hatch slid open, and Avery Sampson walked tentatively into the office. "I'm sorry to disturb you, Admiral…"

"Come in, Avery." West gestured for her aide to sit across from her desk. "Is anything wrong?"

"No, Admiral…at least nothing to do with the tactical situation. The enemy fleet is still keeping back a system and following. We've picked up flashes of stealth drones here and there, but I can only assume they've got more of them out there. I'd say there's no chance of losing them."

"I don't want to lose them, Avery."

A hint of surprise flashed across Sampson's face. West knew she was speaking far more casually than she usually did. A lifetime as the fleet's ramrod stiff commander had been tiring. Or, perhaps she just needed a friend, one that was there, sharing the situation with her.

"Then, what are we doing?" Sampson hesitated, looking as though she thought she'd gone too far with the brusqueness of her question. "I'm sorry, Admiral…I just mean, there's no way I believe you lost your nerve back there. And, you would never lead these bastards back to Earth Two. Something is going on, but for the life of me, I can't guess what it is."

West almost reverted back to her old form and told Sampson to worry about her duties and not where the fleet was going. But, she didn't.

"I'm glad you don't believe I've run, Avery." A pause. "I'm

afraid not everyone agrees with you, though."

Sampson paused, looking uncomfortable.

"It's okay…I'm not blind. They think I've lost my nerve. Some of them probably figure losing Nicki was too much for me, or that I'm just too old, worn out."

"It's…it's mostly the younger spacers, Admiral. I wouldn't say they are convinced you broke and ran…but, they're… confused."

"I'm sure they are, Avery. But, you're not?"

About whether you lost your nerve? No. Not a bit. About what you're planning…yes, I'm very confused."

West took a deep breath. She hadn't planned to tell any of her people what was happening, not until the last possible moment. She'd always tended toward the maximum possible security around any of her operations. But, perhaps even more important, she wasn't sure she should give them too much time to think about it. Cursing their admiral for cowardice at least gave them the hope that they were moving away from battle… not right into the worst one any of them had ever imagined.

She knew she should leave Sampson in the dark, but she needed some moral support, at least one trusted comrade in on the secret she'd been carrying alone. The only other people anywhere who knew exactly what she was doing were Max Harmon and Josie Strand.

And, she knew she shouldn't have told Strand everything… but she'd felt compelled to tell her second-in-command what she was fighting for. And, what her comrades were doing to give her and her people the chance to obliterate the antimatter factory.

"We're not running, Avery. And, we're not going back to Earth Two…not exactly." West took a deep breath and looked across the desk at her aide. "We walked into the enemy's trap, because we couldn't pass up the chance to eliminate their anti-matter supply…but, that's not all of it. Their trap was the bait in *our* trap. We *want* that fleet following us. We *need* it following us."

Another pause, longer this time.

"We're going to…" She told Sampson everything, the entire

plan. All she'd discussed with Harmon before the fleet left…and everything she'd put in her message to Josie Strand.

She knew unloading it all didn't have any real tactical value, that Sampson of all people would have obeyed her orders without explanation. It wouldn't help with the morale of the crews either, or of their resentment to their commander, since none of them would know anything until it was all upon them. It was a pointless indulgence, she knew.

But it felt good to confide in someone…to have one comrade in on what she was doing.

Someone who wasn't hundreds of lightyears away.

Chapter Twenty-Seven

Landing Zone Red Fist
Planet G48-II
Earth Two Date 02.24.43

Cameron stood next to the jagged crater, staring at the rough path leading down. His Marines had been fighting for days on the surface, one enemy attack after another pouring out from hidden access points and hitting his camps and defensive positions.

The First Imperium warbots were the stuff of pure nightmare, but Cameron and his people were ready in ways the Marines that had come before them couldn't have imagined. Their armor was the most powerful and advanced human beings had ever worn into battle…and at their side, lined up almost in serried ranks silently waiting for the combat to begin, were mechanical warriors, bots looking very much like the ones the Marines were fighting against.

Cameron had never been entirely comfortable with the inclusion of bots in the Marines' combat formations, though he hadn't hated the development as much as General Frasier and the other Pilgrims, who'd faced the First Imperium in battle so many times, had.

Now, though, after days of fighting off relentless First Imperium attacks, he understood that hatred a bit more…though

214

he'd also seen the Mules' creations fighting at his peoples' sides, taking down the attacking enemy as effectively as his most elite Marine units. He didn't have a large number of the bots, nothing like the thousands the Mules had built for the defense of Earth Two. Transport had been the limiting factor, and both he and Frasier had agreed that actual living, breathing Marines should be the heart of the strike force.

A lot of those Marines were dead now.

The first two days had been the toughest, and his perimeter had almost collapsed in half a dozen spots. He'd rushed to the front line himself several times, and on at least one of those occasions, he truly believed his fire, and that of his immediate aides, had been the razor-thin difference that beat back the enemy.

The third day had looked to be even worse, as the First Imperium forces brought massive reinforcements to the surface. But, then a miracle happened. Josie Strand and her spacers showed up in orbit. They'd won the battle for control of the space around the planet, though, from what Cameron had been able to ascertain, they'd paid one hell of a price for that victory. Strand had lost at least half of her ships, and the rest were damaged, most severely so. Cameron had gotten the impression from his brief communications with her that she had ships floating all across the system, some crippled, others working on repairs sufficient to restore at least some level of navigation.

But, there were ships around the planet, too, orbiting in the space were the now-destroyed fortifications had once stood. A few battered and disordered ships didn't make up a decisive force, not against an enemy that had any defenses to throw against them. But, the First Imperium orbital defenses were gone, and for all the raw fury of their ground attacks, the bots didn't have a weapon that could reach ships in orbit.

Josie Strand's vessels, as worn down and almost wrecked as they were, did have orbital bombardment capability…and a vengeful need to inflict damage on the First Imperium any way they could.

Cameron could still remember the relief he felt when

Strand's first communique had reached him that morning. He'd been reshuffling what remained of his defensive forces, preparing for the attack he was certain would be the final one. And, then, literally moments later, the heavens opened up and Strand's survivors unleashed all they had on the attacking enemy robots.

The first barrage stalled the enemy attack and drove the First Imperium bots back on their starting positions. But, Cameron had known that wouldn't be enough to turn things around, and he'd called back up to the admiral, setting up linked comm networks between the battleships in orbit and select teams of spotters on the ground. The Marines advanced and targeted the most vulnerable enemy positions…and the ships in orbit opened up and pounded them with everything they had.

It took a few more days, and a good number of ground assaults to back up the bombardments, to clear the enemy from the surface, but now Brigadier General Devon Cameron watched as his lead pickets began climbing down into the mouth of the crater, toward the location their scans had shown led to one of the enemy's sally points…and deep into the heart of the enemy production facility.

His people had come a long way to strike a blow that would even the score between Earth Two and the First Imperium… and now he was going to see it done.

Whatever the cost.

* * *

"Finish packing up his things, Henri." Josie Strand stood along the far wall of the small room, holding a tablet in her hand. It was a compact one, and it seemed to be filled mostly with photos…images of men and women Strand didn't know. Not that there was any reason she should have known them. Cooper McDaid had been a comrade for most of her adult life, and she'd considered the pilot a friend. Even a close friend. But, she realized now that their camaraderie was the sort so common among those who work together—serve together. She thought she knew the essence of the man, but now she was shocked at how little she knew of his personal life, his family and those close to him.

"I'll take care of it, Admiral." There was compassion in Hercules' voice. Strand knew her aide was aware just how hard McDaid's loss had hit her. And, she was surprised how much better it made her feel to have Hercule carefully packing McDaid's things rather than just ordering a few spacers to do it. Hercule hadn't been close to McDaid the way Strand had been, but he'd known the pilot…and he was someone Strand herself trusted to handle things carefully. Respectfully.

One last consideration for a lost friend. Not much…but all she had left to give him.

"Thank you, Hercule. I appreciate it." Strictly speaking, she didn't have to thank her subordinate for doing what she could have simply ordered him to do. But, Hercule was offering her more than obedience, he was giving all he could in the way of support, and she understood that well. And, as she'd told him she appreciated it.

She'd put off dealing with McDaid's personal effects as long as she could. There had been no shortage of excuses. The battle had lasted nearly two days after the pilot's death, and his people had gone back out four more times. By the battle's end, there were twenty-eight pilots still active and ready for duty, less than one quarter the number that had started under McDaid. That grim total was somewhat mitigated by five pilots who'd been rescued after the fight, and another six in sickbay, wounded but expected to survive. But, even with those eleven added in, there was no disguising the fact that the fighter corps had done more than its part…and paid the price for it.

The desperate rush to the planet, and the orbital support for the beleaguered Marines on the surface had given her more time, more reasons to leave McDaid's quarters empty and unattended. But, now, Cameron's warriors were on their way down into the subterranean depths of the planet, on their almost hopeless quest. There was almost nothing Strand could do for the Marines now, save sending them best wishes and, of course, waiting to retrieve them, in the hope that they would succeed…

and survive.

Watching on the scanner as Cameron's people descended into the nightmare that awaited them had stripped her of her self-pity, though, and she decided then and there, it was time. Time to clean out her friend's quarters. Time to write a note to his loved ones. Time to meet her obligations.

But, she realized she hardly knew anything about McDaid's family. He'd rarely talked about them, or about his home life at all. She knew he was married, and that his wife's name was Jasmine. He had two children as well, she thought she remembered, both grown by now, but that was the extent of her knowledge. She wasn't even sure she'd ever seen a picture of his family... at least not until she pulled the tablet from the small nightstand next to the bed.

She shook her head, feeling bad that she'd never gotten to know him better beyond duty, that she'd called a man friend but been utterly detached from his life beyond war.

She paused for a moment, and then she caught Hercule glancing in her direction, looking like he wasn't sure if he should say something else.

She just nodded toward her aide. She held up the tablet and said, "I'll take care of this myself, Henri." Then a few seconds later, "I'm going back to the bridge now."

She had another friend out there. Cameron and his Marines were deep underground, out of communications range. The ground station had been making regular reports, but the main strike force was cut off from their comrades on the surface as completely as they were from the fleet units in orbit.

She knew there was nothing she could do but wait...but she owed it to Cameron and his Marines to do it on the bridge, listening to every silent, frustrating moment on the comm.

Until she heard something.

Or, until she knew she couldn't do anymore for Cameron than she could for McDaid.

*   *   *

The Intelligence activated its auxiliary processors. It sensed danger, and it was struggling to craft its response. The enemy fleet had performed above expectations…it had defeated the forces retained to destroy it. The main fleet was lightyears away, pursuing the enemy's main force…and the surviving human ships completely controlled the system. The Intelligence would have sent any available forces to contest the enemy fleet, to wrest back control of the space around the planet at all costs, but there were none remaining.

The loss of control of the system was disturbing, but not critical. The base had been well-protected by ground forces, and the Intelligence had launched a massive attack, one that had been on the verge of eliminating the human ground forces… until the surviving ships arrived and provided orbital bombardment support.

The Intelligence's surface forces had been destroyed, and now the humans were following up, entering the tunnels leading to the main installation. Perhaps more disturbing, among their forces were warbots, clearly copies of the First Imperium forces. The Intelligence was uncertain if the Regent was aware that the enemy had the capability to copy its own robot warriors.

It had to report that news to the Regent. But, there was no way, not with the enemy in control of the system…and of the planet's surface. All the Intelligence could do was defend the base, repel the attack, and wait for the main fleet to destroy the enemy's navy and return to the system to finish off the survivors there.

It reviewed every tactical file, analyzed every force manifest, every piece of ordnance that remained to it, from the most advanced warbots to the smallest security units. It reviewed the maps of the complex, and the path of the enemy's advance. It selected choke points, positions where it could defend most effectively.

Perhaps most importantly, it organized its defenses to keep the enemy from the vital areas…the main accelerators, and perhaps even more crucially, the vast antimatter storage units. The slightest failure of any of the huge magnetic bottles stored there would mean the destruction of the entire facility.

Not just the factory, nor the Intelligence…but the Regent's sole source of antimatter production.

No, that could not be allowed to happen. The Intelligence questioned the original plan, considered whether luring the enemy fleet to its destruction had been worth the risk.

It couldn't reach a final conclusion. It was not within its range of abilities to question the Regent.

It had one purpose now…one alone.

Defeat the enemy. Stop them from reaching the inner chambers.

Chapter Twenty-Eight

Note From Erika West to Nicki Frette:

I am writing this more for myself than for you, no doubt. After twelve years of what hope I could cling to, what efforts the medical community could make, I finally have to accept that you are gone from me forever. I cannot express the pain caused, even by writing those fateful words here, now. Even if you somehow, against all odds and reason, recover one day, and I do not return from the terrible battle looming before me, what chance is there of this message reaching Earth Two? The battle about to begin is likely to see most of my people—if not all—killed in action. And, even if any of us survive, we can't return to Earth Two, not unless we annihilate the enemy completely, leaving nothing to follow us back.

No, I know you will never see these words, that I will never hear your voice again, so I simply sit here in the calm quiet, knowing you are there. We did share so many things once, and now they are a part of me. You are part of me. This war, our deadly enemy, could take you away, but it could never take from me what you've given me, the part of me that will always include something of you.

Goodbye, Nicki. I know that this will likely never reach Earth Two, and even if it does, you cannot read it...but I am confident you already know all I have said here. I am ready for whatever fate is waiting for me here, and though there is the deepest sorrow in the place you should fill in my life, I am profoundly grateful for the years we had together, however few they may have been.

Flag Bridge, E2S Garret
F-76 System
Earth Two Date 02.26.43

"Scanner report?" West snapped out the order, her tone sharper than she'd intended, especially toward Avery Sampson. Her aide had listened to every aspect of the wild and desperate plan behind the fleet's actions…and then she hadn't said another word about it. But, she'd been on duty almost non-stop since, refusing to leave the admiral's side almost to the point of mutiny.

"The enemy picket ships are definitely moving closer, Admiral. It's pretty clear they aren't even making a token effort to hide their presence anymore."

That made some sense to West. She couldn't imagine a First Imperium Fleet Intelligence would assume that none of her scouts or drones or probes had picked up the massive force following her ships.

She'd also expected the machine's patience to wear out eventually, for its great processing cells to give up and realize that, whatever had driven her to pull her fleet out of G48 and make a run for it, it wasn't a blind enough panic for her to lead it back to Earth Two.

That was fine…the enemy didn't really need to believe she was heading back to Earth Two. But, what she did need was time, just a bit more now. The hope that she would lead the enemy to Earth Two, whatever probability the Intelligence had assigned to it, had been enough to buy her the respite she needed…most of it. West wasn't just running…she was heading somewhere.

One more jump. One more jump, and we're there.

But, she wasn't sure the enemy was going to give her the last bits of time she needed.

Not if they're moving up to attack now…

"Commander…get me Captain Starr. Direct laser communication." Thomas Starr was another Pilgrim, a man she'd known for almost fifty years. If any of her people still had faith that she was doing more than running from the enemy, it was Starr.

"On your line, Admiral."

"Captain, I need your help."

"Yes, Admiral. Of course."

"Tom...you know I haven't lost my nerve and brought us all the way here in some kind of panic, don't you?" She felt a hitch, a feeling that she shouldn't be letting go on the security surrounding her plans, not in the middle of the bridge, at least. But the secrecy had mostly served its purpose now. It wouldn't be long before she told all her people what she expected of them. A tight beam comm line to an old friend and some open talk in front of her officers were tolerable risks.

"I figured you were just as likely to panic as you were back at Regulus VII."

She had to force back an unexpected smile. It wasn't everyday someone threw a forty-five-year-old reference at you.

"Thanks, Tom." It was all that had to be said. West was surprised how much it meant to her to know an old comrade still believed in her. "Tom...the fleet *has* to get through the next warp gate. All of this, the flight, the systems we've been through, it was all to get us here. There."

"And, you think the enemy is going to hit us now. In this system."

"Yes." A pause. "We can't let that happen. We've got to do something to hold them back." She hoped he wouldn't make her say it...and she was grateful when he didn't.

"My people can hold them off, Admiral. At least long enough for you to get the fleet through."

West felt a wave of relief...and one of guilt and sorrow as well. Starr commanded a task force of lighter ships, small cruisers and several types of escorts. Fast ships.

And expendable ones. At least compared with the battleships and heavy cruisers of the line.

"Just long enough for us to get through, Tom. Then your ships can follow." She was upset with herself for that last bit. She knew she was sending Starr on a virtual suicide mission, and she was damned close to certain he knew it, too. She owed him the honesty to admit it.

"Don't worry about anything, Admiral. My people have this.

Get the rest of the fleet through the gate…to whatever you've got planned. These bastards won't catch you…you've got my word on that."

"Thank you, Tom." She wanted to say something more, but she couldn't find the words. Suddenly she felt sorry that she hadn't confided in Starr earlier, that she hadn't shared her plan with him. It was bad enough that few if any of his people were likely to survive the battle she was sending them into, but it really cut at her to think none of them would even know what they were dying for, what desperate effort they were saving.

"We've got this, Admiral. You focus on the big picture." A pause. "I never thought for a second that you lost your nerve. I just feel sorry for those miserable robots. They have no idea what they're up against."

West tried to answer, but she couldn't force out the words. She was still looking down at the comm unit when the signal cut out.

She took a deep breath, her eyes fixed on the workstation screen as Starr's ships began to move out of the formation, decelerating to turn and face the approaching enemy. She felt the urge to hesitate, to stay and not to abandon Starr and his people. But she knew that would just strip their sacrifice of its meaning…and throw away any chance she had to strike a blow against the First Imperium.

She turned toward Sampson's station, breathing in and exhaling again, slowly regaining her usual steely control. She had a job to do, and no more time for indulging emotions. She had a reputation for icy coolness in battle, and by God, she was going to live up to it.

"Commander…all ships in the main force are to accelerate at full power…directly for the warp gate."

* * *

The Fleet Intelligence had run its calculations as it entered each system. It reviewed vast reams of data, comparing previous search and scanning reports with an analysis of the position within the known portions of the warp gate network. It also took into account the number of transits from the starting point in the first system.

It tried to take human emotions into consideration, as well, though it assigned a lesser importance to these, not because it considered them a lesser factor in what the enemy might do, but because it understood its own limitations in such analysis.

It crunched millions of factors, countless possibilities, and it drilled all of it down to a single number, one that had assigned a probability of 1.0 or greater to continued pursuit as the optimal course of action after each warp gate jump. Until this last transit. The result now was 0.999762, virtually indistinguishable from 1.0, for a biologic certainly, but not for a thinking machine of its sophistication. Its orders were clear. Follow the enemy fleet as long as the probability was 1.0 or greater that their course was toward their mysterious homeworld.

That was no longer the case.

The Intelligence's orders in the new circumstance had changed. Attack the human fleet and destroy it, at once. There was no reason to wait, no condition that justified or allowed further delay. It was time to attack.

The Intelligence began transmitting orders, directing the components of the massive fleet. Entire task forces fired thrusters in perfect synchronization. The Intelligence reviewed multiple approach vectors…and selected an interception point.

Then…it put a hold on all maneuvers.

There was new data. The enemy fleet had increased its acceleration. They were moving at what appeared to be maximum thrust toward the system's third warp gate.

All except one sub-fleet.

The nearest ships were decelerating. They appeared to be forming up to engage the Intelligence's forces. The Intelligence considered detaching a single task force to destroy the enemy ships while the rest of the fleet pursued and attacked the main human force before they reached the warp gate. The calculations confirmed that it could intercept the main enemy formation short of the warp gate.

But, the Intelligence ordered all units to decelerate slightly, to engage the single enemy task force before proceeding to pursue the main human fleet. There was no disadvantage to fighting the final battle in the next system instead of the current one…and with all the fleet's firepower, destroying the enemy's rearguard would take almost no time at all.

Then the entire fleet would advance…and overtake the humans in the next system.

And destroy them utterly.

* * *

"Task Force Beta has completed transit, Admiral." All fleet units are through except for the command task force.

West heard Sampson's report, but she didn't answer. Not right away. She knew she had to order the last of her ships to move through the gate. The mission depended on it…and the nightmare she'd watched engulf Starr and his people would be for naught if she squandered the time they had paid so much to give her. Still, she was frozen, her eyes fixed on the display, watching as the last of her friend's battered cruisers tried to break off and run for their lives.

Thomas Starr wasn't one of those trying to get away. The officer had died with his ship, fighting to the last. West had been watching when it happened. She hadn't reacted, hadn't allowed the slightest chink in her ice-cold armor.

She'd struggled with her demons on this mission, thoughts of Nick Frette, of the people she'd lost—and the ones she was almost certain to lose in the battle to come—even remembrances of friends and comrades long gone. She had wondered if the technology that sustained life had kept her going too long, if there was a limit to how much pain and loss a person could endure, no matter how long drug and genetic treatments kept hearts pumping and lungs breathing.

But now she was back…ready for the fight she knew would be the climactic one of her distinguished career. She'd been considered a cold-blooded combat commander for that entire time, and now she embraced that label more fully than she ever had before. The blood flowing in her veins was frigid, and her eyes blazed with an intensity that seemed almost enough to bore through *Garret*'s hyper-steel hull. She had banished all weakness, personal loss, fear, even concern about the outcome of the fight she was leading her people into. She was death now, darkness… and she embraced every cold and negative thought, channeled unfiltered rage toward the enemy that had cost her—and her people—so much.

"Admiral…" Sampson's voice was tentative. It was obvious the aide could sense West's grim determination.

West looked at the display, watching as the lead enemy ships blasted toward her position at nearly 100g. They would be in missile range in just a few minutes…and it would take that long to get the entire task force through. But, still, she said nothing. She didn't move, didn't flinch. She just stared at the oncoming enemy forces, watching as they caught and destroyed the last of Starr's ships.

The bridge was silent, the tension palpable, hovering over the officers and workstations like a dense fog. Sampson sat at her station, rigid, staring at her screens, clearly trying not to look over at West.

Finally, the admiral spoke. She didn't turn her head, didn't move at all. She just said, calmly, even quietly, "Forward, Commander. The rest of the fleet will move through the warp gate."

"Yes, Admiral." The relief was obvious in Sampson's voice, as she acknowledged, and as she turned and repeated the order into her comm unit.

West didn't watch, didn't even listen. Her mind was already through the warp gate…with what she knew was waiting.

The massive battle she planned, the Armageddon into which she'd led her spacers. The one she'd spent her life preparing to fight.

Chapter Twenty-Nine

Planet G-48 II
Somewhere Below the Surface
Earth Two Date 02.26.43

"God damn it…send a runner then!" Devon Cameron stood in the middle of the large cavern, surrounded by about sixty of his Marines. His forces were strung out all across the network of caves and tunnels, moving quickly, combining what scanner readings they could get with geological advice from the tactical AIs…and perhaps more than anything, a healthy dose of gut instinct.

"Yes, General!" The aide's sharp response came back in an instant, and a few seconds later, one of the armored figures that had been standing around turned and took off at a slow jog. That was just about as quickly as one could move in the tight confines of the tunnels.

Whatever difficulties the operation presented—and they were many and varied—his people were as sharp as he'd ever seen them. He knew they had to be scared, but he was sure they also understood just how important a mission they were on.

Cameron took a deep breath of the slightly oxygen-rich mixture his suit fed him, and he shook his head. The planet might have been a perfect choice for the production of anti-matter, but it was a nightmare in terms of tactical operations, especially below ground. The crust was thick with radioactive elements, and the massive volcanic and tectonic activity caused all sorts of interference with communications and scanning. He had Marines scattered over more than a hundred square kilometers of underground mazes, tunnels, and caves…but his comm range through the heavy metals and dense radiation was less than a klick…especially in areas where the rock was particularly dense. The lack of communications was a nightmare for any operation, much less one as desperate and dangerous as this one.

He sent a thought to his AI, and an instant later the display inside his visor switched to a map. The neural connection that allowed him to connect by thought to the computer that ran his suit had been an amazing leap forward, an area of technology that researchers had stumbled around for half a century… before the Mules made it work. Cameron knew his predecessors had fumbled with all kinds of tiny switches and buttons in their suits in past years, or shouted out verbal commands to their AIs. All of that was still there, of course, backup systems in case the primary ones failed. But Cameron hadn't twisted his finger around to tap a button in ten years. Directing his suit to do something was no more difficult than raising his hand or turning his head.

His eyes darted back and forth across the map. It was as up to date as possible, though the communications difficulties had really slowed progress in updating the dynamic mapping database. Half his people were tied up on a daisy chain of sorts, creating a system that could relay reports and data upstream to headquarters in links that were a kilometer or less in distance.

And, headquarters was Cameron himself, and maybe a dozen and a half Marines following him around as he moved deeper into the planet's crust. There was a command post on the surface, but his attempts to keep it in the net had been largely futile. The radiation and seismic activity on the surface, from the initial nuclear assault, and then Strand's sustained bombardment, had played havoc with comms.

The pathways on the map were color-coded. Most were blue, signifying fully plotted tunnels and chambers his people had moved through. There were a few spots where the scouts had discovered clear signs that the First Imperium bots had passed as they'd moved to the surface days earlier, and they were displayed in yellow.

And now, there was one small section of tunnel, shown in bright red.

Finished corridor instead of natural or bored out tunnel. An actual part of the complex his people were searching for.

But, the signal had been brief, the report sketchy. A single fireteam had apparently pushed through into the finished corridor…and after they sent that basic info back, they went silent.

Cameron had sent word down through the makeshift comm chain, but there were breaks in several places in the line. Finally, he just started using messengers. It was a throwback to methods of warfare from centuries earlier, but it still worked…slowly.

It had been frustrating enough during the exploratory efforts, but he didn't relish the idea of his Marines being in trouble somewhere they couldn't call for help. The enemy had expended massive forces in its failed attack on the surface, but Cameron was pretty sure his people weren't done fighting.

Even as he considered that fact, he heard a commotion down the hall, and his comm unit crackled to life.

"We've got First Imperium bots…sector four and sector six. Hitting us in multiple locations."

It was just what he'd feared. "Alright, Decker, Willis…get your sections moving. It looks like we found the fight we came here for."

He paused for just a few seconds, and then he reached around, pulling the assault rifle from its harness. "The rest of you…with me. Victory—or defeat—is down in those two sectors, and that's where we're heading. It's time to finish this."

He held the rifle up in his hand, and then he moved toward the cavern's exit, trying to ignore his aides as they called to him to stop and remain in the rear area.

He was a Marine, and no pair of tiny little stars was going to keep him out of the action…not in a fight like the one his people faced now.

* * *

"Admiral…we're picking something up on the scanners."

Strand's head snapped around so quickly, she almost pulled a muscle in her neck. Her forces had been adequate to give the Marines orbital support—and to wait around and try to pick them up if they were able to complete their mission—but if another First Imperium task force showed up, the fight would be over in the blink of an eye. All her ships had full damage control operations underway, but the hard truth was, her fleet wouldn't be combat ready again for months, if ever, and that only with the use of Earth Two's massive spacedock facilities. Her vessels could limp home, most of them, at least, but that's about all they had left in them.

"Enemy ships?" She thought she managed to keep the dread she felt out of her tone.

"I don't think so, Admiral." A pause. "It's just a single contact, and the energy level is very low. Enough for minimal life support…maybe…but not much else."

Strand looked back at her own screen, quickly checking the comm feed from the surface. The main command post was still in contact, but they hadn't had a signal from the forces underground for nine hours. Strand's stomach tensed when she looked at that report, with the time listed increasing each time. She knew the problems affecting the comm on the planet, but it still fed her worst concerns. For all she knew, every Marine who'd gone down there was already dead, the mission a complete failure.

Or, they're about to hit the main facility even now…

That made her feel better…for a few seconds. But, then she realized, even if the Marines got through and were able to take out the enemy production facility and storage tanks, they'd probably kill themselves in the process.

Whatever is going to happen, there's nothing you can do but wait…

So…go check this out, whatever it is. It's not like you're doing anything sitting here in orbit…

"Bring us out of orbit, Commander. Direct course for that contact." She wondered for a moment if she should send another vessel, but then she put the thought aside. *Midway* was in as good shape of any of her ships, and was probably kilo for kilo, the strongest vessel she had left. Besides, if she was sending anyone to check out some unknown ship, she was damned sure going.

"Yes, Admiral."

"Let's not take any chances. I want active scanners on that contact at full power. If there's enough of an energy spike to light a candle, I want to know about it." She paused, just for an instant. "And, bring us to battlestations." She didn't *really* expect a fight. Mostly likely, the contact was some wrecked ship, perhaps from the original fleet that had explored the system, with some minimal remaining power, but otherwise a ghost ship.

But, she wasn't taking chances. It could also be some kind of First Imperium trap.

"Battlestations, Admiral." Hercule's words beat the klaxon, but only by a few seconds. Then, *Midway*'s flag bridge was bathed in the red glow of the battlestations lamps.

Again.

* * *

There were bodies strewn through the shattered corridor, dead Marines half buried under sections of the roof that had collapsed in the fury of combat. Cameron shook his armored head, trying but failing to keep count of how many of his people had died in the fighting. Normally, his AI would have those stats for him in an instant, but the comm failures were wreaking havoc with data transmission.

He knew it didn't matter, not really…whatever that number was, it was definitely not a final one. The battle still raged, and even as so many fell, his Marines pushed on, deeper into the bowels of the enemy base.

He stepped over a pile of twisted wreckage, all that remained of a First Imperium warbot. His Marines were dying, but they weren't dying alone. All along the route to the forward positions, bits and pieces of enemy bots were scattered around.

Cameron was still back a bit from the heaviest fighting, but he was closer now...and he could hear the gunfire ahead. The chambers he'd passed had been badly damaged as the desperate struggle had moved through them, and he hadn't been able to discern what the equipment his people had passed was used for. He hadn't seen anything that could have been part of a system of huge magnetic bottles used to store antimatter, and even less structures looking anything like the massive, kilometers long accelerators he knew were needed to produce the precious substance.

The power appeared to be out in the area, the overhead lights dead, even where they hadn't been smashed by gunfire. He didn't know if his people had taken out a local reactor or a section of power conduit—or if the Intelligence in command of the facility had cut power intentionally. It didn't matter. Every one of his Marines had a fusion reactor on his back, and more than enough energy to scan infrared wavelengths...or to light up sections of corridor with blinding spotlights.

Cameron pushed forward, swinging to the side each time one of his aides tried to slip around him. He appreciated their desire to protect him, but he was a Marine, too. His whole life had been the Corps, and he'd spent most of his career on Earth Two, waiting for a desperate battle that hadn't come...until now. He wasn't about to sit it out or hang to the rear, just because that crucial fight had waited until his rank had escalated him beyond the normal level of a combat Marine.

His assault rifle was extended out in front of him, one of the oversized combat clips in the magazine. The cartridge held twelve hundred projectiles, each of them an almost impossibly slim shard of super-heavy metal that would be hurled out from the atomic-powered weapon at hyper-sonic velocities. It didn't take a lot of mass to cause damage at that kind of speed, and even the dense armor of a First Imperium warbot was at risk when one of Earth Two's Marines opened fire.

He quickened his pace as he heard the sounds of fighting

getting louder. As far as he could tell, his Marines were engaged in at least three locations…though, with the communications problems they were having, he knew there could be another half dozen hotspots he didn't know about.

He'd hoped the comm troubles would improve once his people entered the actual facility, but they'd only gotten worse, as enemy jamming was added to the list of things interfering with the Marines' signals. He'd continued using runners, but, with the losses, and the way his people were spread all over the complex, out of easy supporting range, he found he didn't have enough Marines to spare. He'd had to cut loose his other teams from his direction, leave them on their own to make their way as well as they could. He hated not knowing what was happening to so many of his Marines, but in the end, he did what he had to do. As all those who served with him did.

He stopped suddenly. He heard something from up ahead. At first, it was just a slight sound, one he only heard because his suit amplified distant noises and replayed them through his internal speakers. But, then he realized…something was coming.

He gestured to the Marines behind him, and he knelt down, and aimed his assault rifle.

"General…"

The sound crackled through his comm unit. For an instant, he wasn't sure who it was, or where the signal had come from. But then he realized, and he relaxed his pose ever so slightly… just as an armored Marine came running down the corridor, moving side to side to keep from launching himself up into the ceiling.

"General Cameron…" The man stated his name, Sergeant Toland Arneson, but Cameron's AI had identified the Marine first, as soon as he turned the corner and his comm connected with the general's.

"What is it, Sergeant?"

"Major Stanton sent me to find you, sir." The man was clearly flustered, more than Cameron liked to see in his Marines. But, he realized, however dedicated his people were, or how well trained, the Earth Two Corps had simply not seen the kind of action the Marines of the original fleet, or the forces back on the other side of the Barrier, had.

"What is it, son?" *When did I get old enough to call Marines, 'son?'*

"Sir, Major Stanton has found something. He thinks it might be an acceleration chamber."

Cameron felt a burst of his own excitement...but he was enough of a veteran, at least, to hide it.

"That's good news, Sergeant." He turned back toward the rest of his column, a needless gesture since he was speaking to them on the comm. "Alright, all of you...let's move out." He looked back at the sergeant. "What are you waiting for, Arneson? We've got work to do."

Chapter Thirty

Flag Bridge, E2S Garret
F-74 System
Earth Two Date 02.26.43

West stared into the deep blackness of the display, waiting for the system to reboot, for *Midway*'s scanners and comm to come alive and reveal what the F74 system had to offer…to her fleet, and to the enemy forces she knew would be right behind her.

The warp gate transit itself had been short, no more than a few seconds of strange disorientation, but it was the minutes that followed that tended to test the mettle of spacers. It was unnerving enough in normal circumstances, sitting, blind, deaf, with even life support systems shut down for a brief time…it was something else entirely to do it under combat conditions, knowing hundreds and hundreds of enemy ships were right behind you.

West could feel the tension from the others on the bridge. As far as any of them knew, in moments they'd be fighting the fleet that had followed them so far from G48. That much was true, West knew…but there was more.

Or, at least there was supposed to be. She wouldn't know for certain until *Garret*'s systems reactivated and gave her a first look around.

Time seemed to move at a fraction of its normal speed, a phenomenon most spacers experienced in such moments, but West was accustomed to the whole thing, and her discipline was like iron. She'd planned for this moment, left Strand and the Marines in G48 to accomplish it, misled the officers and spacers she commanded to bring herself to this point.

She watched, unmoving and unmoved, as the display began to sparkle slightly. Across the bridge, she could hear faint static, as the communications systems restarted. She knew that far forward, where the main scanners were located, systems were rebooting as well. In just a few seconds, her people would know what awaited them in G74.

And, she would know if her plans had come to fruition. If her people had the chance she hoped they did.

She watched and waited, as the display became brighter, and as lights began to appear, a large orange sphere representing the system's primary, and then a series of smaller globes…the six planets that orbited it. More detail appeared as the seconds passed, a faint cluster of tiny dots…the system's asteroid belt. And then, around several dozen of the asteroids, small circles, energy readings.

And, finally, in front of the system's third planet, several lines of small icons.

Ships.

West smiled. The symbols were familiar, and even as she looked forward, unemotional save for the small grin she wore, her officers began to recognize the icons.

Earth Two ships…lined up and ready for battle.

But how? She could almost feel the thought from her people.

"Admiral…I have an incoming message." A pause, and then Sampson continued, the wonder in her voice evident despite the fact that West had told her of the plan. "It's Admiral Chandra."

West allowed herself a tiny grin, a momentary chink in the cold granite stare on her face. Then she tapped the controls at the side of her headset. "Raj…I'm so glad you could make it." The stunned silence on the rest of the bridge was palpable, her people in utter shock, even as they waited for her signal to traverse the two light minutes to Chandra's flagship and back.

West's thoughts drifted to the New Regent, and her hatred flared.

You're not the only one who can lay a trap...

* * *

The Intelligence sent out orders, and it monitored the scanner readings as its ships approached the warp gate. The enemy fleet had transited. The small task force they had sacrificed had bought them just enough time to get their ships through before the First Imperium fleet closed to combat range.

The Intelligence had almost ordered its forces to separate, for one formation to engage the enemy delaying force while the rest continued ahead at maximum acceleration and intercepted the fleeing humans before they could jump. But it had opted for a more conservative tactic, and it had brought all its force to bear against the human rearguard, destroying it utterly.

The enemy couldn't escape. Their ships did not have the acceleration to outrun its own. It made no difference in which system the humans were destroyed. The next one would serve as well as the current one.

The fleet was approaching the warp gate rapidly, its velocity nearly 0.02c. The Intelligence considered decelerating, bringing the fleet to a much lower velocity before transiting.

It assigned a lower risk to that option, one that offered more operational flexibility and ability to respond to unexpected enemy actions. But it did not believe the difference in risk was meaningful. The enemy was clearly trying to escape, and reducing its own ships' velocities would only prolong the chase. The next system was uncharted, and the Intelligence had no data on its composition, or on the number and position of any warp gates located there. It was unlikely the enemy would be able to escape before they were intercepted, but a reduction in velocity might possibly allow the enemy to reach a very close in warp gate and transit to yet another system.

No...there was no advantage to further delay. It was time to destroy the enemy fleet, and then to return to the system from where it had commenced its pursuit. The Intelligence assigned a ninety-four percent likelihood that all human forces in the factory system had been destroyed by the ships left there. Still, there was little to be gained by leaving an inadequate garrison to defend so vital a resource for longer than necessary.

The Intelligence calculated insertion vectors for all of its ships, and it sent out thrust orders and directives. Seconds later, as the nearest ships received and executed the commands, it watched as each vessel changed its thrust angles, positioning for the coming jump.

Hundreds of ships formed up, taking position behind the forward line of heavy battleships. The fleet was the greatest force the First Imperium had fielded since the original Regent's destruction, the fruits of four decades of constant production.

Now, the Intelligence would complete its mission. It would crush the human fleet...and the way would be open to find and destroy the enemy homeworld.

Then, the New Regent would rule the Imperium...even the entire galaxy.

* * *

"All ships, decelerate at full thrust." West snapped out the order even before her people had time to process what they had seen and heard. "Now!" she added, as much to instill a sense of urgency in all her staff than because Sampson had been slow to follow the first order.

She was still waiting for Chandra's response. Lightspeed remained a limiting factor in all forms of communication, save physically carrying a message through a warp gate. But, she knew the old Pilgrim officer well...and she trusted him, both his courage and his judgment. He knew what to do.

And, so did she.

She leaned back as the wave of g forces hit her, *Midway* decelerating with all the power its great reactors could produce. Her fleet was strung out more than she would have liked, but there was no way around that. The task forces that had gone in before hers had already slowed their velocities. Each commander had received orders, delivered by their ships' AIs, and even as *Midway*, and the vessels that had transited with her, shuddered under the massive thrust of deceleration, many of her other ships had already slowed to a near standstill.

Just as she had commanded.

There were few battle tactics that called for meeting a fast-moving enemy at a near halt, but that's just what she wanted now. She just needed the enemy to do what she expected of them…and she didn't' have to wait long to see that they had.

"We've got massive energy spikes at the warp gate, Admiral. It looks like they're transiting."

West felt a wave of relief. The enemy had come through close on her heels…and that meant they were going to come tearing out of the warp gate at something like two percent of lightspeed.

That would take them right past her ships…and toward Chandra's fleet and the fortifications all around it. G74 wasn't just any system…it was one of the decoys the navy had built to simulate Earth Two. The planet was uninhabited, save for the crew manning the defenses, but there were fake energy readings and drones moving about the system, posing as freighters and other commercial traffic. And, right behind Chandra's ships, there were two dozen asteroid bases, bristling with weapons.

West had sprung her own trap, lured the enemy fleet into the teeth of defenses far more powerful than they expected to encounter. She'd done everything she could, convinced Harmon to send Chandra with virtually every ship that had been left to defend Earth Two, made the desperate flight across ten systems to deliver the enemy to all the force the navy could muster.

And, still, she knew it would be a close fight, that her people were lucky to have a fifty-fifty chance of victory. But, that was a lot better than none.

She was still watching as the first wave of enemy ships emerged, ripping into the system at the expected velocity.

"Welcome to G74, Admiral West." Chandra's response

finally came through on her comm. "I think we prepared the party you wanted…I hope our guests enjoy it as much as you hoped they would."

She stared at the waves and waves of ships emerging from the warp gate, a feral glare on her face. "I'm sure they will, Raj… you are quite the hospitable host." she said softly, to herself and not anyone else. Any signal from her would take minutes just to reach Chandra.

"I'm sure they will."

Chapter Thirty-One

Planet G-48 II
Somewhere Below the Surface
Earth Two Date 02.26.43

The fire was loud and heavy…and getting worse. Cameron had pushed Arneson and the rest of his people hard, and now it sounded like they were almost there.

"Just around that corner, sir," Arneson said anxiously. The sergeant was definitely nervous. Cameron wasn't sure if it was fear at the fighting going on, the pressure of standing next to one of the Corps' two officers of general rank, or just the magnitude of the entire operation…but as long as the Marine did his job—which he was doing—Cameron was willing to cut the non-com some slack.

"With me…all of you." From the sounds of the fighting up ahead, whatever forces Stanton had seemed to be hard-pressed. Cameron knew the difference between the sound of First Imperium and Earth Two weaponry, and at least two thirds of the fire was coming from the enemy.

"Sir…perhaps you should…" It was one of his aides. Kerrigan.

"Noted, Lieutenant." Cameron had neither the time nor the inclination to argue with his aide again about who should be at the head of the column.

He rushed forward, pausing for an instant before peering around the corner.

He was looking out into a large open space, extending well out of sight. The whole area was dark, lit only by the searingly bright, but focused, headlamps of Stanton and his Marines, and the light of assault rifle projectiles glowing as they ripped through the thick atmosphere at ten thousand kilometers per second.

Stanton's Marines were crouched down below a giant chunk of machinery, perhaps fifty meters in length and ten high. It was heavy and thick, and it was providing good quality cover from the hail of projectiles coming from the darkness at the far end of the room.

"Stanton…report."

"Sir…" The major seemed surprised that Cameron was there, and a bit relieved as well. "There are at least half a dozen warbots down at the far end. The big bastards, General. We've tried to get some locational scans, but the jamming in here is just too strong."

Cameron turned and looked back at the Marines lined up behind him, and then he stared out again at the four meters or so of open space between the corner and the giant hunk of steel protecting Stanton and his people. He waited for a few seconds, looking out into the darkness of the room…and then he lunged forward, pushing off with the enormous strength he could exert with his armored legs. He covered the distance in an instant, and he careened hard into the heavy chunk of machinery with a loud crash.

He was looking up, suddenly it seemed to his slightly dazed senses, and he realized he was lying on his back. He started to get up, and then he saw another form was hovering over him, great armored hands reaching down to help him up.

Stanton.

"I'm okay, Major," he said, as he pushed himself over to his side and then stood up without any help, just the way he'd been taught in basic training so many years before. "What's your status?"

"We've got eight still in action, sir. Five dead…two others badly wounded." He turned and gestured behind him, and Cameron caught the glimpse of two armored Marines lying against the wall. Neither one of them was moving *at all*, and the general had an idea how badly wounded they had to be completely out of the action in a situation as desperate the current one.

"I've got twelve with me," he said, looking back as he did, watching as two of his aides repeated his desperate lunge across the tiny sliver of no-man's land. They both made it, more gracefully that he had…but the third Marine—Corporal Josten, Cameron told himself, beating the AI to it—wasn't so lucky. He made it about half way before a stream of projectiles hit him and sent him flying back the way he had come.

Cameron told himself Josten might still be alive, but he'd gotten too good of a view of the whole thing to believe that, especially when his readout confirmed the Marine was dead. Then, he got a good glimpse at the torn and blood-soaked wreckage that was all that remained of the man's armored chest, and all doubt was gone.

He glanced back across to the others, concerned for a moment Josten's fate might unnerve the rest of his small column. But, two more of his people jumped out as he was watching, and the others followed, without any noticeable delay… despite the fact that two more went down trying.

One of those, at least survived. Sergeant Polk had taken a hit to the midsection, but his trauma control system managed to treat the wound and patch the breach in his armor before the noxious atmosphere or dangerously high temperature did him in. Cameron was still worried about radiation, and how big a dose the sergeant had gotten when his suit was holed, but he didn't have time to obsess about a single casualty, especially not one who still seemed reasonably mobile.

"Sir…"

"Yes, Major…I know." He turned back toward Stanton, more out of habit that necessity.

"This has *got* to be part of the production facility…maybe we should be setting charges. If we can't get any farther, perhaps we can…"

"No, Major. We didn't come here to knock out a small part of their production…we came here to take it all." Cameron was far from as certain as he sounded. In theory, what he said was correct. Realistically, though, his Marines were scattered to hell, cut off from each other, with minimal comms. And, he had no idea how many warbots the enemy still had down the in tunnels. If he pushed too far, his people might not inflict any meaningful damage at all.

He turned and looked back at the small cluster of Marines behind him. Warrick was there, and Tolbert, too. They both had atomic charges. They weren't heavy thermonuclear jobs, just twenty-five kiloton fission bombs, but that was still a healthy blast, especially underground in confined quarters. He had no idea where the rest of the acceleration chambers were, if they were close enough that charges set off there would take them all out.

He was pretty sure of one thing, though. If he started popping off nukes, he was basically giving up on any of his people getting out. He'd already decided he would do that, sacrifice himself and every Marine he'd brought down to the planet, if that's what it took to really hurt the enemy. But, he wanted to be damned sure he got a lot more than some peripheral damage in return for that.

And, he wasn't sure. Not yet.

That meant there was only one choice…pushing forward.

"Alright, Major. We've got to see what is ahead of our position, and that means taking these bots out." He paused, looking at the armored forms surrounding him. "Okay, let's take an inventory and see what we've got…and we'll come up with an attack plan. I've got four hypersonic rockets, and two dozen grenades…"

* * *

"The beacon's out, but the warbook says it's definitely a *Tor-rance*-class cruiser. She looks like she's been through hell, Admiral." Hercule paused. "It's got to be *Vaughn*."

Strand had been thinking the same thing…she suspected everyone on *Midway* had been. But she wasn't one to be comfortable with unconfirmed assumptions.

Vaughn had been in the system, of course, and she was the only recently-active *Torrance*-class ship missing. There had been two other vessels of the class lost in its history, but the most recent had been nearly four years before, and its last report position was nowhere near to G48. Strand worked through her doubts, realizing that the derelict ship her scanners had picked up was, in fact, *Vaughn*. It had to be. She was still edgy, though, troubled in some way she couldn't quite pinpoint.

"Okay…well, we'll soon know for sure. Launch the rescue shuttle." It was pointless, at least to her way of thinking. There was no way she could see that Captain Graham or any of his people could possibly have survived…not with the number of First Imperium ships that had been present in the system.

But, the navy looked after its own, and she couldn't leave the wreck to simply drift through space, not without confirming absolutely there were no survivors in its tortured hull.

"Very well, Admiral. Rescue shuttle launching now."

Strand leaned to the side of her chair, placing her weight on the right armrest. She was exhausted, the fatigue of days of stress and combat finally threatening to overtake her. It took some considerable effort to stay awake over the twenty minutes or so it took the shuttle to reach its destination.

"Admiral…shuttle one has docked with the ship." A few seconds passed, perhaps half a minute. "Lieutenant Glynn reports the vessel *is Vaughn*. He has confirmed with the airlock registry."

That wasn't any real surprise, though Strand appreciated the confirmation. Her nerves had been working on her the entire time the shuttle made its way to the ship, all kinds of bizarre thoughts that it was some kind of enemy trick, that they had built a replica of an Earth Two ship, and a few other equally crazy ideas. She realized it was all insane conspiracy stuff, but the intensity of the battle, and the days of waiting, hoping no new enemy ships came pouring through one of the warp gates while the Marines were still down on the planet, had worn her to a nub. She was ready to believe just about any nightmare that worked its way into her mind.

"Very well, Commander. Advise Lieutenant Glynn she may proceed."

Strand watched on the main screen, as the view from Glynn's helmet cam was relayed and displayed for all on the bridge to see. The airlock appeared to be functional…though Glynn and her people would keep their suits on no matter what conditions they found. Strand wasn't about to allow anyone to get careless…especially since the mission was most likely a grim one, its likeliest purpose to find some bodies and confirm that *Vaughn*'s crew had all died with the rest of their fleet.

"We're through the airlock. The ship appears to have minimal life support. My scanners read low oxygen levels, but within survivable parameters. Temperature two-eighty-two Kelvin… chilly, but also in the habitable range."

Strand could hear the hope in the lieutenant's voice, but she didn't share it. She waited calmly, sadly, for the report that Glynn had found dead crew members. She just hoped they had died quickly, and not agonizingly, crawling through shattered corridors as they bled to death from wounds or writhed in agony from radiation sickness.

"Ship status?" Strand couldn't understand why the enemy forces hadn't finished off the vessel. *Vaughn* appeared to be pretty badly beaten up, but *she'd* never have left an enemy ship still floating through space, no matter how dead it looked. She didn't think a First Imperium Intelligence would either.

Maybe they just missed it…

That was the only answer, but she still couldn't quite accept it.

The ship's trajectory was odd as well. *Vaughn* was heading slowly in system, along roughly a trajectory leading in from one of the uncharted warp gates. She could understand the ship desperately escaping into unexplored space, through a warp gate leading out of the system…but how did it end up moving back toward the inner system?

"Admiral!" She could hear the excitement in Glynn's voice. She knew instantly what the tone meant…but it still took her some time to accept what she was hearing. "There are survivors! We've got at least four…" There was a pause, then: "No, seven!"

Strand was stunned. She was still suspicious, her mind picking at the inconsistencies she couldn't explain, even as the bridge erupted into applause.

She turned and looked at her people, at the raw joy they felt at finding a few survivors after a fight that had cost the lives of hundreds of their comrades. Then, she let herself feel it, too. She realized she might have ignored the wreck of *Vaughn* if regulations hadn't required her to investigate. And, the idea that she might have left survivors behind to die slowly…it was too much to take.

She drove the cynicism and suspicion from her mind, and let a smile slip onto her lips. "Search that ship from top to bottom, Lieutenant…and get any survivors back here as soon as possible."

Another round of cheers swept the bridge, and Strand participated herself this time.

But, deep in the back of her mind, shoved aside, her unease remained, the sensation that the whole thing was some kind of trap.

"I want a fresh spread of probes launched, Commander. We're going to make absolutely sure there's nothing out there but *Vaughn*."

She could celebrate and be cautious, too.

* * *

Cameron dove forward, even as the spray of automatic fire opened up, ripping through the space he'd occupied a second before. He landed hard, but the cushioning of his suit absorbed most of the impact. He was a little winded, but between the combat stims and the natural adrenalin, he barely noticed.

The combat had been heavy, the entire advance a series of leapfrogs forward, the Marines wiping out a cluster of warbots and then regrouping for the next advance. They'd paid heavily for every meter of ground, but now they were deep in the center of the facility.

They'd been through four acceleration chambers, each one of them a vast tunnel stretching far into the distant darkness. Cameron didn't know much about antimatter production, but what knowledge he did have told him the accelerators were kilometers long, and that when they were active, they produced antimatter continuously.

The ones his Marines had discovered so far had all been shut down, as he suspected the entire facility was. Ongoing production would make the complex too difficult to defend...and even a small amount of loose antimatter could lead to a catastrophic explosion.

The whole operation was still in disarray, though things were a little better than they'd been. Captain Ness and his team had managed to cut the power to the enemy's jamming setup. Communications were still far from ideal, but Cameron had been able to reach about half his people. Several groups of them were moving deeper into the facility, but his own small cluster of Marines seemed to have gotten the farthest.

"How many of these chambers do you think there are?" Major Stanton spoke slowly, and it was clear to Cameron that every word was a struggle. The major—and his second in command now that he'd been able to confirm Colonel Desmond's death—had been wounded twice, and Cameron wasn't sure what it was besides pure stubbornness keeping the Marine going.

"A lot, probably. I don't know how much antimatter one of these produces when its operating, but it doesn't seem like the Regent to do anything in half measures."

"No, I guess not." A pause, and a couple of gasps it sounded like Stanton had tried to hide. "Where do you think we should plant the charges? We can't just keep pushing forward...you know we don't have the strength for that. This complex could go on for a hundred kilometers...even more."

"You're right..." Cameron knew his officer was correct... but he was just as aware that a few small nuclear charges weren't going to do the job the Marines had come there to do. "There's only one way to take out this entire complex."

"The entire complex?" Stanton took a deep breath, one noticeably more ragged than the last few.

"We've *got* to take it all out, Mike. Nothing less is going to be enough. Look at this place...the Regent doesn't need all this antimatter to defeat Earth Two. If we knock out half the production here, even three-quarters, is that going to make a difference?"

Stanton didn't respond right away, but Cameron didn't need an answer. He knew already. And, he could only think of one way to destroy the entire factory.

"We've got to find the storage units. That's the only way. A couple nukes here will do some damage, knock out sections of the base. But, one well-placed bomb next to a storage facility..."

Stanton coughed, trying to clear his throat, and then he said, "Do you realize what kind of explosion you're going to let loose?"

Cameron knew, well enough, at least. He was just as glad Hieronymus Cutter or one of the Mules wasn't there to give him gory details about exactly what unleashing that kind of energy would do to the planet. He was just as happy without knowing how many millions of cubic meters of rock would be vaporized, or whether the atmosphere would be torn away in the cataclysm.

He didn't care about any of that. He only cared about two things. First, if he could get the charge in the right place, he could take out the Regent's antimatter production *and* supply in one fell swoop.

And, two...any of his Marines who were going to escape had to be not only out of the underground complex, but well on their way into orbit before he blew the charges.

Chapter Thirty-Two

Compton Square
Victory City, Earth Two
Earth Two Date 02.26.43

"Are you sure about this, Max?" Ana Zhukov stood next to Harmon, one of the dignitaries invited to watch the spectacle from the comfort and security of the Presidential Box, and a member of the select group that called Earth Two's dictator by his first name. Harmon was one of her closest friends, and she loved and respected him…but she thought what he was about to do was wrong…and she wasn't afraid to tell him.

"I don't want to do this, Ana. I *have* to." Harmon's tone was grim, morose. It was clear he didn't like what was about to happen, but just as evident he wasn't about to change his mind.

"I'm not saying you don't have to execute the real perpetrators, but there are sixty-four people waiting down there. Some of them are just kids."

Harmon turned toward her, the pain in his expression mixing with anger and determination. "Kids who were perfectly capable of plotting to murder their fellow citizens, Ana. I don't find the fact that they are a few years below legal adulthood all that compelling an argument for mercy, not considering what they did." The cadence of his voice suggested he *did* feel that way, actually, at least on some level. But, he still didn't budge.

251

"Ana…you have to understand. This is not just a matter of a terrible crime, or even of terrorist groups plotting against the government." Mariko Fujin was standing on the other side of her husband, and her voice lacked the doubt his still carried. "Erika West is not here. Neither is Cooper McDaid, Josie Strand, Raj Chandra, Devon Cameron. They are all out somewhere in deep space, fighting what is at best a desperate struggle…and, at worst a trap that will see them all lost. We are not only a new civilization, facing a hundred challenges to securing a future… we are still a group of refugees being pursued by a murderous power that would destroy us all given the chance."

She turned and gestured toward the square, where even then, Marines were leading the condemned to the scaffold the work crews had hastily assembled during the night. "Given different circumstances, we could debate endlessly how a just society should handle such situations. We could argue the points of view calling for mercy against those of the families of the innocent dead. But, it is not vengeance for the lost that is important now, nor even justice…if such a thing can be objectively defined. It is survival. Survival for all of us, as a people."

Zhukov leaned forward and looked over at Fujin. She'd been friends with the retired fighter pilot almost as long as she had been with Fujin's husband. She might have reacted angrily to someone else making the argument Fujin was, but she knew very well that Mariko was not a cold and uncaring person. There was realism in all she said, and Zhukov understood the idea that saving a few people at the risk of endangering an entire civilization was a dangerous, and perhaps unbalanced, point of view. But, she couldn't quite bring herself to look at things that way. Her efforts weren't helped when she saw two of the condemned dragged out onto the scaffold, both of them young men, no older than sixteen…and both slouched over, sobbing, begging their captors for mercy.

"I know this is difficult for you, Ana…but you must consider other images, the sky aflame, great mushrooms clouds obliterating all we have built, killing hundreds of thousands, until Earth Two is a silent tomb, our own people lost to the enemy even as the Ancients who preceded us." Harmon didn't sound any less miserable when he spoke, but she could hear the conviction growing stronger in his words.

She understood—she even agreed to an extent—but she couldn't bring herself to support what was about to happen. "Is this how you want to rule? To lead us to victory? With fear?"

She could tell immediately she'd hit a weak spot, and as firmly as she felt the executions, some of them at least, were wrong, she felt guilty for what she had just said.

"Yes…with fear." It was Fujin again, answering for her husband, and her voice was like ice. "I have watched for more than forty years, waiting for the day when my husband could set aside his burdens…and for the last twelve, we have lived in a house that looks more like a fortress, protected by Marines day and night. All that time, I have craved another way, a path to victory, to survival for Earth Two…but that has been nothing but a tortured dream. Max has dedicated his life to Earth Two, given all he has to secure a future for our people. I will not see that goal lost now for lack of the willingness to do what must be done." She looked at Harmon, her gaze one of unrelenting intensity. "It is time, Max…is it not?"

Harmon stood stone still for a moment. For the briefest of instants, he looked like he might back down, change his mind. But then he turned toward the Marine officer standing next to him, and he just nodded.

Down on the scaffold, Connor Frasier stood at rigid attention, the condemned men and women shackled to the long wall, and two rows of Marines waiting with assault rifles in their hands. The firing squads were not armored, but there were hundreds of Marines in full combat gear, positioned along the edges of the scaffold, and throughout the crowd.

Ana looked out over the silent masses, toward the Marines, and her husband. She was determined to force herself to watch, but in the end, her will failed her, and she closed her eyes, right before the assault rifles opened up, dealing out punishment to the terrorists…and a lesson to those in the crowds, and at home watching on the vids, one that made clear violent opposition would not be tolerated.

Max Harmon had been Earth Two's absolute rulers for twelve years, but he'd always been hesitant to use real force on the population, even those who plotted against him.

That was over now…and no one who had watched the spectacle in the center of Compton Square would every doubt that.

* * *

Max Harmon walked down the corridor, feeling his pace increase with excitement as he neared the Institute's infirmary. He'd almost leapt up from his desk when he'd gotten the call from Achilles, and he'd raced out of his office, barely giving his Marine escort time to catch up to him.

Harmon had known what the Mules were doing, the status of their research and the long list of potential uses for their Plague cure…but he'd never really believed he would hear the words Achilles had just spoken to him.

Nicki Frette was conscious.

Frette had long been one of Harmon's best friends, and he still accounted that he owed her his life. It wasn't everyone, friend or no, who would basically crash land a spaceship to save you. Frette had been one of the prime movers in the development and growth of Earth Two's navy over its formative years, and she'd led the fleet that had defeated the Regent's forces twelve years before…though she'd come back from that struggle gravely wounded.

Harmon had maintained hope for her recovery, for public consumption, at least, but, deep down, he'd long ago given up. And, as excited as he was, as much as he believed Achilles, he knew he wouldn't truly know it was true until he saw her himself.

"Mr. President…" Achilles was waiting for him outside the room.

"Achilles, I want to see her immediately."

"Of course, sir. But…" The Mule hesitated, an affectation to which he was rarely prone. "But, please…be calm with her. She is still disoriented. The med-field preserved her body and musculature quite well, but we have not yet been able to ascertain whether she has memories from her time in the coma. She is fragile…please do not push her too hard."

Harmon stood still for a moment and nodded. He felt he'd been punched in the stomach as he considered the possibility that his friend had spent a dozen years, still and unmoving… but *aware*. He couldn't imagine what kind of torture that would have been.

"Yes, Achilles, of course." He was grateful for the Mule's words. He'd been about to barge into the room with a million questions, and now he thought about Frette, about what she was had endured…about what she was likely going through trying to adapt.

Harmon followed the Mule into the room. His eyes fixed immediately on the cot against the far wall. There was a woman in it, propped up slightly, looking tired and worn, but most definitely awake.

"Nicki…" He took a few more steps forward, stopping at the side of the bed.

She turned her head slowly, the effort the movement took clear in her facial expression. But, she paused for a moment, looking up at him, and then her lips curled up into a feeble smile.

"Max," she said softly, her voice barely audible. She was looking at him, but her eyes didn't seem to be quite focused. Still, he felt a flush of excitement that she recognized him.

"I'd ask how you're feeling, but I'm afraid it's pretty obvious." He smiled, and then he dropped down to one knee, moving his face closer to hers. "I'm so glad to see you, my old friend."

"Has…it…really been…twelve…years?"

Harmon paused for a moment, but then he nodded. "Yes, Nicki. You gave us quite a scare for a long while." Another pause. "But, I always knew you were a tough one. Anybody who will crash a cruiser into a planet shouldn't be taken lightly."

Her smile widened, and she even managed a few soft chuckles. Then, she looked up at Harmon, and he could see concern in her eyes.

"Erika," she said softly, barely able to force the words from her parched throat. "Is Erika here?"

Chapter Thirty-Three

Flag Bridge, E2S Garret
F-74 System
Earth Two Date 02.26.43

Erika West watched as the asteroid fortresses opened fire, sending dense clouds of missiles toward the rapidly-approaching First Imperium vessels. Dense, of course, was a bit of embellishment, a testament to the huge number of warheads rather than their concentration. In actuality, there were kilometers between each of the weapons, and the entire barrage was spread out over tens of thousands of klicks.

The massive barrages from the forts joined the waves of missiles from Raj Chandra's ships...basically every one of the republic's vessels West hadn't already taken from Earth Two for her own fleet. She'd been surprised the night before her departure, when Harmon had accepted her proposal and agreed to strip Earth Two of every mobile defensive unit it possessed, but she realized later she shouldn't have been. Max Harmon was a gifted naval officer, one who had learned his craft at the feet of no less of a colossus than Terrance Compton. He knew as well as she did that a true defense of Earth Two was all but impossible, and that victory—survival—depended on finding and destroying the Regent before it did the same to them.

"All ships...arm missiles. Prepare to launch." Her tone was

frozen.

"Yes, Admiral."

Her people had watched the arriving enemy rip through the warp gate and past them at nearly .02c…right into the maw of Chandra's waiting fleet and the line of fortresses. The enemy ships were frantically decelerating, trying to form up to face the forces now threatening them from all sides…but it took time to offset two percent of lightspeed, even for First Imperium antimatter-powered engines.

West had calmly ordered her own ships, by far the larger of the two human fleets in the system, to advance on the enemy's rear…or, more accurately, to chase after the ships still moving away from her positions. In just a moment her forces would add every missile they had to the already monstrous volley streaming toward the enemy, though hers would be coming from the opposite direction. If her people could time things just right, they might give the Intelligences on those ships a bit of a headache trying to defend against attacks from two directions arriving more or less simultaneously.

"All ships report missiles ready, Admiral."

She didn't answer right away. She sat quietly, watching. Then, a few minutes later, at a moment she'd determined half by detailed analysis and half by what her stomach told her, she said coolly, "Launch all missiles."

She sat for the next ten minutes, watching as wave after wave of warheads spat forth from the magazines of her ships. It was a massive show of force, a tidal wave of looming destruction unparalleled by anything else imaginable.

Except the gargantuan cloud of missiles heading toward both her ships and Chandra's from the First Imperium fleet.

The force arrayed in the system was all the combined might of Earth Two, everything the republic could cobble together, save for Strand's ships still back in G48. West had chosen one of the decoy systems as the site of her great stand, in spite of the distance and the very real danger the enemy would attack before her fleet arrived.

The decoys had been developed to confuse the enemy, and

for years, they had been supported by false commercial traffic and made up communications. The Regent's forces had discovered one of the systems, and its forces had taken considerable losses from the fortified positions there before obliterating the planet...and subsequently realizing they had been deceived.

Now, West was using another of the decoys, augmenting her outnumbered ships with the fixed defenses...and Chandra's waiting fleet.

She watched as her fleet sent all its missiles out toward the enemy. Her escorts, and even the cruisers, quickly emptied their magazines, but her massive battleships continued to fire, sending wave after wave of deadly weapons toward the enemy. The largest of her ships, *Garret*, *Holm*, and *LeGrand*, finally launched the last of their missiles...moments before the leading edge of the enemy wave entered tactical range.

"All defensive batteries, prepare for point defense operations. All batteries are to fire at will as targets come into range."

Sampson turned and relayed the order on the fleetcom. West sat quietly and watched for a minute, perhaps ninety seconds... and then she heard the distant whine of *Garret*'s point defense turrets opening fire.

* * *

The Intelligence reviewed the scanner reports. The system was occupied, the planet located in the zone habitable for biologics. There was a considerable energy signature, and freighter traffic between the inhabited world and those deeper out in the system.

Was it possible the enemy had, in fact, returned to its homeworld? Was this the target for which the Regent had searched all these years?

There was no certainty. The enemy had lured the Regent's forces to a false homeworld once before, a trick that had caused the fleet to suffer considerable losses, both in ships and materiel, and slowed its search for the true target. The Intelligence was leery of another trap, but it could not discount the possibility that it *had* discovered the target world. The forces waiting in the system had clearly expected its arrival, and that increased the probability that the entire situation, perhaps even the enemy's flight itself, was part of some kind of ambush planned by the humans.

The Intelligence considered withdrawing, but it rejected that option almost immediately. Its velocity was too great to quickly come about, and it would endure extensive attacks from the humans before it could reach the warp gate and transit back. Besides, though the odds of combat were not as advantageous as it had expected, it still had the greater force. Losses would likely be high, but it determined that it could defeat the humans deployed in the system. If this was their homeworld, the war itself would be won at a stroke. If it was a trap, some sort of deception—as the Intelligence suspected—the battle would at least destroy the enemy fleet, which was its primary goal anyway. After that, it would only be a matter of time before the human homeworld was found and obliterated.

The Intelligence analyzed its position. Its fleet was stronger than the combined enemy forces, but it position was disadvantageous. It was compelled to decelerate rapidly, reducing the energy that could be deployed to weapons systems, at least initially. And, the enemy bracketed it on two sides, closing from both directions.

The Intelligence had launched all its missiles, dividing its barrage between the two enemy forces. That had been done before it had assembled the full data on what it faced, and it considered now that perhaps it should have concentrated the volley against a single target. It quickly set aside that line of computation… there was no point in reconsidering tactical options it could no longer implement. But, now, it had decided on its course of action.

It would decelerate, but it would reduce the rate of thrust it applied, feeding more energy into its energy weapons. It would focus on the enemy forces to its front, the fortresses and the smaller fleet. Slowing the rate of deceleration would buy time before the larger human fleet could close to its own energy weapons range, giving the Intelligence time to destroy the forward force. Then it would turn about and engage the fleet it had been pursuing originally…and complete its victory.

It sent the orders to all ships. Prepare to defend against enemy missiles…and charge all energy offensive batteries.

*   *   *

"Captain, all ships are to prepare for laser barrage. I'm going to want all batteries at one hundred five percent power when those enemy ships move into range, and I want all the power conduits and arming circuits checked now."

Terrance Compton sat at his workstation, listening to Admiral Chandra's orders. He was edgy, nervous, but he put all he had into maintaining a calm demeanor, one that would make his famous father proud. "Yes, Admiral."

Compton leaned forward and repeated the admiral's commands over the fleetcom. The orders weren't exactly unexpected, but Compton still found it difficult to stay focused and confirm the acknowledgements from each of the fleet's ships. He was distracted, in truth, because he was scared out of his mind.

He'd read accounts of his father's many battles, and he wondered how the elder Compton had managed to remain so stoic in the face of constant, deadly danger. Terrance felt shame, even as he hid that along with his fear. He'd come with the fleet by his own choice, to prove he could be his father's son…but now he wasn't sure he could manage it.

He understood why Admiral Chandra had chosen him as an aide—perhaps more likely, felt he'd *had* to choose him—but he wished he had a lower profile job. He'd come to regret the courtesy rank President Harmon had given him. The captain's insignia on his collar made it too hard to give him some faceless post in the bowels of one of the ships, one where his duties— and his failure if it came to that—would be someplace not quite so visible, and with consequences far less severe.

He'd been relieved at first at his posting in one respect—he'd been deathly afraid he'd be put in command of one of the fleet's ships—but now he realized he had even greater responsibility, that even more lives depended on his keeping his shit together.

He realized with a start that his board showed that every fleet unit had responded. He wasn't sure how long the indicators had been alight, but he turned hurriedly and reported, "All fleet units acknowledge, Admiral."

He moved back toward his bank of screens, watching as the waves of newly-launched missiles moved toward the enemy… and those launched by the First Imperium forces streaked toward the fleet.

Toward *Cain*, and on the great ship's flag bridge…him. He tried to suppress a shiver.

"Defensive batteries…open fire. Full point defense operations."

Compton heard Chandra's orders, and he spun around and forwarded them through the fleetcom as he had the previous set, perhaps with a bit more noticeable urgency this time. Prepping the heavy guns in advance entering range was one thing, but now the fleet would be shooting at missiles, deadly antimatter weapons that were coming right for them. An extra few seconds could save lives. Chandra's life. *His* life.

He sat and watched his workstation, feeling almost frozen in place. It would still be a few minutes before the missiles would reach detonation range, but the danger began to weigh heavily on him. A few seconds later, his screens lit up with the antimissile fire of the waiting vessels, defensive rockets and pinpoint lasers targeting the approaching warheads with all the skill the fleet's AIs and gunners could muster.

The shots were deadly, many of them at least, and dozens of incoming missiles vanished in massive explosions. The fleet's fusion warheads didn't usually detonate when intercepted, they just blew apart with muted blasts that barely showed up on scanners…but even a grazing hit from a defensive gun could shatter containment on an antimatter weapon, triggering an immediate—and massive—detonation. It made for quite a fireworks display, but it was unnerving, as well, to see the power of the weapons when hundreds of them were still moving relentlessly forward, their engines blasting at nearly 100g, attempting to close with the waiting warships of the fleet.

Compton took a deep breath, and held it for a moment, trying to hold things together, to find the courage he desperately wanted to believe lived inside him.

His life, for all the privilege he'd always enjoyed, had been a difficult and chaotic one in many ways, and he'd handled the pressure he'd inherited poorly. He was embarrassed about his youthful behavior, and he was determined to prove he was a valuable member of Earth Two society.

That he could become something that would have brought his father pride.

He didn't know yet if he could…but he was pretty sure he was about to find out.

* * *

"*Cain*'s thrust has dropped almost fifty percent, Admiral. We're still too far out for close scans, but it looks like she's bleeding air from multiple locations."

West sat stone faced, not acknowledging Sampson's report, not even turning her head slightly toward the aide's direction. She was in battle mode, and as grim and resolute as her reputation made her, she was determined to exceed even that standard. Raj Chandra was there in the system because she'd asked Max Harmon to send him, because she'd needed one more command-level officer she trusted completely, and he *was* the entirety of the list of available names. She couldn't let herself feel anything now, not fear, not intimidation at the size of the enemy fleet…and not guilt for dragging her friend from a well-deserved retirement to what was beginning to look like it could very well be an apocalypse.

The First Imperium missile barrages had been particularly effective, more so than they typically were. A dozen of her ships were broken, bleeding hulls, half of them dead in space, the others still moving forward with some small remnant of thrust. But, Chandra's ships and the asteroids had taken the brunt of the enemy's attack. Six of the asteroids had been hit directly, victims of their inability to conduct evasive maneuvers. The antimatter warheads were enormously powerful, not enough to pulverize the asteroids themselves, except in one case, but each hit obliterated all manmade structures on the great chunks of rock…and killed the crews of the bases to a man.

The accuracy of the enemy assault might have cost her the battle right then and there, if her people hadn't matched and even exceeded the First Imperium marksmanship. Her missiles, and to a lesser extent, Chandra's, bracketed target after target, melting hulls and blasting the enemy ships with blistering levels of radiation. All told, the two sides had hurt each other roughly equally. West knew that was a win for her people, since they'd only had nuclear warheads to match the enemy's antimatter bombs. But, she also knew the gods of war did not adjust for advantages and disadvantages. One side would win the battle, and one side only, and the victory would be no less complete if it was won by superior weaponry than by tactics or determination.

"We need to close faster." She'd been keeping her fleet together, trying to hold the formation together, save only for the most damaged ships. But, now she realized Chandra's force would be wiped out if she didn't get there and add the firepower of her batteries to his. "All ships are to engage their maximum available thrust. We need to get whatever we can into range… now!"

"Understood, Admiral." Sampson turned toward her station and relayed the orders. A few seconds later, *Garret*'s acceleration increased, and the bridge crew felt the equivalent of almost 5g. West's flagship had been among her most fortunate vessels—or perhaps more accurately, she'd benefitted from the calm brilliance of her crew as the gunnery stations intercepted every missile that came close. One warhead had detonated about two and a half kilometers out, but that had only caused some minor damage to surface scanners. The ships of her fleet were in varying conditions, but the flagship was one hundred percent ready for battle.

"Course adjustment, Commander…*Garret* only. Vector

230.012.309." West's eyes were fixed straight ahead toward the display. Three enemy battleships had targeted *Cain*, and she knew the battleship wouldn't hold out long against those odds. She had to get there and join in the fight. "And get me Admiral Chandra." *Garret* was close enough now, so the communications lag would just be annoying rather than crippling.

"Course adjustment laid in." A moment later. "*Cain* on our line, Admiral."

"Raj...hang in there. We're on our way."

"Admiral West?"

The voice wasn't Chandra's. It was familiar, but she couldn't place it.

"Admiral Chandra is wounded, Admiral," the voice continued.

West paused another few seconds, and then she realized...

"Captain Compton?"

"Yes, sir. I'm at *Cain*'s tactical station right now." A pause, then nervously, "Actually, I guess I'm in command...of *Cain*, at least. I'm not sure who's in charge of the fleet now."

West stared forward, her frozen concentration blown. What the hell was Terrance Compton doing at that station? She knew Harmon had given him a captain's commission...and promised him a combat position...but how could he have sent him on this mission?

Shit...

She was disoriented for a moment, struggling to stay focused...but then she regained her control.

"Well, Captain Compton...I guess *you're* in command of the fleet...at least until I get there and take over." A pause. She almost said something about his father, tried to put together some words of encouragement...but then she realized every officer had to be himself. "You've got the training, Terrance... and you're a good man. Keep that fleet in the fight until my ships get there...you hear me?"

"Yes, Admiral." His voice was shaky, but there was strength in it, too.

She just hoped it was enough.

Chapter Thirty-Four

Planet G-48 II
Somewhere Below the Surface
Earth Two Date 02.27.43

Cameron was firing down the vast open chamber, his assault rifle blasting out bursts of a dozen shots at a time. The battle had been going on for over an hour, the enemy seemingly throwing everything it had at the Marines. He was exhausted, despite the steady dose of stims, and he was trying to keep his mind away from the losses his people had suffered.

But, Cameron saw a ray of hope in the deadly carnage. The intensity of the enemy assault only confirmed his guess that his people had reached the deeply-buried storage units, the great magnetic bottles that held tons of antimatter, keeping particles of the dangerous substance from any cataclysmic interactions with regular matter. For all the defenses the Regent had in place around its precious treasure, Cameron knew such a storage facility was inherently vulnerable.

Cameron had taken advantage of the destruction of the enemy's jamming mechanisms to contact his scattered groups of Marines, and he credited the improved comms with a lot of the assault's success. He'd called down a large number of reinforcements, and he knew there was no way the advance would have gotten so far without the help. Now, however, he was hesitating on calling more reserves. If his people were indeed standing in the center of the storage facility, it was time to do what they'd come to do…and getting his Marines out of the tunnels and off the planet before detonating tons of antimatter had become crucial.

"Major…get two of your people over to that far flank. We don't want any of those bots moving up and getting another line of fire on us." His mind was jerking around wildly, from one thing to the next, trying to keep track of everything from the withdrawal he was about to order to the continuing firefight going on around him.

"Yes, sir." Stanton stood where he was, his bulky suit still, and Cameron knew the officer was on the comm, passing on the order…something that became even clearer, when two of the Marines positioned near that end of the small line jumped up and moved down to the end of the giant bulkhead they were all using for cover. Stanton was doing a reasonable job hiding the fact that he was wounded—as far as Cameron could tell, badly wounded. In any other operation, Cameron would have relieved his second in command and sent him back to the field hospital. Only there were no Marines to spare, not now…and there wasn't a field hospital either. The atmosphere was toxic, the temperature far too hot to sustain life for long, and the radiation levels were lethal. The only hospital Stanton was going to get to this side of retrieval and landing on one of the orbiting ships was the one built into his suit.

Fortunately, that was the most sophisticated portable medsystem ever developed, and Cameron suspected his officer would be dead already without it. He had no doubt Stanton was in a lot of pain, nor that every move was a colossal effort for the officer…but he also figured his number two could make it, at least if he was able to get him out.

Cameron's mind was racing. His first thoughts had been to gather as much strength as possible and continue to push forward. But now, as he looked around and realized the great cylinders in the room were very likely the storage units his people had been searching for, he felt another hesitation about bringing more of his Marines—those who had survived the fighting throughout the facility—down deeper.

Farther from an escape that already seemed hopeless enough…

"Status on that thing, Lieutenant?" He'd had two of his Marines setting up a portable scanner to confirm whether or not the giant constructs in the room were, in fact, full of anti-matter. The enemy's fire had been restrained, which had added to his belief that his Marines had indeed reached what they had sought. First Imperium warbots were not known for the delicate way they conducted themselves…but Cameron was pretty sure the fire coming in was a fraction of what it could have been. Should have been.

If those robots were not trying to avoid vulnerable targets, we'd be eating three or four times this much fire…

"We've got it up now, sir. Just a few seconds, and we should have some readings."

Cameron nodded, forgetting as he sometimes did that it was a pretty ineffectual gesture when fully armored. "Very well," he added, almost as an afterthought. His mind had already moved forward, feeling the fateful decision coming down on him.

What to do next.

"General, those cylinders…whatever they're made of, they seem to block scanner beams." The Marine at the scanning setup sounded frustrated. "We can't get a look inside, no matter how much power we pour on."

Cameron felt deflated for a few seconds. But, then the Marine at the scanner continued. "But, we're picking up energy readings anyway. It almost doesn't make sense. We can't penetrate the casings with *our* beams, but the scanner is still reporting signs of internal energy levels, substantial ones.

Cameron's excitement returned. The First Imperium and its dark energy infused metals were still a mystery to human science. Even the Mules had been unable to come up with more than a few fringe hypotheses. But, there was no doubt the materials were largely scanproof.

And, if there is enough energy in those cylinders to give off a signature anyway, through all that blockage…

"That has to be it." *Antimatter.*

Cameron wasn't sure, of course…he couldn't be absolutely sure. Still, he hadn't been willing to risk everything on destroying the cylinders before he had those readings…

But, he was now.

"Alright, Lieutenant Livermore…I want those charges set up right now." He hesitated and looked around the edge of the massive chunk of metal his people were using for cover. They were about sixty meters from the closest cylinder. Close enough to destroy anything with twenty kilotons.

Anything we know of…

His mind raced, the losses, the suffering, the desperate, hurried retreat he hoped his people could make to the surface… only to see the cylinders survive the explosion. For the mission to end in failure.

No, he couldn't take any chances. None that were within his power to avoid.

"Wait," he said, pausing for a few seconds after. "Not here… we've got to push closer. I want each of those charges right next to one of the cylinders." He took a deep breath, focusing his determination. "And, I mean *right* next to them."

He reached behind him, pulling his assault rifle around again. "Major…you will stay here with the explosives teams. You are to move forward toward the two closest cylinders as soon as we've cleared the way. All teams are to set up and arm the charges the instant they're in position."

"Yes, sir." Stanton didn't sound happy about staying in the rear…but Marines didn't argue with orders, not in the middle of battle.

"Alright…everybody else, on me. We're moving forward, and we're taking out everything in our way. There is no stopping, no hesitating. We need to get the bomb teams up to those cylinders…whatever it takes. Are you with me?" It was a needless question, he knew, but its purpose wasn't to determine if his Marines would follow him. It was to fire them up, get them ready for the attack Cameron knew, for many of them, at least, would be their last.

And, the roar that blasted through his speakers didn't disappoint him.

He took one more deep breath and tightened his armored fingers around the assault rifle. Then he lunged out, firing on full automatic, as he raced down the gargantuan chamber…heading toward the darkness at the far end, and right into the enemy.

* * *

"Admiral…we just got a flash transmission from the surface. General Cameron was able to get a message through." A pause, then: "He thinks they found the antimatter storage units!" Sampson was a disciplined officer, but she couldn't hide her excitement at the news.

Strand was a bit more circumspect. She'd come to G48 to see the antimatter factory destroyed, of course, and there didn't seem to be any more certain way to achieve that that blasting open containment vessels and releasing kilograms—if not tons—of antimatter to annihilate with the regular matter all around. But, a report was not a certainty, and she still harbored worries that Cameron was wrong.

Or, perhaps it was more her almost relentless certainty that every Marine she'd landed on the planet would die there. Part of her knew the importance of destroying the factory, and of all her people had sacrificed to make it a possibility—not to mention whatever nightmare Erika West and her fleet were enduring—but she realized on some level, she'd been telling herself it couldn't work, preparing herself for failure.

Now, success seemed possible…and all she could think of were the Marines, the men and women who'd voluntarily gone down there, and marched their way down, deep below the surface of a world so alien, the only comparisons that came to a human mind thinking about it were various incarnations of hell.

"Very well," she said softly, realizing she still didn't believe Cameron's people could complete their mission, no matter what the communique said.

"Admiral…General Cameron requests we begin evacuation operations of all surface forces." A short pause. "He is also sending up any of the underground teams not involved in his immediate operations."

Strand listened to the words, and she understood. She didn't know General Cameron well, but from everything she did know, she'd always suspected she would have liked him.

Now, she was sure.

"Bring the fleet to yellow alert, Commander. I want all ships with landing craft capable of getting down to the surface and back again to get them ready." She could feel her resolve building, even as her doubts persisted. "I want medical teams on as many of the retrieval boats as possible." A short pause. "And, I want everything ready to launch in fifteen minutes."

Sampson hesitated, but then she said, simply, "Yes, Admiral."

Strand knew her orders, and the timetable she'd given, were impossible. But, she didn't care. All she could think of was Devon Cameron and the Marines with him down in that chamber so deep…so far from escape.

And, in some small corner of her mind, she was beginning to believe Cameron's people might actually succeed. She didn't have a doubt in her mind the Marine general would pay for that victory with his life, however, and the last thing she was going to do was fail his final request. Fail to save as many of his Marines as she could.

No…fifteen minutes might have seem impossible, but it's God damned not, no matter what it takes.

* * *

"Surface command post reports retrieval boats inbound, Sir."

Cameron felt a smile forming on his face as the words, staticky and distorted, but understandable enough, at least after his AI had cleaned up the signal, poured out into his helmet. His Marines were going to get off the planet in time.

Some of them, at least.

"Very well, Sergeant. All stations are to sound withdrawal signals. Any Marines not down here with us, should be on their way to the surface."

"Yes, General." If there was any hint of resentment about his ordering everyone out save for those in the cavern, he couldn't detect it in the non-com's voice.

He knew Marines would still die beyond his immediate location. Half his people were *already* gone. More than that, probably. He'd regained some comms, but he still had units out of touch, and he suspected some of them, at least were still alive.

They won't be for long…not unless they get a signal soon and get the hell out…

He pushed that out of his mind, though. There was nothing he could do, and the task in front of him had now become his obsession. All his people who'd died already, and those who were still going to…it was about them. The next hour or two would determine if they died for nothing…or to strike a blow to save their friends and loved ones.

And, Devon Cameron was going to give everything he had to make sure it was the second option.

Everything.

The room was quiet, nothing save for the sounds of his Marines moving around and working on the charges. The fight had been a fierce one, a struggle that had seen few of his people come away from without a wound of some kind.

Himself included.

He'd managed to hide the severity of his injury, and cover up the effects with painkillers and stimulants. But, he was pretty sure of two things.

One, he was going to keep himself functioning as long as it took to see the mission completed…whatever it took.

And, two, there was no way he was going to make it back up to the surface.

He took a breath, ragged and full of fluid. Then, he turned toward the team setting up the second charge.

"Status?" he said, trying to sound as normal as he could.

"Ready, sir." A short pause. "Setting up the charges was easy enough. The tough part was getting them synchronize. We want them both to blow, not for one to go off a few microseconds early, and blast the other one to bits before the reaction fires off."

"Are they synchronized now?" Cameron understood the problem, but he wasn't sure he had a good grasp on what it took to address it.

"The best we can manage down here, sir. There's still a chance we'll only get one blast—which should be enough, anyway—but I think we've got a good chance of both of them going at the same time."

"Alright...if you're all finished, get your people together and get ready to head out to the surface. There isn't much time." Cameron glanced back toward the nearer charge, positioned just up against the large cylinder about three meters from where Cameron stood.

"We've set the charges to detonate in one hour, and we've connected the activation switch to your channel. Your AI will activate the sequence on your command, and then it's sixty minutes before they blow. They're also rigged to go immediately if they pick up any energy readings or motion coming into the room. So, even if more enemy forces show up, they won't have a chance to disarm the weapons." Left unsaid was the fact that an early detonation would bring an instant a tragic end to any evacuation operations.

"Well done, Lieutenant. Get your people moving." His eyes darted up to the top of his helmet display, to the flashing yellow light he knew signified the detonation switch.

He paused, standing still for a few seconds, fighting off a burst of dizziness. His trauma system had just started giving him another round of blood substitute, and, as he stood for a moment, he started to feel a bit better. He was uncomfortable, not just from the pain, but from the general messiness inside his suit. The med system had soaked up as much blood and other fluids as possible, but the inside of his armor was still a sticky mess.

He took as deep a breath as he could imagine, trying to center himself, to pull up enough strength to follow his Marines back to the surface. But, he just didn't think he could make it… and the last thing he was going to allow was for anyone to stay behind to help him. He'd already sent Stanton and most of the others back up, and he knew it was going to take everything the remaining Marines had to make it in time…and that did *not* include carrying their wounded commander through the corridors at a snail's pace.

"Sir…everything here is set. Shouldn't we all leave together?"

Cameron felt a flush of anger, but it quickly subsided. He'd known his Marines would question why he wasn't coming. They knew he'd been wounded, of course—anyone who'd seen the huge gash on the front of his suit, patched up with sterile packing, knew that. But, he'd done a good job of misleading them, of telegraphing that his injuries were less severe than they were…a bit of deception made a lot easier by the fact that, as commander, he was the only one with control over his own medical readouts.

He stood for a moment, uncertain what to say. He'd planned on staying behind, seeing the mission through to the bitter end. But, he found the idea of surviving, or at least having a chance at it, to be an appealing one.

Besides, with the motion sensors, his rationale for staying, to detonate the charges if the enemy appeared to be on the verge of reaching them, was no longer operative. He questioned if he would be able to keep up with the others…and, he knew they would slow down to accommodate them if he couldn't. And, that, he couldn't allow.

But, that was easy enough to handle. One quick thought to his AI, and a massive overdose of sedatives would end his Marines' burden.

"Okay then…let's go…"

Cameron froze, his eyes darting to the scanner projection inside his helmet, just as his AI warned him of what he was seeing.

"Enemy forces approaching…"

Chapter Thirty-Five

Terror. Absolute, utterly frozen fear ripped through Terrance Compton's body, pushing him to the limits of his control. It wasn't primarily fear of death, though he was scared out of his mind of that as well. No, it was the responsibility, the deep and mournful bell of Erika West's voice telling him he was in command of Raj Chandra's fleet.

He would have argued with her...if he hadn't been shocked to speechlessness by her words. But, even as he sat there, silent, trying to keep his body from shaking uncontrollably, he started to try to grasp for some kind of stability. There wasn't time to argue, nor to debate who was better prepared to take command than he was. The fleet was in a desperate fight, a struggle for survival, and uncertainty was almost as much an enemy as the First Imperium forces currently closing to point blank range.

Admiral West had the larger force, but the enemy was clearly focused on his ships—he struggled to think of them as *his* ships. Her forces were coming on at maximum thrust, but Compton knew that his outnumbered comrades had to hold out somehow...and the first step to making that happen was to give them the commander they needed.

275

His thoughts argued with themselves. He knew he didn't have the experience to lead a force like the one he now seemed to command. No, not *seemed*. Erika West was the navy's commanding officer, and she'd put him in charge. The other captain's, the ship commanders locked in desperate battle, would be looking to him for orders.

It doesn't make sense…why would she put me in command?

But, even as he wondered, he grasped at seeds of understanding.

The fleet was locked in battle, ships matched off against their First Imperium counterparts. There were no fleet strategies now, no desperate maneuvers. Just a fight to the finish. And, morale was the vital thing now.

She wants to invoke the memories of my father…

He felt an instant of resentment, but then it passed, and he realized, Admiral Terrance Compton would have been the first on to use whatever worked.

And Erika West learned at his feet…

"Lieutenant Brickell…all ships are to increase reactor output to one hundred ten percent. All excess power to the main batteries."

The bridge officer looked back across the wide space of *Cain*'s control center, pausing, appearing uncertain for a moment. They had all heard West's orders…but there was hesitancy, too.

Compton paused himself, his mind tearing at itself, even as West's words repeated themselves again and again in his head. *You wanted to prove you were your father's son…was that just shit? Or did you mean any of it?*

He could feel a chasm opening up, threatening to pull him away, to break what resolve he'd managed to scrape together… but then there was something else, a feeling he'd never experienced before, a strength of sorts, even an anger.

"You heard me, Lieutenant," he said, surprising even himself with the raw determination in his tone. "Now!"

"Yes, sir." The officer spun around and passed on the orders, even as Compton stood up from his station, tearing off the straps of his harness and walking across the bridge. He hesitated, just for a few seconds, staring down at the command chair...the one still stained with Raj Chandra's blood. Then he turned around and sat down, sitting as bolt upright as he could manage, as his eyes glared out across *Cain*'s bridge.

"All ships acknowledge, Captain."

"Very well, Lieutenant." He looked straight ahead toward the main display, his eyes coldly focused, feeling as he never had before. He was still scared...but that didn't matter now. He knew what he had to do, and he wasn't going to let his comrades down, not this time.

He could feel a coldness taking him, and he opened himself to it, yielded to the strange sensation. He'd heard his friends many times, Admiral West certainly, and President Harmon as well, speak of the feeling of a predator that took them in battle. Now, he felt it too, and his blood almost cried out for the destruction of the enemy...the foe his father had died fighting against. The enemy his people had battled for more than half a century.

The deadly foe he would fight now...with all he could muster.

* * *

"All ships, maintain full fire." Erika West sat like a carven statue on *Garret*'s bridge, shouting out commands like some angel of death, come to bring ruin and devastation on her enemies. There was no fear, no hesitation, no regret. Not while the battle still raged.

She had no time for personal thoughts, nor even emotions. What little concern had remained of what her people thought of her was gone, too...though she suspected any spacers' inclinations that their fighting admiral had lost her nerve were gone now. They might curse her as an insane demon, one who'd brought them to their deaths, but the briefest look at the maelstrom into which she'd led them had washed away any hints of cowardice.

Cain shook hard, and West smiled. Not because her ship

took a hit, but because it had entered into firing range. The battle had raged for hours now, and the system was full of debris, battered ships bleeding atmosphere, clouds of radiation that were all that remained of vessels where moments before, human and robot crews had battled each other, neither side seeking nor granting quarter. The battle would be one to annihilation, and West's ships had been mostly out of the action as they pursued the First Imperium fleet, desperately trying to accelerate and reach the enemy forces before they wiped out Chandra's—now Compton's—fleet.

West knew she should be worried about Compton, that her friend's son didn't have the skill and experience to command a fleet, even if he did have his father's heart buried in there somewhere. Even more shocking, the younger Compton had made his share of mistakes, and West wasn't usually the type to give second chances, and most who'd served with her considered her cold and unforgiving. She'd always smarted a bit knowing those views were out there, but she'd long ago decided that, true or not, she could turn the opinions to her advantage. The 'ice admiral' and 'West the merciless' had helped her build her reputation…and that had been a huge part of what she'd turned into the successes she'd won. In the end, victory came from the men and women who fought each battle, and they could be driven to give their best by love of a leader, as they had been with the senior Compton…or by fear and intimidation, as West knew had been the case with many who had followed her.

For all the analysis West put into her battles, the matchups and the tactical plans, she knew this battle would be won—or lost—as all ultimately were, by the hearts of men and women. And, for all Terrance Compton had failed to live up to Earth Two's unreasonable expectations in his youth, she believed he had it in him. And, perhaps more importantly, she knew her people would follow him if he showed it.

So, she'd taken a gamble, made a spot decision and placed him in command when he'd told her Chandra was wounded. Despite her reputation for stone cold tactics, Erika West relied on her gut, too…far more often than almost anyone knew. And her gut told her to trust Terrance Compton.

"Engineering reports reactor output up to eighty-three percent, Admiral."

"Very well," she said coolly, doing all she could to play on the persona she'd built over a lifetime. "All ships are to accelerate to maximum thrust and close on the enemy's main body." Her ships were facing a rearguard that had pulled away from the main First Imperium fleet. She knew its purpose—to hold her forces back until the Regent's main body finished off Compton and the rest of the fleet. The fortresses were already mostly gone, the curse of all non-mobile platforms once an advancing enemy got into close range. She'd told herself some of the crews, at least, had managed to evacuate, but she didn't really believe it. She'd watched most of the bases fighting to the very end.

She'd planned the battle going on now…basing it heavily on her intuition for how the First Imperium forces would react. She'd considered every possibility, every action the enemy might take, but until those ships had taken off after hers back in the G48 system, she hadn't known it was going to succeed.

Even then, she'd sweated the whole trip to the decoy system, deathly afraid the enemy fleet would advance and attack… and overwhelm her outnumbered forces before they reached the help she'd been pretty sure, but far from certain, had been waiting for them in F74.

She pushed those thoughts aside. There was no use wasting time on what might have happened. Carefully planned or a wild gamble, her scheme had worked, at least as far as luring the enemy to the desired location.

It was still an open question how that fight would go.

She looked across the display, her eyes moving along the pointed lights of her battleline. There were a lot of ships gone already, including more than ten blown to dust by the antimatter missile barrage of the enemy fleet…and her fleet had endured the lighter side of the attack. Chandra's ships—Compton's now—had been battered brutally, thousands of gigatons of warheads screaming in and detonating all around. The survival of any semblance of Chandra's battleline was another debt she owed to the crews of the fortresses. The Regent's ships had been forced to blast the asteroids with massive waves of warheads, weapons that hadn't been available to come at the ships of the fleet.

She closed her eyes for just a second, recalling the fire and death that had surrounded the bases. Then she opened them again, and she was focused, the emotions creeping around the outside of her psyche gone, back where they belonged.

At least as long as the battle went on…which seemed like it would be for quite some time.

* * *

Cain shook wildly, and along the port side of the bridge, a massive panel fell, slamming into the deck and sending a shower of sparks flying all around. The battleship was immense, a dark monolith of metal that made the ships that had served in the wars of its namesake seem almost tiny slivers by comparison. The automation and the ancient technology unlocked by the Mules had made something like *Cain* possible…but there was little difference between the driving force that made men and women ride the behemoth to war. Terrance Compton looked around his command chair, at his people, at their steadfastness, even as the great chunk of metal that carried them through space's deadly vacuum began to break apart.

"Bring us around, one hundred eighty degrees in the Y plane." Compton wasn't even sure where the orders were coming from inside him, or the deep and strong voice with which he delivered them…but he didn't let that stop him. He'd never met his father, save for his conversations with the machine that bore what remained of his knowledge and memories, but he felt proud—more so, for the first time in his life he believed his father would be proud. His people were dying all around him, but he believed he was leading them well…and that his presence invoked the legend of the great Admiral Compton, inspired the sweating, bleeding men and women to find a way to dig deeper, push harder. Terrance was no philosopher, but he believed warriors facing death deserved to believe in whatever things aided them in their time of trials. And, for many of Earth Two's people, even the Next Gens and Tanks who'd never known the man as Terrance himself had never known him, that was Admiral Compton, the great commander who had led them through the First Imperium to Earth Two.

"Captain, I've got Admiral West for you." He could even hear the respect in the officer's voice, where a few hours before there had been uncertainty and doubt. He was terrified, still… that hadn't changed. But he drew some gratification from the redemption he felt, far more quickly than he'd imagined possible.

"Admiral…Captain Compton here." West's forces were finally closing in, and even as the enemy was pushing hard, striking to finish off his battered survivors, her ships were moving up behind them, ripping past their rearguards and coming hard at their biggest and toughest ships, ignoring damage and danger as they moved inexorably forward.

"Terrance…you've done a spectacular job. You've pulled your people together, and despite your lack of experience, you knew what to do. You've got me believing the spirit of your father *is* alive in you."

"Thank you, Admiral." Compton wasn't sure how much he believed West and how much she was manipulating him—even for his own good—driving him to do what he had to do. And, he didn't care, not now. He'd longed to hear the words she'd just spoken for so many years, it almost didn't matter how sincere she was.

"Listen to me, Terrance…we've hurt these bastards, but the battle isn't over yet. They still outnumber us, and their ordnance and supplies will probably outlast ours, so we've got to win this fight and win it now. Bring your people forward, right at mine. Let's put these damned robots in a vice and squeeze until there's nothing left." She hesitated. "Are you with me, Terrance?"

He could feel the wave building in him, the combination of pride, rage, vengeance. He knew West was working him, but it didn't matter. She was right.

It was time.

Time to win one for his father.

"I'm with you, Admiral."

Chapter Thirty-Six

"The first wave is coming up now, Admiral. Three hundred six Marines aboard..." A short pause. "One hundred ninety-four wounded."

Nothing Hercule had just said surprised Strand, but she felt the impact of the words just the same. Just over three hundred Marines out of the nearly two thousand she'd landed, and almost two-thirds of them were wounded. She was sure there would be more in the next waves—her pilots had reported as much—but, she also knew the first group was almost certainly the largest. No matter how she did the math in her head, Cameron's Marines had lost two-thirds of their number.

Perhaps even three-quarters.

"Anything else from General Cameron?" She'd managed to piece together the fact that Cameron had gone down to the designated ground zero...to supervise the final operations himself. There had been combat down there, heavy combat, but from the last reports to come in, it seemed like the Marines had cleared the area.

It was anyone's guess how long it would stay cleared, but it was still about the best news she could have hoped to get.

"Second wave status, Commander?"

"Projected launch in seven minutes, Admiral." Hercule hesitated, holding back on reporting any numbers.

"Continue, Commander." Strand had an idea what had held her aide's tongue. But, she had to hear it. She had to know.

"Forty-three Marines, Admiral. Approximately half wounded."

"Any sign of General Cameron?"

Hercule looked back across the bridge. "Negative."

Strand wasn't surprised, but she was disappointed nevertheless. She was really rooting for Cameron.

She sat still in her chair, watching, even as the ships of the first wave began to dock...and those of the second lifted off. Still, without Devon Cameron aboard.

She stared at the display, at the grim and hellish surface of the planet, trying to imagine what kind of nightmare it was about to become. She realized, analytically, at least, that when those charges blew—if they blew—the fleet would have accomplished its mission, destroyed the Regent's source of antimatter. For such a blow against the enemy, casualties barely figured into the calculation. Whatever devilish plan that twisted machine had planned, she couldn't imagine it had included her people actually destroying the entire factory. It would be a victory, a massive one that, on a spreadsheet, justified all the losses her forces had suffered.

But, she still couldn't think of anything but the dead, the hundreds of spacers and Marines already lost...and the ones who would never make it off that cursed planet.

Including Devon Cameron.

*   *   *

"Get moving, all of you!" Cameron was standing against a wall of metal, leaning around and firing out across the room as he yelled into his comm. The shooting volume had slowed, but there were still spurts of fire coming in...from a single remaining enemy bot, he thought. Half a dozen of his Marines, all volunteers, had stayed behind with him to hold off the enemy attack while the others withdrew. Cameron didn't think there was any way First Imperium bots could stop him from blowing up the facility—it was too late for that—but he also knew he had to buy time for the rest of his people to get back to the surface.

"Sir…we can't leave you here."

"That's an order, Sergeant." He fired again, sending three semi-automatic bursts out into the shadowy darkness. "Leave me your extra cartridges and go." A pause. "Now, move!"

"No, sir!" The sergeant was standing across from Cameron, wedged behind a large pillar he was using for cover. "There's only one more of them down there. We can finish it off, and then we can all get going."

"There's no time, Sergeant. Now, follow my orders, and get the hell out of here!"

Cameron was angry…but he was also overcome by the loyalty of his last few comrades. He was proud of the spirit of the Corps, the grim comradeship…but he wasn't going to let them sacrifice what slim chances they all had left. The remaining Marines had a poor enough chance to get out…waiting any longer, and dragging his wounded carcass with them, was only going to turn unlikely into impossible.

"No, General…we're all leaving together, or we're not leaving at all."

Cameron turned his head abruptly in anger, bringing on a wave of dizziness as he did. The disorientation blunted his rage at the Marine's insubordination, and he stood where he was, trying to stay focused, to decide how to handle the situation.

He was about to repeat his order, but then he realized the Marines weren't going to listen. They were determined to stay with him, to get him out of there…or to ensure that he didn't die alone, abandoned, kilometers below the surface. He could feel his fists squeezing tight, anger, frustration, gratitude, all combining together in a storm of uncontrolled emotions.

Finally, he said, "Alright then…we've got to take that thing down now, so we can get the hell out of here." He paused for a few seconds. "So, on three…everyone with me." He didn't want any time to think about what he was doing.

"One." He leaned forward, his tired grip tightening on his rifle.

"Two." He took in a deep breath, ignoring the pain in his battered chest and sucking in every drop of oxygen-rich air he could.

"Three." He lunged ahead an instant early, an attempt to put himself out in front of his Marines…but there, he met with limited success. As far as he could tell, every one of them had jumped forward early, and now they were charging across the room, opening up with all the firepower they had left in their depleted stocks.

There were no storage tanks in the enemy bot's direction, at least, so there was no need to exert any care at all in where they fired. The whole thing was a desperate attempt to clear out the last of the enemy, to score a lucky hit and clear the way to make a desperate last dash to escape.

Cameron kept running…until he realized the incoming fire had gone silent. He raised up his hand as he snapped out, "Halt," and then he stopped and checked his scanner display. Nothing. No fire at all. No enemy movement within the range of his detection capability.

He'd been resigned to death, but now he felt a surge of enthusiasm, a desire to get the hell out of the enemy base, to survive, somehow, against the odds. He knew the chances were poor, but even if he'd been ready to give up on himself, he wasn't about to surrender the lives of his last companions who had stayed with him.

"Activate countdown," he said to his AI, watching as the small clock display appeared on his projection. His eyes were fixed as one hour gave way to fifty-nine minutes, fifty-nine seconds. "Let's go, Marines…we're on the clock." He shot a thought toward his AI, a demand for a massive hit of stimulants. He disregarded the computer's compulsory warning that the dose he'd requested was dangerous, and he renewed the order. Nothing was more dangerous that being slowed now by wounds and fatigue.

He could feel the drug pouring into his bloodstream, replacing the exhaustion with a surge of energy. He knew all the damage such a big injection could cause him…but none of it seemed to compare much to still being in the tunnels when some undetermined but massive amount of antimatter escaped containment and annihilated.

*   *   *

"We're out of time, Major." Strand hated herself for the words coming from her mouth, but Stanton's report had only confirmed what she already knew. The charges were activated… and they were set to go off in less than twenty minutes.

Unless an enemy bot moved into the area…in which case the explosion would be immediate. Every second Stanton and the last few Marines stayed down there, they risked utter destruction.

Strand had almost given up on Cameron…at least until the Marine general and his tiny rear guard had gotten close enough to reestablish contact with the surface station. Cameron had brought news that the charges were in place, that the mission was moments away from success…and also that, somehow, he and his companions had managed to get three-quarters of the way back up to the surface.

It was unexpected, miraculous, inspiring. It was also too late.

She'd run the calculations a dozen times, instructed *Midway*'s AI to process every signal received and update the reported locations of the Marines. Every one of them had told her the same thing. There wasn't enough time.

"You've got to leave yourselves time to get out of the atmosphere, Major. That's no normal explosive down there." Strand understood the hesitancy of Cameron's Marines to leave him behind. She even agreed, on a personal level. But, she was the fleet commander, and she had her own responsibilities…to *all* the men and women under her authority.

She might have let the Marines decide to stay if they insisted…but she had a ship crew down there as well, and she felt responsible for their lives…so much so, that she'd ordered them to lift off at once, whether the Marines liked it or not.

And, they had refused. Her crew had thrown in with the Marines, and they had told her, with all the respect it was possible to attach to insubordination, that they were waiting for General Cameron and his people no matter what.

She'd gotten angry at first, furious even that her own spacers would disobey her in such a desperate situation. But, then it passed…and on some level she was even grateful to them for relieving her of the burden to give up on Cameron.

She watched as the time passed, each second seeming almost like an eternity, even as she saw the report that the Marines had reached the surface, that they were racing toward the waiting ship. Her hopeful thoughts were quickly squashed, however, when she saw the countdown clock.

Less than three minutes. Not enough time.

She watched, a feeling of helplessness growing on her, even as the ship sent back a flash comm, confirming everyone was aboard, and the hatches were bolted shut. Strand had calculated the minimum amount of time to get the retrieval boat to a safe altitude, even abandoning all safety precautions.

Six minutes.

Her people had one minute, forty seconds. She'd dreaded having to leave Cameron behind, but now she was going to have to watch all of them die…moments from the fleet. Her mind raced, wondering if there was some way to delay the explosion, get some kind of signal to the charges…but even before her mind focused, she knew there wasn't.

She watched as the small dot appeared on the scanner…the ship blasting up, heading toward orbit at a dangerous, almost crazed trajectory, especially in the thick atmosphere. She stared, knowing the ship could break up at any second from the insane maneuvers, even before the charges detonated, but somehow the vessel held together. It was farther up than she'd imagined, but any excitement she felt was quickly crushed as she saw the countdown clock slip under ten seconds.

She lurched her had back, checking the ship's location. It was still too close.

No…they can't come so close and miss it…not after what they did…

She could feel tears starting to well up in her eyes. It was her people in that ship, spacers and Marines…and a lot more she'd lost over the past few days, finally pushing past her ability to control it all.

She could feel the wetness streaming down her cheeks, even as the countdown hit zero.

For an instant, nothing seemed to happen…but then every instrument on the ship went crazy. The display went almost blindingly white. She waited for the screen to reset itself, to feed in scanning data on what was happening on the surface. But, even without the reports, she could see the image in her eyes.

Mountains surging up, their deep roots giving way as the rock that made them melted, and even vaporized. Earthquakes tearing thousand-kilometer-wide fissures in the planet's crust, loosing giant eruptions of radiation. The atmosphere itself, virtually torn from the ruined planet and blasted off into the frozen depths of interplanetary space.

Strand had been a combat veteran her entire adult life, but she had never seen devastation like that she imagined—and seconds later, actually saw—on the doomed planet beneath her ships.

She realized the mission had been a complete success. Nothing functional could have survived that cataclysm, however deeply buried. Whatever accelerators or storage facilities or warbots that had been down there were gone…completely and utterly gone.

She knew she should be excited. The mission had been a desperate gamble…and somehow her people had seen it done. They were heroes, all of them.

But, she had no joy for the 'victory.' All she could see was the cost…and the men and women most responsible for the victory gone, killed right before her eyes.

"Admiral…I think we're getting a signal."

She turned, shaking her head as she did. There was no way Hercule could pick any scanner signal out of the apocalyptic mess down below *Midway*. "It's got to be from the explosion, Henri." She couldn't imagine the billions of tons of earth obliterated, and the great clouds thrown up into what remained of the atmosphere. There was no way…

"Negative, Admiral, I've got a *signal*. It's faint…but I've definitely got it." He spun his head around a few seconds later. "It's the retrieval boat, Admiral. It's drifting, its engines and reactor are out…" A pause, and then Hercule continued, the excitement in his voice ramping up considerably. "But, all hands are accounted for…including the Marines."

The aide stared across the bridge at Strand, and even as he did, she felt his words sinking in almost as if in slow motion. It was too much to believe…and a small number of men and women compared to those she had already lost, but it was a miracle beyond any she'd dared hope for. She struggled to hold back the tears, but a few made it past even her focused vigilance.

She wiped her hand across her face, and she let out a deep breath.

Then, she turned toward Hercule. "Let's get the rescue ships out, Commander. We've got some of our people to pick up."

"Yes, Admiral."

A smile pushed out on her lips. She knew she'd feel the guilt for all those she'd lost…and the aching, almost unimaginable worry about what was happening to Erika and the rest of the fleet was there, a dark shadow over every thought. But, for that moment, all Strand could think about was Cameron and his Marines…and the almost inexplicable miracle that had brought them back out of those tunnels in time.

Not to mention Captain Graham, and his people from *Vaughn*. She'd almost forgotten the survivors they'd found still alive in *Vaughn*'s crippled innards. There had been twelve survivors in all, and every one of them was back aboard *Midway*, resting in sickbay. They had radiation sickness, dehydration, and a host of other conditions…but none of them were life threatening.

Strand had trouble reconciling herself with two unexpected rays of light amid the darkness and despair of the past weeks…

and, she wasn't about to push her luck any farther.

"Tell the shuttle crews to hurry, Henri. Because once we've got them all aboard, the way I see it, we're done here." A paused, and a deep sigh. "And that means it's time to go home."

Chapter Thirty-Seven

Ships exploded all around *Cain*, great blasts of hard radiation roiling through the vacuum of space as more and more of Compton's vessels were blasted to chunks of useless wreckage, or simply vaporized when their fusion reactions lost containment before they could scrag. Hundreds of spacers he'd served with on the journey to F74, that he'd commanded since Raj Chandra had been nearly electrocuted on the bridge and carried away unconscious hours before. For a few fleeting moments, perhaps an hour, of the most intense combat he'd ever imagined, he'd done all he could to sustain the spirit West had helped to cultivate. He'd spoken silently to the shade of his father trying to find the strength to continue, shouted encouragements to his officer and spacers. But, now, he could feel his spirit slipping away despite his desperate efforts to cling to hope. There just seemed no possible victory in F74, no defeat of the enemy. Just death, and then more death.

The First Imperium forces were suffering as badly as his own, and for all the damage that had been exchanged, the battle was no more decided than it had been hours before.

The last of the fortresses were gone now, the single laser

pit that had outlasted every other emplacement on the twenty asteroids, finally taken out by the concerted attack of two First Imperium battleships. Even in death, however, that valiant crew continued to strike back as *Cain* had moved in and taken the first of the attackers in flank. Compton had burned out two of his laser turrets to do it, cranking the power to one hundred thirty percent and holding the shot until point blank range.

The enemy ship had tried to pull away, to escape the deadly assault coming upon it, but it had been too late. The great beams ripped forward, fusing their own turrets into useless scrap as they lanced out and slammed into the enemy Colossus.

The enemy battleship shuddered hard, and it rolled over in an uncontrolled spin as its engines gave out and internal explosions wracked its dying frame. Compton stared at the display, feeling the predator's joy of the kill...but only for a second or two. Then, his eyes were on the second target.

The next fight was a tougher one, more even a contest, and the two ships exchanged all they could at each other, one volley after the next tearing across the narrow gap of space. Great sections of Compton's ships were shattered, bulkheads blown out and whole compartments ripped open to the ravages of space. The intraship comm systems were damaged in areas, and he had no idea how many of his people had been killed...blown out through great rents in the hull or blasted to death by radiation. But, what he did know, finally, was that the second enemy ship was no more. He'd been watching when the last hit struck... and seconds later when the great vessel exploded with an almost unimaginable ferocity.

Cain had taken down two of the First Imperium's frontline battleships...but Compton knew his flagship was nearing its own limit. He looked around the display, at the battered chunks of wreckage that had once been his fleet. He knew his force had little left to give, that he was lucky if ten percent of his original firepower remained. But now, West's vessels had taken over most of the fight.

The enemy had come far to close to completing its goal of destroying his fleet before the main Earth Two forces could engage…but his people had held out, just long enough.

Long enough to see West's ships hit the enemy main body like a thunderclap. A cheer went up across *Cain*'s bridge, as Compton suspected one had on most of his ships. Help had finally arrived. His weary and battered crews deserved a chance to break off, to pull away from the fight and regroup.

But, that was not to be.

Even as West's ships plunged into the battle, it was clear that the enemy forces still held the upper hand. Whatever Compton's people had left, whatever power and weapons their broken and damaged ships could muster, it was desperately needed. The battle had entered its final stages, and it was beginning to look like some mythical nightmare, a horrible struggle to the end that no one seemed like to survive.

Terrance Compton found himself in the terrible fighting, even as he mourned for his lost spacers. He was still scared—anyone in F74 who said he wasn't scared was a liar—but that didn't matter anymore. There was one thing left among those gasping, sweating, bleeding spacers…the ongoing battle to endure the longest, to emerge from the carnage with some kind of victory, Pyrrhic or otherwise. To die, if they had to die, holding back the deadly enemy, fighting with their last breaths to keep family and loved ones safe.

"Bring us in. Order *Saratoga* forward to our starboard." *Cain* didn't have much left to give, but what she had, Compton was going to extract from her. *Saratoga* was another of his battleships, the last besides the flagship still moving under its own power. The name was a mystery to him, another swiped from some old ship on the other side of the Barrier, he suspected, but the vessel and her crew had fought hard, next to *Cain* in the line, and now the two great ships were going back in one more time.

He was staring straight ahead, waiting for *Cain* to come into arc and open fire…when his eyes caught *Garret*.

He sat still, distracted, his gaze fixed on Admiral West's flagship.

Oh my God…

* * *

"All batteries charged and ready, Admiral."

West could hear the tension in Avery Sampson's voice. Hell, the outright fear. It was no shame to admit fear, especially when starting death in the face. West had devised the plan, led her people to this place knowing most of them would die there. But, as ready as she was, as broken by sadness and driven by duty…as ready as she thought she'd been to face her end, she was scared, too.

But, that didn't matter. Not now. The battle was almost over, a deadly apocalypse where it was beginning to look like no one would escape. That, she knew, would be a victory of sorts… especially if Josie Strand and the Marines had somehow managed to take down the enemy's antimatter factory. In one way, that was the part of looming death that troubled her the most… dying without knowing if the plan worked.

If Earth Two had bought more years of relative safety. More time to prepare for the final battle.

She tried to take it on faith—she had great respect for Josie Strand—but it had just been too difficult of a mission to assume success. She'd find out what had happened…but only if she was able to lead her people out of the graveyard of a system. And, she just wasn't sure if that was going to happen.

"Entering close firing range, Admiral."

West listened to Sampson's words, but she didn't answer. Not yet. *Garret* was damaged, at least a third of her crew killed or wounded, a huge section of her sternward side bleeding from a dozen great gashes in her hull. But, she still packed a punch… and Erika West was going to see that power delivered where it would do the most good.

"Admiral…"

"Not yet, Avery. We're going to bring this one in close."

Closer than close…

She watched as the range ticked down. She could feel the tension on the bridge, increasing as the two target ships saw the attack coming at them and opened up with everything they had.

Garret rocked hard, as much from the wild evasive maneuvers of its advance as the hits the enemy scored. Still, there was damage everywhere, systems blowing out, even one of the batteries West had held back for her broadside blown to scrap along with a big chunk of starboard hull.

But, still, the admiral stayed firm, her frozen nerves setting an example to her people, a rock they could hold on to as they moved forward. She knew they were all waiting for her to issue the command to fire, but no one said a word…not even when another hit slammed into the battleship's side and half the bridge lights flickered and went out.

West sat still, even as the emergency lights snapped on, replacing the lost power feed. The targets were close now, almost unimaginably so. Her eyes were fixed, as the range slipped down below two thousand kilometers…and then to fifteen hundred.

West had never taken a ship this close to enemies…she'd never even heard of such ranges, save for the few instances of ramming that had gone down in the legends of warfare. But, she was going to go even closer…under one thousand klicks.

She was counting now, trying to keep track of the enemy guns recharging. Any shot at this range would be devastating, and while she wanted to get as close as possible, she knew *Garret* had to fire first. She waited, watched…and then she saw the energy spike.

The enemy preparing to shoot.

"All batteries…fire."

She sat in her chair, watching, waiting…seeing *Garret*'s great turrets unload on the enemy ships.

Even as the First Imperium vessels fired their own guns almost simultaneously…

Erika West saw that her shots had hit—both targets—and she knew their aim had been true. But the incoming fire from the two enemy battleships struck *Garret* before she could see anything more detailed.

Her elation gave way almost at once to shock. She'd waited too long striving for a closer in shot, and she'd given the enemy enough chance to fire its own guns. That thought was still in her head, along with the desperate curiosity to know if *Garret* had taken out its two targets…when a series of structural supports crashed along the port side of the bridge. Erika West looked up an instant before she was buried under it all.

She lay there, covered in debris, drawing a few ragged breaths through her lungs.

Then, Erika West, who had fought her enemies without pause for almost seventy years, who had served with Augustus Garret and Terrance Compton—and a host of other heroes—died where she'd always known she would. On the bridge of her flagship.

* * *

Compton had heard Avery Sampson's words over the comm, but try as he might he couldn't make himself understand, not truly. *Admiral West is dead.* He replayed the words over and over again, trying to force the meaning into his head. But, it just seemed like gibberish.

He could hear the tears in Sampson's voice, the grief coming to the verge of silencing West's aide in her final duty for the admiral. Compton had wanted to throw the headset down and run from the bridge, to find someplace to hide and wait for the end. But, he couldn't think of a poorer tribute to Erika West… to the woman who'd put an almost unimaginable amount of faith into him hours before.

He felt the anger building inside him, a firestorm he knew was growing beyond control. His hands were down at his side, balled up into tight fists, and his head pounded with rage.

The battle was almost over, and moments before, Compton hadn't had a sense for which side would win, who would wipe out the enemy while they still had a few ships left. But, that doubt was gone now. He knew the battle was won. West had given her people one last weapon, a deadly tool to use to secure the final triumph.

He reached to the side of his headset and tapped the fleet-com channel. "Attention all officers and spacers of the fleet.

Admiral West is dead, killed even as she led her ship to take out two enemy battleships. We have served Admiral West, respected her, feared her at times. But, I defy any man or woman of the fleet to say mankind has every produced a greater warrior…or a more resolute defender. Erika West gave her entire life, not just these last few moments, to defend her people…and now it is for us to do one last thing for her."

He paused, shaking, with furious rage still pouring from him.

"They say this war is with a second Regent, one seeking to avenge the destruction of the first. These things think they want vengeance for the Regent? These coldblooded buckets of bolts? Well, I'm no substitute for Erika West, but I know one thing. We can show the Regent and its minions a thing or two about bloody, frozen vengeance. So, forward now, every ship, with whatever power you have left…forward for Admiral West."

Compton sat stone-still, his hands clenched tightly into fists.

"Forward to take our vengeance."

Epilogue

"I wish Erika could have known that her death pushed her people forward that last little bit…that they'd won the battle to claim vengeance for her." Max Harmon knew Erika West had never complained about the cold attitude with which so many of her comrades had viewed her, but he was just as sure it had always upset her. He wished she had gotten the chance to see the devotion her spacers held for her.

"I bet she knew, Max…at least on some level. She was a hard woman, strong in a way few people can understand. I think some part of her craved a softer side, but I don't think it was in her. In the end, we all are what we are…even you, my husband." Mariko Fujin's voice was somber. Erika West had been her friend as well as his, and both of them were mourning one last link to their old comrades gone.

Harmon was grateful, at least, that Raj Chandra had made it back, though his wounds would have him in the hospital for months. The old Pilgrim had experienced a very rough transition to retirement, but Harmon truly hoped it would stick when the officer was discharged and sent back home.

"I still can't believe she's gone." Josie Strand walked on Harmon's other side, clearly trying to hold back the tears that threatened to come out every time she talked about West. "She didn't even tell me what she was planning, Mr. President. Not until she sent the signal releasing the message hidden in my AI." A pause.

"I never got the chance to speak with her after I knew, to wish her well, to say…"

Strand never finished what she was saying, but Harmon heard the word anyway. *Goodbye.*

"She would be proud of you, Josie…and insufferably pleased with her choice of you to follow in her footsteps. I know it's hard to see through the losses, but between the two of you and your spacers and Marines, you have not only helped us avoid a trap set by the enemy, but you have sprung our own. The fleet is virtually destroyed, that is true. But, the enemy's forces are equally devastated, and their antimatter stores *have* to be depleted. They have some stored in other locations, no doubt, but with luck, not enough to shift the strategic matchup too seriously. For the first time since humanity has faced the First Imperium, we can look to a next struggle that will be fought on something close to equal terms."

He stopped walking and took a breath. "We must make the next battle the last. For Erika…and for all the others we've lost. This endless war cannot be allowed to go on."

They all nodded quietly. Harmon had no doubt they were thinking about lost friends…as he himself would have been, if his thoughts weren't fixed on a final duty he had to perform, one for a friend who had been lost, but who was now back.

"I have to go see Nicki," he said softly. The others all nodded again, and they slowly turned and walked away. All except for Mariko.

"I don't know how to tell her, Mariko. For twelve years, Erika sat at her bedside, kept vigil, never gave up on her. Now, against all odds, she is back to us, likely to make something like a full recovery." He looked at his wife, his eyes wide, the pain in them on full display. "Now, I have to go in there and tell her Erika is gone…that they will never even got a moment together." Harmon had been a warrior all his life. He'd mourned his father as a teenager and his mother when she'd been left behind on the other side of the Barrier. He'd lost countless friends and comrades, including a second father in Terrance Compton. But, this was the most relentlessly crushing thing he'd ever had to do…

and he had no idea what he was going to say.

Mariko leaned in and hugged him. She'd looked like she was going to say something, but then she just gazed at him, her normally bright and cold eyes cloudy and choked with tears. She tried to speak, but she couldn't. Finally, she just hugged him a second time, and then she turned and walked down the hall, leaving him to his thoughts…and the cold gray door closed in front of him.

He stayed there—he remembered for how long. Then, finally, he tapped the entry stud and walked into the room.

* * *

Graham sat quietly, watching as his companions walked slowly into the room. They'd been welcomed back home as heroes, all of them, and him the most. The battles against the Regent had been cataclysmic, and the losses had gutted Earth Two's military…but the Regent's fleet had been annihilated as well, and its antimatter production obliterated. It was widely regarded as a great victory, if a somber and pyrrhic one…and Graham, who might have found himself ostracized and court martialed for risking the transmission of a message to Earth Two, was instead regaled as a hero. He'd received a decoration from President Harmon himself, and his people had all been promised plum assignments as soon as they had rested and recovered…and as soon as the new ships already under construction were ready to receive their crews.

It had been two months since the remnants of the fleet had returned. Strand's fleet had found that the remnants of West's force, led back under the command of none other than Terrance Compton II, had arrived just two days before they had. Together, the two forces were barely a tithe of what they had been, though there were damaged and crippled ships slowly limping in behind the main forces that would bolster the numbers somewhat when they arrived.

Graham had dutifully played the role of the returned hero, accepting medals, even giving speeches on occasion…but now it was time to address another duty, a more vital one.

He waited as all eleven of his comrades walked in and sat down, the door closing swiftly behind them. It was a risk, of course, gathering so many from *Vaughn*'s crew in one place. Earth Two, for all the effects of forty years of emphasis on reproduction and population growth, was still a small society, and one where unnoticed seclusion was a difficult thing to find. But, he had to speak with them now. They had been back far too long…and they had work to do.

"Thank you all for coming," he said, a few seconds after the door closed. "I have kept communication among us to a minimum to date, as a security measure. But we have a purpose, and one that can no longer wait. We must be careful, however, for we cannot succeed if we are suspected."

Roland Graham, or at least the part of him that remained true to himself, tried to stop the words from escaping, struggled to assert control over his voice and his actions…but to no avail. He had memories of what had happened, spotty, fuzzy images of what the robots had…done…to him, the pain that even now drove him close to madness just in its recollection. The stark terror of watching the surgical implements moving toward his motionless body, being helpless to even try to move away…

He remembered the First Imperium ship docking with his crippled vessel, the warbots moving onto the ship. His people had prepared to fight to the last, but the enemy robots had used powerful stun guns, and they'd rendered *Vaughn*'s survivors unconscious. Graham had been prepared for one last fight—to the death—but he hadn't even considered capture as a possibility.

He could hear his voice, the words he was speaking to his companions despite his efforts to stop. He was aware of the nanobots inside him, controlling his actions, some of his thoughts, even, but he couldn't do anything about it. He was trapped, everything that made him who he was held in a section of his mind, as deep and inaccessible as the darkest prison. He could watch…watch himself commit the gravest treason imaginable. But, he couldn't do anything to stop it.

He could *feel* the nanobots, or at least the effect they had on his mind. They controlled every external function. He could reel in horror at what he was saying and doing, but he couldn't stop it, no matter how hard he tried. All he could do was listen, with growing horror.

"As you are all aware, we have been regaled as heroes by the president and many others. This will be extremely useful. We must make our plans, secure the positions we need to attain our goals. And then, we must strike. The republic feels it has a respite, a period of time before the Regent can renew its attacks...but there are other threats than battlefleets, other ways to bring down Earth Two and its government."

* * *

"Welcome home, Terrance. You did well, beyond even the highest expectations. You should be proud of yourself." A pause. "I believe your father would have been proud of you, too."

Terrance walked into the room, moving up toward the single chair where he'd spent so many hours of his life conversing with a machine that had always told him it wasn't his father. Now, he looked at the cold metal cylinders, listened to the same voice he'd heard so many thousands of times, and something was different. The magic he had once felt was gone. The entity before him for all its abilities, and all the hours they'd spent together, was just a machine. He'd known that before of course, but now it was clear in ways he hadn't seen then.

"It wasn't...what I thought it would be."

"My files on the subject suggest that that war is rarely what humans expect. Some of your father's early writings suggest rather strongly that he found the entire thing very surprising and difficult to handle at first."

Terrance listened to the words, but he found himself restless, impatient. Before he'd left, gone to war, he would have talked for hours to the machine...but now, he felt the urge to leave. He made excuses, not really necessary for an AI, he knew, and he left, finding himself jogging as he moved down the corridor. He'd come back, at least he thought he would, but for now he needed to be somewhere else, someplace he could be alone. Where he could think about his father...*truly* think about the man for the first time.

His father might be gone, but he still had something to share with his son, something Terrance couldn't entirely understand yet, but knew he needed. There would be at least one more battle to fight...and Terrance Compton II knew the next time he went to war, the spirit of his father would ride with him.

To secure the future of Earth Two...or to fall before the enemy. It would be one or the other, he knew. The next fight would be the last, and it would end in victory...or death.

Crimson Worlds Refugees Concludes With

Crusade of Vengeance

(Coming Summer 2018)

Notes on Earth Two Society

The fleet that colonized Earth Two had journeyed across vast distances, fighting desperate battles every step along the way. By the time they defeated the Regent and reached their new home, the refugees had lost two-thirds of their number.

When the survivors arrived at Earth Two, battered and exhausted, they immediately recognized the need to increase the population as rapidly as possible, both to create a truly functional civilian society and to ensure that they would be strong enough to face any future threats that might arise.

The discovery that First Imperium forces did, in fact, survive thirty years later, combined with subsequent fears that a second Regent existed—an entity likely determined to finish the job the original had failed to complete—added to the urgency.

Earth Two faced a desperate fight against the old enemy, and the nascent civilization needed people...soldiers, spacers, workers, scientists. The drive to increase the population, by any means necessary, continued the move toward a fractured society, one consisting of various factions, each differing in the means of their birth and genetic makeup...and each resenting and fearing the others, at least to a degree.

The societal groups of Earth Two face a common enemy, one that will destroy them all if it can, and this danger has held the troubled society together...so far. Nevertheless, beneath the surface cooperation, tensions seethe and resentments build, generating an internal threat almost as dire as the external one presented by the New Regent and its First Imperium fleets.

Earth Two Genetic Groupings

Pilgrims

Pilgrims are the men and women who crewed the original fleet and arrived to settle Earth Two. They were born on Earth or its colonies on the other side of the Barrier. At the start of Storm of Vengeance, the youngest pilgrims are in their mid-60s.

Natural Borns (NBs)

Children born conventionally to the pilgrims (and subsequently to succeeding generations of NBs). There is roughly a twenty-five-year gap between the ages of the youngest Pilgrims and the oldest Natural Borns, as no children were conceived while the fleet was in transit. As of the start of Storm of Vengeance, the oldest generation of Natural Borns are in their early forties.

Tanks

Tanks are Clones created from selected individuals, pilgrims at first, but later also NBs. As their foundational genetic material is chosen from selected genetic donors, Tanks tend to be well-above average in terms of physical and mental abilities. In addition, they are genetically manipulated during the cloning process to eliminate most diseases and chromosomal abnormalities, resulting in the development of considerably stronger immune systems and overall constitutions than their naturally-born cousins. In general, Tanks are stronger and faster than NBs, and they also benefit from attributes like higher resistance to radiation.

Despite their many strengths, the Tank population suffers from one terrible weakness, an unexplained mutation or anomaly that causes sudden and painful death, occurring initially in approximately four percent of those quickened. Known colloquially as the Plague, this affliction typically strikes in a period ranging from late-adolescence to early adulthood. While its exact cause remains a mystery, it is known that specific DNA donor lines experience increased rates of incidence. Donor screening has reduced the percentage of the population affected to approximately 2.5% over the decade preceding Storm of Vengeance. Nevertheless, it remains a feared shadow looming over the Tank population.

The name "Tank" is based on the artificial wombs used to nurture clone fetuses. As tensions between the clone and naturally-born populations have increased, the term, initially practical in nature, has come to be regarded as mildly derogatory by some...though many of the clones still use it to refer to themselves.

Doubles

Doubles are clones created from the DNA of other clones (Tanks). They suffer from an array of problems and dysfunctions as a result of increased incidence of replicative failure, as well as Plague rates nearly three times those of the overall clone population. The quickening of more doubles was forbidden after the problems experienced by the initial generations became understood, but there is still resistance among many of the Tanks, who feel this prohibition makes their kind genetically dependent on NBs. This is a cause of some resentment and tension in the Tank population, despite the fact that they are able to reproduce by natural means with no restrictions.

Clone Borns (CBs)

Clone Borns are children born conventionally to Tanks. CBs are genetically almost identical to NBs, but they nevertheless suffer from some discriminatory attitudes, mostly from NB purists, but also from some militant elements of the Tank population, who eschew conventional forms of reproduction in favor of continued cloning.

Clone Borns can inherit the Plague, though the incidence is far lower than in their lab-quickened parents, averaging about one half of one percent. Children born conventionally to a Tank and an NB are sometimes called "Halfies," though this is not generally considered a socially acceptable term.

Double Borns

Double Borns are children born naturally to Doubles. They inherit many of the genetic abnormalities afflicting their parents, often in exacerbated forms. Reproduction among Doubles is discouraged, but not outright illegal.

Mules (Hybrids)

Mules are genetically-engineered beings, created from fusing human DNA with recovered First Imperium genetic material. The Mules are very advanced in terms of physical and intellectual abilities, and are considerably more capable than any of the other groups on Earth Two, both mentally and physically. Their only genetic weakness is the inability to reproduce by natural means. Mules quickened after the first group of 116 are sometimes called Next Gens (NGs or "Nexies"), though generally, most outside the hybrid group simply refer to them all as simply, "Mules."

The first generation of 116 Mules were subject to the Prohibition for more than twenty-five years, a mandate that forbade the creation of more of their kind, and was only repealed after a near-revolution. Even now, the number of new Mules allowed to be quickened is strictly controlled, creating a continuing tension between the hybrids and their purely human cousins.

The Mules feel a definite kinship to the other humans, and

somewhat of an obligation to protect them as well, especially the original 116, but they all view themselves as *different*, more a new life form than the same species as those they consider to be more primitive cousins. Mules are prone to arrogance, and this has been exacerbated by the more or less inarguable fact that the they have done more than all the others combined to comprehend and adapt the technology of the First Imperium and to assist in keeping Earth Two strong and hidden from the Second Regent's forces.

Also By Jay Allan

Marines (Crimson Worlds I)
The Cost of Victory (Crimson Worlds II)
A Little Rebellion (Crimson Worlds III)
The First Imperium (Crimson Worlds IV)
The Line Must Hold (Crimson Worlds V)
To Hell's Heart (Crimson Worlds VI)
The Shadow Legions(Crimson Worlds VII)
Even Legends Die (Crimson Worlds VIII)
The Fall (Crimson Worlds IX)
War Stories (Crimson World Prequels)
MERCS (Successors I)
The Prisoner of Eldaron (Successors II)
Into the Darkness (Refugees I)
Shadows of the Gods (Refugees II)
Revenge of the Ancients (Refugees III)
Winds of Vengeance (Refugees IV)
Storm of Vengeance (Refugees V)
Shadow of Empire (Far Stars I)
Enemy in the Dark (Far Stars II)
Funeral Games (Far Stars III)
Blackhawk (Far Stars Legends I)
The Dragon's Banner
Gehenna Dawn (Portal Wars I)
The Ten Thousand (Portal Wars II)
Homefront (Portal Wars III)
Red Team Alpha (CW Adventures I)
Duel in the Dark (Blood on the Stars I)
Call to Arms (Blood on the Stars II)
Ruins of Empire (Blood on the Stars III)
Echoes of Glory (Blood on the Stars IV)
Cauldron of Fire (Blood on the Stars V)
Dauntless (Blood on the Stars VI)
Flames of Rebellion (Flames of Rebellion I)

www.jayallanbooks.com

71500928R00189